Natasha Lester worked as a marketing executive for L'Oréal, managing the Maybelline brand, before returning to university to study creative writing. She completed a Master of Creative Arts as well as her first novel, *What Is Left Over, After*, which won the T.A.G. Hungerford Award for Fiction.

In her spare time Natasha loves to teach writing, is a sought after public speaker and can often be found playing dress-up with her three children. She lives in Perth.

For all the latest news from Natasha visit:
natashalester.com.au
Twitter: @Natasha_Lester
#TheParisSeamstress
Instagram: /natashalesterauthor
Facebook: /NatashaLesterAuthor

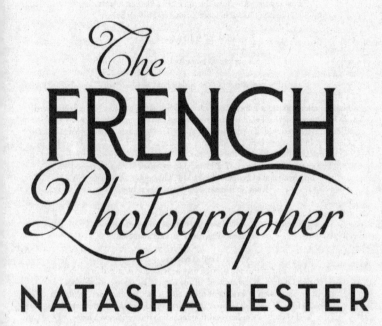

The FRENCH Photographer

NATASHA LESTER

sphere

SPHERE

First published in Australia in 2019 by Hachette Australia
First published in Great Britain in 2019 by Sphere

1 3 5 7 9 10 8 6 4 2

Copyright © Natasha Lester 2019

The moral right of the author has been asserted.

The quotations on pages 1 and 121 by David E. Scherman and Lee Miller reproduced
with kind permission of Palazzo Editions Limited and © Lee Miller Archives, England
2018. All rights reserved. The quotation on page 335 by Audrey Withers/Vogue © *The
Condé Nast* Publications Ltd. The quotations on pages 47 and 307 © *The Face of War* by
Martha Gellhorn (Granta Publications, 1993). Reproduced with permission.
The quotations on pages 237, 298 and 335 by Susan Sontag are reproduced
by permission of Penguin Books Ltd. The quotation on page 296
from *No Woman's World* by Iris Carpenter.

A CIP catalogue record for this book is available from the British Library.

ISBN 978-0-7515-7309-1

Papers used by Sphere are from well-managed forests
and other responsible sources.

MIX
Paper from
responsible sources
FSC® C001695

Sphere
An imprint of
Little, Brown Book Group
Carmelite House
50 Victoria Embankment
London EC4Y 0DZ

An Hachette UK Company
www.hachette.co.uk

www.littlebrown.co.uk

To Rebecca Saunders, publisher extraordinaire, whose belief in me is the greatest gift any writer could have. Thank you.

PART ONE
Jess

It is almost impossible today, almost fifty years later, to conceive how difficult it was for a woman correspondent to get beyond a rear-echelon military position, in other words to the front, where the action was.

David E. Scherman, *LIFE* magazine correspondent

One

*J*essica May turned on her famous smile and raised her arm aloft, her movements as repetitive as those of the riveters and welders and all the other jobs women were doing these days. Except that she wasn't in a factory and she wasn't wearing overalls.

Instead, she stood on a white platform, backdropped by a brilliant autumnal sky, wearing a white silk dress, bridal in length. It was designed to cling to the front of her body – helped along by the fans blowing over her – and then billow behind her in the artificial breeze, goddess-like. A white cape tied at her neck rippled too, adding to the celestial effect. Two large American flags fluttered proudly beside her, and her outstretched arm made it appear as if she might declaim something important at any moment. But that was also part of the make-believe; since when did a model have anything momentous to say about patriotism and war?

Once upon a time she'd marched passionately in the streets of Paris protesting against fascism, first as its vile ideology swept through Spain, then as it turned Italy and Germany into grotesqueries. Now Jessica May was simply the figurehead of a ship. Or Toni Frissell, the photographer, would make her into one after the photograph had been cropped and manipulated in just the right

1

way for the cover of *Vogue*, a cover that would be as galvanising as everyone needed it to be in late 1942. Nobody would ever know that there was no ship, no water, no sea breeze, no goddess; just a few props in a field in upstate New York, beside a herd of cows with quizzical eyes chewing over the interruption to their ordinarily pastoral outlook.

Toni asked her to rearrange her face. To look solemn. To respect the flag and the men and her country and the fighting. Jess did as she was asked.

'Perfect,' Toni said soon after. 'I don't need any more.'

So Jess stepped off the platform, batting away the wardrobe assistant who wanted to help her down. She unhooked the cape and moved behind a screen where the assistant helped her change into the next outfit, a Claire McCardell bathing suit made of black wool jersey with a very low-cut v-neckline and a row of brass hook-and-eye closures down the front.

This time, when Jess climbed onto the platform, she sat between the flags, pretending to dip her toes into the imaginary water that readers of *Vogue* would think lay just out of shot. She smiled and tipped her face up to the sun, leaning back on her elbows. A cow bellowed its approval and she laughed. Toni caught the shot at just the right moment.

Then a car drew up in a hurry on the dirt road alongside the field. Belinda Bower, *Vogue* editor and Jess's friend, stepped out and picked her way across the field in a pencil skirt and heels, wobbling, but clearly determined not to appear as out of place as a tuxedo at the seaside. Toni lowered the camera and Jess straightened. Bel never interfered with photo shoots. Something was up.

Which Belinda confirmed moments later when she reached Jess and showed her a full-page Kotex advertisement in *McCall's*. The words, *It has women's enthusiastic approval!* were emblazoned across the top of the page. Underneath, Jessica May posed idly in an evening gown as if she hadn't a care in the world, and especially not about the taboo subject of menstruation.

'Goddammit!' Jess said.

'Goddammit,' Bel agreed. 'Shoot's off,' she called to the makeup artists, the hairstylists, Toni's assistant, and Toni.

Toni packed her camera away without asking any questions. But the eyes of everyone else remained fixed on Jess and Bel. There was no good reason to call off a shoot that everyone could see had been going exceptionally well. Unless Jessica May was in some kind of trouble. And that was both likely and a toothsome piece of gossip nobody wanted to miss.

'It had to be Emile,' Jess muttered as they walked across to the privacy of the cows. 'He took that picture of me last year. He must have sold it to Kotex.'

'I thought so,' Bel replied. 'I tried to get Condé to change his mind; hell, he wanted me to change his mind – you know he adores you – but we also know the advertisers would abandon us quicker than Joan Blondell can remove her clothes.'

Despite everything, Jess grinned at the quip. Then she sighed. Bel was right. None of *Vogue*'s advertisers would want their products appearing in the magazine that had the Kotex girl on the cover. Because the Kotex girl was what she'd be known as from now on. Even living with Emile out of wedlock wasn't as great a sin as menstruation. 'How long will I be on the blacklist?' she asked.

'I don't know,' Belinda said honestly. 'It depends how long Kotex run the ad for. Condé hopes we can have you back modelling for us next year, but . . .'

'Until then, I should murder Emile and find some other way to pay the rent,' Jess finished.

'Condé still wants you at his party tonight. He won't drop you for everything.'

Just my livelihood, Jess thought grimly. At the age of twenty-two and after almost three years, hundreds of outfits, countless lipstick re-applications, innumerable images of Jessica May in the pages of *Vogue* and *Harper's Bazaar* and *Glamour* and much fussing over her blonde hair, it was over. She would no longer perpetuate a fantasy that, despite the war, a world still existed in which a woman might buy a low-cut bathing suit and, on a trip to the seaside, meet a prince and fall in love.

'Besides,' Bel continued, pushing the nose of a cow away from her Mainbocher jacket with the same force she used when disposing of hapless interns, 'now you'll have time to take more pictures for me. And to write for me.'

'Will Condé agree to that?'

Bel eyed Jess, who was still wearing the bathing suit in which her cleavage was displayed so winningly. 'Your by-line won't be anywhere near as intimidating to advertisers as a full-page of Jessica May in the flesh and not much else.'

A peal of laughter rang from Jess's mouth, so loudly that the team from the shoot all turned to look their way.

'Think about it,' Bel urged. 'You know how much I loved the few pieces you've done for me.'

'I will,' Jess said. 'But right now I need to change, go back to the city, and deal with Emile.'

'What will you say to him?' Bel asked as they walked over to the makeshift dressing room.

Jess unhooked the bathing suit, unconcerned that Belinda was with her, so used to undressing in front of people that it now seemed strange when she was alone in the apartment taking her clothes off without an audience. 'Something I would have said to him six months ago had he not returned from the training camp missing two fingers,' she said bleakly.

Hours later, Jess swept through the Stork Club, past the ostentatiously large flower displays and voluptuous velvet drapes, her eye fixed on a booth she regularly occupied. She was brought up short by two men who wouldn't move aside to let her through and she dealt with them the same way she always dealt with men who thought the face and body of Jessica-May-the-model was theirs for the groping. 'You've left them there,' she said, indicating a spot on the floor.

As both men looked down, she shouldered her way past and called back to them, 'Your eyeballs, I mean.'

Emile smiled at her when she reached the booth, a smile she'd once thought suave and sensual. As usual, he wore his hair slicked back, his suit just the right side of louche to allow him entry into the Stork Club. He pushed a Manhattan across to her as she slid into the seat opposite. She took the drink and, in return, pushed Bel's copy of *McCall's* over to him.

'I thought you'd be pleased.' His smile widened, as if he thought one of his signature grins was all it took to have her thank him for ruining her career.

'You knew I wouldn't be. Otherwise you'd have told me.'

His smile stayed on. 'You're always saying I should start working again. I took your advice.'

They both looked at his right hand; at the remaining two fingers and thumb. Once upon a time, the handsome Frenchman, Emile Robard, had been one of the darlings of fashion photography, peer to Man Ray and Cecil Beaton, first in France and then in New York City, where he'd decamped in 1939 when war was declared. To where he and Jess had both decamped, to be precise – Jess might have been an American but she'd lived more than half her life in France with her parents, which is where she'd met Emile.

After arriving in New York, it took only a year for Emile Robard and Jessica May to become the darlings of both the scandal sheets and the social pages, the royalty of Greenwich Village artistes. A sought-after model and a French photographer, both, according to the press, blessed with enough beauty to lift any gathering to greatness.

That she'd shockingly dared to live with Emile, to be his *mistress*, was both titillating and thrilling to most Manhattanites whose values were far more conservative than their cosmopolitan facades implied. What she hated most about it was the word – *mistress* – implying she lived off Emile's largesse. But her modelling career meant she had more than enough money of her own. In fact, over the last few months, he'd been the one burning through *her* money like packs of Lucky Strikes. He'd taught her photography, the press said – another lie, although he had bettered her skills. He'd ensured she was the face most loved by the fashion magazines – another untruth; she was perfectly capable of finding her own work and hadn't had to attend a go-see for two years.

And then earlier in the year, having witnessed the glory surrounding photographers like Robert Capa and Edward Steichen who were taking pictures of war, Emile had decided he wanted some of that lustre for himself. He'd cast off models and magazines and got himself assigned to an army training camp in Texas. Jess had been glad to have some time apart from him; the six months prior had seen Emile throwing himself at parties with the same passion he used to save for photography, and consuming whiskey as if it were air. It wasn't a lifestyle that Jess desired, given that late nights were incompatible with a magazine-worthy face, and nor did she want to be the vapid party-girl whose only concern was locating a suitable sofa to pass out on at three in the morning. She'd hoped that Emile's sudden urge to shoot training manoeuvres would result in him finding inspiration in something other than late nights and drunkenness, but he got into an argument with a private at the camp and ended up being shot himself, losing two fingers in the process.

When he returned with a bandaged hand, Emile told Jess he'd been defending her honour, that the private had made lewd comments about a photograph of her naked back in a magazine. It was her fault he'd lost his fingers and could no longer hold a camera properly. So she'd stayed with Emile even though she wasn't sure that she still loved him.

But now they were done. Jess could no longer go to work in the morning, leaving him in her apartment to drink whiskey all day, could no longer dance with him in the evenings with a model's empty smile pasted on her face, could no longer help him home and to bed because he was too drunk to walk. Could not ignore the fact that he'd lined his pockets with Kotex money at her expense.

Jess sent the martini glass the same way as the magazine. 'I meant that you should go out and take photographs. Not sell old pictures of me to Kotex to use for an ad you know will make me persona non grata in the modelling world. The only reason you can't hold a camera steady is because you drink too much. Your hand would be fine with just a little practice.'

Emile finished his drink, then picked up hers and took a long swallow. 'I did nothing wrong.'

Jess sighed. She had to say it. *It's over.* She had to forget looking up at a jazz club in Paris and seeing this man smile rakishly at her, had to forget dancing with him into the early hours of the morning, had to forget doing that most romantic of all things: walking hand in hand through the streets of Paris as the sun came up, stopping to buy espresso, stopping to kiss. Had to forget that what she'd had with him was a kind of love; hedonistic, exciting, suited to that time in her life when she'd thought she might go mad because both her parents had just died and she had nobody. Except Emile.

'*The New Yorker* telephoned for you this morning,' Emile said.

Jess wished she could ask him at another time, when he was less drunk and more merciful, but she had to know. 'What did they say?'

'They said your idea didn't interest them.' Emile's eyes roamed the room, settling on Gene Tierney, which was lucky; he wouldn't see the sting of his words made manifest in the clench of her jaw.

Being rejected at a go-see had never bothered her as much as a rejection by *The New Yorker*. She'd hoped her pitch might be a way to build on the handful of articles she'd written and photographed for *Vogue*, about the female artists from Parsons School of Design who were now painting camouflage on aeroplanes and designing propaganda posters instead of creating their own artworks. This time, Jess had wanted to write about what might happen to all those women when the war ended and the men returned and reclaimed their old jobs. What would the women do with all their new skills? Would there still be jobs for them?

Jess had wanted to stand up high on a ladder and take photographs in the factories, pictures that showed how many women there were; not just one or two but an entire generation. She knew nobody could dismiss a photograph the same way they might consider words to be exaggerated. And she'd wanted to feel as if she was doing something that mattered; instead of screaming her outrage about fascism into the wind at the Place de la Concorde as she'd done when she was younger, she could show that war reverberated in ways beyond bullets, that the ramifications could be found in the hands of a woman who'd once sculpted bronze and who now fashioned aircraft propellers.

'They liked my idea,' Emile went on, leaning back and lighting a cigarette.

'Your idea?'

'I told them I'd write a piece about the jobs women aren't doing as well as the men who used to do them. I'd photograph the mistakes, expose the money it costs to make do with labour that isn't suited to the job. You Americans have been asked to believe a story about how well everyone is getting on with the new way of things but perhaps it's not true.'

'You didn't really.' She stared at him, expecting he would laugh and tell her she was mad; as if he'd write a story like that.

But he just stared back. 'I did.'

Her legs pushed her upright and the words came to her easily now that she no longer cared about kindness. 'You know this is over. We're holding on to something that happened a long time ago when I was young and didn't know any better and when you were . . .' How to finish that sentence? 'A better man than you are now. And I'm not referring to your fingers.'

'Nobody ever refers to my fingers,' he retorted. 'But everyone thinks about them. About poor Emile who used to have the models falling at his feet.'

'That's what you miss?' she asked sadly. 'I'm sure if you're still able to stand by the end of the night, you'll be able to get someone to fall at your feet. I'll stay elsewhere for the next few days while you move your things out of the apartment.'

'How will I find somewhere to live on such short notice?' His voice was petulant, like a child's.

'I'll get the bank to transfer you enough money to pay your rent for a month. After that, your *articles*,' she couldn't quite keep the anger from her voice, 'will surely support you.' Then she left before either of them could say any more hurtful things.

The only thing to do after that was to go to a party. She arrived at midnight, which was late, but not impolitely so – the party never started at Condé Nast's Park Avenue apartment until ten at the earliest. Condé kissed Jess's cheeks and apologised for the stance he'd had to take with the Kotex ad.

He'd been the one to discover her, not long after she'd arrived back in New York City. She'd taken a different ship home than her parents because Emile hadn't been ready to leave on the SS *Athenia* – she couldn't even remember now why he'd prevaricated. Which was, everyone said, lucky for her because the *Athenia* had sunk and her parents had died. But how was that lucky?

A month after she'd arrived in Manhattan, when she'd at last made herself stop crying, she walked into Parsons School of Design to enrol in photography classes. Condé Nast had been at Parsons delivering a lecture to the fashion students and he'd seen her, as poignant as any Madonna, he would say later when he told the fantastical story, her brown eyes wet with tears from a month of weeping. The rest, as they say, was Jess's history.

Now, Condé released her from his embrace, told her that she was still his favourite model and commanded her to enjoy herself.

Which was not going to be difficult, she supposed, when the bar was fully stocked with impossible-to-get French champagne – a man like Condé probably had a cellar big enough to outlast the war – when everyone around them was attired in expensive gowns, when the air smelled heavy with French perfume. The orchestra played Cole Porter, George Gershwin sat at a table chatting to a group of admirers, overladen buffets were set up, as usual, on the terrace under the forgivingly warm fall sky, and the dancers took up most of the space in the room. Dancers, Jess noted, who included Emile, almost lip to lip with a girl she knew, another model, four years younger than Jess, barely eighteen. She waited for jealousy to swirl through her but she felt, if anything, relieved. She sat at a table, lit a cigarette and heard a woman say her name.

'Martha Gellhorn,' Jess replied with a grin.

'I see my fame goes before me,' Martha said with a wry smile, sitting beside Jess and lighting a cigarette too. 'Which you must also be used to.'

'Perhaps not as much as Ernest Hemingway's wife,' Jess said. 'Does it make your blood boil every time they call you that?'

Martha laughed. 'I've considered wearing a label that lists my other achievements but few seem interested.'

Jess shook her head; she knew that although Martha was one of the few women – perhaps the only woman – reporting on the war from Europe, her single biggest claim to fame in most people's eyes was as Ernest Hemingway's other half.

'I've read all of your pieces,' Jess said. 'I can't say that I enjoyed them because nobody could enjoy stories of war and death, but I appreciated them.'

'I've read yours too.' Martha eyed Jess appraisingly. 'And seen your photographs. The one you took of the artist's canvas sitting beside the propaganda posters she now paints was better than any newspaper report. I like the way you blurred one image into the other –'

'Solarisation,' Jess explained. 'I wanted to make it look like one painting was literally bleeding into the other.'

Martha nodded. 'I thought that might have been it. It was the subtlest commentary; you didn't need words to explain the conundrum: the wish to appear selfless and donate one's talents to one's country at the same time as mourning the loss of true art.'

'Thank you.' Jess felt herself blush, which was something she hadn't done in a very long time.

'What are you working on now?' Martha asked, sipping whiskey rather than champagne.

'That's a very good question. Besides asking my paramour to move out,' Jess nodded at Emile, 'not much.'

'I heard about his hand,' Martha said without sympathy. 'I also heard that if it hadn't been for his hand –'

'I'd probably have asked him to move out a long time ago.' Jess finished the sentence for her.

'So why don't you look happier? I believe you used to be quite something of a couple – like Hem and I – but wasn't that a while ago?'

'Jessica May and Emile Robard. Model and photographer. Bohemian artistes,' Jess mused.

'You're selling yourself a little short by calling yourself a model. From what I've seen, you're as good a photographer as he is. You've had work published.'

'It's what everyone thinks. See.' Jess reached out and opened the newspaper on the sideboard to the social pages, pointing to a picture from a party two nights ago. *Celebrated photographer Emile Robard with Jessica May, model.* 'Apparently I'm not even celebrated,' she said with a sardonic smile. 'The thing is, only this morning I was thinking that I didn't know how much longer I could parade around in dresses and smile at cameras. You're doing something useful,' she said to Martha. 'What am I doing?'

'Keeping up morale?' Martha said teasingly. 'I bet there's a soldier or two who has a picture of you posted above his bed in his training camp.'

Jess rolled her eyes. 'Just what I want to be remembered for.'

'There you are.' Bel joined them, kissing both Jess's and Martha's cheeks.

'You look as frowny as I feel,' Jess noted as Belinda sat down.

'You never look frowny, Jessica May,' Bel said. 'You two look as if you're having the most interesting conversation at this party.'

'Cheers to that,' Martha said, raising her glass.

'Maybe we can wipe your frown away,' Jess said to Bel. 'A problem shared and all that.'

Bel took a sip of champagne. 'I spent the afternoon foxtrotting with the government. The price of paper has gone sky high since the war started, and they're talking about paper rationing. I need to stay on the good side of the politicians if I want to keep *Vogue* alive during the war. But during today's meeting, I was asked if I could do more to contribute to the war effort than it's felt we're currently doing.'

'I take it by "asked" you mean "blackmailed"?' Jess said.

'Exactly. I told the government that women are a valuable part of the propaganda machine and that *Vogue* can and should help with that. The government wants women here to let their men go and fight, to shrug off rationing as their moral duty, to work in order to keep the economy going. And *Vogue*'s market is the women the government wants on their side. But I need pictures, not just words; *Vogue* is visual. I don't suppose you'd quit *Collier's* and come work for me?' Bel said pleadingly to Martha.

As Bel spoke, an idea at once so outrageous and so perfect began to form in Jess's mind. Four years ago in Paris, when she'd joined the anti-fascism demonstrations, she would never have imagined that, in the near future, while fascism claimed life after life and country after country, she would be sitting at a party in a Park Avenue penthouse drinking champagne. Back then she had marched and she had protested and, most of all, she had cared deeply about what was happening in the world. She still cared, but in a helpless and hopeless way. Writing and photographing those pieces for Bel had re-inflamed that care and given her a sense that she could do something more, like Martha did. Jess couldn't shoot or fly or fight but she could write and she could photograph.

Martha leaned back in her chair, pointed her cigarette in Jess's direction and said exactly what Jess was thinking. 'You don't need me,' Martha said. 'You've got Jess.'

'Yes. Send me,' Jess said, turning to Bel as her restlessness fell away, replaced by an animation she hadn't felt for a long time.

Bel laughed. 'I appreciate you trying to cheer me up but –'

'I'm serious.' Jess put down her glass and eyeballed Bel. 'I can be *Vogue*'s correspondent.'

'I'm not sending you into a war zone. It's ridiculous.' Bel took a large sip of champagne, then said, 'Brilliant, but ridiculous.'

Jess felt the chink in Bel's Mainbocher armour. 'It *is* brilliant. And I'm *asking* to go into a war zone; you're not sending me. There are other women over there.'

Bel arched her eyebrows. 'About two of them.'

'So with me, there'll be three. Lucky number three.'

'Actually, you're about right,' Martha said. 'Margaret Bourke-White's the only female photojournalist I know of in the Mediterranean. There are a couple of other correspondents like me. But that's all.'

This time, Bel's eyebrows performed such a feat of acrobatics that Jess had to stifle a laugh. 'I was joking when I said two!' Bel protested.

'I want to do this.' Jess kept her voice level. 'I *need* to do this. Please.'

Bel gesticulated at the waiter for more champagne. 'How on earth am I going to get you accredited? Former model, Emile's lover – or are you? I can see he's finding comfort in another girl's lips just over there – unconventional as all get-out. I've heard the woman at the passport office is as easy to get past as Hitler. She's never going to let a model, who I'm sure she imagines will sleep only on silk sheets at the finest hotels, go to a war zone.'

'You're selling me short,' Jess said. 'You know what my childhood was like, that I've lived in tents, slept under the stars, roughed it in a way that probably most of the men going to war couldn't even imagine.'

'When I landed in Spain in '37 to report the war over there, I'd never slept in a tent,' Martha added. 'Or seen a man shot. I survived. Best way to learn is to throw yourself into the thick of it, bombs and all.'

Bel inhaled smoke, breathed it out, inhaled again. 'If only you weren't so damn right,' she said to Jess. 'You *would* be perfect. And I've always known you wouldn't be a model forever.' She reached out and squeezed Jess's hand. 'Martha, you've been over there. Shouldn't I try harder to dissuade her?'

'On the contrary,' Martha replied. 'If you do, we'll only hear stories of men, told by men. Given I'm married to the biggest chauvinist in the country, I have a vested interest in opening up the discourse.'

'You're the only person in the world who would make me feel like I was doing her a favour if I said yes to sending her into a war zone,' Bel said to Jess.

'Let's try,' Jess said. 'We can only fail spectacularly.'

$\mathcal{T}$WO

$\mathcal{W}$*e can only fail spectacularly.* The words rang in Jess's mind as she sat, in early 1943 – bureaucracy was unfamiliar with the concept of speed – at the State Department offices for one of the meetings that would decide her future. *Remove all objections*, she told herself as she stared at the ticking clock, more nervous than she'd ever been at any go-see.

At a go-see, she knew there was nothing she could do that hadn't already been done. Her portfolio had been shot, she had the face and body that she'd been blessed with – dark brown eyes that every photographer she'd ever worked with said they could never do justice to, naturally waving blonde hair that sat a couple of inches above her shoulders, and a figure that had curves in all the right places. But, with this interview at the State Department, everything depended on what she said, not on the way she looked. Perhaps on the way she smiled too – how much would be too much in the eyes of a woman holding all the power to grant Jess a passport to Europe?

Stop it, she told herself, studying the demure and practical Stella Designs black crepe tuxedo trousers and the prim and subdued white cotton shirt she'd paired them with – Stella too, because only Stella

15

shirts came with the white peony over the left breast, which made the outfit more like herself than the person she was pretending to be.

'Miss Jessica May,' a voice called out.

Jessica stood, straightened her back and then realised she was striding down the hall like a model on a catwalk. She tried to correct herself but then couldn't remember how to walk normally so, in the end, she marched on, hoping to God they'd think she had military precision rather than modelistic pretensions.

'You may sit.' A tall woman – tall enough to have been a damn good model – gestured to a chair.

Jess sat down, and arranged her face in a way that she hoped indicated strength, hardiness and determination.

'I thought I should explain myself,' she began. 'I know I must seem an unusual candidate for a passport to Europe to work as a photojournalist. But I possess many advantages that I'm sure some of the men currently over there reporting the war do not. My parents were paleobotanists, you see, and I led a somewhat peripatetic childhood. We followed plant fossils around the world; I lived in or visited South America, the northern territories of Australia, Tahiti and then we made our way to Europe after my parents' work began to receive recognition. I lived in France for ten years; I speak the language fluently.' She felt her voice relax as she spoke, confident of her bona fides.

She went on. 'As soon as I was old enough, I became my parents' photographer every summer and often during term time; if they thought they were on the trail of a discovery, my parents would simply take me along, put the Rolleiflex in my hand and ask me to capture whatever they'd found. Since then, I've studied at Parsons and received more training in photography from Emile Robard.'

As she spoke, images appeared and disappeared in her mind like a shutter opening and closing: fern fossils fronding delicately over rock, cotyledons puncturing the surface of a stone, the barest tracing of Zamites leaves carved into limestone. And then pictures of herself, very few, taken on the rare occasions her mother picked up the camera, showing a Jessica yet to grow into her gangly limbs and too-large smile, her blonde hair a ferocious tangle down her back, skin tanned to a then-unfashionable brownness, nose freckled by the sun.

More snapshots: Jess playing in mud, scrambling over rocks until her kneecaps were bereft of skin, swimming in the lakes and rivers even though her parents were warned about parasites and crocodiles. Her mother wearing a floppy hat, stained by mud and dust, grinning at Jess. Happy, always so happy to have her hands in the dirt, to prise away stories of a time long past, to clatter out papers and findings on the old typewriter. And her father, the quieter of the two, not quite of this world, his head always in the past, dreaming, perhaps imagining Ginkgoales into being.

It was an unorthodox childhood of intermittent schooling, of having to grasp German, Italian and French; she had to either learn the language or be excluded from playing with the other children during the short spells she had at various schools. Her education was propped up by as much reading as her parents were able to obtain books to supply. And so Jess's life had formed from two seemingly opposite sources: the mysteries of what the ground held and the stories recorded in books. Which meant she'd always done well at English, History and Science but had never had any interest in or flair for Mathematics.

'May I speak?' The woman's voice was smoothly polite and Jess blinked, shutting out the past and cursing herself for being so distracted.

'Europe is at war; you've photographed plants,' the woman stated.

Jess realised that she hadn't even waited for the woman to introduce herself; that she'd barged in and, rather than confidently stating her qualifications, probably arrogantly confirmed everything the woman might assume about models – that they were used to having the floor and thought far too highly of themselves.

'I'm sorry,' she apologised. Should she admit to nerves? They'd hardly send someone into a war zone if they suffered from nerves in an office in broad daylight. 'I've photographed more than plants. I had some pictures and articles published in French *Vogue* in 1939, showing the exodus of Americans out of Paris. American *Vogue* have also published my work about female camouflage and propaganda artists.'

Jess stopped speaking. She waited. And waited. And waited.

She was used to being appraised; she couldn't walk into a party or a club without feeling dozens of pairs of eyes wash over her. But this was different. This was scrutiny of a kind so intense she could feel herself melting back into her chair, looking down at her lap, not wanting the woman to find anything within her that made her the wrong choice of person to be granted a passport.

'It is not my goal to allow women into a war zone.' The woman said it matter-of-factly, politely even. But her words were a boot pushing down on the back of Jess's neck, telling her that she should stay where she was, doing what she was doing; that being a clothes hanger with a nice smile was the right job for her.

Jess matched the woman's pragmatic tone of voice. 'I speak German. Not fluently, but certainly well enough to make myself understood, and to understand what's being said. I also speak Italian. I wonder if you can tell me the names of any men you've given passports to in order to report the war who can speak French, German and Italian?'

The woman didn't shift her gaze. 'I cannot,' she said.

And there it was, a tiny advantage, but an advantage nonetheless.

The woman finally let go of Jess's eyes. 'I will inform your editor at *Vogue* of my decision. It will take some time.'

She'd been dismissed. She'd either given it her best shot or her worst; it was hard to tell. If this didn't work, she'd be back in a field, if she was lucky, or on a beach, or outside a steel-grey skyscraper wearing next season's clothes, smiling as if she were happy, as unremarkable as a Jurassic fern leaf imprinted into volcanic rock by the years and then long forgotten.

⁓

Two months later she got her passport. The year was marching on and Jess had achieved nothing except to substantially reduce her savings, living off house model work for companies like Stella Designs. It was lucky she had her parents' apartment and didn't have to pay rent.

Then she had to be screened by the War Department's Bureau of Public Relations Overseas Liaison Branch, who had the power to accredit her as a correspondent. Or not. Just getting the appointment took another month. And if she'd thought her parents were particularly skilled at uncovering secrets that the earth tried to hold on to, nothing prepared Jess for the rigour of the War Department. Martha had forewarned her. 'By the time they've finished with you, you'll feel like you're sitting in front of them in your underwear.'

Which she did. They showed her a photograph of her mother; Jess couldn't imagine how they'd got hold of it but, that night, when she returned to her apartment and looked through her boxes, it wasn't in her photo album, which only proved that Emile was more of a bastard than she'd realised.

Just as she'd done the day she and Emile stepped off their ship in New York City to be greeted by the news of her parents' death, Jess sat on the floor of the Greenwich Village apartment, weeping. Back then, she'd been watched over by the angelic forms of dust sheets and the brooding presence of Emile, standing in the doorway, not knowing what to do. Now she was alone. She hadn't wept for such a long time. But seeing the photograph of her mother, knowing that she and her father and botany had never been enough for her, if what the War Department had said was true, brought back the grief.

Then she heard the ghost of her mother's voice telling her to be practical, to stand up, to not wallow. To not let the War Department get to her. So, just as her mother had always been the one to find the best camping spot, to give everyone errands so that food would be cooked and supplies purchased, Jess scrubbed her cheeks dry with a Kleenex and took out her own supplies.

To start with, the Rolleiflex her mother had given her. Then she hunted around for the Leica Emile had bought for her birthday their first year in Manhattan. She preferred the Rollei but knew it would be an advantage to take two cameras with her.

She ran her hand over her typewriter; it had been her mother's. Each night of her childhood, Jess had fallen asleep to the sound of keys striking paper, the lullaby of her youth. It wouldn't do for Europe though. A baby Hermes would be just the ticket. How much paper could she feasibly take? Martha had said there were shortages across Europe. She made herself keep thinking along those lines – as if she was going – because the idea that she might have to stay working as a house model, waiting for advertisers to consent to her returning to the pages of magazines, had become unbearable.

A knock at the door startled her and she opened it to find Bel bearing a pot of soup and a bottle of wine.

'The last supper,' Bel said cheerily as she made her way into the kitchen. 'I thought if we acted it out, it might come true.'

Jess managed a smile and took bowls and glasses out of the cupboard, then hugged her friend. 'Thank you. What the hell will I do in Europe without you?'

'You'll find someone. You're the kind of girl who always lands on her feet.' Bel put the soup on the stove and they sat at the kitchen table, waiting for it to warm. 'How did it go?' Bel asked shrewdly, studying Jess's face.

Jess reached for a cigarette. 'As badly as Martha said it would.' She hesitated. 'They showed me a picture of my mother. I took it in a club in Montmartre during one of my parents' rare visits out of the field and into civilisation. I was at boarding school there and they picked me up on their way out for the night; I don't think it ever occurred to them that Montmartre jazz clubs weren't really the place for sixteen-year-old girls.'

Bel smiled. 'Sounds like your parents were the kind every sixteen-year-old thought they wanted. I imagine the reality was a little different.'

'I didn't think so at the time but now . . .' Jess pictured the photograph. Her mother sitting at a table in the club in the centre of a group of artistes, having always been a part of that circle; her college training had been in illustration and drawing as well as botany. In the background, her father stood by the bar, watching her mother as if she was the most precious thing in the world. He always sat at the edges, eyes fixed to her mother's face, content to listen and admire. Jess used to sit with him until, later, it transpired that Jess could tell a better story than anyone – or so she'd thought at the time – and she took her place at the table. She'd soon understood that her moving into the centre actually coincided with her growing into her body and into her smile rather than her abilities as a raconteur.

'I had my first gin when I was fifteen,' Jess said to Bel, inhaling smoke deep into her lungs. 'My first kiss that same night, and you could say that I quenched my curiosity of all things sexual by the time I was seventeen. My parents were either oblivious or had a different moral compass to most – I've never been sure – although I'm fairly certain my mother wasn't faithful to my father.'

'Which the War Department was only too happy to confirm,' Bel said slowly, piecing together the story of what had happened that morning.

Jess nodded. 'They listed the names of men my mother had had affairs with. And they listed the names of men I was suspected of sleeping with. They were trying to establish a pattern, they said. A pattern of licentiousness that would preclude me from ever being let loose among an army of men. Of course, their list of my paramours was long and hugely exaggerated.'

'So you're not going?'

'I don't know. I told them . . .' She hesitated, wondering now how she'd ever had the bravado to retaliate when all she'd wanted to do was cry, because the irony of it all was that Jess might have lived openly with a man for three years but it was only one man; she would never cheat on anyone, no matter what the War Department thought.

'I hope you said something typically Jessica May and left their filthy mouths hanging open.' Bel reached across the table for Jess's hand.

Something typically Jessica May. It was the first time, sitting in the War Department offices, that she'd ever wanted to be anything other than typically Jessica May. But why should she change for a group of condescending men?

'I said,' Jess stood theatrically, hand on hip, '"My, my, it's a wonder I have any energy left to apply to be a correspondent. Do you provide the men who apply with a list of their conquests? Or is that something you all drink to at the bar later? Perhaps I might write about this *screening process* for *Vogue*, seeing as how I apparently don't have a reputation left to lose."'

Bel laughed. 'Bravo!'

Jess walked over to the stove to stir the soup. Of course she'd been dismissed after that, her threat hanging in the air like cheap perfume, tawdry but essential; if she capitulated, then how would she ever survive in the European Theatre of Operations?

'Sometimes I feel like I'm always saying goodbye,' Jess said suddenly, back turned to Bel. 'It's one of the things I remember about growing up. That I had to be funny and fabulous so I'd make friends and then, once I'd made the friends, we'd leave. Even when I was at boarding school in Paris, my parents would pull me out every few weeks when they needed photographs taken. Then I'd come back and, even though it was the same school, it was like starting again.'

Starting again. Which was what she'd be doing now if she was ever accredited by the War Department.

She continued. 'There's just one girl, Amelia – she was English – who I still write to. Her parents had left her at school when she was seven and she'd only seen them twice in nine years. We bonded over a certain kind of parental ignorance, although our parents were nothing alike. Her father was in the army and always away somewhere. My father had the social skills of a mollusc, so my mother thought that taking me to all their parties would teach me both how to look after myself and how to win people over.'

'Did it work?' Bel asked with a trace of irony.

'I won you over, didn't I?' Jess teased, facing her friend and pushing the past back down to where it belonged.

She ladled soup into bowls and pushed a pile of clippings across the table towards Bel. 'Martha told me to read these. Ruth Cowan and Inez Robb got themselves assigned to the WACs – the Women's Army Corp – in North Africa and they've been reporting from there. About what it's like to have to wear trousers instead of skirts and the trials of only going to the hair salon every few months. In this one,' Jess pointed to a page, 'Cowan even says she'd prefer to have a bomb fall on her than share a ditch with a spider. I wonder if any of those things cross the minds of the soldiers out there? Every one of their by-lines carries the words "Girl Reporter". If you put that on any of my pieces I'll never speak to you again.'

'What are they going to do with you if you do get yourself over there?' Bel said, shaking her head and starting to laugh. 'I'd hate to be the first man to try calling *you* a girl reporter. Don't forget you're probably subject to military law so you might have to eat your words occasionally. Although I can't imagine how a woman who had her first kiss at age fifteen will tolerate censorship.'

'My plan is not to kiss anybody while I'm away,' Jess informed her primly. 'If I do, then I just reinforce every suspicion they already have about me. I'm sure they're itching for me to seduce an entire division of the US Army. I'm not planning to give them the satisfaction.'

'Sounds like you won't be having any satisfaction while you're away, then.' Bel grinned, and that did it.

Jess felt her eyes tear up and her throat tighten. 'I think Emile has cured me of wanting that kind of satisfaction for a good while.'

'I wanted to make you laugh,' Bel said. 'Don't cry. The formidable Jessica May does not cry. Even when our art director excoriated you in front of a whole team of graphic designers for framing a picture with too much surrealist ambition, I never saw you cry.'

Jess gave a small laugh and wiped her eyes, hoping to wipe away all thoughts of Emile. 'I'd forgotten about that,' she said to Bel. 'That was the day you told me you were going to run my first piece. We went and drank too much champagne at the Stork Club afterwards.'

'And here you are now, waiting to take more photos and write a whole lot more pieces about a war.'

'Perhaps it pays to be publicly excoriated and then to go out and get drunk.'

'Sounds like a motto that might hold you in good stead for the next couple of years.' Bel hugged Jess. 'I'm going to miss you. *When* you go. Not if. When.'

Three

The War Department did let her go. Thankfully, the Condé Nast empire's influence was vast. They made Jess cut her teeth on some home-front reporting of the training of WACs, which *Vogue* published, and when she managed to do that to everyone's satisfaction, she was finally given orders to go overseas, not long after her twenty-third birthday.

Thus she became a captain in the US Army – her rank and uniform a courtesy meant only to provide camouflage and to stop her being shot as a spy if she was captured. She was inoculated against tetanus, typhoid and typhus, and given a card from the Adjutant General's Office of the War Department showing her fingerprints and stating her birth date, hair colour, eye colour, height, weight, and including a photograph of her looking stunned – it would never make it into the pages of *Vogue*, she thought with a smile. She kitted herself out in trousers – she packed the two skirts they thrust on her but doubted if skirts and combat zones were a terribly good combination – two men's army shirts, a tie, her pinks and a green US War Correspondent patch for her jacket and cap.

Her embarkation point was in Brooklyn, where a sergeant looked her over and said, 'Virgin?'

Jess couldn't help laughing. 'Only in matters of war,' she replied smoothly and saw every visible piece of his skin flush bright red.

He led her to a warehouse, punishing her with silence for turning his attempt to embarrass her back on him. She was issued a musette bag, a canteen, a helmet, sunglasses that she surreptitiously slipped back into the pile – she knew from being out with her parents that her sunglasses were probably better than anything the United States Army could issue her with. Next came insect powder, which she was used to from paleobotany expeditions, chocolate, mosquito netting and gloves. She added the items to everything she'd brought with her: socks, underwear, cold cream, lipstick and powder, her two cameras, film, lenses, flash bulbs, repair parts, and typewriter paper. Plus a Stella Designs dress, made especially for her by Estella Bissette, from the lightest silk, which folded down to fit into the palm of her hand. Thankfully she'd been allowed to have her Hermes baby typewriter go as an extra piece of baggage, rather than having to fit that into her bag as well.

She'd done her homework and asked to go to Italy where the nurses, she'd been told, were closer to the front than they'd been in any other war. As a woman, Jess wasn't allowed to cover the actual war. Just the ancillaries. So her destination was Naples, recently liberated by the US Army, and her orders were to record the work of the nurses for the readers of *Vogue*.

In Naples, the Public Relations Officer – or PRO – a man she discovered she'd have to mollify despite the papers in her hand, let her cool her heels for a fortnight while he verified that her orders were real and that some *damn fool in Washington* had actually let a woman come to Italy to report on the Medical Corps and that Stone, *the damn fool PRO in London* – hadn't warned him about it.

'You can go out to the Eleventh Field Hospital,' he told her at last. 'But you'll have to wait until someone's heading that way. I don't have a jeep for you.'

'Where do you suggest I wait?' she enquired coolly. 'By the side of the road with my thumb out? Or does the US Army have a more orderly approach to hitchhiking?'

'If I were you,' he said evenly, 'I'd concentrate on keeping myself safe. Women are absolutely *not* allowed near a combat zone. I'm not taking any shit if you get yourself hurt.'

~

How exactly does one stay safe when one is taken to an area that is supposed to be out of the combat zone, but which turns out to be the scene of a conflagration?

In Naples, on the dance floor at the Orange Club, Jess had learned that the Eleventh Field Hospital was near Mignano on the ridge of hills surrounding the Cassino Valley. It had sounded lovely but, in a jeep that had come to a sudden halt in the place where the field hospital should be, there was nothing lovely: only sound beyond anything she'd ever imagined, so loud that she couldn't distinguish individual noises but rather one catastrophic roar, like a gargantuan lion provoked.

The drive north from Naples had given her no indication of what she was heading into. She'd sat in the jeep, which had the floor sandbagged to minimise the effect of any mines they might drive over, one of a constant stream of olive-coloured vehicles – tanks, trucks, ambulances, command cars with names like Black Devil and Death Dodger painted on them. They passed tent camps that stretched for miles in a sea of mud, dotted with soldiers stripped to the waist, shaving. Mounds of rubble that must once have been villages; occasionally they passed a pink wall still standing. Italian women washing clothes in troughs because laundry still had to be done even in the midst of war. Coils of communications wire that stretched on as if the veins of the earth were unexpectedly and horribly on display. Children playing in wrecked munitions carriers.

And then, suddenly and magnificently in front of her stood the mountains, snow-capped and wild, perforating the sky. The peaks rose above a valley from which white puffs of smoke erupted, the scars of shells gouging the once beautiful land, artillery tracks making a crazed, circular pattern. The view was obliterated a moment later by the rain that had been threatening. It came in thick and grey, engulfing everything.

Immediately afterwards, the driver skidded to a halt. They'd rounded a bend and found a battle instead of a hospital. The sound became something Jess heard not only in her ears but all through her body, thudding on irresolutely like a secondary, even a tertiary heartbeat. A sound she couldn't escape from and could hardly bear, such was the pressure of it in her head and her chest. The driver made to turn the car around but Jess opened the door of the jeep – Rollei around her neck, Leica in hand – and jumped out before he could stop her.

'You should help them,' she cried when the driver hesitated. To her, it looked as if the soldiers on their side were capable of nothing more than defence in the face of what was being thrown and shot and hurled at them.

He hopped out too and hit the ground, diving straight into a mud so viscous it was hard to believe solid ground could exist anywhere beneath the mire. 'Stay by the car,' he ordered, clambering across the ground, the camouflage patterns on his uniform no longer needed because his whole body was now covered in clay.

'Stay by the car?' Jess shouted. It was a ridiculous command; the car was exposed. A horrific scream that seemed to be right above her head had her instinctively mimicking the driver: making for the ground as fast as she could. By sheer luck, she fell into a ditch, which provided a semblance of cover and she thanked God that the person there wore an American uniform rather than a German one.

'What the hell are you doing here?' the owner of the uniform barked.

'This was supposed to be a field hospital,' Jess snapped back. 'He,' Jess indicated the driver, who was hunched over a couple of feet away in the same ditch, 'was meant to know where we were going.'

'If he's come from Naples, then he doesn't know shit. It *was* a field hospital. It was evacuated last night.' The GI, whose rank insignia proclaimed him a captain, raised his head and fired his gun into the blindness in front of them.

Jess crouched where she was, unmoving. It was inconceivable that this was battle: a huddle of men in a boggy ditch popping their heads up every few seconds to shoot in the general direction from which a cannonade of machine gun fire emanated. And she knew, as surely as the fact that she could actually die at any moment, that she'd been a damn fool. She hadn't thought about what armed conflict would be like. She'd understood she'd be roughing it, that her accommodations would likely be tents, that there would be no luxuries. But she'd been so busy fighting to get herself here that she hadn't stopped to imagine how it would feel to be in range of enemy bullets. Because she wasn't supposed to be in range of enemy bullets.

Thank God for the noise and the physical echo of the sound inside her body. It deafened her to the usual physical reactions to fear; she couldn't feel her heart or her breath and whether both were faster than usual, she couldn't even comprehend that she had hands, let alone that they might be sweating. Her eyes were almost the only thing that seemed to be within her control and she tried to fix her gaze on one thing, rather than everything. As she did so, she realised that she was the only one in the hole who was frozen; none of the men looked scared. After their first flicker of surprise at seeing she was a woman, each one had settled back into a state that looked a lot like resignation. Which meant they'd done this before. Too many times. And they'd survived or else they wouldn't be here. It gave her hope.

She concentrated on her fingers. They responded to her thoughts, flexing, and she remembered the cameras in her hands. She flicked the Leica around her back and lifted the Rollei. *Look through the lens*, she told herself. A camera reduced things to the size of a frame and she could certainly do with the chaos being minimised in some way.

Her mind was functioning enough for her to know that it would be lethal to move suddenly or distract the attention of the American soldiers. But the benefit of a twin lens reflex like the Rollei was that she shot from the waist and could be unobtrusive. The captain was too close to her for perfect focus but, rather than fiddling with the focusing knob, she leaned back a little, allowing her position to focus the shot. Then, while he shot bullets at a small posse of German soldiers she could just make out when she lifted her head to the edge of the ditch, she shot photographs.

Focus, shoot. Focus, shoot. She repeated the words over and over in her head. And she concentrated on deliberately blurring the background of each picture so that the flashes of light from the bullets or shells or God only knew what were rendered flamelike, dancing around the captain's hands, which were so rigid and black with dirt they almost appeared to be a part of the gun they held.

How does one grow accustomed to the noise, she wondered as she at last began to discern individual sounds within the roar: a sudden loud shriek and bellow, which made her flinch, followed by the earth lifting into the air and then raining down just a few feet away as the jeep, with most of her belongings in it, blew up.

After a time, the rain cleared enough for Jess to see that the Germans were far closer than she'd realised – thank God she hadn't noticed that when she'd first landed in the hole or she might never have found a way through the terror. They looked bewildered, not at all like the devilish beings she'd imagined them to be. In fact, they seemed just like the captain next to her: youngish, mid-twenties perhaps, filthy, tired, wet, caked in mud and oblivious to anything other than the sighting and shooting of an enemy.

Then the captain began to make a series of complicated hand gestures – which she gathered were a way of communicating through the noise – to the other soldiers, and she saw some of them climb out and race a hundred yards forward before disappearing into another ditch. She lifted her head up just enough to record their flight on her camera.

'You can't do that!' the captain yelled.

'Why the hell not?' she retorted. If he stopped her from taking pictures then she would have nothing to distract her from the still-terrifying reality of being in the Nazis' line of fire. Like a reflex, her body defaulted to the wit and the smile that had always got her what she wanted, and she was once again amazed at how she was still able to function amidst the inferno. 'Stop worrying about me,' she said. 'I'm much less deadly than the Germans.'

She thought she saw a flicker of a smile; at any rate, he turned his attention away from her and back to the exploding stars that burst into life and flickered out before them, into the smoke, thicker than any fog rolling up the Hudson, into the choking smog of earth and ammunition and adrenaline that hung in the air.

Who knew how long she crouched there, recording every moment first with the Rolleiflex and then, when it only had one shot left – which she wanted to save – with the Leica. In between bouts of fire, the GIs wisecracked to one another, finding time to light cigarettes from the ubiquitous white and red packs of Lucky Strikes. She remembered reading one of Martha's articles about Spain in which she'd said that you couldn't wait forever for the shell to fall on you; you couldn't cower in expectation of death all day. Watching the men around her, Jess understood what those words meant.

Then, just as she had the Leica lined up, her finger depressing the button, she saw, through the viewfinder, a man in a German uniform fall, the consequence of a shot from her partner's gun. The captain didn't react, just lined up the next one and shot him, too. The men died, not gloriously, not spectacularly and certainly without anyone to mourn them, disappearing into the mud beneath their feet. Two lives had just ended, one of them was frozen in time inside her camera. She didn't know how she would bring herself to look at that negative, didn't know that she could ever allow herself to discover exactly what it meant to die.

She was supposed to be glad; two fewer Germans was a good thing for her country. But how could anyone be glad of a boy dying alone, an unthought-of consequence in this grand mess called war?

∼

'I need to send you out with the medics,' her companion said a while later when the shooting had lessened and the men were drinking from their canteens.

'Where are the medics?' Jess asked. 'All the noise has mixed my head up into jigsaw pieces. It's my first day on the job – and I'm not saying that for sympathy, but by way of explanation.'

'Explanation accepted and no sympathy given.'

'How long has it been like this?' she asked, indicating the mud and the rain, knowing her job was to get answers to go with her pictures, and that conversation was, like the Rollei, a good diversion from fear.

The captain rubbed his temple tiredly. 'Weeks. Since we arrived in September. Apparently nobody thought to check what an Italian winter was like.'

He was a veteran, then. Very few US Army units had served in Europe, but he'd already done two months in Italy. His words reminded Jess of her father who, like the people who hadn't understood what havoc Italian rain could wreak, was always the one wanting to go to faraway places in winter, who never considered the weather, who would never remember where exactly they'd pitched the tent. It was as if men like her father were running the war, although that probably wasn't fair. It was just that, out here in slime and sludge that roiled around them like a living thing, in rain like nothing seen since the time of Noah, in the midst of men who were alive one minute and dead the next, organisation must be impossible. And Jess thanked God that she wasn't a dumb debutante model like they all thought, that she was her mother's child, that she had learned from a young age to organise herself amidst the worst kind of shambles.

'What?' he asked, studying her face.

'I was just being thankful for being caught in a hurricane in Tahiti when I was six. It wasn't as bad as this, but . . .' she shrugged.

'Tahiti?' he asked, eyebrows raised.

'Tahiti,' she repeated.

'Sure as shit would give anything to be there now,' he said. 'Hurricane and all. Let's go.'

Jess began to stand, to revive her cramped legs, but immediately ducked upon hearing the whistling sound she'd come to realise preceded a shell explosion.

'No need to duck,' he said. 'That one's ours. We try not to hit ourselves too often.'

'How can you tell?'

'Listen,' he said, cocking his ear as if they were straining to hear when in fact it was impossible to do anything else. 'If you hear the whistle first and then the thump, it's theirs. Thump first, echo after is ours. You learn to tell a thump from a whistle from an echo pretty damn quick. We're heading for that foxhole over there. Should be a medic inside. You'll be okay.' He glanced up at the sky as if he had the power to stop shells from falling in their vicinity during the time it took them to scramble to the back of the line.

Jess was thankful for the mini-lesson on the intricacies of shells. There was so damn much she didn't know. But Martha had said that she knew nothing about war when she arrived in Spain in 1937. And Martha had survived and learned from men like the one beside Jess now and done a damn good job. It wasn't in Jessica May's make-up to give up after one frightening encounter. But she said none of this to the captain as they hurried along, although hurried was the wrong word – the ground was so slippery she was terrified of falling over and ruining her film, if not her pride.

'Wouldn't it be easier to slide along on our stomachs like penguins?' she asked at one point after she'd had to drop her pride and grab his arm just in time to save herself from landing face first in the slime.

He laughed. 'It probably would be.'

They found the medic and the scramble continued to a point even further back, where a jeep was parked. An injured man was laid in the back and the captain climbed in after Jess.

'You don't have to escort me,' she said.

'Jerry's retreated for now. Won't be back till tomorrow if we're lucky. I can spare half an hour. Besides, if anyone finds out I had a woman in my foxhole and didn't deliver her to a point out of shooting range, then I'll be serving as a private in a company in a training camp rather than running a company in the field. And yes,' he grinned, 'there are so many jokes you could make about what I just said that it's hard to know where to start.'

She burst out laughing. If anyone had said to Jess that it was possible to smile or laugh at the most dangerous moment one had ever faced in one's life, she wouldn't have believed them. But now she saw that was all you could do to get through; that on the other side of jocularity lay despair and nobody could afford to waste a single moment on that out here otherwise they might as well run without a weapon straight into the open arms of the Germans.

It was only a short drive to the field hospital, which was altogether too fine a word to describe the tents, the stretchers, the bodies, the stink of mud and flesh, the too few people unloading the ambulances with the too many bodies. 'Flick!' he called to a woman who'd come out to check over the wounded men in their vehicle, 'Can you take Captain . . .' He stopped.

'Oh, Jessica May. Lovely to meet you,' she quipped, holding out a filthy hand for him to shake.

Before he could reply, Flick accosted him. 'Where've you been hiding, stranger?' She gave him the kind of easy smile that suggested they'd done more than share war stories.

And Jess knew it was why she'd saved that one shot on the Rollei – for just such a moment. She took it. The grubby officer looking back over his shoulder to the battle he'd left, to the men he probably needed to check on, and the nurse gazing up at him with adoration.

~

That night at the Eleventh Field Hospital was almost worse than the battlefield. The Germans controlled the high ground of the mountains, and the hospital was within shelling range, the place of greater safety it had moved to proving only to be the better of two bad choices, rather than a sensible position.

Within minutes of her arrival, Flick had shown Jess a spare cot in a tent with five other nurses, the cot only available because the nurse who'd once occupied it was now a patient. That was the cost of having nurses closer to the front line than they'd ever been in any other war but it was counterbalanced by the fact that they could have a man in the shock tent and hooked up to life-saving plasma within one hour rather than five.

Jess was lucky enough to cadge a roll of film for her Leica from the supply store – someone had died with it on them and nobody else had a use for it. But that was the only piece of luck in one long and unlucky day as the Germans began to toss shells at the hospital with deadly intensity.

'Never shelled us before,' Anne, a nurse – a small woman who looked as if she would hardly be able to help lift a stretcher but here she was, carrying the weight of every injured man's survival on her tiny shoulders – said grimly to Jess. 'First time we thought it was an accident. Now we think Jerry means it.'

And Jerry did mean it. Before long, a shell made a direct hit on the mess tent, leaving a stew of ration boxes, canned eggs, salted peanuts and onions embedded in the mud. It was fortunately empty of people at the time but the result was that the electrical system, which had been wired through the mess tent, went out and the night continued on through the beams of flashlights.

So Jess found herself in an operating theatre holding one of the flashlights when all other hands were busy, watching doctors operate with their boots covered in mud, their surgical gowns covered in blood. Jess's camera caught them as she concentrated once more on looking only through the frame; it was the best way to keep her stomach calm. And she had to stay calm because what did anyone back in America know of any of this?

Of exactly what a mortar could do to a leg, tearing away flesh so that only bone held the limb to the body, of the screaming sound of a shell, which caused everyone to drop to the floor of the theatre – but only after, Jess noticed, petite but gutsy Anne had paused to check the position of the plasma needle in the boy's arm – and then, once the explosion was heard and the shell thus detonated, to stand up, retake their positions and continue operating as if they wouldn't all die at any moment. And so it went on, the whooshing sound, the dive to the floor, the explosion, the standing up, the return to the operation, the endless changing of blood and plasma bags.

Man after injured man came in, faces lacerated, bones smashed. So many men needing so much blood that, after midnight, supplies ran dangerously low. The staff gave their arms over to needles to draw out their blood and so did Jess. She saw a surgeon, Major Henderson he'd said his name was, trying to stop an injured soldier – whose lungs were full of blood – from drowning, by drawing the blood out of his lungs with a tracheotomy tube and feeding that same blood back to the soldier intravenously. Wounded men arrived unabated and Jess couldn't believe that ambulances were still driving through the sleeting rain and pitch dark outside.

'Hold his foot,' Major Henderson ordered Jess at one point.

Jess put down her camera and found herself staring at a leg being sawn off. She followed instructions, forcing herself to look at the face of the injured soldier without crying; he was the one losing his legs, not her.

The soldier grabbed Jess's hand. 'My feet are cold,' he murmured. 'Blanket.'

And even though the soldier had no feet, Jess found a blanket and tucked it around the empty space. It was that one small act of comfort that finally tipped her over into tears. She tried to dam them but Anne saw her face and touched her shoulder gently.

'Keep busy,' Anne said. 'When it's quiet, we have too much time to think, which only leads to crying. Try not to think, as much as you can.'

Jess tried, she really did. But when she saw the pile of amputated legs stacked against the side of the tent, she had to stop, breathing hard to keep the nothing in her stomach from pouring out. She wanted to go home.

Thankfully, the shelling lessened around the same time and Jess and three other nurses were sent off to bed where Jess struggled not to let the sudden and aching homesickness show on her face.

'Best put your bedroll under the cot,' Anne advised. 'If this keeps up we might need the protection.'

So Jess did as she was told, watching while Anne heated water in an empty ration can on a little oil stove in the middle of the tent before tipping the water into her helmet to begin a rudimentary wash. One of the other nurses scrubbed her thin and shivering back. Anne kept her boots on throughout because even the dams the women had built around the tent couldn't stop the rainwater from oozing across the floor. She finished by removing one foot at a time from her boots and sprinkling each one liberally with the contents of a yellow tin of Marathon foot powder.

'You can have the next bath,' Anne said, nodding at the fresh batch of water that was heating.

'We're going to have to dig the trench around the powder room a bit deeper tomorrow,' another nurse said as she entered the tent. 'I think the entire Volturno River has been redirected at us.'

All that night, Jess sobbed in her bed and nobody could hear her through the noise. If Emile had been there, she would have taken him into her bed because the familiarity of his physical presence, his connection to a world she could comprehend, would at least be a kind of comfort. Instead, she saw all the photos she'd taken, the combat pictures the less powerful of them all: the nurse who'd called their forlorn latrine, its walls made from piles of folded blankets, a powder room; Anne's insistence that her rudimentary wash out of her helmet was a bath; Flick's bright pink painted fingernails; the full-length mirror one of the nurses had picked up from a wrecked palace on their way north into Italy and which hung from a rope attached to the tent roof. And the photo she hadn't taken, of the boy who'd died despite the tracheotomy – the boy who'd asked for watermelon just before his heart stopped; his ghost was there in every image.

The world needed to know that Monte Cassino, a speck on a map, the name of a battle to anyone in America, was a boy with no feet searching for comfort in a blanket. But what if Jess couldn't convey that? Her job was so much more than she'd understood it to be. And that was another reason she cried: because she doubted she had the talent, the stamina and the stomach to do her job the way it ought to be done.

Perhaps she should admit that she'd made a mistake. Perhaps she should ask Bel to send somebody over to take her place.

Four

She didn't have a chance to ask to be replaced. Instead, the enraged PRO from Naples – the one who'd told her to make sure she wasn't responsible for any shit landing on him – arrived at the hospital in a furious spray of mud, telling her she'd completely disregarded his directives when she waltzed out into a battlefield.

'It was a little tricky to think about you while I was in a ditch being shot at,' she retaliated, sounding more like her old self than she had for the past two days.

Somehow, word had spread, quicker than lice in a foxhole, that there'd been a woman at the Italian front, which was a violation of the terms of her accreditation and was also, apparently, a crime worse than slaughter. She was put on a plane in Naples and sent back to England. She'd thought she wanted to get out of the hell that had left the underworld and landed on a mountain in Italy, but the way she'd been yelled at and ordered away had made her seethe and not give anyone the satisfaction of telling them she didn't want to be in Cassino anyway.

She was collected at the airfield by Warren Stone, the London-based PRO. Stone was tall, blond, with too many white teeth and he spoke to her in the kind of soothing tones she imagined a vet might use with a temperamental mare. He even put a hand on her arm, the same way one approached a horse's rump, gingerly.

'I know that a mistake was made,' he said.

'Exactly,' Jess said, relieved that somebody understood she hadn't purposely gone out looking to photograph a fight. 'I was told I'd find a hospital there, which is what I was supposed to be writing about, not a battle.'

'I can get you a more suitable assignment,' Warren said, smiling at her. 'We like the women to focus on women's interest, for the women's pages. Like this.' He passed her a newspaper folded to a piece written by Inez Robb in North Africa. The headline read 'War Fails to Spoil Midwinter Cruise on the Mediterranean' and was accompanied by a cartoon drawing of Robb standing before a mirror applying lipstick. 'I have no idea why you were sent to Italy. Like I said, now that I'm looking after you, it won't happen again.'

'I asked to go to Italy,' Jess said quietly, while her mind processed both what he'd said and the way he'd said it, as if he were her protector, ready to guide her, with his sharp white teeth, towards the things seemly for a woman, rather than the unladylike.

'But now that you've seen Italy, you'll know you made a mistake.'

He let the sentence hang in the air, giving her the out she'd thought she wanted. But to tell him, with all his condescension, that yes, she couldn't face Italy and would rather report on cruises was something she found herself unable to do. Instead she said, testing, still unsure if she was reading the situation correctly, 'I wouldn't have been sent back to England if I was a man who'd been driven to a battlefield, would I? So it's not just that I took photographs that were beyond the scope of my orders to report on the hospital, is it?'

'Women are not permitted in combat zones. But I can get you plenty of other assignments.' Again that touch on the arm, that smile – which suggested he was used to having some kind of potent effect when he flashed his teeth around – and Jess realised that, as well as wanting to relegate her to the kind of reporting she could just as easily do for *Vogue* back in America, he was flirting. And doing it with such assurance, as if he really thought she'd bat her eyelashes at him, be grateful that he'd rescued her and be only too happy to let him take her womanliness out to dinner — so long as the restaurant wasn't on the same land area as the war that was forbidden to her by that same femaleness.

'I should limit myself to cruises and cosmetics?' she asked coolly, dumping the newspaper on the floor of the jeep.

'Perhaps just cosmetics,' he said, taking his eyes off the road, raking them over her face and then her body and grinning at her as if she'd appreciate the joke. 'I believe it's your area of expertise.'

He knew who she was. She gritted her teeth. 'I'm here because I possess other kinds of expertise as well.'

'We can definitely talk about that over a drink.'

'I just want to do my job,' Jess said formally, as if it wasn't a personal rejection; it wasn't a good idea to get the PRO offside although she had no idea if she still had work, if she even wanted to do the work or if this uncomfortable meeting in a car was the end of it all.

'Women don't belong in the European Theatre.' His tone was harder now and his eyes carried a warning: she should back off and accept his interest, his veiled offer of, not a date, but an assignation. She imagined that the women he allowed into the cosmetic arena of the European Theatre must fall for his smile and his offers — or at least pretend to do so in order to keep the peace. But she had never been very good at pretending. The jeep pulled to a stop outside the Dorchester Hotel.

'Why not?' She wished she could just walk away, certain his answer wouldn't make her feel any better.

'Well,' he smiled again, 'there's the latrine business. Where would you —'

'Don't,' she interrupted, unable to listen any more. Men were losing their limbs and their lives and the PROs were worried about where a woman might empty her bladder. She climbed out of the jeep.

As she did, Warren said, 'You're confined to your room until the penalty for disobeying your orders is decided by the Public Relations Office.'

~

Jailed. She was, she realised over the next week, effectively jailed. She'd been given a chance to scramble out of this mess, to go back to New York, or to write filler pieces about frivolities but instead she'd antagonised someone she would have to work with, if she stayed. *If.*

For days she stared out the window at London, a dismal, bombed-up mess of rubble and dismembered buildings. How would the world ever be put back together again? There was hardly food enough to eat in the city, cigarettes and toothbrushes were non-existent or worth a small fortune, all of which would make replacing the things she'd lost in the jeep explosion more difficult. London felt trapped in an eternal night; no sooner had the sun struggled to rise than it was dark by four in the afternoon, a darkness unrelieved by blackout conditions. Outside, along the street at the back of the hotel, she watched two girls dressed in homemade nurses' uniforms bury their dolls in the crumbled brick and concrete remains of a house and then dig them out, put them in prams and administer to their wounds. They were playing at war, as if it were a game, as if it were the only reality they knew how to mimic. What happened to children who'd been born while the fighting was on, who didn't understand that it wasn't normal for bombs to fall from the sky like Chicken Licken's acorns, who believed that streets were comprised of both intact buildings and desecrated ones, who had never seen a night alight with electricity?

She sat at her chair before her desk, pen poised over paper, thinking to write down her thoughts and then perhaps type them up when she was able to replace her typewriter. But Warren Stone's obvious belief that women should only write about – or provide – decoration made her both unable to write and unwilling to prove his theory that women and war didn't mix. So she waited, reasoning that if the Public Relations Office threw her out, then she'd have to go; she wouldn't be quitting. Would she?

A tap at the door roused her and she opened it to find one of the hotel staff with a telegram for her.

Sorry Darl, she read, *none of your photographs made it through, not even the ones at the hospital. The War Department censored them all. What can I say, better luck next time? Bel xx*

Jess crumpled the paper in her hand.

It had all been for nothing. Worse than nothing; her one attempt at getting a story had resulted in her being confined to a hotel room, waiting to be fired. But when had Jessica May ever waited to be fired? She hurled the telegram at the wall, then stormed over to the dressing table and stared at herself in the mirror.

You're not a coward, she told herself. So what if she wasn't talented enough to take the photos she saw in her head? It was her job to *make* herself that talented. Nobody else would take those pictures; a male photojournalist would never think nurses worthy of any interest besides the prurient. And of course the War Department wouldn't let Bel have Jess's pictures because then everyone would know that a woman had been in a combat zone and *that*, apparently, was the real problem, not the death and dying and undocumented bravery of that small tent full of women in Monte Cassino. Not the children who were paying the price with their childhoods for a war they had never wished for.

Jess watched the girls outside wrapping lengths of white fabric around their dolls' heads, their faces serious, adult. Her mind whirled. The photos she'd taken in Italy, the photos she could keep taking if only she stayed on, were not like other journalists' pictures from Europe: soldiers in trenches with guns, pictures declaring that war was about men and battles and bullets. Her pictures from Italy would have been clarifications: miniaturised explanations that these were the consequences of that war. In every photograph, Jess had held both horror and beauty in her hands – a thing as precious and rare as an asymmetrical butterfly. It was her duty to transmit that to the world, no matter what it did to her stomach. She picked up the Rollei, pressed it to the glass and captured on film exactly what, now, child's play had become.

Then she put the camera down and made for the door. She would put her case to the Public Relations Office. Because she *had* to stay.

A tap at the door drew her up short. 'Marty!' she cried.

'I thought you might need these.' Martha Gellhorn marched into the room. 'Don't ask what I had to do to get them.' In her hand was a large bottle of whiskey, and a new Baby Hermes typewriter. 'I heard what happened.' Marty settled into a chair and poured out two whiskeys, glasses full to the brim. 'Cheers. Here's to breaking the rules.'

'You mean this has happened to you too?' Jess took the whiskey and propped herself up on the bed. To look at Martha, legs crossed louchely, glass held casually in her fingertips, one would never think it.

'I'm thirty-five years old and I've covered four theatres of war. Yet all I'm allowed to do here is sit on the sidelines. I spent the week at Bomber Command but nobody will take me up in a plane. I watched two male correspondents go up though.' Marty swallowed her drink. 'There was a press conference while you were in Italy and I asked, as I always do, if I could get a posting to a Press Camp – they're right near the front. The delightful Warren Stone leered at me like I was a hooker and said, "Last time I checked, Martha, you were a woman." Every single person in the room guffawed as if it was the funniest thing they'd ever heard – that Warren Stone had had the luck to discover I was a woman, which of course he hasn't. Wolfing, I've decided to call it – when they treat you like all they want from you is your breasts and your legs and the space in between.'

'You didn't think to tell me any of this when you were so busy convincing Bel to send me here? What will they do to me? I don't want to go back to New York.' Jess said it with conviction.

'Depends if someone speaks up for you and says what really happened,' Martha said sagely, clearly the veteran of many a battle with the rules and those enforcing them.

'Nobody will do that. It was my first day.'

'Maybe they'll let you off for naiveté. Don't be afraid to wear a skirt; beg, borrow or steal a pair of silk stockings, cross your legs and bat your lashes,' Martha advised. 'You can soap off your principles later.'

Jess stood up, a little unsteadily – the large glass of whiskey had found its way into her bloodstream quickly – and stroked the typewriter Martha had brought her. 'Do you ever get scared?' she asked, her voice low.

Marty lit a cigarette and offered Jess a smile. 'Do you remember that piece I wrote about the hospital in Barcelona?'

Jess thought for a moment. Then she nodded. Martha had written about seeing a ward full of injured children, one boy sobbing for his mother. She'd been asked if she wanted to see the medical ward and in her article she'd written: *'Well,' I said. Well, no, I thought.* Martha had wanted to turn away too.

Jess looked up and caught the same look in Marty's eyes that she could feel at the back of her own. Trepidation, which was, she supposed, somewhat different to fear or cowardice.

'It means you're human,' Martha said gently. 'Not that you're incapable of doing your job. Channel it into your pictures. And your words.'

It was good advice. Before she could say so, before they could both get caught any further in the sticky emotions of war, Marty turned the conversation. 'I heard that Warren Stone didn't get the promotion he's been hankering after. Which maybe means there's going to be some good news for you.'

A knock sounded on the door. Jess opened it and her heart sank at the sight of an officer in dress uniform. 'You've come to escort me to my doom,' she said.

The officer shook his head. 'You don't remember me, do you?' He removed his cap, as if that might help.

Jess studied his face. There was something familiar about him. 'Shit,' she said when she realised it was the captain from the foxhole in Italy. Then she winced.

'I seem to remember that my language in the ditch was probably more colourful than it should have been. So I'd say we're even,' he said.

'I didn't recognise you without the mud,' she said grimly. Now, in the light and without rain, she could see that his hair was actually dark even minus the dirt. His eyes were the grey-blue of dusk and his face was serious. 'I really am doomed if they've brought you in to bear witness.'

'I'm Dan Hallworth. I did come to bear witness.' His mouth turned up a little and she felt herself stiffen at the thought that he would enjoy ruining her career as a correspondent before it had even begun.

'And?' she said despairingly. She felt Marty step in behind her.

'And I told them it wasn't your fault. That you had no choice but to be there because the US Army brought you there. I told them that you put no one in danger and got out the minute you could.'

'You did?' Jess wrapped both her hands around the now-empty glass of whiskey to stop from flinging herself in thanks at Dan Hallworth. 'What did they say?'

'That you should keep out of trouble in future. But,' he added, looking at Martha, 'I can see that's probably not going to happen. How are you, Gellhorn?'

'I'm damned fine, Captain, no, Major Hallworth. Look at that,' she said, fingering the golden oak leaf insignia on his uniform. 'You outrank us both.'

He smiled at Martha. 'I should have known you two would join forces. You even look like sisters.'

Martha touched her hair, which was short and blonde like Jess's, but even curlier. 'If I was ten years younger, perhaps.'

'Do you know *everyone*?' Jess asked Martha.

'Just the ones worth knowing.' Marty winked at Major Hallworth. 'I met Dan in Italy a few weeks back. He took the time to explain to me how fast our men are dying around Cassino.'

'Nothing's changed,' he said, then looked at Jess. 'You're allowed back to Italy. I think your PRO is coming to tell you. But I know from Gellhorn that you ladies don't get a jeep, so I thought I'd pick you up here at 0700 on Tuesday. We'll be back in Purple Heart Valley by the end of the week.' Dan turned to leave.

'Purple Heart Valley?' Jess asked, stopping him.

'They've given out more Purple Hearts in Italy than ever before.'

'It's a beautiful name for a terrible place.'

Before Dan could reply, Jess saw Warren Stone striding down the hallway towards her room.

'I might leave you to it,' Dan said.

'Thank you,' Jess called to his departing back.

'Officer Stone,' Martha drawled, hardly bothering to blow her cigarette smoke away from Warren. 'Always such a pleasure.'

'Cut the shit, Martha,' he said.

'I bet if I was in a nurse's uniform you'd be a lot friendlier,' Martha replied, raising an eyebrow.

Jess drew strength from Martha's lack of fear. 'So I'm off to Italy again?'

Warren grimaced. 'Apparently you are. And I've been given the job of keeping you in line. So if you do as you're told this time, then I won't have to take the blame for your mistakes again.'

Something in his tone, a mortification when he said the words — *take the blame* — made her wonder if Marty had been right. If there was some link between him not getting his promotion and her victory. She tried for appeasement; perhaps they could start again. 'It was never my intention to go to a battlefield.'

'But then you photographed it and sent those photos to the censors for everyone to see.' This time his voice was hard and Jess sensed there was definitely something more going on — that he had decided she was the one at fault and that whatever had made him angry, he was channelling it into resentment towards her.

It would be best to end the conversation before things deteriorated any further. 'I will avoid all battlefields from now on,' she said before she shut the door. 'What a jerk,' she said to Marty after she'd heard his footsteps fade away.

Martha shrugged. 'That's being kind. Like I said, he's been after a promotion. When you met him, did he spin you a line about being able to get you whatever assignments you wanted? And did he ask you out for dinner?'

Jess nodded.

'He did the same to me and I, like you, was canny enough to be wary. He can't action press assignments; he can only administer them. With a promotion, he'd be able to do more. But thankfully he hasn't got it and I suspect it might be because Dan Hallworth — a CO who's seen more than enough battles and actually knows what's what, as opposed to Warren who hasn't ever seen a battle — has come here and told them that they were wrong and you were right. The powers that be would have seen your photos and been irate that you were so close to combat and told Warren to deal with it. He hasn't. And it sounds as if his punishment is to look after you.' Martha ended with a smirk, as if she relished the chance to see fireworks erupt between Jess and Warren. 'He, like many others, hates the idea of women doing this job — apparently it goes against nature, unless the women also agree to dine with him.'

'I'm not sure that makes me feel any better.'

'Getting a CO like Dan on your side is what you need. Some people call it an unfair advantage. I say that if you're lucky enough to find one of the few men in the US Army who couldn't care less if you were a woman or a flamingo – and they do exist; the French are much less concerned about women at the front – then use it. Besides,' Martha added, 'he's very easy on the eye.'

'Easy on the eye!' Jess exploded. 'I think being a jerk precludes anyone from being attractive.'

Marty laughed. 'Not Warren. Your Major Hallworth. And we all need a little love – or bodily comfort – in the midst of war.'

Bodily comfort. It was what she'd craved that night in Italy. But Jessica May could stand on her own two feet; witnessing war broke her heart enough without needing to involve herself with a man again. She shook her head firmly. 'He's not *my* major. He's just proven himself a friend. And I'm going to need a few of those if I want to last more than a month over here.'

~

As much as she wanted to, on the day she was due to leave for Italy, Jess wasn't able to avoid Warren Stone. He met her in the lobby at six in the morning and she tried to deflect anything he might say or do with an apology.

'I'm sorry about your promotion,' she said honestly. 'If I can speak to somebody to let them know that, as much as it wasn't my fault, it wasn't your fault either, then I will.'

As soon as she said it she knew she'd made a huge mistake. His face contorted, at first surprised, and then anger flared, covering up what might have been embarrassment, or indeed humiliation. Of course he wouldn't want a woman to know of his failures, or for that same woman to then hurtle in and offer assistance in rectifying them.

'I don't need help from a model,' he said slowly.

'I know,' she said quickly, wanting to leave.

'Go to Italy,' he said suddenly. 'And just so you know, I didn't lose. I let you stay. It'll be more fun to watch you leave in disgrace later, just when you think you've settled in.'

'I don't intend to do anything disgraceful.' Jess drew herself up to modelish height, despite knowing that the best course of action would be to collect her bags and go.

'I read over the War Department's screening notes. You won't be able to help yourself.'

'Nothing in those notes was true.'

He laughed. 'Well, that's a shame. Because I may have drunk a little too much last night and my loose tongue may have let a few details about your fondness for bedtime activities slip to some of the other correspondents.' And then, before she was able to let the full blaze of her fury unleash itself upon Warren Stone, his demeanour changed and he began to recite, blandly, a list of rules. 'Gal reporters must never put themselves closer to the front than the nurses in the field.'

Jess stared at him, bewildered by the swift shift of the conversation.

'Good work, Stone,' another PRO said approvingly as he passed.

'Thank you, Sir,' Warren replied obsequiously, falling into step with his superior and following him out of the lobby.

Jess gathered her belongings and sat down to wait for Major Hallworth, riled by everything Stone had said, but trying not to be.

Thankfully Dan soon arrived and greeted her cordially as she seated herself in the jeep. He introduced her to the two men in the back, Private Sparrow and Private Jennings – one blond and tall, the other red-headed and short – and both as green as her. 'They're replacements,' Dan said.

Jess winced at everything the term implied.

The two men gaped at her, then Sparrow, obviously the bolder of the two, gave her a suggestive hello and started to ask, 'Say, aren't you . . .' before Dan quashed the flirtation with a look.

As they pulled out onto the road, Jess asked, 'Shouldn't they be driving you? Don't majors get drivers?'

'As you found out in Italy, just because someone's driving a jeep, it doesn't mean they know where they're going. Those two haven't a clue.' Dan lowered his voice when he said it and she knew he didn't mean they were unsure of the route, but that they wouldn't be able to conceive of what awaited them in Italy.

She turned back to the two privates and gave them a smile; it was all she had to offer. Jennings looked like the kind of man she didn't realise still existed: innocent, a newly baptised babe who blushed furiously at her. Sparrow, on the other hand, took the smile as if it were his due, leaning back in the seat, arm casually outflung, but then a car backfired nearby and she could have sworn she saw him jump and whiten. He immediately reached for a cigarette, no longer meeting her eye.

Jess returned her attention to Dan and decided to risk asking a few questions. 'You were a captain. Now you're the major of a . . . what? And are you infantry?' She tried to see his division patch. 'I'm still coming to terms with army structures and ranks and, at the risk of sounding stupid, I need some education.'

'It's not stupid,' Dan said. 'The US Army is a world unto itself. I'm a paratrooper. Airborne division.' He pointed to the AA on his sleeve. 'In charge of a company.'

A paratrooper. The Italian campaign was the first time paratroopers had ever been used, an elite squad of men trained within an inch of their lives to be dropped by plane behind enemy lines to wreak havoc and provide land support to an amphibious assault, such as that at Sicily. Jess was impressed but she only asked, 'What were you doing in London? I don't imagine you came all the way here just for me.'

'My company had been in combat for sixty-nine days. Mightn't sound like a lot but in those conditions it's too much. We got leave and I didn't have the patience to jitterbug around the dance floor at the Orange Club in Naples, which is crawling with VD anyway . . .' It was his turn to wince. 'Sorry,' he said.

'Don't be.' Jess shook her head. 'When I was in Naples, I heard that one in ten GIs has VD. That you can buy a woman in exchange for a ration box.'

'Women and typhus are the cheapest and most plentiful things in Italy. There's hardly any food for the locals. The women have children they need to feed. The GIs have the only currency worth anything — rations. And some of them spend it any chance they get.'

He spoke quietly, and Jess knew from his tone that he wasn't one of the GIs trading his rations for women. 'What a mess,' she said.

'A mess I was happy to escape from for a week,' he finished. 'When I landed in England, I heard you needed a hand. Then I had meetings about . . .' He shrugged. 'Forward planning.'

'Invasion plans?' Jess guessed. An invasion was being talked about more and more. Everyone knew it was coming but nobody knew when or how.

'Yes. Now I need to say,' he veered off the subject, 'that I have some rules.'

'My God!' she snapped. For the last half hour she'd started to think he was an ordinary person but now he sounded just like Warren Stone. 'I've been told the rules so many times, I could recite them backwards. I'm to stay out of combat zones. Not flirt with any of your men or act in any way befitting my reputation as a model who has, for the past three years, lived with a man in a scandalously unmarried state and slept with at least half of America. Is that about it?'

'No,' he said evenly.

'What have I forgotten? Oh, of course, bat my eyelashes and wrap my legs in silk stockings so you all have something to look at besides the mud?'

She realised, once her outburst was over, that the two men in the back had gone completely silent. So had Dan.

'Your past doesn't mean a damn out there in Purple Heart Valley,' Dan said eventually. 'It's the present that's going to get you blown up. Which is what my rules are about, if you'd let me finish.'

'Oh.'

'I didn't know you were a model or . . . anything else.' The tough paratrooper actually blushed.

Jess couldn't help it. She began to laugh. To have finally found someone who didn't know or care who she was and to have blurted it all out was not one of her finest moments.

'I'm sorry,' she said between gasps of laughter. 'I think I might sit quietly and not say anything for the rest of the trip. I was mad with Warren Stone and I paid you the discourtesy of thinking you were just like him. Tell me your rules and I promise to listen.' She tried to compose her face but she knew the corners of her mouth were still twitching.

He laughed too and his eyes caught the light, glinting silvery blue in the sunshine. 'I know you're pissed off. I can't help that. My only rule is that the safety of my men comes first and if you jeopardise that, I'll boot you back to New York quicker than Warren Stone will. Fair enough?'

'Fair enough,' she agreed.

'Just so you know, I have the same rule for everyone, male or female.'

'Thank you. And perhaps you could forget everything I said a moment ago?'

'I'm not very good at forgetting.' He grinned. 'But I won't tell anyone.'

'And I'll pray they're all as ignorant as you were.'

Which of course they weren't. The minute she stepped out of the jeep and into the crowd of men waiting to board the troopship to Italy, she felt eyes on her. She heard whispers. One GI elbowed his friend in the ribs and said loudly, 'A model and not a virgin. This ship just got a lot more fun.'

Fear. There it was again. She'd thought bullets were the only things to be scared of in a war zone. But her reputation was proving to be the one obstacle she couldn't surmount. She couldn't help the hand that strayed to her face. The face she'd never truly understood. Of course she knew, when she looked in the mirror, that her features were good. That she'd been gifted with blonde hair, deep brown eyes, well-honed cheekbones, full lips, skin that never spotted, and a figure that didn't look out of place in a bathing suit on a beach. But, being a model meant that she'd also seen many other girls similarly gifted, all pretty, but somehow lacking a quality that only a few had. A quality difficult to understand or explain; it was more a feeling than a solid fact. A face that was entrancing, one you could stare at all day and never grow tired of, one that attracted a crowd at a party, or a chorus of catcalls on the way to a field hospital in Italy. Even over here, she was still window dressing, of the kind they'd obviously all like to handle. It was time, again, to fight.

'Excuse me,' she said to Dan. 'I need to borrow your jeep.'

Before he could reply, she climbed onto the bonnet, stood up and whistled for quiet.

'Yes, I'm Jessica May.' Jess's voice rang through the air, clear, unwavering, not betraying the fact that her stomach had dropped to the floor and she wondered what they'd all do right now if she fainted. 'Yes, I was a model. Yes, I lived with a man I wasn't married to. Like a very wise man recently said to me, none of it matters to the Germans. Over here, I'm a photojournalist. I intend to take pictures and write words that will be published in *Vogue*; words and pictures that will tell your mothers and sisters and girlfriends and wives back in America your stories.'

She jumped down from the jeep and picked up her bags, pretending that she was simply on a stage at a fashion showing, albeit the subject of more intense eyeballing than ever before.

A voice broke through the silence. 'I think you can probably all close your mouths and board ship.' Dan's words were a command, and they were instantly obeyed.

Jess obeyed too. And she was surprised to hear, as she stepped across the gangplank, Private Jennings say to her shyly, 'Say, do you think they'd ever put my face in a magazine?'

Sparrow guffawed, but good-naturedly; the idea of any of them adorning the pages of *Vogue* a ridiculous fantasy.

In reply, Jess unslung her camera from her shoulder, dropped her bags, focused and snapped a picture of Jennings and Sparrow, whose names should have been exchanged. Sparrow's height and build made him look distinctly un-bird-like, whereas Jennings was lean and not even as tall as Jess, as if he were still young enough that he hadn't yet finished growing and mightn't ever finish if the war had its way.

Then a flurry of men descended on them and it became clear that something she'd taken for granted – her face in a magazine – was a novelty, a moment of whimsy, an unbelievable possibility. All the way to Italy, the men asked her to take their picture and she tried her hardest to capture the sense of them, incongruously young in their uniforms, setting off to war, but caring only if their mothers might see them and be proud of them if Jess got their faces into the pages of *Vogue*.

Five

At the port in Naples, she disembarked and was about to try sweet-talking her way into a truck going north when she felt a tap on her shoulder. 'I'll give you a ride,' Dan said. 'Anything to stick it to Warren Stone, who wants nothing more than for you to have to mope around Naples waiting for days for transport.'

'Jeez, a few months ago in Manhattan, I had a line of men offering to take me for a ride at the end of a party. Now it's a form of retaliation? How the mighty have fallen,' she said with a smile.

Dan laughed.

Jess eyed the overfull trucks lined up behind the command cars and officers' jeeps. 'You don't have to drive me around. I know you have better things to do.'

'Climb in,' Dan said. 'I have to stop at the field hospital anyway.'

'You don't look sick,' Jess said doubtfully.

He leaned his arms on the jeep as he spoke, his cropped dark hair almost hidden by his helmet, but the light of an Italian morning showed plainly his youth – he could only be a couple of years older than Jess – and his handsomeness. Not like Warren Stone, who looked too perfectly put together, almost a simulation. Dan was a man who knew himself, self-assured but without hubris, the hint of a smile at her words charismatic rather than leering.

Suddenly, she understood; he probably had at least one or two nurses chasing after him. 'Someone special you'd like to see at the hospital?' she asked.

'Something like that,' he replied.

At the receiving tent of the hospital, a nurse smiled at Dan as they walked in. 'She's been asking for you,' the nurse said. 'I think she's with Anne.'

'That's where I'm headed,' Jess said, eyeing Dan appraisingly as they threaded through a maze of tents and guy ropes. First Flick, now a woman in Anne's quarters; he really did seem to take Martha's philosophy — that you needed love, or at least bodily comfort, in the midst of war — to heart.

After a few minutes they stopped at one tent from which Jess could hear, incongruously, a child's laugh. She picked up the Rollei, feeling a prickle of alertness creep over her skin, and readied it.

'Victorine?' Dan called and Jess heard an excited gasp, followed by the tent flap opening and then a little girl tore out and into Dan's arms.

Jess had the camera in the perfect position to catch the moment of their embrace, Dan's back to her, the girl's smiling, ecstatic face full to the camera.

'You're back!' the little girl cried.

The faces of the two nurses who'd emerged from the tent reflected everything Jess felt: that the ordinary moment of an embrace had been transformed by war into something precious. And she was so glad that she'd come back to Italy. These were the stories she could tell, the pictures she would take: of the humanity behind the guns. The compassion beyond the bloodshed, and the fact that, as a counterbalance to evil, charity, mercy and love still existed and could therefore triumph.

'I am Victorine,' the little girl announced to Jess. 'What is that?' She slithered out of Dan's arms and pointed to Jess's camera.

'Pleased to meet you, Victorine,' Jess said. Then she switched to French, detecting the girl's accent. 'It's my camera. Would you like to see?'

Victorine clapped her hands. 'You speak like Papa,' she said, also in French, and Jess wondered who the hell her papa was and why he'd left her in such danger.

Jess squatted closer to the ground, held out the camera and pointed to the viewing lens. 'You look through here,' Jess said, 'and then this here,' she pointed to the lens that would capture the image, 'will copy a picture of what you see when you press the button. But the picture will stay inside the camera until I go back to London and have it printed out for you. I promise I'll bring it back next time I'm here. It'll probably take a few weeks.'

'Everything takes a long time,' Victorine said with a sigh of resignation well beyond her years.

Jess looked up at Dan. What was a child doing in a field hospital? Was she his? She'd said her papa spoke French, and Dan was about as French as the Empire State Building. But the way Dan and the girl had greeted one another; it was as intimate as a father and child.

'Where's Vicki?' Jess heard another voice shout and two soldiers appeared. 'We got you some chocolate, Vicki,' one of them said, holding out a white packet emblazoned with the words, 'US Army Field Ration D'.

'It's Victorine,' the little girl said crossly. 'But thank you.' She stood on tiptoes to kiss each soldier on the cheek, all the while never letting go of Dan's hand.

'Are you boys discharged?' Dan asked them and they nodded.

'Yes, Sir. That's why we needed our kisses,' one of them said, indicating Victorine..

'Thought we could get a ride back with you, Sir,' the other one added.

'Sure,' Dan said. 'Give me five minutes.'

'Thanks, little Vicki,' one of the soldiers said. The other added, 'Bye Vicki!' before they both moved off in the direction of the jeep.

'Victorine,' the girl called after them. 'I'm French!' Then she turned her attention back to Jess. 'Are you Dan's friend?'

'I think so,' Jess said.

'You can be my friend, too. But Dan is my best friend.'

Dan crouched down beside Victorine. 'I have to go. I'll come back whenever I can. I promise.'

The little girl's face crumpled. 'I want you to stay.'

'What about if I show you my camera some more?' Jess said, with a smile.

Victorine nodded, her eyes tear-filled. Dan used the moment to unravel himself from the girl, who kissed his cheeks.

'Let me walk Dan back to the car and then we'll look at the camera, okay?' Jess said, before she hurried after Dan, scrambling over the mud and slime to keep up. 'Who is she?'

'You need a pair of jump boots,' he said as he walked.

'Jump boots?'

He nodded at her boots, which she'd thought, before encountering Italy, would keep her feet dry. 'Paratrooper boots. Like these.' He pointed at his boots and Jess felt a serious pang of envy at the sturdy, thick, high leather boots that would indeed be perfect.

'The US Army gave me a pair of brown Oxfords and I knew enough about roughing it to understand they'd be useless, so I got these.' She pointed ruefully at her own inadequate boots, which had been the most serviceable she could find in Manhattan.

Dan studied her feet. 'I'll get you a pair. They're in demand though. No sooner has an airborne GI died and someone from infantry is claiming his boots.'

Jess shuddered. 'I don't know if I could wear a dead man's boots.'

'If I died I'd rather someone who needed them had my boots than they were buried in this muck,' Dan said prosaically. 'Major

Henderson, the surgeon you met that night at the field hospital, has my brother Laurie's stethoscope because it was a damn good one, too good to waste.'

He paused, stopped walking all of a sudden, and Jess heard herself ask, even though what he'd said implied its own dreadful answer, 'What happened?'

Dan's words came fast, as if he didn't say it all at once, he wouldn't be able to. 'Laurie was a doctor. On vacation in Europe, he met a French girl, fell in love, married and moved to Paris. He worked with the French Army as a surgeon in 1940, the same year – June 1940, in fact – that his wife was due to give birth. It was the worst damn time to have a baby.'

Jess remembered that the end of May was when the British Army had fled France, and that June was when Paris surrendered, when the Germans took France for themselves. It was worse than the worst damn time to have a baby.

'There was a mass exodus of people out of Paris in June, trying to keep ahead of the Germans. My sister-in-law was one of them,' Dan continued, starting to walk again, slowly. 'The roads were so jammed with cars that it took days to travel a few miles, there was no water and no food and the Krauts bombed the lines of refugees. So everyone did what they could to protect their children. They gave them to convoys of French soldiers fleeing south, anyone with a vehicle. They thought they would all get to somewhere south of the Loire and it would be safe and they would be reunited.'

'Oh God,' Jess said quietly, unable to think what it would be like to hand your child over to strangers because it seemed the better choice.

'My brother was with a convoy of medics and a woman handed him two children through the window just after the Stukas had strafed a line of civilians. One was older, a boy; he'd been shot and he died soon after. The other was a tiny baby girl, about a week old.'

'Victorine,' Jess said. 'But why isn't she with your brother's wife?'

Dan didn't answer that question. Instead, a long stream of terrible words filled the air like mortar explosions as he told her that his brother had waited in Moulins for a fortnight, trying to find the baby's mother as she'd said that's where she was going. But there were too many lost children and no possible way to reunite them all. His brother hadn't been able to give the baby to another family as nobody had enough milk for their own children. So he'd taken the child to Toulouse where his wife had gone to be with family.

'He thought he and his wife could care for the baby for a couple of weeks, then he'd go back to Moulins and try again once everything had settled down. But at his wife's family's home, he found . . .' Dan paused.

They were back at the jeep, the men he'd promised a ride to huddled into their coats in their seats. 'Fucking rain,' he swore as the relentless drizzle turned into a torrent that really couldn't make them any wetter than they already were. 'Sorry.'

'If you think that's the first time I've heard someone say that then you really have forgotten everything I told you in London,' she said gently.

It made the corners of his mouth turn up a little and he leaned his back against the jeep, away from the waiting men and went on, his voice low. 'His wife and their baby had died in childbirth. There were no doctors left in Toulouse. His mother-in-law was ill from grief and his father-in-law refused to so much as look at Victorine because he thought she was a changeling who had taken his daughter's and granddaughter's place.'

Dan stopped speaking, his jaw tight. Jess leaned back against the jeep too, next to him, but not looking at him so he could speak out into the rain, rather than to her. 'The baby wouldn't settle with anyone but Laurie. And his father-in-law had made everyone suspicious of Victorine; you've no idea the kinds of beliefs people in the countryside have. The final straw was when Laurie walked in on his father-in-law shaking her. He knew he had to leave or Victorine would be dead too. He got to London. As soon as the American troops rolled into Italy, he signed on as a medical officer. He brought Victorine with him.'

'But how?' Jess asked. 'If they won't let a woman go anywhere near a combat zone, I can't imagine they'd allow a child.'

'He didn't have a choice,' Dan said simply. 'Nobody has a choice. We all do what we hope is for the best. How all this is for the best is anyone's guess,' he added, hand gesturing to the ambulance driving in, the injured man lifted out. 'He thought the hospital would be safe. That the nurses would help him look after her. Nobody, nobody,' he repeated, 'understood what a field hospital on the Italian front would be like.'

Jess risked a glance at him, remembering the horror of last month. The thickness of the blood beneath her shoes, the latrines walled with a teetering pile of sodden blankets, the proximity of the shells. It *was* incomprehensible. 'So your brother was the man she calls Papa? She doesn't know about her real parents?'

'She doesn't.'

With the cover of rain, almost impossible to see through, Jess couldn't be sure how Dan felt at that moment but his stance suggested a remoteness that made her heart crack a little. How old was he? Twenty-five at most. In charge of how many men? Knowing that whatever he ordered them to do could kill them. And a child to protect too. She understood now why he could shoot a man and not look as if he felt anything; he had so many people to care about and to keep alive that he couldn't afford to expend any visible emotion on an enemy. Which didn't mean he didn't feel it though.

She waited for what he would say next, sensing by the tension dripping off him more thickly than the rain that it wouldn't be good.

'A shell landed on the operating tent in September. Laurie was killed.'

Jess instinctively reached out a hand to touch his arm. 'So now she's yours?'

'Yes,' he said simply.

'Victorine means victory,' she said when she thought she could speak.

Dan nodded. 'And nobody will dare to send her away. She's our lucky charm. Almost a deity.' He drew in a breath. 'The boys bring her chocolate. They believe that if she kisses them on the cheek before they go out to fight, they'll survive. The boys who don't believe it are always the ones who get shot. I can't explain it. But it's what happens. No one in the upper reaches of the army wants to send away something the men believe in. So they turn a blind eye. The nurses look after her for me. I owe them a whole goddamn lot.'

Jess couldn't believe she'd assumed he'd wanted to drive her to the hospital so he could charm one of the nurses. He clearly had no time and no energy to be charming anyone. 'I'll go and show Victorine my camera,' Jess said. 'And you'd better watch out,' she added mischievously, wanting him to leave to face the enemy with lightness rather than sadness, 'you might find that *I'm* her best friend by the time you return.'

Over the next week, Jess settled into life as a photojournalist. She propped her typewriter on a small table she'd found that would also double nicely as a shelter to roll under should the Germans start bombing the hospital again and she sat there every day, wearing everything she owned, layered in double socks, trousers, shirt, jacket, overcoat, scarf. It still wasn't enough to keep out the cold, nor was the oil stove enough to warm the tent; it was only when she stepped outside that she realised it was actually a couple of degrees warmer inside — freezing, instead of several degrees below. The stories she collected were about Victorine, who was a small sun bringing light and warmth to a place otherwise bereft of those things.

Each day, she and Victorine visited the convalescent tent to sit with the men and, each day as they entered, like today, someone would call out for her. 'Vicki?'

Victorine spun around crossly and stalked, as much as a four-year-old could stalk, into the ward. 'You are one of Dan's men,' she pronounced to the man who'd called her name. 'My name is Victorine.'

'Sorry, Miss,' the soldier apologised, and Jess realised it was Private Jennings, the man who'd wanted his face in *Vogue*.

'Captain May,' he nodded at Jess.

'You have a dirty arm,' Victorine scolded him.

'What happened?' Jess asked, remembering that he was a new replacement and here he was, already in the hospital, his face pale against his shock of red hair, his leanness all the more childlike against the hospital blankets.

Jennings flushed. 'Hurt my head,' he mumbled and Jess could see that he had a row of stitches holding together a split eyebrow.

'Somehow he managed to trip over and crack his head on a long Tom,' a nurse said sardonically and when Jennings' cheeks coloured so red he looked as if he might explode, Jess again had the impression of enduring innocence, a wholesomeness worth preserving.

'Look!' Victorine cried, pointing to the patch of clay on Jennings' arm. 'The mud is shaped like a . . .'

Puppy. Bird. Fairy. Rabbit, Jess waited for Victorine to say, imagining it was like the game she'd played as a child when she'd lain on her back on a sandy beach before a Tahitian storm watching clouds coalesce into giants' faces and unicorns.

'One of the silver pineapples nobody lets me touch,' Victorine grumbled, as if it were wrong that nobody would let her touch a grenade. 'See,' Victorine continued, 'it has lines across it. And the funny bit on top.'

Jess met Jennings' eye and saw in them a shock she imagined was mirrored in her own. Then she took the photograph of the little girl tracing the mud on a man's arm that she'd compared to a deadly weapon, such were the limitations of what she'd been exposed to in her short life.

'Doesn't matter how you got to hospital,' Jess said to Jennings, hoping to make him feel better, and herself too. 'Now you'll be in the pages of *Vogue*.'

Jennings grinned and whooped.

After that, Jess took Victorine back to her tent where Victorine had, without asking, been staying in Jess's bed since Jess arrived. Jess lay down next to Victorine and began to tell her the fairytale *Le Petit Poucet*, but she made the tiny thumb-sized boy into a little girl who defeats the ogre at the end instead.

Later that night, as nurses came in and out, always exhausted, always cold, always wet, always with bloodstains on their bodies because having a shower in the middle of an Italian winter was a feat of hardihood that most hadn't the energy for, Jess continued to write her story, in between heating cocoa in empty plasma cans on the stove. She wrote about Dan, the oh so young major who had not only a company but a little girl to think of, both of which he did without question, without resentment, with true valour of the kind, Jess realised, she'd never before witnessed.

When she'd finished, she unrolled the paper from the typewriter and re-read her words. It was good, she thought, and it told a story no one else would ever tell: that of the cost exacted by war on a four-year-old child. But she had to show it to Dan. She couldn't send it to Bel without making sure he was okay with it.

Victorine was sound asleep as Jess set her body against the wind and propelled herself through the rain to the receiving tent. Luckily she arrived during a lull; no ambulances were arriving, no bodies were lying on stretchers waiting to be attended to, and Anne, whose smile was always large as if to compensate for her diminutive stature, had a tin of Nescafé in her hand.

'I was just thinking it'd be nice to have someone to talk to,' Anne said, shaking the tin at Jess.

'Oh, yes please,' Jess said gratefully.

Anne made her a coffee and Jess leaned back against the desk to drink it.

'I don't know if it's just my imagination but it tastes so much better in a mug than a plasma can.' Jess wriggled her toes, wishing the hot liquid would somehow find its way down to her feet, which she hadn't felt properly for a couple of days. 'How long until spring?' she asked ruefully.

'I thought you were going back to cosy London next week,' Anne said. 'Think of me when you're having a shower.'

'I'm not allowed to stay longer than my orders. The PROs in London like to keep me in their sights.'

'I'm teasing,' Anne said with a smile. 'You go back and tell your story. I've seen you talking to the nurses, writing down what they do and recording it all with your camera. If I wrote a letter to my momma and told her what it was like here, she'd laugh. Nobody will laugh at your pictures.'

'So you won't mind if I come back and take up a bed in your quarters again as soon as they let me?'

'Not a bit.' Anne took Jess's empty cup from her and refilled it.

'How do I see Dan if I need to?'

Anne groaned. 'That man could thread all the hearts he's won onto a string and it'd reach New York. Don't tell me he can add another one to his chain?'

Jess laughed. 'My heart is safe in my chest. He does seem popular though.'

'Popular is an understatement. Most of the nurses would follow him into battle if it meant spending another minute with him. Glad you've got more sense.'

'Why? Is he . . .' Jess stopped. Did she want to know the answer to her question: *Is he not worth their hearts?*

'Oh no, he's as good a man as he is good-looking. Says he made major because everyone else was dead and they didn't have a choice, but a couple of months ago he went out into no-man's-land and brought back a boy who'd been injured out there; they could hear his groans between shell bursts. Nothing makes a company more panicky than hearing one of their own, injured and alone. He saved that GI's life.'

'She doesn't want to hear about that.'

Jess whirled around at the sound of Dan's voice. He was standing behind them, cheeks pinked with embarrassment, tiredness fixed deep in his eyes, an ugly graze on the back of his hand. 'How long have you been there?' she asked.

'Long enough to learn my charms are wasted on you,' he grinned, clearly eager to turn the conversation away from Anne's recitation of his acts of good.

'You've come to get that boy Jennings, haven't you?' Anne asked. 'Wait there.' She disappeared into the ward.

'Surely it's not a major's job to escort privates back to the front?' Jess said, offering him her mug before she realised what she was doing and that he probably didn't want her half-finished coffee. 'Sorry,' she apologised.

But he took the mug from her. 'Hey, you can't take it back once you've offered it.' He finished it in one long swallow. 'Damn that's good. And no, majors don't normally escort privates around but I've known Jennings since we were kids and his mom told me she'd kill me if anything happened to him. Given his ability to not require actual shelling and bullets in order to injure himself, I thought I'd better look after him. Don't want to survive the war only to be killed by Jennings' mom,' he added.

Jess laughed. This was why all the nurses were in love with him. He was that rarest of all things: a nice man. 'Do you want to see Victorine before you go?'

'Do you know where she is?' he asked, tiredness suddenly erased from his face, which was now filled with an eagerness of the kind Jess hadn't seen him turn towards any of the nurses who wanted to give him their hearts.

Jess nodded and he followed her outside where she stopped short.

'What is it?' he asked after he nearly collided with her.

'It's not raining,' she whispered, awe-struck by something as simple as the cessation of water falling from the sky.

'About goddamned time,' he said, reflexively doing the same as she had, tipping his head up to the sky.

All of a sudden, the deluge began again, striking them full in the face with drops as hard and stinging as rocks. They *were* rocks, Jess realised. Hailstones, and for some reason, rather than wincing as one hit her brow, she laughed, and so did Dan and they started to run as best they could.

'Next time, don't say anything and the reprieve might last a little longer,' Dan mock-grouched as they reached her tent.

'I jinxed it, didn't I?' Jess said, pulling open the tent flap.

Dan smiled when he saw Victorine, soundly sleeping. 'Is this your bed?' he asked as he took in Jess's typewriter and the crate containing her cameras and paper, held up off the ground by rocks. 'I thought she was staying in the convalescent tent.'

'She kind of invited herself here. I don't mind. She keeps me warm.'

'Jess . . .'

She held up her hand. 'I don't need any thanks. It's what anyone would do. You love her, the men love her, hell, I've half fallen in love with her in one week . . .' Her voice trailed off at the look on Dan's face.

'What?' she asked.

He shook his head. 'You can't say that.'

Can't say what? Jess was about to ask when she suddenly realised. *Jinx.* If you say the rain has stopped, then it's bound to start up again. If you say you love someone, then they're bound to . . . *die*.

'I take it back,' she said. 'Her bony elbows stick into me all night and you should see the bruises on my legs. She can kick in her sleep harder than any horse.'

Victorine stirred in her sleep, her leg shooting out suddenly and they both laughed. The girl's eyes flew open. 'You came back,' she said sleepily to Dan and he sat on the bed beside her and stroked her hair. Within half a minute she was asleep again.

'Will you read this?' Jess asked abruptly.

In the faint glow of the kerosene lamp, sitting on her bed, Victorine asleep beside him, Dan read her words about Victorine while Jess kept her back turned studiously towards him. When she could no longer hear pages rustling, she said, 'I don't want to send it to my editor unless you approve.'

'You should definitely send it,' was all he said before he gave Victorine a quick kiss on the cheek and left to get Jennings.

Six

*J*ess's story about Victorine and the accompanying pictures were syndicated worldwide. *I can't thank you enough*, Bel had written. *You've given* Vogue *credibility during this period of war that it wouldn't otherwise have.* Jess's name was one people now knew for something other than how she looked in a dress.

When she'd first learned how far and wide her photographs would travel, Jess sat in the near empty bath at the Savoy Hotel and cried. She cried for Victorine, for the men who made it off the mountain that day only to die by nightfall, for the nurses who had to patch up the men and send them back out into the field, for the people who saw her pictures and didn't understand that each moment was underlit, hauntingly so, by what had come before, and what would come after.

Beneath the tears, she was so thankful that she'd returned to Italy, despite the fear, and that she'd told a story worth telling.

But that night she saw Warren Stone in the bar shaking his head over a newspaper and she knew her picture well enough to recognise it as the one of Victorine and Dan. Warren still didn't have his promotion. But Jess had a set of well-regarded pictures behind her name. It would be best if she kept well out of his way and did nothing to provoke him. Not that she really thought there was anything much he could do to her, other than waste her time with disagreeable exchanges.

So, after a short break, where she spent as much time as she could outside, tracing the unfamiliar geography of a wounded city where bedrolls littered tube stations and women with scarves wrapped around their hair sat atop piles of rubble and drank cups of tea and children pretended to shoot one another with crumpled iron bars fallen from buildings, she got herself another set of orders to go back to Italy, to search out another story, thankful that Warren Stone was now on a week's leave and she didn't have to deal with him.

She waited in London for a few more days, hoping to see Martha – who was on her way back from visiting her husband in the States – and had almost given up when Martha phoned her room and told Jess she was downstairs. Jess made her way across the black-and-white marble floors and through the mahogany opulence of the lobby until she reached the American Bar where the US Army Press Office had set itself up. She sank into a booth opposite Martha, who had two large whiskies in front of her.

'Wait till you hear this,' Martha said to Jess.

'What?'

'*Collier's* has made my dear husband their war correspondent.'

'But you're the *Collier's* war correspondent,' Jess said uncomprehendingly.

'They want someone who can go into combat zones. Especially now that rumour confidently predicts an Allied invasion of Europe within two months. Because I'm a woman, I can't do the job they want done.' Martha downed her whiskey in one swallow. 'The RAF even flew him to London. I had to hitch a ride on a Norwegian freighter.'

'How could he do that to you?'

Martha shrugged, a gesture that might seem nonchalant on anyone else but on Martha it was like a cowering in, an enfolding of herself into something that could not, would not, be hurt. But of course she had been hurt, and not just emotionally, as her next words confirmed, making her action — her attempt to deflect what was likely still to follow from her husband — all the more affecting. 'That's Hem for you,' she said dully. 'I asked him for a divorce, of course. He laughed, after he hit me.'

'I'm so sorry.' Jess reached for her friend's hand. But that wasn't enough. She moved across and wrapped her arms around Marty, all the while knowing that no matter how much they tried to shield themselves, the wounds were still getting through.

'Last year, if you'd told me this would happen, I wouldn't have believed you. We were in love.' Martha blinked, hard. 'Then when I told him I was returning to Europe, he said to me, "Are you a war correspondent, or wife in my bed?"'

Two opposing choices. A binary the world seemed determined to force upon the women who wanted something more inclusive, limiting them to this single moment of a shared embrace, a shared pain, a broken heart and the uncertainty of what was to come when they declared that an either/or choice was not enough.

Into the silence following Martha's words, Jess heard her name spoken by the men at the next table, accompanied by uproarious laughter and she knew that the bar at the Savoy was not a place she wanted to spend any more time in. And nor should Martha, especially if her husband was here too. 'Let's go to Italy.'

'Not so fast.' Warren Stone shifted into the seat beside Jess.

Damn. She'd waited in London too long and now Warren's leave was obviously over, or he'd been recalled. And he was cockier than ever. Why?

'You haven't heard?' Martha said sardonically to Jess.

'Heard what? That a nude painting of me is on display at the Tate Gallery or something equally ridiculous?' Jess said, smiling sweetly at Warren.

'You know they show the men a picture of a naked woman painted in camouflage colours at the infantry training school to arrest the men's attention when it wanders,' Warren said as he sipped his whiskey.

Jess knew she was gaping, open-mouthed. 'That's a lie,' she insisted.

'It's not,' Martha said sadly.

'And it's not what's important right now,' Warren said, a grin spreading wide across his face. 'There are a lot of shiny new women being sent here and they're very inexperienced. We want to protect you all. So every female correspondent is quarantined in London for now.'

Jess knew that half of what Warren had said was true. As well as wanting to have reporters on the ground if the rumoured invasion really was imminent, the American newspapers had seen the success among readers of Ruth Cowan's pieces on the WACs in North Africa, Iris Carpenter's reportage of the Blitz, and Martha's by-line, albeit hidden behind the 'Mrs Ernest Hemingway' title. Which had meant the arrival in England of a dozen more unblooded female reporters, raising the latrine business and the cloakroom question – as the British more politely put it – to bar-room conversation status. And if they were quarantining women already, then it confirmed the invasion was not a rumour, but an action soon to be taken.

'How long are you going to keep us here?' Jess asked, provoked by his comments into breaking her pact not to deliberately antagonise him. 'And *you* can't keep us here. I'll speak to your boss.'

'But *I* am my boss now. Feel free to congratulate me on my promotion,' Warren said.

Jess and Martha looked at one another in disbelief.

'And in answer to your question,' Warren continued cheerfully, having noted with satisfaction the women's expressions, 'you're to stay here indefinitely.'

'Just because the new reporters are as green as an English paddock, we don't all need to be treated the same way. Marty and I certainly aren't inexperienced, nor are we prone to hysterics,' Jess said flatly. Just last week she'd been so proud that her photographs were being syndicated all over the world and now here she was being told she'd be kept away from the invasion just because she was a woman. From beautiful success to ridiculous failure, with the snap of a finger. 'How do you expect us to report on an invasion in mainland Europe if we're stuck here in London?'

'We don't. The men will do that. You can go with the Red Cross doughnut girls to the camps in the south of England and spread smiles and anything else you care to.' Warren ground out his cigarette.

'You can't make us stay.' Martha was firm.

'Did I forget to mention that we have official rules now?' Warren leaned back, relaxed, legs wide apart, arms stretched along the back of the booth, unlike Jess and Martha who were hunched over their drinks.

'The rules state, in writing at last, everything that's already in practice.' Warren began to recite: '*The inherent difficulties, such as housing facilities, which arise due to the presence of women in the forward areas naturally make their ready acceptance as Correspondents a problem. It is believed that sufficient male Correspondents are available to make it unnecessary to utilise women in the forward areas to cover spot news and technical subjects. It is recognised, however, that certain stories, such as those concerning nurses, can best be handled from a woman's point of view.* I hope you're grateful to me for conceding that you do a better job of writing about nurses. But none of your nurse stories can be filed until the men have filed their war stories. You have to wait at the back of the line for censoring, transmitting; everything. Cheers.' He finished his drink and stood up, having done the damage, leaving them to wallow in it.

'Shit,' Martha said. 'I heard that only the men will be going across with the invasion fleet, whatever and wherever that is. But I didn't know . . .'

'That the heretofore unrecorded rules are now printed in black and white for all the PROs to beat us over the head with,' Jess finished. 'What a joke. It'll never be safe. Not until somebody wins. Does that mean they'll never let us over there?'

Neither woman spoke. They drank instead, and smoked.

Then Jess said, 'It's lucky that I got a set of orders before Warren returned from leave. If I go now, I might just get myself on a transport that doesn't know anything about women being quarantined.'

'Warren will not only kill you when he finds out, he'll do it with his bare hands,' Martha said, staring at her.

'But I can't be a war correspondent in the bar of the Savoy. There's no war here. I've had one piece published. If I'm quarantined now, I might never have another piece published again.'

'Then go pack your bags. And good luck.'

Jess slipped away, heart hammering both at the thought of her own daring, and at what Warren really would do to her when he found out.

Jennings was waiting for Jess when she stepped off the ship, his face obviously hastily scrubbed clean for the assignment, faint dirt streaks showing where his fingers had swiped over his brow and chin.

'Captain May,' he stuttered.

'To whom do I owe the pleasure of being provided with an escort?' Jess asked.

'Anne told Major Hallworth you were coming again and he said he has to provide escorts for all the male correspondents who come over so he didn't see why you should have to hitch through Italy. Last month, I even had to carry one fellow's camera lenses around for a week.'

Jess snorted. How could the army honestly think a woman who didn't get ground transport or ask for assistance was more trouble than a man? A curious rustle of noise made her realise there was quite a line of GIs assembled at port, and that the Naples PRO who'd been so irate with her several months ago was smiling at her in a way that was certainly not friendly.

'Look what I have,' he said, stepping forward to show her a crumpled picture he'd taken from his pocket. It was of Jess. Louise Dahl-Wolfe had shot it for *Harper's Bazaar* in 1940 in the early days of Jess's modelling career. In it, Jess was sitting on the floor reading a book, back to the camera, naked except for her knickers, but all you could see of her in the photograph was her bare back and the very top of her hipbones. She'd been waiting for her next outfit when Louise decided Jess didn't need an outfit; the shoot was meant to show off the diamond clip in Jess's hair, rather than a dress. For the first time, Jess wondered how many people actually noticed the hairclip.

'I've got one too,' another man joined in the fun, pulling a different picture out of his pocket, this time of Jess in a swimsuit.

'One of the public relations guys in London was real helpful in finding these for us,' the Naples PRO said. 'Now, here you are in the flesh.'

He made sure to linger over the word *flesh*, and Jess just stopped herself from shuddering. Warren Stone, Jess knew, was the one who'd made sure the men had so many pictures of her.

But that wasn't the worst of it. 'I have a telegram here for you.' The PRO handed her a piece of paper.

Her orders had been countermanded. She was to return immediately to London. *It'll be more fun to watch you leave in disgrace later, just when you think you've settled in,* Warren had said to her. And she wondered if Warren had let her go, had wanted to make sure that, before he ordered her to come back and sit in a bar and watch the war from a distance, she would see that every man in the US Army had a picture of Jess to paw over.

'When's the next ship back?' she asked, as if she didn't care about any of it.

'Tomorrow. Take her to one of the hotels for the night,' the PRO said to Jennings.

At that, Jennings hitched Jess's bag onto his shoulder and walked away to the jeep. Jess followed. What else could she do? Stand at the port and watch the GIs compare pictures of her? She hadn't won when her story and her photos of Victorine were published. Warren Stone had just wanted her to think she had because he knew that would make the loss hurt all the more.

Jennings pulled the jeep out onto the road. 'My orders from my CO are to take you to the hospital at Cassino,' he said shyly. 'I could bring you back early enough tomorrow to catch the ship.'

Jess leaned over and kissed his cheeks, which were, as always, suffused with the endearing blush that matched the colour of his hair. 'Thank you.'

When Jess woke the next morning, it was to find Victorine curled up in bed beside her, staring at her, obviously willing her to wake. 'You came back too!' Victorine said and Jess realised it was what she said every time she saw Dan, and now Jess. As if the little girl could never quite believe that anyone would return, as if being passed by her mother to a convoy of medics, never to meet again, was trapped in her psyche like a leaf fossil in rock, barely visible to anyone who didn't know what they were looking for.

Jess hugged Victorine. 'I did.'

They climbed out of bed, even though it was before sun-up, and the mundane tasks of the morning were transformed, by both the marvellous lack of rain and Victorine's assistance, into something more delightful than collecting water in her helmet to wash her face, than eating a breakfast K-ration of egg yolk mixed with spam.

They were walking through the tents to visit Anne when Jess heard a voice say, 'I thought I'd better take you somewhere this morning before you leave so that you have your own set of pictures to show Warren Stone.'

She whirled around and saw Victorine leap into Dan's arms.

'I will come too,' Victorine announced but Jess knew that wasn't going to happen. The hospital was dangerous enough, let alone going anywhere else.

'But I have a job for you,' Jess said quickly. 'Come with me.'

She retrieved a stack of *Vogue* magazines from her tent. 'There are pictures of you in here,' Jess said to Victorine, 'and pictures of Anne and some of the soldiers. And one of Dan,' she added. 'Can you show the magazines to Anne and the men in the convalescent tent?'

Victorine hopped up and down with excitement. 'Yes!' she cried.

Jess opened up the magazines and showed Victorine the photograph of the little girl in Dan's arms. Victorine's smile was infinite now, carved onto her face in black and white by Jess's camera, this one moment of immense love unable to ever be destroyed. Dan's face in profile was unguarded and Jess had had to close the covers the first time she'd seen it because it made her realise that he was vulnerable; that, without him, Victorine had nobody. Jess had wanted to shout: *Don't you damn well die!*

She wondered now if he'd be able to look at himself. She understood all too well – because it had been done to her – that a photograph could trap a person in an incarnation unknown to them, that seeing such an image could feel like nakedness, bringing with it the revelation that the photographer had exposed a part of them that would ordinarily be hidden from the world. Jess hadn't comprehended just what she'd caught and it was only in seeing the print that she realised it was a one-in-a-million shot, that she might never photograph anything quite as poignant again.

Dan's head jerked back as Victorine held the magazine aloft and awareness hit him. Then the nurses crowded around and Jess said, 'Let's go,' wanting to get him away from seeing what Jess had seen: evidence of the fracture in his armour.

She knew now that everything Emile had told her about photography, her entire experience of it as both her parents' child-photographer and as a model before the lens was wrong. The chance moment was what mattered out here, that and the premonition before the moment happened so that one was ready. Not the careful positioning of a person or an object or a light source, not the fully imagined outcome of what would be caught after aligning the camera and pressing the button. Her job was to extemporise – not to plan – and thus expose the reality that had been obscured by the reduction of everything around them into three letters and one simple word: war.

And that's what she'd do once again on this outing with Dan. 'Where are we going?' she asked as they neared the jeep.

'It's Easter,' Dan said as if that explained everything.

Jess thought for a moment and realised he was right, but that in this place divorced from real time, each day blended into the next; nameless. 'And we're going to church?' she quipped.

'Sort of,' he said and Jess just about burst with curiosity.

Then he added, 'I'll be in England soon. My division's been recalled. I'm taking Victorine back with me, putting her in a boarding school there.'

Which meant only one thing. It *was* coming. The mammoth attack on Europe. An attack Jess would never be allowed to witness or report on. She wanted to thump her hand on the jeep from the injustice of it. Instead, she said, 'I'll visit her whenever I can. I mean, I'll have plenty of time if Warren Stone has his way.'

Dan stopped in front of the car. 'You're a great photographer, Jess. Keep fighting them.'

And she found herself momentarily speechless at having received admiration of the real kind, not of her face or her cleavage or her legs. 'Thanks,' she said at last, before she climbed into the jeep.

Dan drove fast, but expertly, as if they had somewhere they needed to be, and soon he'd stopped and was jumping out. 'Now we have to walk.'

They joined the column of soldiers winding up the escarpment before them, the dawn sun just beginning to tinge the landscape orange, mist wafting around, then disappearing below them as they climbed higher so that they seemed to have stepped over the clouds and into the sky. Hardly anyone spoke, and all Jess could hear were boots shuffling through sand, guns rattling on shoulders, and the one warning Dan had given her: 'Don't step off the path. There are mines everywhere.'

The shutter on the Rolleiflex clicked intermittently as they hiked and Jess was grateful that nobody had really noticed her yet; her helmet hid her face, her uniform was the same as the men's, and she was tall enough that she didn't look too out of place. The only thing that marked her as different was the camera she carried instead of a gun.

They reached a place where the slope levelled out into a ledge, with a large flat rock in the centre. The men veered off and found positions, seating themselves on the ground or leaning against the face of the mountain. Jess sat near the edge, the daredevil child still hidden inside her making her hang her legs and boots over the side, swinging freely. Dan did the same and they both stared out at the massive Garigliano Valley spread before them. A faint ribbon of distant sea shone blue on one side, the mountains loomed up over the other. Most of the ground in the valley was ruined but, up here, olive trees clung stubbornly to the hillside and anemones bloomed pink and purple in cracks of ground. She drank in the view like whiskey, trying to ignore the fire that burned below them, blazing high even though Jess couldn't believe there was anything down there left to burn.

She lined up the Rolleiflex and shot the once fertile valley, which now grew nothing but guns, then a group of men sprawled on the ground, then a mule with, inexplicably, a small camp organ on its back, then another man with a large book that he placed on the flat rock. Jess realised he was wearing a chaplain's uniform but before she could ask Dan about it, a shell whizzed over the group, dropping harmlessly into the valley below them, more fire marking its detonation.

'How close exactly are the Germans?' she asked Dan.

'About four hundred yards,' he replied cheerfully.

'That sounds a little too close,' she said.

'They won't hit us. It's Easter; a temporary ceasefire. Besides, we're not in range. They'd have to move and they're not going to come out of their dugouts with so many of us sitting here.'

Before Jess could decide if Dan was right, the chaplain began to speak. Somehow, they had a microphone and loudspeakers rigged up and the chaplain's welcome, to both Catholics and Protestants of the US and German armies, and his wish to them all for a joyous Easter, was proclaimed in both German and English, the sound ringing out to where Jess imagined the German dugouts must be, and carrying far out over valley below them.

'After the Sabbath, and towards dawn on the first day of the week, Mary of Magdala and the other Mary went to see the sepulchre,' the chaplain read in German. Then he re-read the gospel in English.

Throughout, nobody spoke. Instead they sat listening to the story of a miracle, all too aware that what everyone wanted, no matter their nationality, was a miracle of the kind that hadn't been seen since the Gospel of Saint Matthew was written.

When the chaplain finished, somebody sat down at the organ and began to play. A nurse stood up from a small group and began to sing *'I Know That My Redeemer Liveth'* from Handel's *Messiah* and the beauty of that lone voice, the sonorous organ ringing out over a desecrated Italian valley, was too much for Jess. She squeezed her hands together and gritted her teeth but her throat burned and the tears were too many for her eyes to hold and they spilled over, running like the Italian winter rain down her cheeks. She closed her eyes and swallowed, trying not to sob aloud, trying to hold herself together, to stop her body from shaking.

Something brushed her hand and took gentle hold of it. Jess opened her eyes to find that Dan had taken it, that his jaw was clenched tight too, that just one drop glistened on his cheek. They sat like that for the entire song, hands pressed painfully together, but it was the only way to listen to the hymn and not fall to pieces like the shell that had burnt out to nothing far below them.

Keep fighting them, Dan had said. And she would, she vowed, as the hymn crescendoed. Warren might well string her up when she got back to London or confine her to the Savoy. But, damn the consequences; she'd press the rules to the limits to find a way to get out of the Savoy and back to Europe, to photograph the moments like this, a lacuna of pathos amidst the firestorm of invasion.

The silence after the song had finished vibrated with the sound of the soprano voice, the final words — *For now is Christ risen from the dead, the first fruits of them that sleep* — bittersweet. Jess knew that none who fell here at Monte Cassino or during the imminent invasion would rise; that all the men around her, including Dan, might tomorrow be the ones to sleep forever.

PART TWO

D'Arcy

Seven

*A*s the train sped out of Charles de Gaulle Airport, D'Arcy's eyes banqueted on the view; she could almost smell the chestnut-and-lily–scented French summer air seeping into the train. It had been too long and she'd missed the church spires in every village, the railway bridges arching like ornate rainbows over river and road, the dusky Van Gogh yellow of the cornfields.

In an hour, she reached Reims, ready to pick up her car, hoping the gallery had remembered to book a small vehicle for her, one designed for navigating French towns, not a typically muscular SUV like everyone in Sydney preferred to drive. She was relieved to find a minuscule blue Renault awaiting her and she promptly opened all the windows, not caring that her long blonde hair would fly about madly as she drove past engorged grapes, so full of champagne juice that it was a wonder the slipstream of her car didn't burst their skins. Oaks – how she wanted one day when she was finally a grown-up to have a grand driveway lined with oak trees – peered majestically down at her, some bowing their heads, others raising their arms to the sky as if they too were celebrating the fact that D'Arcy Hallworth was finally back in France.

She glanced down at the map on the passenger seat occasionally until, after about twenty minutes driving south-east, climbing up high into the Montagne de Reims, the valley spilling out in picturesque impressionist shades below her, she turned off the A-road and onto a D-road towards Verzy, passing a succession of champagne caves. After a short time, she reached a road that was so narrow she found herself breathing in foolishly when she encountered a vine tractor coming in the opposite direction.

All of a sudden she saw the signpost, *Lieu de Rêves*, almost hidden. She swung into the driveway. An avenue of plane trees, densely planted, made it impossible to see where she was headed. And then, all at once, she was there: in a fairytale. The trees opened out onto a true chateau made of white stone with a blue slate roof and an actual drawbridge, turrets and a keep.

'Oh!' she said, unable to stop the exclamation escaping.

She parked the car and stepped out, glad to stretch after the long journey. She tried to smooth down her hair and her dress, which had at least only had to suffer the train and the car as she'd changed at the airport. It was a floral print dress, brightly patterned with orange and blue, the skirt kicking out at her knees, teamed with brown cowboy boots. She crunched over the gravel and crossed the drawbridge, unable to resist straightening her back, holding out her skirt, slowing her pace and pretending she was a princess despite the boots and the fact that she was twenty-nine years old.

She grinned at herself and just managed to let go of her skirt in time as the door to the chateau swung open and a man stepped out to greet her.

'D'Arcy Hallworth?' he asked.

'That's me.' Her smile grew wider when she saw that the man in front of her made all synonyms for handsome meaningless, his almost-black hair sexily ruffled in stark contrast to the perfection of his crisp blue shirt, which was just a shade lighter than his eyes.

'I'm Josh Vaughn.'

'Oh, you're American.' She realised her faux pas the second the words left her mouth.

'Sorry if you were hoping for a dashing Frenchman to go with the castle,' he said, unsmiling.

She decided to risk a joke. 'Well, at least you're dashing,' she said.

He laughed in surprise, which suited him much better than the serious face he'd greeted her with. 'For that, you can come in.'

She stepped through the doorway and her body automatically spiralled around, soaking in the grandeur, the elegance, the lack of excess. Even Josh paled in comparison to the surrounds.

The centuries-old chessboard-patterned black-and-white marble floors echoed with the sound of her boots. The walls, which should have felt forbidding, cut as they were from stone too, receded behind the photographs adorning them. Photographs that D'Arcy recognised, photographs she'd studied over the years, photographs she could now reach out and touch except that would be like stroking the crown jewels – a sacrilege.

'What a pity I can't take all of this back to Australia with me,' she said, indicating the ceiling flying up into the void above them, almost impossible to see without arching both neck and back.

'Excess baggage charges would probably set you back a bit,' he said dryly as he watched her drink in the house, assessing her, but not in a voyeuristic way.

'So do you trust me yet?' she asked.

'No.'

It was her turn to laugh. 'Repaying my flattering honesty with your more brutal version, I see.' Then her eye caught sight of it, just one of the many things she'd wanted to see: a single photograph, not large, but one that made her advance.

It was a picture of a mother and child, inspired, she knew, by an 1883 Christian Krohg painting of an exhausted mother sitting beside a sleeping baby, her head dropped onto the nearby bed, asleep, fatigue etched into every stroke of oil on canvas. In the same way that the painting had eschewed the artistic tradition of the devoted mother and child, the photograph in front of D'Arcy showed the naked torso of a woman, sweat slicked, hair glued to her head, a newly born child screaming on her chest, one arm outflung, protesting. The woman's eyes were shut and her face echoed the exhaustion of the painting, as if she were saying, *Why now after hours of labour must I feed this child?* But then the careful viewer saw the mother's hand, one finger outstretched, caressing the baby's hidden cheek.

'It's . . .' She paused, realising she'd been in a reverie, had been standing with her hand reaching towards the photograph, as if communing with it. 'One of the best pieces of work I've ever seen,' she finished simply. Then she turned to Josh, relocating her professionalism. 'Why is it hanging? I thought it would be packed.'

'The contract was for you to pack some of the more valuable pieces,' he said as if she were an idiot.

'I signed the contract, so I know what it says,' D'Arcy replied testily. 'But I wasn't expecting to pack something like that.' It was a dream, to handle a photograph so exquisite, but it was also a bit of a nightmare. What if she ruined it? 'How many exactly do I have to pack?'

'Most of them,' he said matter-of-factly.

'Most of them?' she repeated. 'I'm only here for two days.'

'You'll have to change your plane ticket. It'll take at least a fortnight.'

'The contract you sent to the gallery – I assume you are the Josh Vaughn who, as the photographer's agent, wrote the contract to which I am subcontracted – mentioned "a *few* valuable pieces". *Most of them* is not a few of them.'

He shrugged, irritatingly, as if it wasn't his problem. 'I called the gallery and explained that the photographer didn't trust anyone else to do the packing. That you'd need to do it and you'd need to stay longer. They emailed back a confirmation to you of your extra fee now that the job will take more time.'

'So you know how much I get paid,' she said, annoyed.

'Didn't seem too bad an amount for the privilege of travelling to France and handling photographs you've obviously been dying to see.' He was stiff, almost adversarial; the artist's agent concerned only about his client.

She couldn't resist the riposte. 'But did they include danger money for dealing with you for a fortnight?'

She saw the corners of his lips twitch up for just a moment and she childishly congratulated herself for the small victory before he handed her a printed page. It was a confirmation from the Art Gallery of New South Wales for her to stay in France for as long as it took to pack the photographs she'd simply thought it was her job to courier. As an art handler, she was used to hiccups and problems and she was also used to managing them to everyone's satisfaction; one only had to spend as much time in transit as she did to know that when planes and trucks and warehouses and customs brokers and art were all thrown together, moments of chaos were to be expected. But adding an extra week or two on to the trip was somewhat unusual. She was beginning to understand why the gallery had asked her to go so early.

'It will be easier if you stay here in the chateau,' Josh said.

'I guess I could handle that.' D'Arcy looked around once more at the magnificent surrounds. 'Is the photographer in residence?'

He nodded.

'Do you ever see her?'

'We don't converse via telepathy.'

She smiled, although she had no idea if he was being sarcastic or joking. 'Will I see her?'

'You're assuming the photographer is female.'

'I know she's female. Her body of work has a degree of compassion for the subject that I've never witnessed in that of a male photographer.'

'Cartier-Bresson. Penn. Mapplethorpe. They're not compassionate enough for you?' He folded his arms across his chest.

'No.' D'Arcy was emphatic. 'They were technically masterful but empathically absent. Like Ansel Adams said, a great photograph gives expression to precisely how the photographer feels about their subject and thus illustrates how one feels about all of life.'

He raised an eyebrow in response and she supposed that throwing Adams into the conversation probably made her sound like either a show-off or a know-it-all. Or both.

But he only asked, 'What about Capa?'

Ordinarily she might concede to Capa. Not today. 'Shouldn't you be defending your client rather than listing the photographic canon, a group of men who need no more recognition?' she replied.

'You didn't just come to babysit photographs on a plane, did you?'

Yes, because that's all an art handler does, she almost snapped back. Instead she said, 'I've been flying for more than a day – Sydney is on the other side of the world, after all – then on a train and a car for another few hours. What I really need to do right now is sleep and then tomorrow I'll get started. If you could show me where my room is? Given you've had notice of my forthcoming stay, I assume you have that organised.'

'Célie will show you.' He indicated a woman who'd just appeared from nowhere. As her travel-fuddled brain shut down, D'Arcy followed the woman up the stairs, which spiralled within the turret, then down a long hallway and into a room that she would peruse tomorrow. Right now, all she wanted was a shower and her bed.

⌒

D'Arcy woke the following morning thankful that her nomadic existence meant she'd learned to sleep whenever and wherever, and that jet lag never bothered her. She yawned and stretched and, for the first time, revelled in the luxury.

Sheets so sumptuous they must be Egyptian cotton. A true French bed of curved and carved wood, the moulded flowers spilling delicately across the headboard, the wood painted a soft creamy white, D'Arcy thought at first, but then she realised the paint held the palest note of blue, offset by the velvety blue-grey wallpaper. Matching carved bedside tables stood on either side.

She sat up and swung her feet over the edge of the bed, walking over to the soft white drapes, pulling them open to reveal doors that led onto her own balcony. Her stomach growled and she realised she was starving and had no idea what to do about breakfast. Would they feed her? Or would she have to drive to the nearest town and grab some coffee and croissants?

In answer to her question, a knock sounded on the door.

'Come in,' D'Arcy called.

Célie appeared, breakfast tray in hand, loaded with croissants and baguettes and cheese and fruit juice and – D'Arcy sniffed the air – coffee.

'Breakfast on the balcony?' Célie asked in French.

'*Oui, merci.*' D'Arcy followed her out and breathed in the wild scents of the French countryside – musky sweet chestnut, the strong fragrance of artemisia, spicy liquorice and citrus. Yellow buttercups frolicked over the garden below and she could see that a loose formality played hide-and-seek with the natural landscape: pleached limes bordered a mass of wild orchids, a separate garden room had been created with drooping mulberry trees to house the *potager*, which was full of strawberry and blackberry bushes, as well as the most vividly orange pumpkins D'Arcy had ever seen, perfect for flamboyantly gilded fairytale carriages. There was even a maze.

D'Arcy sank into a chair, sipped her coffee with closed eyes and felt the kind of contentment wash over her that was an infrequent visitor in her life.

'Would you like anything else?' Célie asked.

'I think everything is perfect,' D'Arcy replied, the French her mother had always spoken with her rolling off her tongue as familiarly as the English she ordinarily spoke.

It was very tempting to sit on the balcony all morning and drink too much coffee and eat too much pungently oozing cheese and fresh baguette. No bread in the whole of Australia ever tasted as good as the bread in France. But she had work to do so she threw on her version of jeans and a white shirt — her choice of shirt being a once lemon-coloured, now faded to cream 1970s Ossie Clark chiffon blouse, with a bow at the collar and the bleached-out lines of a Celia Birtwell print still visible. She eschewed yesterday's cowboy boots in favour of a pair of scuffed vintage boots with the traces of once bright embroidery.

Before she went downstairs, she telephoned her mother to let her know she wouldn't be back in Sydney any time soon.

'Hello, darling,' Victorine Hallworth said as soon as she picked up, and D'Arcy smiled.

'You'll never believe me if I tell you how fabulous this chateau is. And I'm staying for two weeks,' D'Arcy crowed. 'It's like a dream job. Delicious food. Amazing views. And photographs I adore.'

'You sound happy.' D'Arcy could hear her mother smiling down the line.

'I am. In fact, I might write a piece about it. I'll send a pitch to Maya tonight.'

'I'm sure she'd love to have another piece from you. You haven't written for her for a while,' Victorine said.

'I haven't,' D'Arcy agreed, freelance writing being just one of the many things she dabbled in over her peripatetic existence. 'But this place is just begging to be written about. You'd love it. It's the France of everyone's dreams.'

'The France of my dreams is probably a more tarnished vision than the one you have in front of you now. Although you're making me want to come out and see you. Where exactly are you?'

'Not far from Reims.'

'Not my favourite part of the country.' Her mother's voice seemed to catch on the words.

'How can it not be your favourite part?'

Her mother paused before replying. 'Just memories. From a long time ago. You have a wonderful time and enjoy it for both of us.'

'I will. I love you, *Maman*.'

As D'Arcy hung up the phone, she frowned. They hardly ever spoke about her mother's childhood in France, a country Victorine hadn't visited since she was in her twenties, even though she'd insisted on D'Arcy learning French and had always encouraged D'Arcy's own visits there, from exchange trips in high school, to university in Paris. Despite that, her mother had told her to enjoy herself, so she would. She went downstairs, jumped in her car and drove to the nearest *quincaillerie* – the hardware shop – for supplies.

Back at the chateau, she carried everything inside and almost beheaded Josh with a piece of plywood. 'Sorry, I didn't see you,' she said after he'd leapt out of her way.

'I didn't need that ear anyway,' he said, mock-rubbing the side of his head.

'You'd better tell me where to put everything before I injure anyone else. I don't want to risk hurting Célie and not having that divine breakfast tomorrow.'

'Oh, but *I'm* expendable.' He actually smiled.

'Naturally.' She smiled back. Perhaps he'd just needed coffee yesterday. He seemed much nicer today. Although he was still wearing a perfectly pressed shirt and the trousers of an expensive suit, so perhaps the stiffness of demeanour to match would soon reappear.

'Follow me. The *salon de grisailles* might work.'

He led the way through the chateau to an enormous room, a sitting room now, although it looked to D'Arcy as if it must once have held elegant receptions or balls, the columns proudly arching up to the ceiling indicating its history. It had the same view as D'Arcy had seen from her balcony that morning, the grounds rolling away in a riot of colour and perfume down to a canal. The room was furnished as tastefully as D'Arcy's, the soft blues and greys that had lent the room its name present here also in the panelled wood walls, inset by *boiserie*, which arrested D'Arcy's attention. They were painted in silver, pearl, black and white and depicted a child in a forest of strangely stunted and twisted trees; D'Arcy couldn't tell if the child found the trees' presence haunting or soothing.

She tore her gaze away from the panels. 'I'm going to be making a bit of a mess,' she said doubtfully.

'You can work on the terrace if you like.' Josh opened the doors at the back of the room. 'Or there's the winter garden over there.' He pointed to a windowed enclosure that would be ideal on a cooler day but most likely roasting in summer.

'I'll take the terrace,' D'Arcy said, exiting through the doors. She dropped her equipment onto a table that she could use as a workbench. 'I'll build a crate for each photograph that isn't already packed,' she said, 'but they'll need to be double-crated. You must have some insulated crates somewhere?'

He nodded and disappeared, and D'Arcy began to saw and hammer. She did build crates occasionally; certain clients were fussy and D'Arcy had a reputation for being able to take care of an artwork from start to finish. She knew how to pack and how to transport and how to negotiate with customs brokers and sometimes couldn't believe that a fine arts degree had led to her becoming a kind of glorified babysitter for priceless artworks. But she also knew she loved it, even the carpentry that was her job right now.

Once the first crate was ready, she started on the condition report for the accompanying photograph. Josh arrived back with the insulated crates just as she'd finished.

'I need your autograph,' she said, passing him the paperwork.

He read it over, frowning, glancing at the photograph referred to and eventually seemed to concede to her description as being accurate.

'I'll work in the salon this morning so I can read each report and sign as you go,' he said.

'It'll be noisy. Sawing and hammering are hard to do quietly.'

'I don't mind noise. I used to work in the bullpen of a law firm in Manhattan; twenty associates are probably a lot noisier than a saw.'

'Wow, this must be a huge change of pace,' she said.

He shrugged, not elaborating any further.

The morning went on with D'Arcy fashioning crates, completing condition reports, having Josh sign them, which he did wordlessly, but at least never disagreeing or asking her to change what she'd written. In between the whirr of her saw or her drill, she could hear Josh speaking on the phone in impeccable French. It felt as if hardly any time had passed before Célie appeared with food and D'Arcy realised it was after two o'clock. More baguettes. Cheese. Tomatoes. Charcuterie. Her stomach growled loudly.

'I'm starving,' she said to Célie in French, who smiled.

'Wait until you try the tarte tatin I have for dessert,' Célie said.

D'Arcy groaned. 'I'll be sure to leave room for it.'

Josh came out onto the terrace as D'Arcy sat down. 'You speak French much too well for an Australian,' he said.

D'Arcy finished chewing her mouthful of bread. 'Are Australians not known for their linguistic skills?' she asked innocently.

'Not generally, no. You're an island in the middle of nowhere. There's no pressing need to speak anything other than English.'

'And Americans are somehow different? You have a pressing need to learn French because Canada's on your doorstep?'

'Touché,' he said, that hard-to-provoke smile reappearing. 'What I meant to say is, why do you speak French so well?'

'My mother is French. And your mother is . . . ?' she guessed, knowing that to speak the language so well, he must have learned as a child too.

'French Canadian.'

'Aha.' She reached for more bread. 'So tell me about the bullpen. How did you get from there to here?'

'Preventing corporations from being sued for obscene amounts of money, while guaranteed to give you a short-term, fist-pumping high, is pretty soulless,' he said flatly. 'I did a degree in law and art history – the bizarrest combination, but that's what I wanted to do. When an artists' agency was looking for agents with legal and contractual expertise, I applied, not really expecting to get it. But I did. Then, because I could speak French, I was asked to run the French office for the agency after a year or so.'

'Which means you mustn't be too bad at being an agent. But shouldn't you be in Paris, rather than here?'

'I come here at least once a week. The photographer was my first and most important client. And when the photographer's work is travelling across the oceans, it's doubly important that I'm around to make sure it goes safely.'

A short silence followed, into which a chasm of questions opened. *Who is the photographer? Do you speak to her in person? What is she like?*

The work D'Arcy was crating bore no name. The artist was known only as *The Photographer* and, while D'Arcy suspected she was female, nobody really knew for sure. It was a circumstance in which the mystery of anonymity added to the creative genius of the photographs, and created a media storm that hadn't abated for years. Every now and again it flared up, as somebody pushed a new theory about the identity of the photographer, an interest that had been stirred again as the photographs prepared to leave Europe for the first time ever, touring to Australia and then on to America. And D'Arcy, who'd been working as an art handler and sometimes curator for years, had been the one lucky enough to be chosen to go to France and escort the photographs. Of course, the prospect of getting close to brilliance had been a huge incentive, as had the intimation that she'd been specifically requested.

Célie came in with a platter of tarte tatin that filled the air with the vigorous scent of apples and the decadent sweetness of caramel. D'Arcy reached for a slice, before saying to Josh, 'You're not going to tell me anything about the photographer, are you?'

'I'm not,' he agreed.

'You could at least pretend you might drop me a hint to draw out the anticipation.' D'Arcy forked the tarte tatin into her mouth. 'Oh, it's so good.'

'I don't play games,' Josh said simply.

'I'd worked that much out. Luckily the culinary incentives more than make up for your lack of interest in giving me morsels. How can you not stay here all the time? If somebody made me food like this and gave me a bed like the one upstairs and a view so spectacular . . .' D'Arcy flung her arm out to encompass the divine surroundings. 'I'd never leave.'

'Is this your way of warning me I'm going to have to evict you at the end of a fortnight?'

'See,' D'Arcy stood up. 'You can be amusing if you try. Now, I'm going to work off my lunch by sawing some wood. And here are two more condition reports for you to frown at.'

She passed him the reports, catching the upwards quirk of his lips and turned around before he could see her matching smile.

The day sped onwards. Towards late afternoon, she felt someone's eyes on her. She looked up to see Josh, in running gear, watching her.

'I'm going for a run. You can leave any more condition reports on the table.'

'Do you mind if I log in to my email on your computer? I have my laptop but by the time I hook up to your modem, it's probably quicker if I just use yours.'

'Sure.' He nodded. 'It's in the office along the hall.' Before he turned away, he added, 'I told Célie we'd have dinner down in the folly.' He pointed to a structure halfway between the house and the canal, almost lost beneath a clump of startlingly red-leafed beech trees. 'At about eight. If that suits you.'

'Well, a girl's gotta eat. Enjoy your run.'

Eight

Running. Just the thought of it exhausted her. D'Arcy checked her watch and saw that it was after seven o'clock but of course it was still so light, a true European summer. She brushed off the sawdust, located Josh's office and logged into webmail. The email she'd been hoping for was sitting at the top of her inbox and she clicked on it before she could stop and think about it. As she read the words, she flopped into the nearest chair, shoulders sinking.

She hadn't been chosen for the fellowship. She'd applied – she'd thought carelessly, unworried if it didn't come off – for a Jessica May Fellowship for Women Artists. But the rejection hit her with more force than she'd thought it would. It meant the slender hope she'd been holding onto that she might still be able to do something about her dream of being a documentary filmmaker – a dream that had started and been nourished at university but which had since withered under the pressure of finding work that actually paid money – was now something she needed to relinquish. She hadn't pursued it actively for years, had let it flit around in her head in moments of solitude on plane trips and long truck rides couriering others' artworks, had told herself the fellowship would be the thing to get her going again. But, with no fellowship, she couldn't afford to dream.

She finished reading the email, ambitions cruelly resurrected on discovering the sentence: *The board thought your project idea excellent and worthy of a fellowship but we found your explanation of the creative process lacking. We encourage you to apply again, paying particular attention to how you will translate your idea into a documentary, and your plans for how the narrative will unfold.*

It was tempting to curse the board – they didn't know what they were talking about; they wouldn't recognise talent if it came and sat beside them – but D'Arcy knew, in her heart of hearts, that her explanation of the creative process *was* lacking. She'd dashed off the application three hours before deadline in her usual whimsical fashion and probably hadn't provided the rigorous detail required to be truly competitive. Her mother might say that D'Arcy hadn't really wanted to succeed because then she would have to commit to a twelve-month project, whereas D'Arcy's life consisted of short-term contracts and minimal obligations. Which was the best strategy for avoiding disappointments like this one.

D'Arcy went upstairs. She almost headed straight for a long soak in the tub but knew she'd feel better if she stretched first. Her yoga mat was one of her non-negotiables when it came to packing for overseas trips; she retrieved it from her room and laid it out on the balcony, moving through a series of sun salutations, stretches and inversions for almost half an hour. Then she let herself sink into the glorious bath.

Célie had left out a tray of Buly 1803 products, with their eccentric vintage-style bottles, and D'Arcy inhaled the scent of lemon, mint and rosemary as the bubbles rose around her. She lay her head back and closed her eyes, feeling the ache in her muscles from hammering and sawing dissolve into the water. She really could stay here forever, which, for someone known for their nomadic habits, was both a confronting and curious thought.

After a very long time, she dragged herself out and dried herself off, using the Buly moisturiser and hand cream liberally. Then she went to her suitcase and discovered that everything had been hung in the wardrobe, and pressed too. She couldn't remember the last time she'd used an iron, and her clothes wafted lavender and citrus towards her from the bags of herbs strung from the rails.

What did one wear to dinner in the folly of a French chateau? she mused. She pulled out one of her favourite things, a vintage turquoise Courrèges mini-dress that she always took with her when travelling because it didn't crease, could be dressed up or down and, she thought, suited her. The brown cowboy boots from the day before were pulled back on and she checked her watch. Nearly half past eight. Everything was lazily late in France though. She hoped Josh would be too.

Outside, the night was balmy and not yet dark, a crescent moon just beginning to show like the curve of a hipbone glimpsed beneath sheer fabric. The folly was lit with candles and D'Arcy could smell the food from a hundred metres away. 'At this rate, *I'll* have to take up running,' she said as she cast her eyes over the table laden with food, and then at Josh, who looked as delicious as the dinner.

'I don't think you have anything to worry about,' Josh said unexpectedly and she caught the briefest glimmer of something like admiration in his eyes before he poured out the wine.

She couldn't help asking, 'Do you normally have candlelit dinners with art handlers who stay in the chateau?'

He shook his head. 'Art handlers never stay in the chateau. But I often have dinner in the folly, sometimes with the photographer – I usually stay the night when I come down each week and I like being outside.'

'Well, thank you for asking me to join you.'

'Like you said, you have to eat.'

Which meant the admiration she thought she'd seen must have been for the wine, which he was staring at intently, not her. He was so hard to read. She sat down and helped herself to the terrine. 'Who cooks? How many Michelin stars do they have? And can I take them back to Australia with me?'

'Célie cooks. She doesn't get to cook for guests very often so, when she does, she goes all out. She also looks after the house and the photographer's needs. Célie's husband is in charge of the grounds.'

'A true family affair. Are they related to the photographer?' The words came out before she had time to think. She held up her hand. 'Sorry, I wasn't trying to pry. It was just the kind of question you might normally ask.'

D'Arcy sipped the wine and almost groaned again. It was so very good. A true feast for the senses, which must be why she was checking out Josh with one side of her brain, while the other side was telling her to behave. He was *very* good-looking, especially with candles flickering around him, offset by a garden so fecund she could almost hear the buds opening and new shoots pushing forth, and accompanied by a bottle of wine as full-bodied as a burlesque dancer, and paté so rustic and fresh that she wanted to eat it with her hands. Since when did D'Arcy behave anyway? Although she did like to be a little more sure that the other party was interested before she wasted time on flirting.

She dragged her eyes away from Josh's face. *Business*, she told herself. *For once, just stick to business.* 'Speaking of prying, how would you feel about me writing a piece on the chateau and its grounds for a newspaper in Australia?' she asked. 'I'd be careful not to specify where it is so the photographer's anonymity is safe, but I'm not sure how you feel about that kind of publicity. It might be a nice feature to have in the lead-up to the exhibition. As well as being a free-lance art handler, I freelance for arts magazines and newspapers, mainly writing about the arts but, because I travel so much, I sometimes write travel pieces too.' It was quicker and easier than telling a story on film, she didn't add, no matter that making a documentary was an infinitely more satisfying creative experience.

'You like freelancing? Not drawn to a more stable job?'

D'Arcy shook her head adamantly. 'Not for me. I like being able to work where and when it suits me. I like doing a mix of different things. I like that I can say no if I want to.'

'Have you always been like that?' Curiosity flickered in his eyes and she saw herself as he might: flighty, unable to settle, drawn to the unconventional in a way that he, as a lawyer, hadn't been.

'Pretty much. I did a couple of exchanges in high school, one to Italy, and one to France. I went to uni in Paris. The Maison Européenne de la Photographie offered me an assistant curatorship when I finished, which I loved, but I hated the black pencil skirts and sleek ponytails and the hush and the quiet and the seriousness. It wasn't fun, and art should be fun. Like here; I can tell that, whoever the photographer is, she revels in life. Everything is thriving and luscious and gorgeous and you just want to wallow in it. There wasn't a lot of wallowing at the Maison.'

She managed to extract a smile from him, which made her add, 'This won't mean anything to you but I just about mortgaged my apartment to Buly 1803 when I lived in Paris and there's a whole tray of it in the bathroom upstairs. If that doesn't call for some committed wallowing, I don't know what does.'

'I know Buly. I bought an ex-girlfriend some things from there once. She hated them. Too old-fashioned, she said.'

D'Arcy raised an eyebrow. 'I bet she wore pencil skirts and had a slicked-back ponytail, right?'

'She did, actually.'

'Well then.' D'Arcy sipped her wine with satisfaction.

'You say that like you've just proved an important scientific theory.'

'I have. Girls in pencil skirts have never learned to wallow. I'm sure your ex is a case in point.'

He laughed. 'Before we start talking about my ex-girlfriends, let's go back to where we started,' he said. 'I'm not sure we can take the risk of an article about the chateau. But I'll ask the photographer and let you know.'

'Okay,' D'Arcy said, before her head turned at the smell of more extraordinary food bearing down upon them.

Célie placed a platter of whole pan-roasted fish between them, the skin crisp and delicious, the smell of butter and lemon and rosemary wafting out. Another plate contained vegetables so imperfectly shaped and delightful that D'Arcy knew they'd come straight from the garden. 'Oh, dorade,' she said, sniffing the fish. 'Tell me this is a dorade.'

Célie smiled. 'It is. I had a feeling you might like it.'

I'd have liked to show children blue-water dorados, golden fish and fish that sing, D'Arcy quoted.

'Rimbaud,' Josh said quizzically as Célie melted into the night.

'I had a Parisian literature student as a boyfriend for a few months when I was at uni. He rather fancied himself as Rimbaud. I think he just liked the lines about vomit and cheap wine whereas, for some reason, it was always those golden singing fish that I remembered. I've had a fondness for the dorade ever since, even though I know they're different to the ones Rimbaud wrote about.'

'He sounds like a wallower.'

A laugh burst forth from D'Arcy. 'But he wallowed in all the wrong things.'

They began to eat the fish and Josh said, 'So tell me who you think does show compassion in their work,' and D'Arcy was both surprised and pleased that he wanted to keep their earlier discussion going.

The next hour was filled with companionable, lively and stimulating talk and D'Arcy couldn't remember time ever passing by so quickly and so engagingly. Eventually, she pushed her plate away. 'I really can't eat another thing. Don't tell me Célie's made dessert, or is about to appear with artisanal cheeses.'

'If I know Célie –'

'Look!' D'Arcy cut off Josh's words, jumping up suddenly from her chair and moving over to a stand of lobelia on which was perched the most extraordinary butterfly, as white as a bride waiting on an altar of petals for her beloved. She crouched down to inspect it more carefully, resisting the urge to run the soft film of its wings across her fingers.

Josh appeared at her side. 'It's called a Wood White. I always thought it should have a more extravagant name.'

'It should,' D'Arcy breathed.

The butterfly lifted into the air and she felt the slightest brush as it settled on her hair for an instant so unexpected she almost tipped over. Then it rose again, a wraith-like creature luminous against the darkening sky, as startlingly white as a full moon, fading to the merest streak of stardust before disappearing altogether.

'It's moments like that . . .' D'Arcy murmured as she stood. 'Impossible to orchestrate. Like the best photographs.'

She looked up at Josh; he was, she realised now that he was so close to her, several inches taller than she and he smelled as if he belonged to this place. Lemon most certainly, and mint too, with a base of cedar or cinnamon or both. And she would be quite happy to stand there for the rest of the night inhaling him, her eyes travelling over the dark shadow of his jaw, the inky hue of his eyes; without the light of the candles or the sun they were more indigo than she'd realised.

Her hand moved, laying itself lightly against his chest, enough to feel that running had certainly given him a very fine body. She tilted her head higher as his eyes darkened to midnight and rested on her lips. She probably shouldn't kiss him, she knew; she was there to work. But life was about seizing the moment and if a balmy evening in the lush garden of a French chateau with a handsome stranger whose conversation engrossed her wasn't a moment, then she didn't know what was. At least this way she'd find out pretty quickly if he had been admiring her or the wine earlier. And she was used enough to flings in foreign countries – in fact, they were her preferred encounters — that she didn't really mind what happened next; either he'd step away and be exceptionally solemn for the next two weeks and she'd have to find her pleasures in the Buly bath products and the food instead of him, or he'd respond and they'd have a fun night, or a few fun nights together, and that would be that.

So she let her hand drift up to the back of his neck and caress the skin there before exerting a gentle pressure to bring his head down to hers. Even though she'd given him at least a minute's warning of her intentions, he still seemed surprised when her mouth met his, kissing her softly — far too softly. But then she let herself fall into it, this kiss that was all about the caress of lip against lip; he hadn't even stepped closer to her, but had instead let the fact that only their mouths were touching create a kind of intensity, an expectation of what it would be like if she moved towards him, letting her body meet his.

After a long and exquisite time during which she was torn between opening her mouth and kissing him the way she wanted to and just staying in the moment of what was, she had to admit, the most romantic kiss she'd ever had, she felt him at last give way. His hands reached up to cup her jaw, drawing her in more deeply to meet the first touch of his tongue against hers. Then, finally, the oh so sensual feel of his mouth opening, letting her in, of her body shifting into his, of her hands running up his back an inch at a time, feeling every single lovely muscle beneath her palms.

She broke off just long enough to say, 'My room or yours?' and was left momentarily speechless when he stepped back and shook his head.

'Since when does a kiss mean we go straight to a bedroom?' he demanded.

'Well, it was a pretty good kiss,' she said, aiming for jocular but he grimaced.

'Sorry,' she continued, 'For a minute there, I mistook you for somebody attracted to me, not my grandmother.'

This time, he smiled a little and she was, she had to admit, relieved. It didn't bother her if he wasn't interested. But he didn't have to be a dick about it.

'It's just . . .' He paused and studied her as if he was deciding whether or not to say what was on his mind.

'Out with it,' she said. There was nothing worse than tiptoeing around a moment of amorousness as if it had never happened, like teenagers did. Much better to be honest and then move on. 'I can tell you want to say something. I have bad breath. You don't like women who can handle a saw better than you can. You're practising celibacy. Which one?'

'None of the above. I kissed you because I wanted to kiss you, not because I want to have sex with you. Haven't you ever found that something is a million times better when you don't have it straight away?'

She frowned. 'Actually, no. The dorade would be off in a week. The terrine too. Okay, maybe this dress was worth waiting forty-five years for but I generally find that knowing more about a person doesn't necessarily make the sex any better.'

'Maybe you haven't been having sex with the right people.'

She dared to look up at him and wished she hadn't. Yes, she wanted to kiss him all over again but she wouldn't now. 'Well, I'm clearly not going to find out what it would be like with you so do you have anyone else you'd like to recommend?'

His eyes flickered up the hill to the house as if something had caught his attention and she turned to see Célie approaching with yet more food. Josh stepped back and reached out his hand to take the tray from Célie. 'We've decided to do some work,' he said to Célie. 'I'll take that inside for us.'

'Work,' D'Arcy said archly once Célie had gone, wanting to make light of the whole situation. 'You'll be lucky if I can concentrate on anything.'

He prodded her gently in the back with the tray. 'Move,' he said, his voice as close to teasing as she'd heard it. 'Work is the best thing for both of us right now. And turn off the lusty eyes.'

She made sure to give him a long stare before she started towards the house – anything to capitalise on his one definite foray into flirting. 'I had no idea they were lusty in the first place so I won't be able to turn them off. You'll just have to put up with them.'

Nine

*H*er hopes lifted a little when he led her upstairs but sank when he opened the door to an attic filled with boxes and filing cabinets, an archive of the photographer's work, D'Arcy presumed.

'I guess I was still hoping work might be a euphemism for . . .' she began.

'Stop it,' he mock-ordered. 'If this doesn't distract you, nothing will. You're the only person besides me who's ever been allowed into this room.'

'Does the photographer know?' D'Arcy said, then wondered why she'd asked. There was no way Josh was the kind of person who'd have his head turned by one little kiss and give her access to things forbidden by his client. 'Why would the photographer let me in here?'

Josh shrugged. 'I don't know. I was literally speechless when the photographer asked me to contact the gallery in Australia to see if they'd be interested in an exhibition; the photographer had never before wanted the works to travel outside Europe. And then there was the specific request for you to handle the art for the show. I mean, I had heard of you; you've handled work for some of our clients before and there aren't too many art handlers in Australia.'

'Well,' D'Arcy said, 'you've succeeded in completely distracting me. Is this where all her work is kept?'

'It is. It's far from ideal storage conditions but she doesn't care about that. Even I've only been allowed to look through certain boxes and files – the ones on the left side of the room. But tonight . . .' He paused. 'She told Célie to send me up when I finished my run. She said you might like to see some of her older works, to show more of a sense of her career. Things never exhibited. That we could look through anything in the room, even the boxes on the right. I said you weren't the curator and you probably wouldn't have authority to add things to the exhibition. But she was insistent.'

'So the photographer is a she?' D'Arcy grinned, pleased that her intuition had been right.

Josh swore. 'Her telling me to bring you up here has thrown me more than I'd realised. I never slip up like that.'

'Don't worry, I won't tell anyone. And you're right; I can't just send extra photographs over to the gallery. But I know the curator. She'll listen if I think the pieces are worthwhile.'

She knew her face must betray all of her anticipation. As an art historian by training, this was like buried treasure for pirates. 'We need gloves,' she said. 'And the lights.' She looked up at the ceiling but saw that the installed lighting would be kind to artefacts.

'Gloves are over there. But I'm definitely not turning the lights off.'

She laughed. 'There is a funny man lurking beneath the lawyer, Josh. You should let him out more. Pass me the gloves. Can I choose where to start?'

He nodded. 'You look much more excited about this than you did about kissing me.'

'Only because you put a stop to it much too soon. I assume you're not going to do the same here?'

'No.'

'Good. Well, if you've never been allowed to look at anything on the right-hand side, that's where we start.'

She opened the first box. It was an assortment of photographs of the house and the gardens, narrowing in on details: flowers, leaves, insects. They had a feel of uncertainty, as if the photographer wasn't familiar with this kind of subject.

'Look at this,' D'Arcy said, showing Josh a picture of a Wood White, the butterfly that had graced her head earlier. The chateau in the background looked similar to now, but the gardens were less dense, as if they'd only been planted for a few years. Another group of photographs showed four people, two men and two women – taken in the seventies, judging by their clothes – their faces impossible to make out, caught from one of the rooms at the top of the chateau as they wandered through the gardens.

None had the quality of a magic shot that would earn it a position in a retrospective. 'Do you have anything?' she asked Josh, who was working his way through another box.

'Not really. The same woman is in quite a few but I don't know who she is.'

D'Arcy glanced over at the pictures of a young woman. She was striking, but in a wild sort of way, her face so stunning it was hard to look away without scrutinising it to see if it really was as beautiful as it appeared at first glance. Whoever she was, the young woman was definitely not one for slicked-back ponytails, D'Arcy reflected with a smile.

D'Arcy opened another box and frowned when she saw pictures of incorporeal women who were somehow still standing even though they looked dead. Next, pictures of uniformed men, soldiers grinning out at her, and then one shot that she'd seen a thousand times before, a shot used in Kleenex advertisements, department store Father's Day promotions, a photograph reproduced in black-and-white prints in IKEA, the final desecration. But this was the original, the source of all those copies, and she could see that none had ever done it justice, that in being overexposed by cheap copies, the image had been robbed of its true power.

The photograph was sixty years old now and the paper had yellowed and dulled, which only added to the poignancy. A man in a US Army uniform embracing a little girl. His face profiled, his back to the camera, the little girl's face fully on view, exposed in a moment of utter love – it was the kind of love D'Arcy wasn't sure she'd ever witnessed in her life. The kind she wondered, for one quick and painful second, if anyone, besides her mother, would ever express for her.

Her stillness caught Josh's attention and he came over to her side.

'What's that doing in here?' he asked.

'You know the picture, don't you?' she said, looking up at him from where she was crouched on the floor.

'Of course I do. But . . .'

'This whole box is full of war photos. I've seen these ones before too.' D'Arcy indicated the skeletal women. 'A photojournalist by the name of Jessica May took this picture of the man embracing the girl. She worked for *Vogue* during the war. I don't even know if she's still alive.' D'Arcy tried to recollect if she'd read anything about Jessica May's life on the fellowship website when she applied but realised she'd arrogantly thought she knew everything and hadn't bothered. 'I'm sure she never took any more pictures after the war though. She was forgotten, like so many others, besides that one photo of the man and the child. Although it's the photo that's endured not the photographer; most people would have no idea who snapped it. Why would these be here?'

'Maybe Jessica May knew my client?' he guessed. 'Maybe she gave her all her negatives and prints when she died?'

D'Arcy frowned. 'Maybe. But why not tell anyone? Despite May being consigned to the amnesia of history, these prints should be in a museum. Not in here. They're not just interesting as war records; the photos themselves show true artistry.'

D'Arcy pulled out another photo, this one of a nurse on a mountain, singing, surrounded by soldiers. 'See how this one's been solarised so that the woman appears angelic almost,' she said. 'Solarisation was such a new technique back then and this one is done perfectly. The angel singing – I believe it was Handel's *Messiah* – to the troops on Easter Sunday to give them the courage to keep fighting. It's propaganda almost, but so well done.'

She stopped suddenly. 'Sorry, I'm giving you an art history lecture. It's just that . . .' Her voice trailed off.

'It feels a bit unreal,' Josh said, lowering himself down beside her to sift through the crate.

'Exactly. It's an art historian's dream to come across something like this and here I am standing in the middle of it, photographs in hand, and I don't quite know what to make of it.' D'Arcy hesitated, but then her habit of candour made her keep going. 'I studied war photography and it was thought these negatives had been lost. All the reproductions have been made from the print held by *Vogue*, not the negatives.'

'You know so much about it. Why aren't you . . .'

He stopped but D'Arcy knew exactly what he'd been about to say. Why aren't you a curator? Why waste an art history degree on being an art handler? It was what everyone asked her, mostly because so few people had ever heard of an art handler and had no real idea what she did. But he knew, and he still thought he had to ask the question.

She riffled through the box so she didn't have to look at him and be disappointed that he held the same prejudices as everyone else. 'There are too many people to answer to as a curator,' she said crisply. 'Boards, the public, the media: being a curator sometimes seems much less about the art than it is about making everyone happy. And then there's the pencil skirts. I prefer the freedom of being an art handler. And the wardrobe.'

He started to interrupt and she expected he would offer a platitude, say that he hadn't meant to imply that curatorship was the only real job to which an art historian should aspire, but she didn't give him the chance. 'And the reason I know so much about it is because I once thought I wanted to be a documentary filmmaker,' she said. 'That was my art. I studied media, as well as art history at uni. One of the documentaries I made was about what happened to women artists after the war. Women who'd been working as camouflage and propaganda artists, or war photographers, women who'd put their creative ambitions on hold to serve their country and who, once the war was over, were brushed aside as the men returned and took their jobs and reoccupied the artistic world. I'd read a piece in *Art Monthly* that resurrected Linda Nochlin's 1970s essay. You know the one: "Why Have There Been No Great Women Artists?" So I made a documentary arguing both that there had been great women artists and why they'd been overlooked and unremembered.'

D'Arcy drew in a breath. God, that was all such a long time ago. When she'd been a passionate art student and had thought she could be a filmmaker. Even writing her fellowship application hadn't excited as much feeling in her as that speech just had. Regret squeezed her heart in its unfamiliar fist – how easily she'd cast her artistic aspirations aside like thousands of other female artists before her.

'You wanted to resurrect the documentary for the Jessica May Fellowship,' Josh said quietly.

Shit! She must have left the bloody email open on his computer.

'I wasn't prying,' he said. 'I closed it down as soon as I realised it was something of yours but it was impossible not to see some of it. They were right; it is a good idea for a documentary.'

'I felt it deserved more thought than my amateur abilities had lent it ten years ago,' she said. 'But that's not going to happen now. Another reason for me to continue as "just" an art handler,' she finished sarcastically.

'I wasn't going to ask why you weren't a curator,' Josh said. 'I was going to ask you why you didn't write about art instead of travel. But as soon as I thought it, I knew the answer. I bet travel pieces pay a lot more. And more than documentaries, which won't pay you anything until you get a backer. I'm not judging you for spending your time doing the things that pay. I just think you're good at making the theory come to life when you talk about it so I expect you'd write about it well too. Or film it well.'

'Thanks.' D'Arcy managed a quick smile.

'You know that Walter Lippmann quote? The one that goes: *Photographs have the kind of authority over imagination today, which the printed word had yesterday, and the spoken word before that.*'

'*They seem utterly real,*' she finished the quote for him.

'I've always thought it needed amending again,' he continued. 'To say that film has the kind of authority over imagination which photographs had yesterday.'

'Maybe.' She shrugged, wanting to move the focus away from herself. She'd shared more with Josh about her once lofty aspirations and her past than she'd shared with any man ever. 'Why do you think . . .'

'These photos are here?' Josh shook his head. 'I have no idea.'

'You don't think . . .' D'Arcy had started to say: *You don't think your photographer is Jessica May?* But she stopped herself in time. Just because the photographer Josh agented had chosen to be anonymous, it didn't follow that she was a formerly famous war photographer. Even if she did have a formerly famous photographer's archive in her home. That Jessica May had known the person whose chateau D'Arcy was now standing in, as Josh had suggested, was the more realistic option; the other was the stuff of Hollywood movies. And Josh's surprise at finding the photos was genuine; if his client was Jessica May, then surely she would have apprised him of that fact?

'We're going to find a new photographer in each box?' Josh quipped, finishing her sentence in a way different to that which she'd intended.

'You've been sitting on a collection of a once famous photographers' work all this time and not known about it? I doubt it. But let's take a look.' Perhaps there would be something in the boxes that made the reason these photographs were here, and the relationship between Jessica May and The Photographer, clear.

The next box was marked in English — 'Unpublished'. On the top were more pictures from the Easter service, the ones that hadn't made it into *Vogue* if the label on the box was right. Then more of the unsettling, cadaverous women whom D'Arcy almost didn't want to look at, but she knew that was the point. You should never look away from the things that make you uncomfortable. 'These are from one of the concentration camps,' she said quietly, and Josh took them from her, studying them carefully, as if paying tribute to the courage of these barely alive survivors.

'You know that, before the camps were discovered, people didn't believe they existed,' D'Arcy said. 'Photographs like this made them a reality. And people saw the pictures and thought they understood what it must have been like, as if the photos *were* reality. As if looking upon the feelings of the women was some kind of surrogate way of actually feeling their pain. It's what we do now: look at a picture of a tragedy in a newspaper and say, *how awful*, before we turn ruthlessly to the next page.'

'What's the answer?' Josh asked. 'To not photograph? Then nobody would know anything.'

'I know. I think that's why I've always admired the photographer's work. Because it seems to ask the viewer to stop and to feel, not just to stop and to look.'

'Maybe you should be her agent instead of me.' He frowned. 'It's been a long time since I've stopped and felt, or even looked, when I've come here to visit her. Always too damn busy, like everyone is these days.'

They were both quiet for a moment, reflecting on what they'd discussed, and D'Arcy realised she was glad Josh was with her. When he let his guard drop, he was the most interesting man she'd met in a long time. And it was nice to share this discovery with someone like him, who was as intrigued as she.

D'Arcy dug a little deeper into the box and pulled out two more pictures. It was the same man and the same little girl from the iconic shot. One of the prints in her hand was taken moments before the embrace as the girl flew towards the man, arms outstretched; the other one was taken moments after. The first one was blurred and it was easy to see why it hadn't been published but D'Arcy liked it regardless. The blurring underscored the animation of the little girl's body and the way she felt about the man.

In the second shot, the man held the girl up high in the air. D'Arcy could now see that the girl wore an olive drab jacket that obviously had been made for her to look like the nurses' dress uniforms. On the lapels, instead of the nurses' insignia, someone had hand-stitched a name. It was the name that made D'Arcy gasp. Victorine.

'What is it?' Josh glanced across at her quizzically.

D'Arcy shook her head. 'The little girl has the same name as my mother. I've never come across anyone else called Victorine in my life.' She shrugged. 'But I guess during the war it could have been a popular name.'

Josh plucked the photograph from her hand and, as he did so, D'Arcy caught a glimpse of writing on the back. She tipped her head to the side to read it.

Dan Hallworth and Victorine Hallworth. 1944.

This time, she was incapable of gasping. She simply stared, then felt her hand reach out to touch the words, running a finger over them as if she had made some mistake and the real words would soon become apparent beneath her gesture of erasure.

'You've gone very white,' Josh said, putting the photo down. 'Are you okay?' He touched her arm, concern evident on his face.

'I don't think so.' She closed her eyes and opened them again. Then picked up the photograph. Turned it over. But the words were still there: *Dan Hallworth and Victorine Hallworth. 1944.*

'Victorine Hallworth is my mother's name.' D'Arcy's voice sounded as fragile as the Wood White butterfly's wings, as if it would take off and desert her at any moment. There might be other Victorines in the world, but was there more than one Victorine Hallworth of around the same age as her mother?

'That's a very strange coincidence.' Josh's words came out heavily, dropping like thunderclouds into the room. 'Who's Dan Hallworth?'

'I have no idea. Well, actually, I do have some idea but it doesn't make any sense.' She put the photograph down. 'I need a drink.'

'I'll be right back.' Josh vanished through the doors and D'Arcy sank to the floor, knees hugged tight against her chest. Her mind circled around and around the words – *Dan Hallworth and Victorine Hallworth. 1944* – and came up with a long list of unanswerable questions.

'Cognac?'

D'Arcy jumped at the sound of Josh's voice. He'd returned with a decanter and two glasses. She nodded.

Josh sat down beside her, much less awkwardly than she imagined he might be on a dusty floor beside a woman in a mini-dress who needed cognac to restore the colour to her cheeks. He poured them both a drink.

'Which mystery do we start with?' he asked, as if he wanted to help.

'I don't know,' she replied, swallowing the cognac and staring at the ceiling. 'I just don't know.'

PART THREE
Jess

The pattern of liberation is not decorative. There are the gay squiggles of wine and song. There is the beautiful overall colour of freedom, but there is ruin and destruction. There are problems and mistakes, disappointed hopes and broken promises.

– Lee Miller

Ten

As May wore on, Jess and Martha, still shackled to London by the Public Relations Office, made it their business to sit in the bar at the Savoy almost every minute of every day so they could eavesdrop on any conversation that might give them a clue as to what was going on and how to get themselves attached to the invasion fleet. Martha was also doing her best to avoid Hemingway, who was at the Dorchester, thankfully, but he'd developed a nasty habit of accosting her in hallways and remonstrating with her in loud and drunken fury. All the more reason to get back over to the Continent, Jess reasoned.

It was in the bar that they first heard about parachute school.

'I wonder why we haven't been invited to parachute school,' Jess said, smiling sweetly at the two correspondents who were having the conversation that had piqued Martha and Jess's interest.

Martha stood up and slid into the booth beside the men. 'I have a story for you,' she said.

The men looked from Martha to Jess, and Jess knew they were trying to decide which one they'd have the most chance of bedding later if this went the way they thought it would. *It won't*, Jess wanted to say, but she and Martha needed information and if that meant trading on the fact that they were women, then that's what they'd do; it was the mere fact of being women that meant they had to resort to it in the first place.

'Did you know,' Martha said flirtatiously, smiling her beautiful smile, her pale blonde hair curling sweetly around her face, 'that the powers that be have just ordered eight gross of rubbers for the correspondents?'

'Only for the photographers,' Jess said, turning on her magazine smile and trying not to laugh. It was true; more than one thousand rubbers had been ordered for the press, but it was to protect the films they would take in France, rather than their nether regions. 'Perhaps you should learn to take pictures, Marty, so you'll be as well equipped as me.'

'Perhaps I should,' Martha said. 'I don't suppose either of you gentlemen are photographers?'

The men replied in the negative, clearly regretful and also titillated by the conversation.

Martha sighed dramatically. 'Too bad. But perhaps you have some other interesting stories to share. How about I buy everyone a whiskey and you tell us a little more about parachute school.'

Marty and Jess had seated themselves strategically. The correspondents they'd chosen were as callow as children on their first day at school, having arrived in London the previous week. They still thought free whiskey and two women were prizes worth having and had no idea the prize came with a price. And they'd probably heard Warren's stories about Jess and hoped that a bedroom digestif might be the outcome of this cosy chat.

One of the men leaned forward and whispered conspiratorially. 'The public relations guys are in a jam. There are more correspondents wanting to go with the invasion fleet than there are places. So they thought they could drop some of the men in by parachute. You need to do five training jumps, so they're sending any man who's interested to parachute school in a village called Chilton Foliat.'

'So that's where Joe Dearing vanished to,' Martha mused, the *Collier's* photographer having been missing for a couple of days on sanctioned business.

'You haven't heard the best part,' the other man jumped in, eyeing Jess, and she let him sit closer than was comfortable because she was as keen as Martha to hear the rest. 'Bob Capa had a party on the weekend and he and Bill Landry and Larry LeSueur got themselves as full as bedbugs on champagne,' he said. 'They signed a contract with one of the PROs at the party, saying they'd go with him at eleven the next morning to do their training jumps. Only the press guy turns up to collect them and there's no sign of Bob or Bill or Larry. He phones Bill who says he sprained his ankle. He phones Larry who says the same. He can't find Bob anywhere. So –'

'Three places allocated to train male correspondents to handle parachute jumps in preparation for the invasion went to waste because they were drunk,' Martha finished. 'Good to see they take their responsibilities so seriously.'

'Sorry fellas,' Jess said, finishing her whiskey and standing up. 'But we have somewhere to be.'

The men were not polite in their remonstrances to the women as they walked away, causing Marty to add fuel to the fire by blowing them a kiss. Jess led the way to her room where she bashed out a letter on her typewriter, and then she and Martha went upstairs and banged on Warren's door.

He opened it with a smile when he saw who it was. 'Two at once?' he said loudly, no doubt hoping anyone in the rooms beside would hear. 'That's too much even for me.'

'This,' Jess said, ignoring the jibe, 'is a letter officially requesting permission for Martha and me to begin parachute training in preparation for the invasion. I have a copy here for SHAEF PR, filling them in on details of wasted parachute training places, requesting your documented response within a week.'

'Don't,' he said, and this time when he looked at her, his exasperating smile was gone. 'Don't send it to SHAEF PR.'

As he spoke, Jess saw the flicker of humanity in Warren; he didn't want her telling tales to his bosses at the Supreme Headquarters of the Allied Expeditionary Forces, tales that might make the PR men in charge believe that Warren Stone couldn't handle two little women like Jess and Martha.

But any compassion she might once have made herself muster for Warren had abandoned her at the port in Naples, where it remained with the line of men who all had copies of *Vogue*, provided for them by Warren, to taunt her with.

'I have to,' she said quietly.

And then she turned around and stalked off, leaving even Martha's experienced mouth hanging open.

⌒

Warren made them cool their already frozen heels for a week. The only burst of sunshine was a letter from Dan, with whom Jess had entered into a correspondence, by way of Victorine. Victorine had wanted to send Jess some pictures, Dan had explained the first time she'd received an envelope addressed in unfamiliar handwriting. Inside was a child's drawing in smudged black ink of a little girl reading what looked like a book. On closer inspection, Jess realised the squiggly lines on the front of the book were awkward letters spelling *Vogue*.

Jess had written back to both Victorine and Dan, and he'd replied. He'd written that, on returning to England, his company had been put through more training, then finally quarantined somewhere – of course he couldn't tell her where. But Jess knew the US Army had very few battle-experienced soldiers, besides the men from Italy. It was obvious to her that those men would be relied upon to teach the unblooded what to do when faced with an enemy more implacable than anyone had initially anticipated. And that

Dan, as a paratrooper, would be among the very first men in France, parachuted in hours before any amphibious assault, attempting to secure strategic targets that would allow the infantry to advance. In the hands of all the too-young men like Dan, about to jump out of a plane and into the abyss, the future rested. If they couldn't do what they were meant to, what would happen to the world?

It was a line of thought she couldn't let herself pursue. She shook her head and turned her attention back to Dan's letter but then Warren slid into a seat at the bar next to her, his toothiness recovered, and she wondered if the previous week's glimpse behind the facade had been a hallucination.

'Well?' she demanded, stubbing out another of the countless cigarettes she and Marty were working their way through.

'You're to discuss the matter with your editors,' Warren replied as serenely as if they were discussing what to have for afternoon tea.

'Why?' Martha asked.

'It's somewhat . . . delicate,' Warren said, unable to stop the corners of his mouth twitching.

'More delicate than accusing me of sleeping with half the US Army in order to get my stories,' Jess said collectedly.

'You didn't get the information about wasted parachute training places just by asking around.' Warren didn't bother to restrain his smile this time. 'The US Army is very keen to protect your special skills.'

Jess's stomach contracted. She had no idea what he meant but she knew it didn't sound good.

'If you really would prefer to hear it from me, rather than someone who might handle it more sensitively, then here goes,' Warren continued with faux concern. 'As you can see, none of the staff sections could provide any reason why women should be prevented the right to descend by parachute into France.'

He passed a letter to Jess and her nausea somersaulted into excitement. She looked across at Martha and grinned. No reason they couldn't go! Then they'd be at the next jump training session. But if Warren hadn't got his way, his bosses at SHAEF PR were likely furious with him. So he should be downcast at the very least. Instead, he bore a strong resemblance to the proverbial canary-eating cat.

'Except for a major in the office of the Surgeon General,' Warren said, leaning back and draping his arm along the back of Jess's stool. 'He was very concerned about the effects on the female anatomy of dropping out of a plane going 115 miles per hour. Add to that the brusque upward thrust of the opening parachute canopy and one doesn't like to think about what might happen to the delicate female apparatus.'

Absolute silence followed. Neither Jess nor Martha could make their mouths form a single word of response. How Warren must have searched high and low for that major. How he must have relished receiving that report and showing it to his superiors to prove that he was doing such a good job of keeping the women quarantined and out of the invasion fleet.

Then Warren let his hand drop, seemingly accidentally, onto Jess's shoulder.

She shot to her feet. 'And what does the Surgeon General's office have to say about the effect on the dangling male apparatus? Oh, that's right, it's used to brusque upward thrusting but we women are too delicate to know anything about it. And I suppose if one has no balls in the first place, like PROs who sit in hotels rather than fighting for their country – for God's sake, I've seen more of the war than you have! – then we shouldn't be too concerned about any adverse effects on those balls.'

Martha exploded with laughter, which set off the rest of the men at the bar, who'd heard all too clearly Jess's tirade, delivered at full volume.

Stone spoke so softly that Jess had to lean down, despite her dis-inclination to do so, to hear him. This time, there was no humanity, no vulnerability in him at all. 'One day, Captain May, you will regret this conversation very much. And on that day, I will remind you just what you said about the brusque upward thrust.'

With that he left, Jess's victory as empty as any in Italy that had cost a hundred lives. By publicly calling him out on the fact that his 'war' service was confined to hotel bars rather than battlefields, she'd openly and unwittingly skewered another of Warren's most tender spots. Neither she nor Martha would witness the invasion by parachute, and now she had to also try to forget what he'd just said, and what he'd meant by it. Everything he'd done and said to her before had been immature horseplay. But that threat wasn't.

She shivered and swallowed more whiskey.

~

At Portsmouth, it seemed incongruous that, across the Channel, one could see France, see the enemy. Today was invasion day plus one; yesterday, everyone had decamped to the south of England and Jess and Martha had had to sit and watch the flood of male journalists boarding planes that blackened the sky, watch the soldiers who'd never seen battle swarming onto ships bound for France, stand in this very spot and stare across at the war that no female was allowed to witness.

But instead of letting Warren's threat and almost obsessive interest in Jess get them down — what could he really do to her in a hotel full of people? — Jess and Martha decided to use it to their advantage. So long as Jess stayed in Warren's line of sight, Martha could at least try to get herself across the Channel.

It was dawn when Martha embraced Jess and said, 'I sure am glad I saw you at that party in New York.'

'Me too. Now go.'

Jess made sure to stride provocatively into the bar and sit beside Warren, ready to engage him in another battle of words while Martha slipped off to the beach. Then, between taking Warren's barbs, Jess imagined Martha creeping onto the hospital ship as planned, hiding in a bathroom – would it really work? It sounded so simple and foolish now – landing at Omaha Beach and getting her story. The first woman to set foot on French soil post-invasion, the first woman to tell people how it really was. Not the way the men saw it.

After a good hour or two, when she was sure that Martha had got away, Jess turned her attention to a couple of officers and availed herself of a ride to the village school nearby; Warren had, of course, refused her a jeep. She walked up the driveway to the school and heard her name, screamed at the top of tiny lungs, then a little girl in a muddle of dark curls and a too-big uniform ran out to throw herself into Jess's arms. This time it was Jess who picked her up and swung her around, for Dan, who could not.

'You did come!' Victorine beamed and kissed both of Jess's cheeks and Jess returned the gesture.

A woman Jess assumed was the school mistress appeared and nodded at Jess. 'You must be Miss May,' she said, a friendly smile on her face. 'Why don't you take Miss May for a walk, Victorine? You can stop by the kitchen and ask the cook for some cake.'

'Thank you,' Jess said. 'I'm sorry if I've caused any disruption.'

'You haven't,' the woman said firmly. 'She's been pining for Major Hallworth and while we try to supply as many hugs as we can, it's not quite the same. It will do her the world of good to spend the morning with you.'

So Jess and Victorine sat down on a stile in a field and ate chocolate cake. Jess told Victorine about her own parents, how they'd died too, just like Victorine's papa at the hospital in Italy, and how, even though she was older than Victorine, she still missed them. 'I thought maybe we could look after each other,' Jess finished. 'I don't have parents and nor do you anymore, and it would be nice to know that there was someone else who could be my family.'

Victorine beamed. 'I will be your family,' she said seriously. 'And you will be mine. Dan is my family too. So now he is yours as well.'

Jess grinned as she thought about writing *that* in a letter to Dan. All he'd wanted her to do was pay Victorine a visit and now they'd been proclaimed family. But she also knew that the most important thing was to get Victorine through this war. If they could do that, then everything else would work out too. Or so she was trying to make herself believe.

But that belief lay in tatters later that day when she heard from the pilots who'd made three hundred and twenty-five missions over to Normandy the night before to resupply Dan's airborne division. 'We threw the stuff out for the poor bastards and prayed; the Army doesn't know where they are so it's anyone's guess if they find their supplies,' one of them said to her between long drags of cigarette smoke.

'What do you mean?' she made herself ask.

'The fellas in the airborne division got dropped anywhere and everywhere because the Krauts were shooting down the planes. Hardly any of them are where they're meant to be. That's if they even made it to the ground alive, the way Jerry was shooting at them as they dropped.'

Jess held up her hand. 'I get it,' she said.

Now she had yet another reason to find a way into France. To find out if Dan was okay. She wouldn't be able to see Victorine again until she knew because Victorine would see it in her face: her fear that the worst had happened.

———

Warren Stone was waiting for her in the bar when she returned. 'Your friend's been arrested,' he said, triumph in his voice. 'Mrs Ernest Hemingway stowed away in the bathroom of a hospital ship and got herself onto a water ambulance that landed on the beach. As if that wasn't stupid enough, she sent a story through to *Collier's*, reporting what she saw. I picked it up from the censor. She convicted herself.'

'I think that was her intention,' Jess said evenly. 'One doesn't stow away on a ship to get a story and then not write the goddamned story. Wouldn't it be easier if you just let us go?'

'How it must torment you; she got there and you didn't.' Warren folded his arms across his chest as if he'd just made the final, winning rebuttal.

'It doesn't torment me at all.' It was true. Jess was having a hard time holding back the jubilation that Martha had really done it, and had beaten her husband to the story. Hemingway hadn't yet landed on French soil; Martha had. She risked a smile and raised her voice so everyone in the bar would hear. 'When I think about how you must have felt when you found out what she did, all I can do is laugh. And raise a glass to her.'

'Shame you won't have anyone to raise it with. Martha Gellhorn has been confined to a nurses' training camp. She has no passport or accreditation papers. She's not going anywhere.'

'And I don't suppose I should bother asking if I can see her?'

'Only if you want to hear me say no to you one more time.'

'Well, that's just another in a long line of shitty decisions,' Jess said. 'Martha's got more experience reporting war than anybody. But she gets locked up for trying to do her job? Exactly how long am I, and every other female correspondent, going to be stuck here? What started out as a ridiculously sexist notion of imagining we might swoon at the sight of war simply because we're women has become a stubbornly entrenched dictate that nobody in SHAEF wants to relinquish, just to prove a point. It's childish illogic, especially now that the *female* nurses are finally going to France.'

Jess felt someone step up behind her. She was just about to whirl around, thinking it would be someone come to defend Warren from the deranged and wanton Jessica May, when she heard a woman's voice say, 'Yes, we'd all like to know that.' It was Iris Carpenter from *The Boston Globe*. Not one of the novices.

Someone else joined them. Ruth Cowan from Associated Press, another woman with experience. Soon there was a group of women around Jess, all of them staring implacably at Warren Stone, wanting Jess's question answered.

'If you don't answer,' Jess said quietly, 'we might think you don't have the authority to do so.'

'I don't take kindly to being ambushed,' he replied.

Despite the steel in his voice, despite knowing it would only strengthen his resolve to do whatever his obscure threat had promised the other night, despite knowing that she was once again starting a fire that Warren would do anything to extinguish before his superiors felt its heat, Jess made herself say it. 'Then it's a good thing there are better men than you fighting in France.' As she spoke, Jess could feel the held breath of every woman around her, all of them wanting to applaud while at the same time wishing Jess could take it back because what would Warren Stone do now?

Jess didn't wait for his reply. 'Back when you quarantined us, you said we'd be able to go when the nurses did. They're going next week but we still don't have our orders. We'll put our concerns in writing,' she continued. 'We'll expect a reply within twenty-four hours. If that reply says anything about our delicate vaginas, then we will, every single one of us, publish it.'

She turned away and walked over to an empty table. Iris dumped her typewriter in front of Jess. Ruth bought the drinks. And Jess bashed out their words. At the end they had a letter to SHAEF, signed by every single female correspondent who'd been in Europe for more than a month, demanding they be allowed into France.

Eleven

$\mathcal{T}$wo days later, Jess and Iris Carpenter were on their way to Omaha Beach on a plane. The first women into France – besides Martha's unscheduled expedition – after D-day. They had thirty-six hours. No more. While SHAEF might be well aware that *The Boston Globe* wouldn't print any military communication about women's unmentionables, Jess knew they weren't so sure about *Vogue*. And so her threat had worked. But it had come at a price. More new rules for 'girl reporters' arrived from SHAEF as thick and fast as bombers in an invasion sky and any breach would result in court-martial. And she'd also heard that Warren Stone had been bawled out by his boss once again for his inability to keep the gals quiet. Which would only make him hate Jess all the more.

But as she and Iris flew in lower towards the minuscule Saint Laurent airstrip, between Easy Green and Easy Red, Jess forgot about all that and wondered instead how anyone could land on or take off from the beach. Indeed the pilot looked taut enough to snap as they came in low over Dead Man's Gulch through ashen bulges of smoke.

'Do you think we'll make it?' she said to Iris.

'It'd certainly be the definition of irony to have finally been allowed to come, and then to crash land on the beach,' Iris replied.

'Maybe I'll just close my eyes and pray,' Jess said.

In the end she prayed, but she couldn't make herself shut her eyes. The sea, a beautiful holiday blue, was full of battleships and tugboats, all flying silver barrage balloons above like misshapen moons, the sunlight dancing off the silver, off the water. Here and there, drowned tanks and derricks could be seen among the ruins of bombed-out boats. The hulking grey of the Mulberry harbour fingered the ocean and bulldozered piles of metal hedgehogs spiked menacingly from the sand. Foxholes, which just days ago had sheltered men, gaped out of the cliff.

They landed safely and Jess and Iris hopped out, sharing a relieved grimace to find themselves alive and intact and in France. On the beach beside them, medics prodded the sand with spades, removing the bodies that had, until now, been temporarily covered over in the rush. Row after row of sticks marked each resting place, and from each stick wafted a canvas bag. Jess walked among them, in the European Theatre of Operations, a place where the actors would not come back to life once the curtains came down, focusing not on the things one would ordinarily admire on a beach – the colour of the water, an unusual shell – but on the things one should never behold by the seaside.

Worst of all was the tideline. The beach was so wide, the difference between high and low tide so marked, that the high watermark had become the most poignant reminder that what lay now on the beach had once been the living. Yardley hair tonic, bibles, a baseball mitt. Razors, letters from home, pistol belts. Sticks of camouflage cream, a guitar, shoe polish. The remainders of men who would no longer polish their shoes.

Jess made herself walk across the beach. *All you have to do is take photographs*, she told herself. *Your job is the easiest of anyone's in France.* And so she snapped the tideline, knowing she would ask Bel to run a wide-angle shot across a bifold, four pages in all. It would be her attempt to say, without words, that while the official rhetoric was that casualties were lower than expected – which everyone in America would take to mean that few had died – 'lower' still meant thousands and that nobody could sit on Omaha Beach and feel anything other than devastated.

~

Five days later, Jess was still in France. As usual it wasn't her fault; she hadn't been able to get a ride back to London on a plane or a ship as they were full of wounded GIs whose need was greater than hers. She'd lost Iris Carpenter. Warren Stone was probably standing at port in England ready to lock Jess up the moment she returned. But she'd been smart enough to have the pilots and medics sign a paper attesting they had no room for her, which she looked forward to handing to Warren once she reached England.

She was beyond filthy; when she'd been told thirty-six hours, she hadn't bothered to bring a change of clothes, thinking it would only weigh her down. She was almost out of film and she'd had to send all her used films back to London in a press bag despite her misgivings that it might end up in the censors' trash can.

Now, she was picking her way across the sand, towards the cemetery, where she could see someone studying the graves, silent. His stance was familiar – back unbending, the air of command apparent – although his helmeted head and uniform made him look much the same as every other soldier in France.

The figure turned around slowly, face altering when he saw her.

'Major Hallworth,' she said, only just raising a smile.

'Captain May,' he replied, his expression matching hers.

She felt it before it happened, the press of tears at the back of her cowardly eyes, all the goddamned tears she'd refused to allow herself to shed for the past five days because a woman was not allowed to fall to pieces if she ever wanted to be allowed back into France. She didn't say anything, willed her eyes to dry out but they refused to listen and so at last she said, her voice wobbly, 'I think there's a good chance I'm going to cry.'

'Come here,' he said, lifting his arms and she walked into them, helmet pressed awkwardly into his shoulder, crying now, but only for a few minutes because if he could stomach everything he'd seen, which would be so much worse than what she'd witnessed, then so too could she.

'Sorry,' she said, drawing back. 'And thanks. I haven't had a shower for five days. It's an act of bravery in itself coming close to me right now. I think you just repaid the favour you owed me.'

'Jess, holding you while you cry isn't repaying a favour. It's being a friend.' His voice was soft, a lovely caress amidst the savagery.

She shook her head. 'God, don't say that. I'll start crying again.' She smiled. 'It's good to see you alive.'

'It's good to see you too.'

'Do you have to get back?'

He checked his watch. 'Not for an hour.'

'Then come with me.'

She led him to a small ridge, a place she'd sat a few times over the past couple of days, watching the activity on the beach. They sat there now, backs against the rock, flattened blackberry brambles twisting forlornly around them, and she told him about Martha's escapade and the parachute jumps they'd been denied due to having delicate female apparatus and what she'd said to Warren in reply.

He laughed and she saw his face relax for a moment, the lines furrowed on his forehead suddenly fall away, but return just a moment later.

'Oh no,' she said with a sudden flash of horror. 'Not Jennings?' She gestured to the graves behind them.

'Not Jennings. But a hell of a lot of others just like him. Some didn't even make the ground alive. Their time in the US Army consisted of a training camp in England, a plane ride across the Channel, then death in the air.' He rubbed his face but it didn't erase the troubled expression. 'I was ordered to take this afternoon off to sleep; I haven't slept properly for a week. But now that we've secured the causeway and the beachheads have been joined up, I had to come here.'

Jess jumped up. 'I'm keeping you from sleep. You should go.'

But he stayed where he was and patted the ground beside him. 'No, this is what I need. To laugh. To talk . . .' He stopped.

'Tell me about it,' she said, sitting back down.

'Have you ever seen an airborne division in the sky?' he asked.

She shook her head.

'It's kind of beautiful. There are so many parachutes. It's like, I don't know, watching a thousand pure white hankies flutter to the ground. That's if you can shut out the vibration of the C-47s and the fact that you have to carry eighty kilograms of equipment, which is more than what some of the younger GIs weigh. We had to jump before we'd reached the landing zone; Jerry was throwing too much at us. Then we were in the inferno, a sky filled with fire and smoke so thick you couldn't see your hands, the entire carcasses of damaged aeroplanes hurtling at us through the sky; I saw so many men hit by their own plane before they'd even reached the ground.'

He stopped and she waited, knowing he hadn't finished, that the terrible stories of what 'invasion' actually meant were numberless and that he wouldn't have said any of this to anyone else because he was the man in charge, the one who did the ordering and the listening but never the confessing.

'We were supposed to land around Sainte-Mère-Église but we landed all over fucking Normandy, split by the Merderet River,' he continued. 'The men near Carentan landed in mud to their necks and it sucked them under like quicksand. The gliders came down too hard and impaled themselves on Rommel's damned asparagus and all that survived was the equipment. The crickets we use to call to one another to rendezvous were useless because nobody was in hearing distance of anyone else. A brand new private got stuck in a tree, hanging from his chute, and we found him, not taken prisoner by the Krauts as he should have been but riddled with one hundred and sixty-two bullet and bayonet holes. Scattered at his feet were the ripped pages of his prayer book. *Greater love hath no man than this,*' Dan quoted, '*that a man lay down his life for his friends.*'

This time, it was Jess's turn to reach out for Dan's hand, just as he'd done at Easter. Because in spite of the fact that Dan's division had been unable to land in their drop zones, they'd taken the town of Sainte-Mère-Église by the early morning hours of D-day, thus securing a defensive position to prevent German reinforcements arriving on the beaches. That success had been much spoken of, but not what it had cost to gain.

'I was never more relieved than when I found Jennings after only a couple of hours,' he eventually said.

'Thank God,' Jess breathed.

'By D-day plus two our division only had two thousand fighting men left. That's less than half the number who left England.'

They sat in silence after that. Below them, on the beach, they watched litters disgorged from ambulances and onto aeroplanes, a never-ending stream of men who would return home vastly different to how they'd used to be.

Neither let go of the other's hand. At last Dan said, 'Are you waiting for a ride back to England?'

'How did you guess,' she said, ruefully acknowledging her state of extreme dishevelment.

'I remember how well the fellas in public relations look after you. Let's go. I'll find you a chauffeur.'

As they wound their way down to the sand, Jess noticed the more than usually deferential 'sirs' sent Dan's way and she suddenly understood when she saw one man nod at Dan and say, 'Lieutenant Colonel.'

'Lieutenant Colonel?' she asked.

He flushed, reminding her of Jennings. 'And Battalion CO.'

'How many men are you in charge of now?'

'About seven hundred and fifty.'

And she was glad, foolishly glad; with someone like Dan in charge of all those men, the invasion might actually succeed.

Within an hour she was stepping into a plane and Dan was asking her, 'When will you be back?'

'Soon, I hope. None of the female correspondents are allowed to stay over here yet.'

'Make sure you send me a note and come find me when you do. And,' he paused, 'Victorine . . .'

'Is well and happy. I'll go see her again, tell her you're okay.'

'Thanks.'

She saw him waiting by the airstrip as the plane took off into the sky, not waving, just watching her leave, then, at last, turning around to go back to fighting to win a war. All the way back to England, she held her right hand – the one Dan had held – inside her left, but it didn't comfort her the same way he had.

~

When Jess arrived back at the Savoy and handed her uniforms over for cleaning and delousing, she learned that Iris Carpenter had been court-martialled. Iris had strayed from the 'beachhead' and the Ministry of Information was trying to make an example of her. As well as that news, there was a letter waiting from Martha.

I couldn't sit around in a nurses' training camp forever. So I managed to get out and I'm on my way to Naples. I don't have any orders or papers or a goddamned passport – they took everything off me – but I can sweet-talk my way into anything. Everyone's so focused on France I don't think they'll care about me all the way over in Italy. If I can find a unit of French or Canadians who'll let me attach myself to them, then I can avoid the rules of the US Army altogether.

> *You do a damn fine job of France and I'll do a damn fine job of Italy.*
>
> Marty

Jess smiled as she read Martha's words. It would have been nice to have Martha by her side. But Martha was right to go to Italy and escape Warren Stone. SHAEF had managed to get rid of one woman. Jess prayed they wouldn't be able to get rid of any more with Iris's trial.

Thankfully Iris had ambiguity and a colonel on her side. Nobody could define precisely what was meant by the beachhead. 'Colonel Whitcomb, who gave me an escort to Cherbourg, told them the beachhead stretched as far as the town,' Iris told Jess over whiskey that night. 'And none of the PROs were able to produce a different interpretation from anyone as high up as a colonel who'd actually been in France.'

'So they let you off? Will they let you back though?' Jess asked, moving from joy to hopelessness in the space of those two sentences.

Iris grinned. 'Brigadier Turner told me, eyes bulging, that it would be a *very* long while before I got orders to go to Normandy again.'

'Why are you smiling, then?' Jess asked despairingly.

'Before I left Normandy, I had Colonel Whitcomb issue me orders to return to the beachhead as soon as possible.'

'Bravo!' Jess cheered, chinking her glass against Iris's.

'I think you'll find that, after this brouhaha, they'll have to change something about the way they handle women over there,' Iris finished.

Luckily Iris was right. After the bungled court martial, SHAEF PR did have to change the way they let women into France. Every woman who wanted it was issued permanent orders to go to France, and those orders were valid for an entire month. Jess hugged her papers to her chest, unable to hide her smile even from Warren.

His attempt to dampen her spirits by telling her she had to wait a week for transport didn't make a bit of difference. Besides, he looked cowed for once, as if all the fighting and the losing was wearying him. Jess was hopeful that, once she was in France, she wouldn't have to deal with him anymore and he would let go of their feud and they could both just do their jobs.

She used the week before embarkation to say goodbye to Victorine and to visit her friend from boarding school days, Amelia, with whom she had continued to exchange letters. Amelia had been begging Jess to visit since discovering she was in England.

'Jessica May!' Amelia said when Jess arrived on the doorstep of a grand country home in Cornwall. 'I couldn't believe it when you telephoned. Come in.'

Jess hugged Amelia, who looked as devastatingly pretty as she had in school. 'You haven't changed a bit.'

'Oh, but I have.' Amelia waggled her left hand at Jess. 'I got myself married, remember.'

'I can't imagine you a married woman,' Jess said as she followed Amelia into a masculine drawing room adorned with stags' heads and other hunting souvenirs.

'I can't imagine myself a married woman either,' Amelia said with a grin, before commanding a maid to bring them champagne. 'I'm having to work very hard to behave myself.'

Jess laughed. On the rare occasions Jess was actually in school in Paris, she and Amelia had, most weekends, snuck out of the boarding house and into the jazz clubs of Montmartre where they'd refined their drinking and kissing skills even though they were only sixteen.

'Luckily he's a corporal or a colonel or an admiral or something in the Navy – I can never remember all of those ranks – so he's on a ship somewhere and I'm here hosting house parties.'

Jess's hand tightened on her champagne glass. 'Aren't you worried about him?' she asked. For Victorine's sake – at least she thought it was for Victorine's sake rather than her own – Jess worried about Dan every morning when she woke and every night before she slept.

Amelia laughed. 'He's a friend of Daddy's and almost as old so let's just say that the war is very convenient.'

'Why did you marry him?'

'For freedom, of course.' Amelia stared at Jess as if she were being obtuse. 'Married, I have the money and the means to live life as I choose. I wanted a military husband. I well know from having a military father how little time they spend with family. It suits me perfectly; I don't have to behave all that much,' Amelia finished with a wink. 'You're lucky I'm even awake. Last night's party didn't finish until dawn.'

'Shouldn't you be doing war work? I thought all the women in England –'

'Jessica May!' Amelia exclaimed. 'Or are you really an imposter? Bring back my friend. You've become so . . . earnest.'

Jess sighed. She *was* earnest. Where was the laughing girl who'd danced all night at Greenwich Village clubs or at Condé Nast's parties, wearing beautiful gowns and a much-photographed smile, who'd fallen into bed with Emile at all hours of the morning and had damn good sex? Had she really been that person?

She took a large swallow of champagne. How was it possible to see Omaha Beach and not be earnest? 'For today,' she said to Amelia with a weak smile, 'your job is to make me not quite so earnest.'

'Hallelujah.' Amelia raised her glass, sipped, then something like earnestness fell over her face too. 'It really is good to see you,' she said. 'Everyone sleeping it off up there,' she raised her glass to indicate the bedrooms on the upper floors, 'has only known me with all of this.' Her hand swept around to encompass the large room with its expensive but fusty adornments. 'Whereas you knew me before any of it.'

Jess stayed that night for Amelia's party but, rather than finding solace in another man's arms as Amelia did, Jess went to bed early and wrapped her arms around herself, Amelia's words playing through her head: *you knew me before any of it.* And the reply Jess hadn't made: *But where did that world go? And, without it, who are we?*

Twelve

Over the next few days in France, Jess discovered what a goddamn joke the 'rules' designed to 'protect' women were. The press camp for the men was miles further back from the front and thus a hell of a lot safer than the Fifth General Hospital outside Carentan where Jess was posted. As a woman, she had absolutely no access to press camps, which meant no access to briefings, or to maps, or to news about hot spots and likely strafing attacks and the day's objective or anything else that would actually give her an idea which part of the country was safe and which wasn't. When Jess had pointed out that this would put her at more risk than the men, nobody seemed to care. And she still had to wait in line with her stories; hers were sent back to London where the censors tore them apart and then directed them on to Bel, which meant that her words occasionally made no sense as she wasn't allowed to review them. Whereas the men submitted theirs direct from France after their very own censor had checked them and allowed the men a final edit.

Warren had made sure to stress that she wasn't to leave the field hospital without permission from the CO. And then he'd added, smiling, that he was going to France too. It had taken all of Jess's willpower not to say, *But that's a little too close to danger for you, isn't it?*

Instead she'd swallowed the retort and prayed that he'd stay at his cosy press camp and that she'd never have to see him again.

But she did hold on to his words: *without permission from the CO.* She knew a CO who'd give her permission, she was sure of it. It wasn't exactly what Warren had meant but nor had he been precise enough to specify that he was referring to the CO of the hospital – and she would take full advantage.

At her new home on French soil, she quickly became adept at diving into the slit trench behind her tent whenever the Germans flew over at night strafing, at pretending the enormous red welts of mosquito bites didn't itch like the devil, at never being alone, not even on the toilet – the latrine had a row of six seats and more often than not at least one or two of the other places were occupied by nurses clutching their precious rations of Scott paper. It was incredible the conversations that could be had while doing one's business, especially during the rare quiet times, which everyone dreaded, because that was when the nurses would finally break down.

She also became expert at sleeping in spite of the maddening ringing in her ears from the constant boom of shells and guns, at eating in spite of the way the smells of ether and gangrene and blood seemed to coat the inside of her mouth. Most of all, she became proficient at pretending not to be scared, at only crying in the shower, at being the one to tell the new nurses to sleep under their cots rather than on top, or the one to move aside and let the new recruits lie beside her when she heard them sobbing as the Stukas shrieked overhead, at telling them it would be all right.

She remembered her first night in Italy and knew that she was just as scared now as she had been then, but she also knew how to hide it better. Humour and dispensing practical advice were her chosen means for this, making a show of demonstrating how to tip one's head upside down at the end of each day and shake it thoroughly before bed in order to dislodge another day's worth of the thick yellow dust that covered everything; the bombed-out earth of France had taken to the skies in search of refuge, where it floated around them all day long, discovering what everyone in France already knew: there was no place of refuge. France was no longer France.

Once past the seductive vista of silky blue sea at the edge of the country, everything changed. On the beach and between the hedgerows, the land was scarred with shell craters, slashed with foxholes and trenches and wretched with newly dug cemeteries. Boards painted with red skulls and crossbones and menacing warnings about the dangers of mines were as commonplace as apple trees. New roads unfurled brutishly from the maws of bulldozers and were quickly overrun with convoys of military vehicles. Each set of crossroads bore a pole stabbed into the earth with arrows directing traffic to the different units: Madonna Charlie, Missouri Baker, Missouri Charlie. Strung over everything like Christmas tinsel were reams of wire for communications.

Her days consisted of hitching rides on ambulances to collecting posts closer to the front then watching as ambulances brought in men from the battlefield, their faces stark white beneath the dirt and cut through with tears. Many were uninjured bodily, but their minds were lost somewhere in France, and Jess photographed the medics working with especially gentle hands to do whatever they could, which was very little, for those men.

The *bocage* fighting in the area was the dirtiest anyone had ever seen, from the castrator mines that leapt up and detonated at crotch height, to the surrendering lone German soldier who would emerge with hands up until the American GIs came to take him prisoner, whereupon he would leap to the side and the machine guns hidden in the hedgerows would mow down every American soldier who'd thought the white flag was the one thing that could be relied upon in war. But nothing could be relied upon, not anymore.

At an aid station near La Fière she recognised the insignia of Dan's division among the men and heard that his battalion was in the area, that they'd succeeded in cutting a line across the Cherbourg Peninsula, that they'd been fighting unrelieved and without replacements for thirty-three days and had achieved every mission they'd been set and never given up any ground they'd taken. The news that he was alive made her the one crying silently in her cot at the hospital that evening, wondering why she was shedding so many tears over a man who was just a friend, but reasoning she would do the same for Martha if she'd suddenly, after a long silence, heard good news about her.

The day after the Germans, who'd been gathered in the surrounding hedgerows like deadly nesting birds, finally capitulated at Saint-Lô, she begged Major Henderson to allow her a ride on an ambulance out to the town. 'It's been captured, which means it's no longer the front, so I'm allowed to travel there,' she reasoned.

He just shook his head, not to prevent her, but because he knew he couldn't. 'Look after yourself,' he said and she thanked God that the surgeon she'd helped one night in Italy, the one who had Dan's brother's stethoscope, was the one in charge of the field hospital and that he usually did his best to help her get to where she wanted to go.

The reports she'd seen of the siege of Saint-Lô, written by her male counterparts out of the luxury of their very own press camp at Valognes, with their very own set of jeeps, censors and couriers, had spoken grandiosely about the glory of the battle. When Jess climbed out of the ambulance at Saint-Lô, try as she might, she couldn't find the glory.

The town was destroyed, unliveable, another victim of war. In front of one shattered villa, magenta fuchsias bloomed in profusion over the body of a dead American soldier, a fluffy white rabbit hopping over his leg. It was a surrealist composition worthy of Man Ray but Jess didn't photograph it. How war could so easily make a corpse inhuman. This man had died on soil not his own in order to secure one small town and had then been left to the attentions of rabbits. Someone in America was crying for him, imagining him honoured with prayers and farewells, when the only sound to wing him towards death had been the crash of bullets, the boom of exploding shells.

Hours later, Jess walked back to the road, leaning against a wall, thinking, waiting for the next vehicle to drive by. Why was she there? What good would any of her photographs do? Show truths that mothers wouldn't want to know, remind people of things that should never be relived. She needed to get ready to offer a smile and a stream of banter to pay for her ride back to the hospital but the last thing she felt like, after clambering through the carcass of Saint-Lô, was being the Jessica May everyone thought she was. Before she was ready, she saw the distant dust cloud even more thickly and she waved to flag down the oncoming jeep.

The jeep pulled to a stop and she couldn't help but raise a smile when she saw Dan's face.

'Don't tell me, you still don't get a driver or a jeep,' he said, face grim as he jumped out.

She shrugged. 'You know I don't.'

'It's lucky I was coming to find you, then,' he said in a very un-Dan-like tone. 'You can't stand around outside towns that have only just been liberated. You don't know what's about to fall out of the sky, or if there are snipers still around. I stopped at the hospital and Major Henderson said you'd left eight hours ago. I thought you'd had the shit strafed out of you by the Stukas.'

'All I have to rely on are the reports that come in from the wounded men about where the front has moved to. I'm doing my best with the little information I have,' she said. 'So don't be mad. I don't need mad right now.'

'Tell me you at least have a gun.'

She shook her head.

He swore again. 'I've got a spare Colt in the jeep. It's yours. Come to dinner and I'll show you how to shoot it.'

'Dinner?'

'Dinner, as in food. On plates, not out of a ration box. Come to the camp and have dinner.'

'Is that an order?'

'Yes,' he said, smiling at last.

'Well, in that case . . .' She climbed into the jeep and tilted her head back, closing her eyes, the images from the past few days shuttering relentlessly through her mind. She snapped her eyes open and looked at Dan.

'How the hell do you do it?' she asked.

He didn't have to ask, *do what*? Instead he grinned and said, 'Well, my preferred method is to take correspondents out to a fine dinner of C-rations at my equally fine mess tent.'

She hit his arm. 'At least you called me a correspondent rather than a model.'

'I want to finish the evening alive,' he teased.

The banter relaxed her for the first time in days. A friendship like this was almost the only way to stay sane and she knew she would do her damnedest never to do anything to ruin it.

'I have something else for you besides a gun.' Dan said. 'In the back.'

She reached around, past Dan's submachine gun, ammo belt, machete and rope and withdrew a pair of paratroop boots that looked as if they might fit her. 'Are these for me?' she said excitedly, then laughed. 'I'm sure that, once upon a time, I would have saved that sort of excitement for sapphires, not second-hand brown boots.'

She tugged off her now scuffed and almost worn-out boots and replaced them with the almost-new ones. Her toes danced with the satisfaction of being shod in something comfortable, and her ankles, which were sore from walking, now felt as if nothing at all was the matter. 'I think it's probably the best gift I've ever been given,' she said, propping her feet on the dashboard and studying them. 'Although I'm sorry someone had to die for it,' she added quietly.

Dan glanced over at her. 'He didn't die. Just had half his skin burnt off. He's gone back to Texas. He knew I was looking for boots for you and he told me to give you his. He's one of the men you photographed on Easter Sunday.'

Neither spoke for a long moment. Then Dan added, 'And if you think that next time I give you something it'll be sapphires, then you're as nuts as this whole damn war. Now get your filthy feet off my dashboard. That's another order.'

Jess laughed again and saluted. 'Yes, Sir!'

~

When Jess jumped out of the jeep, it was to applause. She looked around, bewildered; was Eisenhower arriving at the same moment? She could see nothing worth applauding until at least two men she recognised, Sparrow and Jennings, stepped forward and warmly shook her hand. Jennings' hand was adorned with a bandage – he'd sliced his palm with a knife, he explained abashed, and Jess smiled at his obvious proneness to fortunately minor accidents.

'My girl is prouder of me now than when I was shipped over here,' Jennings, who looked as if he was at last growing into himself, taller and more filled out – despite the rations – added, using more words than he'd ever managed with her before. 'Every time she shows her friends the picture of me in *Vogue*, they just about die of envy and wish I was theirs instead.'

Sparrow, who obviously hadn't had his confidence shaken out of him by the war, erupted into laughter at the thought of Jennings being so in demand, and Jess smiled. Then another man pressed to the front of the group and, rather than shaking Jess's hand, he embraced her. His face looked somewhat familiar. 'I was on the mountain at Easter,' he said and Jess realised she'd photographed him, the look on his face so fervently prayerful, her camera having caught, in that moment and in that one man, what every man there had been feeling.

Then Sparrow said, rather unexpectedly and seriously for once, 'One of those graves at Omaha was my brother's. My mum was happy to see he'd been buried with friends.'

All Jess could do was squeeze his hand. As each man clamoured to tell her about the picture she'd taken of him, or his brother or friend or neighbour, or of the story she'd written him into, she was swept off to the mess tent by a wave of admiring men, deposited at a table and a tin mess tray was placed in front of her.

'C-rations,' Jess said, breathing in the smell of a meat and vegetable stew she was sure she would never have eaten two years ago but that now looked better than caviar. 'And bread with butter! I haven't seen anything other than a K-ration in two weeks.'

'Then you should have this to go with it.' Jess looked up to see Dan passing her a mug with what she assumed might be coffee and discovered – coughing when she took too large a swallow – was cider.

He gestured behind him to a cider barrel. 'We found it and thought it'd be a shame to waste it. Especially now that we have a week off.' He handed her a cigarette.

'Lucky Strikes,' she sighed, lighting up. 'They only have Chesterfields at the hospital. You know, I might never leave here.'

At which the men cheered, as if they'd be more than happy to have her stay. While she chatted over dinner and put the Rollei into service, all Jess could think was: at last she'd found a place where she belonged.

At dinner, the men who'd known Victorine in Italy asked about her. 'If I'd realised I was coming to dinner,' Jess said, 'I would have brought the pictures she's drawn for you. She thought the pictures might stand in for her good-luck kisses.'

'Some GIs over in the 371st Fighter Group have got their own Victorine,' Sparrow mumbled through a mouthful of food, and the other men nodded. 'A girl called Yvette,' Sparrow continued. 'Krauts killed her sister and wounded Yvette so bad she had both her legs amputated. So the GIs made her a tent from parachute silk and they fly her with them wherever they go. Because she has no one else to look after her. She's their mascot, like Vicki was ours.'

Nobody spoke but the night flickered with the poignancy inherent in what Sparrow had said: both that the men needed something to believe in – anything – in order to keep hope alive, and that somewhere in the darkness there was girl called Yvette who could no longer walk.

'We've all had to find new good-luck charms now we no longer have Vicki.' Sparrow finished both his dinner and his story and Jess wondered if she'd misjudged him when she first met him in the jeep in London, whether he had more substance than she'd thought. Or if war had deepened his character.

'Would you mind if I photographed your lucky charms?' she asked, looking across at Dan for permission, knowing that pictures of the men with their new talismanic objects would be a moving follow-up to her Victorine story.

Dan nodded and the men rose to their feet. They crossed the field, past lines of washing strung from tent to tent, past water bags swinging from tripods, past a phonograph singing into the night. In each tent she saw the same thing: GIs transformed into heartbreakingly young men. The Domino 'Sweeten It' sugar tablet that one had carried with him since Italy because, he said in a terrible understatement, life in Europe was damn short on sweet stuff; the red tin of Tuxedo Club pomade that had sat in another man's pocket and deflected a bullet; the green wrapper from a cake of Camay soap that a WAC with a lovely smile had given another as a keepsake because she'd had nothing else to gift.

There were also the much-folded and studied photographs of mothers or wives or girlfriends or dogs or horses or even strangers like her. So many of the men had pictures of beautiful women from magazines or calendars, their faces and bodies creased into pocket-sized shapes. What did those pictures remind the men of? Jess wondered as she saw, many times, the photograph of her naked back, the one the PRO in Italy had ruined for her.

And another that she'd forgotten: Jessica May in a floor-sweeping Lelong ballgown with a full princess skirt, thin straps crossing her back, which was otherwise bare, the fabric having been scooped away down to her sacrum. She looked as if she had no place in this world she now found herself in, as if she came from another universe entirely and that was, she supposed, the point of the pictures: they were the only means, out here, by which beauty could be held in the men's hands. And perhaps the pictures reminded each GI that there was another world beside this one, a world they could return to, if only they survived.

She kept smiling as if it wasn't at all disconcerting to know that so many men kept pictures of her. After one over-eager private asked if she would go to dinner with him in Paris once it was liberated and she'd deflected him, kindly, she saw Dan studying her face. Before she could ask him why, Jennings interrupted them. 'Sir, there's a man asking for Captain May.'

'A man?' Dan queried.

Jennings flushed. 'He said his name was –'

'Warren Stone.' A voice Jess recognised all too well cut across Jennings.

'It came to my attention that you were missing,' he said to Jess. 'I was about to put an order out on you to be apprehended and taken back to London.'

'Did you miss me?' Jess said glibly, to hide the fact that she was furious. She was acutely aware of the many eyes on her, eyes belonging to men whose stories she'd been photographing for the past hour, men who were treating her like she was one of them, which Warren Stone was about to destroy by making them think she was his possession and worthy only of contempt.

He no longer looked cowed and weary but rejuvenated and as malicious as ever. And his sudden appearance told her that he hadn't let go of his vendetta. Fury clogged her throat at the thought that perhaps this was what he'd meant by his threat in the bar at the Savoy – that every time she thought she was happy, and doing a good job, he would appear and destroy everything. And then she realised he had someone with him, someone she knew. Emile.

She froze, eyes fixed on Emile's face. His smiling face, but the smile was not one of joy at seeing her. It was the same callous smirk he'd tossed her at the Stork Club in Manhattan the night she found out he'd sold her off to the highest bidder. She knew instantly that it wasn't coincidence he'd palled up with Warren. And if she'd thought she was mad a moment ago, now she was raging, the strength of it burning her throat and her eyes like white phosphorus.

'Jessica May,' Emile drawled as if they were breezy acquaintances.

Before Jess could speak – before her anger collided with her hurt that Emile, a man she'd once loved, would betray her again – Dan stepped forward.

'I'm Lieutenant Colonel Hallworth,' Jess heard him say to Warren. 'You might remember me from the last time you tried to lock Captain May up.' Dan didn't let Warren interrupt. 'I'm the CO here. I heard that Captain May had been eating K-rations for two weeks even though the recommended length of time is ten days. I thought she needed to be shown some hospitality. She's not missing. I know, and everyone here knows, exactly where she is. Her orders say she can leave the field hospital with permission from a CO. I gave her permission.'

'That's not what her orders mean,' Warren said, anger roughening his voice. 'It means the CO of the hospital.'

'It doesn't say that,' Dan replied evenly. 'It just says permission from a CO.'

Of course Warren was too good to show how he felt at being dressed down by a lieutenant colonel. 'I'm just looking out for those of the weaker sex. Nobody can blame a man for that. But I see she has you to take over from where Emile left off.'

Warren smirked at Dan. Emile grinned at Warren.

That Emile would find satisfaction in watching someone smear her reputation made Jess finally explode.

'Yes,' Jess spat, 'even though Lieutenant Colonel Hallworth has been fighting for more than thirty days without rest, we've managed to conduct a clandestine sexual relationship in which I, jeep-less, run through the ack-ack bombing each night to find whatever trench or tent or abandoned village his battalion is holed up in, have my way with him without anybody else seeing or hearing, then run back through the ack-ack bombing to arrive at my tent at the hospital just in time to get up and face the new day as fresh as a daisy. It's hard to see how that kind of stamina would make me a member of the weaker sex!'

Silence greeted Jess's outburst, but Warren's eyes held hers, locked there, a kind of acquisitive loathing on his face, and the fury she'd felt before twisted into a sharp and painful fear. *One day, Captain May,* she remembered he'd said. She broke the stare first, her gaze falling away only to land on Emile's face which was, at that moment, the less malevolent of the two.

Then Sparrow, unable to hold it in anymore, exploded into laughter, setting off each of the other men in turn.

Dan's voice broke through the noise, silencing it for the most part although the occasional snort of laughter could still be heard. 'Sparrow, escort Mr Stone and his friend back to his jeep. Jennings, take Captain May back to the hospital.'

Oh God, what had she done? Realisation hit her with the force of a shell explosion. After inviting her to dinner, she'd repaid Dan by publicly losing her temper and saying things that no woman should ever say aloud. No wonder his mouth was set in a very grim line. No wonder he was sending her off with Jennings. She was mortified but she knew better than to give Warren the satisfaction of looking back over her shoulder at Dan and thus confirming his ridiculous suspicions. Instead, she turned on Emile when they reached the jeeps. 'What are you doing here?' she asked, not bothering with ordinary politeness.

'Taking pictures,' he replied. 'I know how to do that, remember.'

'I remember,' she said quietly.

She felt nothing for Emile, she realised then, not even a latent fondness for the man who'd been there for her, albeit unwittingly, when her parents died. Not even dislike for the lover who'd turned traitor on her in New York and who was now palling up to a man who wished her ill. Out here in France, beside men who kept soap wrappers in their pockets so they wouldn't get shot, Emile Robard and Warren Stone were a waste of her time.

Besides, the only thing she could think about on the way to the hospital was Dan's too-stern face after she'd yelled about sleeping with him at the top of her voice to Warren, ensuring everyone in the vicinity could hear. What would Dan think of her now?

Thirteen

ut she had no chance to find out what Dan thought because Rennes was taken soon after and it began again: the pre-D-day sequestering of the women. They were all rounded up, taken out of their hospitals or WAC encampments, a dozen of them, and kept in the custody of Stone and another PRO in a tiny hotel in Rennes until Paris was back in Allied hands and safe. They had to sign in and sign out every day. They had to get a leave pass to have lunch outside the hotel. One of the other female correspondents actually reported two of their number, claiming they'd got away and were making for Paris, which was proved false when they returned to the hotel after the dinner for which they'd been given a pass into town.

'Goddammit!' Jess exploded when she heard. As if it wasn't bad enough having the men in charge treat them like imbeciles, now the women were turning their backs on each other too. If only she hadn't gone to Rennes in the first place. If only she'd done what Lee Carson of the International News Service had done and gone AWOL. Of course an order had been put out on Lee but so far she'd been missing for a week and nobody had managed to locate her.

Jess was only allowed out of Rennes after Paris fell. She and Iris Carpenter hitched a ride to the Hotel Scribe, designated point for all correspondents in Paris. As they came over the hill to the north, Jess could see the city bathed in sunshine, white and innocent, waiting peacefully as if nothing had ever been the matter and they'd all taken too long to arrive. Once through the Porte d'Orléans, a group of women and girls bearing fresh flowers ran up to Jess and filled her arms with blooms, calling her *la femme soldat*.

'Oh no, I'm just a correspondent,' she protested, until Iris grabbed Jess's Leica and took a picture of her, blushing, laden with flowers, the beaming Frenchwomen in the background. She would send the photo to Victorine, Jess decided. Victorine would like the idea that her people thought Jess was a soldier.

It took a while to navigate the Parisians, who were cheering every vehicle on every street, but they finally reached the hotel, standing orderly and Haussmanian just across from the ornate and undamaged splendour of the Opéra. The dead geraniums in the window-boxes were the only visible sign that something of significance had happened in the city.

Over the next few days, the Hotel Scribe filled every corner, every crevice, with correspondents and their associated gear. The Rue Scribe was lined with jeeps and bedrolls, and gas masks and duffel bags lurked in piles in the lobby. The press office took over the entire first floor, where the censors scribbled out all the words they didn't want read and correspondents haggled and begged to keep their stories intact. The transportation room was stacked to the ceiling with jerry cans of gasoline. The mess had nothing but K-rations and coffee but also, somehow, champagne.

As soon as she could, Jess took to the streets, knowing she could find her own damn story rather than waiting for one of the PROs to tell her what to write about. The male correspondents, on the other hand, didn't seem in much of a hurry to hunt down their words, not when the ladies of Montmartre required no hunting down whatsoever and needed little persuasion to give up their wares. Jess lost count of the number of times she witnessed correspondents entering or leaving brothels. The Hotel Scribe was almost as bad — women hurried into elevators under the guise of being someone's cousin even though the correspondent in question had no French blood in his body. Sex, it seemed, was easier to procure than nylon hose, and a hell of a lot cheaper.

So Jess looked for stories of women who, through the occupation, had done remarkable things without thought of consequence — resistance came from the heart and not from the head, they said — things that in her previous life in Manhattan, Jess could never have imagined women might have to do. A group of resistance fighters from the French Forces of the Interior showed her their hideout in the underground sewer system from where they'd planned the rebellion that led to the fall of Paris. She spoke to ordinary women who stole guns from the Germans to help arm the resistance. Those guns fired the shots that had rung out on the day of the rebellion to announce to the city that they should put up their barricades and take back their streets.

She knew *Vogue* would love it, especially the pictures of the Parisians in exotic hats laughing and showing off the guns they'd swiped from under the noses of the Germans. But then the men of the FFI — boys really — took her out to the damp tunnels at Ivry in which the Germans had locked up resisters. Within half an hour of being underground, Jess's bones were frozen; not even a fingernail of light reached down there. The Germans, she discovered, left the men and women they'd captured in the wet and blackly dark tunnels until they died. Through a beam of torchlight, she was shown the fingermarks clawed into the walls as the prisoners tried to dig their way to freedom.

Jess returned to the Hotel Scribe a different person from the one who'd left that morning. To witness both matchless barbarism and matchless desperation in the one day left her incapable of speaking. But the atmosphere at the hotel didn't make her feel any better. She was greeted by Iris Carpenter and the newly arrived Lee Carson with the news that the women were to be locked up. Again. Not allowed out of Paris, and only permitted to report on the stories their PRO allocated them.

'Apparently it's for our own safety,' Lee – who was tall and blonde and whose fluttery eyelashes had caused Major Mayborn, the SHAEF public relations man in charge, to forgive her escaping Rennes – said.

'Every goddamn time,' Jess said between gritted teeth.

'Your pal Warren told me to tell you that he's given you approval to cover the fashion shows that are starting up again,' Iris added dourly. 'He thought it fitted nicely with your "expertise".'

'Did you hit him?' Jess asked.

'I wanted to.'

'Say,' said Lee with a sudden smile. 'Let's use that expertise.'

'What do you mean?' Jess asked.

'Have you looked at yourself lately?' Lee asked, casting her eyes over Jess. 'If I can get out of a court martial by smiling nicely at the major, then a former model, showered, made-up and appropriately attired, could probably do a hell of a lot more.'

Iris nodded in agreement.

Jess caught a glimpse of herself in the mirror; she was filthy as usual but she also carried with her the distinct odour of the sewers she'd visited that day. Nothing about her betrayed the fact that her face and body had once been used to sell dresses. That didn't bother her but the thought that she might be stopped from collecting more stories and more pictures did. What she'd seen in just a few days meant there must be many unreported and unrecorded horrors that had to be brought out of the tunnelled darkness and into the light of words and photographs.

'If this works, you owe me a hell of a lot more than a drink,' she said to Lee and Iris before she left the mess.

She slipped up to her room and bathed. She washed her hair. She applied powder, rouge, lipstick and mascara. She put on her unworn olive drab skirt. She left the gloriously comfortable but decidedly unflattering paratroop boots behind. And then she made sure to bump into Major Mayborn in the lobby.

'Oh, excuse me,' she said to the major after colliding with him. 'I've spent the day interviewing the men from the FFI and my head's full of the story I'll write for *Vogue*.' She smiled, standing like a model with her hand on her hip, showing off the figure that had been hiding beneath trousers and dirty shirts for too long, transforming herself into the Jessica May from the pages of a magazine. 'I wish I could interview some American soldiers about their role in the liberation of Paris otherwise the women who read *Vogue* might start to think their men had nothing to do with it: that it was a French victory rather than an American one.' It was a gamble; he was either going to be furious, which was likely, given that the fight over who won the fight for Paris was ongoing, or he'd see that she was right.

'My dear,' he said, 'I can get you interviews with as many soldiers as you like by tomorrow if you just tell me what you need.'

'Oh, but you can't,' Jess actually pouted. 'I'm not allowed out to the front to talk to the men because apparently women are better than men at attracting enemy gunfire. Which is strange, since I managed to survive Italy and Normandy, and get myself all the way to Paris without a scratch.'

'Italy? You've seen Italy?' The major sounded impressed and Jess pounced.

'Yes I have. I believe I'm one of the most experienced female correspondents in Paris. Why don't I buy you a drink and tell you more?'

He agreed with relish and so Jess, in the bar at the Scribe, with the beseeching eyes of Lee and Iris looking on, and beneath the hard gaze of the few men who hadn't bothered to seek fleshly comforts, dropped the names of field hospitals she'd worked out of. And she reminded him that she was the one who'd taken the photograph of one of his majors holding a little French girl, a photograph that had come, she understood, to represent the acts of charity the army was capable of, even under fire from the most brutal enemy the country had ever known.

'You're the gal Stone's been talking about,' the major said once she'd finished her tale. 'I can see why.'

Jess kept her smile on, made it wider even, dropped her chin a little as if a photographer had just told her to seduce his lens. She overheard one of the correspondents at the poker table say her name and all the men laughed and she knew it would be all over the Scribe tomorrow that Jess was sleeping with the SHAEF PR man in charge, but she no longer cared.

Well, that wasn't true; she did care. She cared deeply that she had to behave like this to get what she wanted. She cared deeply that Stone had laid such a solid foundation of rumour and innuendo that all it took was one smile and a drink with a man and everyone would think she was doing what they all did – sleeping around – but only when she was accused of it did it become a crime; the men were free to be as openly promiscuous as they chose. She'd tried letting her photographs speak for her and it wasn't working. Time to unleash a different weapon.

After two whiskeys, Major Mayborn was laughing as she told him about Jennings' misfortunes; after three, he was congratulating her for having done so much to keep the women of America behind their men. After four, she stood up and flashed the smile that had once adorned magazine covers. 'Thank you so much for listening. I really should go and write my story, one-sided as it might be. If only someone would let the women go where the men are allowed.' Leaving him with that final thought, she turned and sashayed through the lobby as if it were a catwalk and she its star.

The next morning in the mess, Jess, Iris and Lee sat together, praying that Jess's conversation with Major Mayborn had had an effect. But then Warren moved in, and allocated Jess a fashion show to cover and Lee and Iris a puff piece on how the Allied forces were helping the people of Paris to rebuild – and they knew she'd failed.

'I can't even flirt properly anymore,' Jess said dismally. Her prospects of being anything more than a woman who'd once taken one or two good photos seemed as luridly disappointing as an overexposed negative.

'Give it some time,' Iris said, but time was the one thing they didn't have. The war was marching on without them. Their male counterparts were the only ones reporting anything worth reading.

For two long weeks Jess grouched around Paris, drinking and complaining with Lee and Iris. Every night, she remembered how Dan's face had looked the last time she'd seen him, when she'd exploded so publicly in front of his entire battalion. She had no idea if she'd ever see him again.

She was never so glad as when, one evening upon returning to the Scribe, she found herself engulfed by a set of arms.

'Marty!' she cried when she realised who it was. 'You must have heard my prayers.'

'Couldn't let you have all the fun,' Martha replied with a grin.

Their greeting was interrupted by the sound of a band striking up in the lobby. A young blonde girl in a very low-cut dress began to sing for the appreciative audience of correspondents who couldn't take their eyes off her cleavage. Warren Stone was leading the chorus of cheers. Someone – probably Major Mayborn – had thought to prop a sign on the piano saying: 'Anyone caught fraternising with the singer will have his head shaved!'

'I'm sure that will deter them,' Jess said, arms folded. 'And I'd hazard a guess that my extra $4.75 weekly payment for food supplies and entertainment has gone into her pocket.'

'I'd say you're right,' Martha replied, shaking her head. 'Don't tell me it's worse? Maybe I should have stayed in Italy.'

'No!' Jess said, taking Marty's arm and leading her upstairs. 'I need someone to mope with. Lee's got Iris. You can share my room. Unless you've got your accreditation papers back? Or reunited with your husband?'

'Nope on both accounts. I'm not really here. I'll be sneaking around and doing my best to remain unnoticed. By Hem, too. Let's not talk about him now, though.'

Once the women were in Jess's room, surrounded by paper, the typewriter, cameras, lenses, films, cosmetics and cognac, they both let out a breath.

'It's like a frat party without rules down there,' Martha observed.

Jess filled her in on what she'd witnessed since arriving in Paris. 'But I've heard worse things are happening,' Jess added.

She began to tell Martha what a number of Parisiennes had hinted at over the past few days: that US Army soldiers were raping Frenchwomen and nobody was doing anything about it. Who would believe a young French girl over an Allied soldier, one of the men who'd helped free their city? 'Chanel is giving away perfume to any Allied soldier. So the men take their perfume, find a girl, show her the bottle and tell her what she needs to do to get it. And that's the best-case scenario,' Jess finished bitterly.

'You going to write about it?' Martha asked, eyebrows raised as she lit a cigarette.

Jess shook her head. 'The censors would never let it through. Besides, I need more evidence first.'

'It's a story that needs to be told.'

'Like so many others,' Jess sighed. 'You know that nobody planned beyond Paris? In the original invasion plan, we were meant to take Paris by D-day plus seventy-four. We made it by D-day plus seventy-five. But that's it. Apparently the Germans were supposed to capitulate after Paris. So getting a briefing on the army's next move, although impossible for us *gals* anyway, is now about as easy as finding a Nazi in Paris.'

Cognac solved nothing, so the next morning she and Marty took the elevator down to breakfast as gloomy as the night before.

'Any word of my husband?' Martha asked on the way, not looking at Jess.

'I heard he's at the Ritz,' Jess said. 'Apparently the Hotel Scribe isn't able to withstand his reputation.'

'I know I have to go there and see him,' Martha said, with a hesitancy that wasn't at all her ordinary way of speaking. 'I know I have to ask him for a divorce. But at the same time . . .'

'It will hurt to end it,' Jess finished for her. 'You know that if I could do it for you, I would.'

Martha gave her a small and desolate smile. 'It's just so hard to say that a love like mine and Hem's failed after all.'

'I wonder what actually survives a war?'

Martha shook her head as the elevator doors opened.

'You'll definitely need breakfast if you want to face off with *mon general*,' Jess said, fixing on the practicalities. 'Hemingway's attracted a band of followers and you'll want something to line your stomach before you fight your way through them to be admitted into his presence.'

Her words came to an abrupt halt when they reached the mess and Emile, with shaven head, pushed past them into the room and was greeted with cheers and applause. He looked back over his shoulder at Jess, face triumphant.

'On second thought, breakfast might make me sick,' Jess said, turning away, nausea rising in her throat as if her body wanted to purge itself of her past with Emile, knowing that while she hadn't done anything wrong, she felt ashamed of herself for ever having loved him. 'How are we going to stand any more of this?' she said quietly.

'You know he shaved his own head,' Martha said.

'It doesn't matter. They all think that having sex with a woman is a joke they must share with the world.' Jess shook her head. 'They're never going to let us out of here, are they? Every morning I wake up and think, today will be the day, and Iris and Lee agree and then it doesn't happen and we all drag our heels off to a story nobody cares about. What are we doing? Should we just quit?'

'I don't know,' Martha said, uncharacteristically short of a perky comeback. 'I just don't know.'

After covering another fashion show, Jess returned to the Scribe late in the evening, more than ready for a drink – but nothing as bubbly as champagne – her words from that morning echoing in her head like the concussion of shell bursts: *Should we just quit?* She was doing nothing of use and every day that she took pictures of fashion shows her self-respect and her dignity withered a little more; people were dying and that was what mattered, not what dresses might be in fashion next season. Soon she would have no pride left. Warren would have prevailed and Jess would be just someone who'd once had something important to say.

'Anyone got whiskey?' she muttered to Martha, who was at their usual table in the bar with Lee and Iris.

'We're going to be alcoholics by the end of the war at this rate,' Iris said glumly as Martha organised the drinks for what felt like a funeral and they all began to drink steadily and not at all slowly.

'What are we going to do?' Jess asked.

Before anyone could reply, Major Mayborn appeared and Jess felt herself default to her once infamous smile.

'I thought you might be happy with this,' the major said, saluting Jess, Iris and Lee, handing them all a piece of paper, and then walking away.

Confused, Jess watched him leave, the paper squashed in her hand. 'It's not a goddamn court martial, surely?' she said. 'We haven't done anything, have we?'

'We don't have to do anything more than exist to get into trouble around here,' Lee said bitterly.

'Open it,' Martha said.

So Jess did, Martha, Iris and Lee all watching her. She read the major's words. When she'd finished, she rested her elbows on the table, her head in her hands, and began to sob.

'What is it?' Martha's voice sounded desperate and at last Lee and Iris began to read their own letters.

Wordlessly, Jess passed hers to Martha.

She read it through without speaking, then Jess saw her eyes return to the beginning and read it over again.

'Well, I'll be damned,' Marty said slowly. 'We are going to get drunk, very drunk. But on champagne. No more whiskey.'

At last Jess laughed, and Iris and Lee cheered. For the letter had given Jessica May, Lee Carson and Iris Carpenter permission to access all areas. They were no longer only allowed to stay with the nurses. They were allocated jeeps. They were allowed to attend press briefings. To stay at press camps outside Paris. To be told about the day's hot spots and military objectives. To send copy to their newspapers or magazines as soon as the censor had passed it; they no longer had to wait until all the men had filed theirs. They even got a cigarette ration.

So long as they found a unit to attach themselves to – which would mean, Jess thought, her joy evaporating a little, that she had to think of a way to get Dan to forgive her outburst – Europe was as much theirs as it was the men's.

Fourteen

It was late morning when Jess awoke with a groan. Her headache confirmed that she'd definitely drunk more than she should have.

'That was a night and a half,' Martha muttered.

'It sure was.' Jess blinked and tried to focus. 'Will you come with me when I go out to the front? Be my jeep partner. It might be easier for you to sneak around out there; Stone won't let you have a room of your own here without accreditation. And you can get away from Hemingway.'

When Martha had visited her husband at the Ritz, she'd discovered him in the bedroom of *Time* correspondent Mary Welsh. The outcome had been one more blow to Marty's heart, but also, at last, an agreement to dissolve their marriage.

'That,' Martha sighed, 'is just what I need. Are you joining Dan's division?'

Jess stood up and walked over to the window. 'I don't know whether he'll have me,' she said at last. She explained what had happened at the camp dinner. 'He's in charge of hundreds of men, he's meant to set an example, and I, his dinner guest, shout about sex in front of all the men he's supposed to be leading. Warren deserved it but I shouldn't have handled it like that.'

'Only one way to find out,' Martha said practically. 'Besides, with all the COs you and I have met over the past year or so, we'll find someone to take us on.'

'I suppose you're right.' But Jess knew she'd much prefer to work alongside Dan and his men, GIs she already knew and cared something for. So the only thing to do was to drive out there and hope he'd forgiven her and not think about where she'd go if he hadn't.

Soon she and Marty were on their way downstairs with their bags. In the lobby, they found a huddle of correspondents and PROs, obviously waiting for someone. Jess soon found out it wasn't what had happened in battle overnight that had got everyone so excited; it was what had happened at the Hotel Scribe right under their noses.

'If only I were blonde,' one said loudly as Jess walked past.

'You'd need nice long legs too,' another added.

'Don't forget the breasts,' Warren added.

Jess stopped. 'I assume you're making some kind of point directed at me?'

'You got access to the front. We're just interested to know how you did it,' a reporter for a third-rate paper smirked.

'Yes,' said Jess. 'It is interesting, isn't it? Now I have the same access to the war as you do. No more, no less. I have no extra privileges. But it's taken me a year to earn the rights you were handed the minute you turned up. So the only reason you might be so concerned is because you think I'm going to get better stories than you, and get them first. If that's the case, then I don't know why you're sitting in the bar. War's out that way, fellas.'

Jess pointed to the doors and strode off, tongue having got the better of her again.

When Jess and Martha pulled into the driveway where Dan's division had been billeted, not far from Reims, they both found themselves uncharacteristically speechless. Before them stood a fairytale chateau — it actually had a turret. Yes, it showed some signs of misuse from German occupation but even the circling of khaki tents spread throughout the once manicured grounds and across the fields stretching down to the canal couldn't diminish the splendour. *Lieu de Rêves*: Jess saw the chateau's name on a sign before them and knew it had been appropriately named. It really was a place for dreaming.

Her eyes took in the overgrown maze that she imagined must provide the GIs and WACs the perfect opportunity to become lost together, the plane trees that stood proudly above the tangled branches of chestnut trees, and the vibrant splashes of colour provided by the wild orchids that had just begun to flower, and the still-lingering butterflies. Hiding here and there were contorted dwarf beech trees that had lost most of their leaves, branches covered with moss, looking haunted. Jess knew from her parents that legends abounded that the trees — *Les Faux de Verzy*, as they were known — were either blessed or cursed: there were stories that woodland trolls had caused the stunting, or a monk had cursed them, or that to dance beneath the canopy of leaves might grant one both love and fertility.

'I'm not going to the field hospital,' Marty said, still gazing at the chateau. 'I mightn't have accreditation but I'm staying here too.'

'You're assuming I'll be welcome,' Jess said as she drove forward, adding her jeep to the long row parked down one side of the chateau.

She was certainly welcomed by the men. Sparrow clapped her on the back and Jennings offered his usual shy hello. The ruckus drew the attention of those inside the chateau, and some of the WACs came out to see what was going on, before Dan appeared.

'Jess,' he said, obviously surprised.

'Lieutenant Colonel Hallworth,' she replied, determined to behave impeccably. 'Can I have five minutes of your time?'

He frowned, but at least he said, 'Come in.'

Jess followed him into a magnificent entry foyer that made her head tip up, and then into a huge room – a former ballroom, surely – panelled with grey, the wood inset with faded paintings. Judging by the tables lined up in rows, it was now the mess.

'Coffee?' he asked.

She shook her head. Thankfully it was quiet and there were few people around. She didn't even wait until they were sitting before she spoke. 'I'm sorry about what happened last time I saw you. I promise I won't yell at people like that again. At least not in front of you and your men – I might yell at them more privately next time. I've finally been allowed out of Paris.' She thrust her papers at him. 'And not only that but I'm allowed to go wherever I want and I was hoping you wouldn't mind if I attached myself to your battalion – but I understand if you would rather I didn't.'

He didn't even look at the papers. Instead he grinned at her. 'I was wondering why your greeting was so formal. You know why I invited you over for dinner that night?' he said.

She shook her head.

'To remind us all what it's like to laugh,' he said. 'I almost behaved in a very un-CO-like manner and laughed at Stone in front of everyone because he absolutely deserved it and nobody could have said it better than you did. Sorry if I looked angry; I was actually trying to keep it together. And I didn't drive you back because I didn't want to add any fuel to Stone's idiotic fire; I know it's hard enough for you already without me giving anyone cause to gossip.'

Jess finally smiled. 'Well, I'm glad that I keep everyone's spirits up. In exchange for my special skills at that, will you let me have a room in this grand chateau?'

'Jess, you can have a room without needing to provide anything in exchange. I'll get one of the WACs to organise it; there's plenty of space and a spare bed or two in the attic. And the champagne at dinner tonight to celebrate this,' he pointed to her letter, 'is on me. Congratulations.'

'Thank you, but you might want to take all of that back when I tell you that Marty is here with me and she still doesn't have her accreditation papers back and she wants to stay too.' The words came out in a rush and, as she said them, she felt sure Dan would have to turn them both away but he just smiled again.

'Luckily my division has been put into reserve so there's no one particularly official around here at the moment. Gellhorn might just be able to get away with staying.'

With Dan's division enjoying a well-deserved rest, life was almost normal for a few weeks. Having an address of sorts meant that Jess received the occasional letter from Amelia, who plied Jess with hilarious tales of her nightly antics, over which Jess wasn't sure whether to laugh or to cry, as it seemed like Amelia was talking about a different world, one Jess could never really return to. Dan had moved Victorine to a boarding school in Paris, which meant Jess could visit her occasionally as Reims wasn't far, and Dan had been making the most of the quiet time to visit her too. And Martha was allowing the natural beauty around them to provide a balm for Hemingway's betrayal and to slowly mend her heart.

Just lately, Jess had been writing a story that had nothing to do with battles and war, but about what each man most missed from home. They were such simple things – the coffee mug they always used even though it was chipped around the rim, the crocheted blanket that had been on their bed since they were a boy, the particular creak of a step that meant their mother was up and in the kitchen making bacon and eggs for breakfast. She planned to accompany her words with photographs of each man's young and smiling face, wanting to show that every man here was his own story, taking shots that were simple and very close up so the viewer could see every one of Jennings' freckles, see the strange sadness that now lurked in the back of Sparrow's once confident eyes.

So she gathered up her cameras one morning in December as close to happy as she'd ever been. The advance into Germany had been stopped by the early winter and nobody expected they would be doing any more fighting until the spring of 1945. News *had* come down that the Germans had pushed into the Ardennes, but no one really believed it.

She threaded her way through the tents, dotted always with bare-chested men shaving out of their helmets, past GIs lounging around reading letters and smoking, playing cards, feeling a restlessness in the air that hung around Dan too, a sense that they'd all forgotten how to be still, how to be unafraid. Only last night at dinner, Dan had complained to her that his men were all bored and that boredom led to mischief and that he wished they'd be called up to the Ardennes to join the rumoured fight going on there. She hadn't been surprised to find that he'd gone out early that morning to drive to the front to see what was happening.

'Jess!' Jennings, newly returned from the hospital after setting his foot alight by accidentally stepping into a campfire – much to Dan's resigned amusement – called out eagerly when he saw her. 'Everyone's ready.'

She'd chosen a place that had a magical feel to it in an attempt to convey the spell-working that had somehow kept this group of men together and alive and intact through so much bloodshed. Fairy rings of mushrooms spiralled across the ground. Two of the enchanted trees twisted over the men, providing both the protection of a canopy of naked boughs and the eerie strangeness of the distorted branches. The moss, in the pale midwinter sun, was just a shade brighter than the men's uniforms and when they sat beneath *Les Faux*, they looked as if they were mingling into the forest, becoming a part of the French landscape in such a way that it would be almost impossible to return to chipped coffee mugs and creaking stairs.

'I'm first.' It was Sparrow, of course, using his height and size to manoeuvre his way to the front of the pack of men.

Sparrow's claim was followed by the usual jostling for position that happened every time the GIs saw her camera. She laughed with them as they razzed each man when he sat for his portrait, calling him ugly, telling him he had a face only a mother could love.

'A lot more people love this face than you know.' Sparrow grinned broadly, the torment in his eyes shoved aside by a glint of something Jess didn't like, and the quality of laughter changed: shifty, with an overtone of nuance she didn't understand.

Then another man said, sotto voce to Sparrow, 'Hey, you're not the only one,' and the laughter continued on, starkly.

She put it out of her mind; it was probably a lewd joke they thought might singe her ears. Instead, she concentrated on the focusing and positioning of the Rollei until she had everything she needed.

'Thanks,' she said, standing up at last from the crouched position she'd been occupying. 'I guarantee this will keep your sweethearts' attention fixed on you for at least another few months.'

'Except if you're Jennings,' Sparrow said, punching the other man in the arm. The laughter chorused again.

Jess caught a glimpse of Jennings' reddened face but she had no idea what was going on. She collected her things and hadn't quite reached the chateau when she realised she'd left her notebook behind. She turned around and was almost past the tents and back to the pocket of dwarf beech trees where they'd taken the pictures when she heard her name, spoken heatedly, the voices raised beyond ordinary conversation. For just a moment she felt the tree before her reach out, its curious and beautiful arms pleading with her to step away. She shook her head. The tree, odd and curling as it was, was just a tree. Sparrow and Jennings' discussion cut through her strange hallucination.

'Of course I'm a member,' Jennings was protesting.

Sparrow replied, goading. 'Where's your evidence? To get your J Club badge you need proof. Like we all have.'

Jess was about to move forward and tease them about their mysterious club when she heard Sparrow continue. 'Soon you'll be the only man in the battalion without a badge. Maybe Jess is immune to your charms.'

'But she can't resist yours?' Jennings spoke with more anger than Jess had ever heard in him. 'What was your proof?'

'Her accreditation pass.'

Jess whipped around, not wanting to hear any more. Because it all began to make sense. The little things that kept disappearing from her room. One day her accreditation pass was missing, the next day it was back where she'd thought she'd left it. Her little vial of perfume had vanished but never reappeared. Socks gone one day and then back the next. A precious pair of the very few knickers she'd brought with her evaporating into the general miasma of war. She'd imagined that when she'd washed them and hung them over the bushes to dry they'd been taken by the wind. That the perfume had perhaps been borrowed by one of the WACs who'd forgotten to return it.

But what she'd just heard meant that everything she'd believed — that the men had accepted her presence and thought of her as nothing more than one of their number — wasn't true. The misogynist cabal was just as bad here as in Paris.

They'd started a club. A club that required one of her possessions as an entry pass, possessions gained, she gathered, after she'd supposedly succumbed to the men's charms. *Goddamn you, Warren Stone*, Jess seethed. *Goddamn you Sparrow and every other member of the J Club.* Then her heart stopped. Did Dan know about it?

She didn't bother to retrieve her notebook. She stormed back into the chateau and found Marty, who'd been laid low in her room the past two days. 'Let's go find a story,' Jess said. 'We'll drive up to the Ardennes. See if it's true.'

Martha groaned. 'My stomach is turning itself inside out. I don't know how you bounce around here looking so goddamn young and beautiful and healthy while my guts have turned to water and I feel like a crone.'

Jess sat down beside her friend, anger momentarily quelled and determined not to burden her sick friend with her own problems. 'I'll take you to the hospital. They can get you rehydrated and up and about more quickly than if you stay here eating rations.'

'They won't want me taking up a bed.'

'Anne's there. She won't mind. Besides, you're supposed to be staying there anyway and with the fighting having slowed, they'll have room. Let's go.'

Jess bullied Martha until she acquiesced. It gave her something to think about other than the club and whether Dan knew. She packed Marty, weak as a newborn kitten, into her jeep. At the field hospital, Anne promised to get Martha on a drip and told Jess to pick her up in two days. Which left Jess without a jeep partner to travel to the Belgian border.

'I'll come,' said Catherine Coyne, another correspondent who'd been posted at the field hospital.

'There are reports that the Germans are attacking the front,' Jess said. 'It could be bloody.'

'I see the results of it here,' Catherine said, waving her arms around the hospital. 'It can't be much worse out there.'

Jess supposed she was right so they drove north, only to discover, as the noise of shelling and bombing and gunning grew louder, that the stories were true. The Allies really had needed to launch an Ardennes counteroffensive to hold their lines, and it was failing. The women met a tank near a bombed house, the tank crew perched on top to get the best view of a village being blown up just down the hill.

'This whole area's full of Krauts,' one of the soldiers said to Jess. 'I wouldn't take that road. Although who knows which road you should take. We don't even know where the infantry is, let alone where the front is. But they said thirty Panzers are coming down that road. So . . .' He shrugged, fatalistic, as if thirty Panzers against one Sherman tank wasn't a big deal.

'We'll go back,' Jess said to Catherine, knowing that such a fluid situation wasn't the best way to initiate someone into battle.

She turned the jeep around and, not long after, had to jump out and hit the ditch when a Stuka flew overhead, shooting. The noise was so loud and the concussion so fierce that it robbed their breath. Catherine clutched Jess's hand.

'You okay?' Jess asked.

Catherine nodded.

As they were cautiously preparing to stand, another jeep, driving furiously, churning up dirt and snow, pulled to a halt. Jess waved when she recognised Iris Carpenter and Lee Carson in the vehicle. Emile, whom Jess thankfully hadn't seen since Paris, was with them, hunched in the passenger seat of the jeep, cameras around his neck as if he'd actually been working rather than playing cruel jokes on singers, as had been his main occupation at the Hotel Scribe.

'We're pulling out of Spa,' Iris said. She and Lee had both managed to stick with the press camp and ignore the crude First Army Press Song which was sung daily by the male correspondents – Jess suspected this had a lot to do with a certain relationship Iris had formed with one of the PROs up there. 'Headquarters and the press camp is moving to Liège.'

'Christ,' Jess said. 'Things *are* bad.'

'Come and see.' Iris beckoned.

'Let's just go,' Emile muttered.

Lee rolled her eyes. 'You wanted a ride out of Spa,' she said impatiently to Emile. 'It means you go where we go.'

Jess and Catherine followed Lee up the hill to a ridge where a flood of traffic appeared. Bumper to bumper, the most dangerous way to travel with the Luftwaffe strafing above, a convoy of retreating US Army trucks and tanks was coming towards them.

'We're leaving,' Jess said to Catherine, knowing there was nothing more perilous than sitting in a slow-moving column of vehicles, unable to speed up if needed.

Before they could, the Stukas screamed through the air once more. The Sherman tank they'd seen earlier, the one whose crew they'd spoken with, was bombed barely one hundred yards away. The sound was hellish and they all dived for the ground, covering their heads with their arms but not before Jess, and Catherine too, saw the tank light up and incinerate before anyone could get out of it. Jess knew that every single man had died in the infernal flames.

Catherine broke down then, sobbing into Jess's shoulder, while Jess tried to keep her own tears in her eyes and not break down too.

'Shhh,' Jess whispered as she rubbed Catherine's back, praying that the Stukas wouldn't fly past again, cursing herself for bringing the girl with her. The girl. The boys. They were all the same age as Jess but sometimes she felt a thousand years old: how could anyone ever laugh again after seeing men imprisoned in flame, dying a terrible death.

A long moan had rent the air as the tank exploded. Jess had somehow imagined it came from the tank but as she lifted her head she saw that it had come from Emile, that his mind was desiccated by slaughter. 'Go home,' she said to him, not unkindly. 'There's nothing for you here. There's nothing here for any of us.'

It was the truth but Emile still glared at her. 'That's why it suits you,' he said bitterly. 'Because you are nothing. Nothing more than a face and a smile.'

'You forgot to mention the body,' she said, the words acid on her tongue, before she stood up with Catherine and walked away.

It was a long four-hour trek back to Reims with a nervous Catherine, who wanted Jess to stay at the hospital rather than go back to the chateau on her own. It was tempting, Jess had to admit. But she didn't want to give Jennings or Sparrow or anyone else a chance to take any more souvenirs from her room, nor did she want to admit that she was scared to go back, scared to walk into a chateau with men she'd thought were on her side but who, she now understood, still saw her first and foremost as the woman in the picture with the naked back, the woman whom any man would want warming his godforsaken bed. She wanted to cry, and she couldn't do it there.

She made it back near midnight and didn't bother to eat, just fell into bed in her nest in the attic. But sleep was on the wrong side of the front and she couldn't reach it. Every time she closed her eyes, the image of the burning men inside the tank scalded her eyes. Instead she lay, staring up at the ceiling, listening to the sounds of the officers on the floors below, the laughter of the men in the tents in the fields drifting through her windows, Emile's words — *you are nothing* — striking her ears like machine gun fire. It was what every man at Reims thought. Emile had been the only one brave enough to say it to her face.

The GIs' laughter rang on through the night. Jess's nightmares were of fire, and of men gathered in packs in their tents, sniggering over a woman they'd turned into a coin-operated machine. All they had to do was put in enough whiskey or perfume or money and her body would be theirs, for as long as it continued to amuse them.

The intermittent sleep and the dreams made her angrier and angrier. As soon as the sun rose, she marched down to the first floor, so livid that she forgot to knock when she reached Dan's room.

'How many of your men do you think I've slept with?' Jess demanded as she shoved open the door and stormed inside, only to find him naked from the waist up, shaving over an old porcelain wash basin, a relic of the chateau's once gracious past.

He paused, razor in hand to stare at her. 'What?'

'Can't give me the exact number?' she continued. 'Let's try a range. Stop me when I'm close. One to five? No? Five to ten? More? Forty to fifty? Jesus!' She advanced into the room. 'None!' she continued.

'I have slept with exactly none of your men. Zero, null, nada, zilch. And now I don't know why I bothered with abstinence. I like sex. I could have been having sex. But no, I told myself not to behave the way everyone thinks I will. So I've spent twelve bloody frustrating months celibate and now I discover that, according to your men, I've slept with at least half of them!'

Dan's mouth twitched, and then he convulsed into helpless laughter.

Jess stared at him with disbelief. And everything she'd feared suddenly seemed unbearably true. That he was in on it too. '*What* is so funny?'

He was laughing so hard now that he collapsed into a chair, unable to speak. Jess was unable to speak too, could only feel the God-awful punch of knowledge that Dan might not have been the friend she thought he was.

When he finally managed to take hold of himself, he said, 'It's just that you're the only woman I know who would tell me how much she likes having sex and how frustrated she is and not even realise that it isn't the kind of conversation I could ever have imagined having with any woman just two years ago.'

As he spoke, Jess's words replayed in her mind. 'Oh God!' she sighed. 'I came in here to convince you of my unimpeachable reputation and I've just convinced you of the exact opposite, haven't I?'

'You haven't convinced me of anything because I have no idea what you're talking about,' he said. His face became grave. 'Tell me.'

She shook her head, determined to leave before she embarrassed herself any further. 'It doesn't matter. Temporary insanity.'

He stood up, took her gently by the shoulders and led her back to his chair. 'I want to know.'

This time, when she spoke, all her anger was gone and she could hear that her voice sounded so tired and so resigned, and so – sad. 'I overheard Sparrow and Jennings talking. Sparrow was asking Jennings why he didn't have his J Club badge, which is apparently an honorary award bestowed on everyone in your battalion to have slept with me. And I just . . .' She paused to hide the cracking in her voice, which she knew wasn't just because of Jennings and Sparrow; it was because of the tank and Catherine and every dead and damaged body she'd seen over the past year. 'I thought they'd moved beyond the fact I was a woman. But I don't think they'll ever move past that. I'm a woman first and everything else comes a long way after.'

She stood up, fists clenched, jaw tight. 'And now I'm being everything they expect me to be. Weak. Unable to put up with the teasing. A tale-teller. Forget I said anything. But I guess . . .' She hesitated. 'I think of you as a friend first and the guy in charge second. Which I should probably stop doing.'

She turned and hurried out, taking the jeep and pushing it out along the road to the north, camera ready for whatever she might find in the land that lay beyond reality.

Fifteen

As Jess drove, she remembered the story she'd wanted to write but had been too scared to pursue. Until now. So she didn't go as far as the Ardennes. Instead, almost hating herself for doing it because how could she betray the men she'd seen burned alive in the tank yesterday, but knowing that if she didn't, she was betraying all of the women instead, she stopped near Sedan. She knocked on doors, spoke to the women, asked them about the soldiers who'd passed through, both German and American. What were they like? How did they treat the villagers? Did they ask for what they wanted or did they just take whatever they thought they had a right to?

Not many women would speak to her once her questions changed from the general to the specific. But she kept asking, kept taking notes, kept photographing these women who'd seen more than anyone knew since 1940. One woman, Marie-Laure, whose husband was a prisoner of war in Germany and whose father had been killed by the Germans for helping downed British airmen evade capture, asked Jess to dine with her and her mother.

'We only have a little bread, and some cheese,' Marie-Laure said. She looked to be about eighteen, but that could just be the effect of poor diet over the long years of war.

'I have chocolate, and cigarettes,' Jess said, offering the two items that were more sought after than money.

Marie-Laure's mother accepted both with a silent nod. In fact, she didn't speak at all over dinner. But her daughter did.

'We always give our food and our cows and our chickens to the soldiers,' Marie-Laure said as she smoked a Lucky Strike, ignoring the food. 'But then there were no more chickens or cows to give, and the vegetables in the garden were too small. Unsatisfactory. My father had a pilot hiding in the cellar. The Germans came. Perhaps . . . perhaps we should have given them the pilot. But then they would have taken my father too. So –'

Marie-Laure shrugged, stood up and walked over to kiss the top of her mother's head.

'They told us to choose,' Marie-Laure continued quietly. 'Me, or my mother. So I went with them to the bedroom. There were four men. The fifth was given the job of keeping my mother and father in the kitchen.'

Jess's pen moved over her paper. She did not look up as Marie-Laure spoke because she sensed her shame, that she did not want Jess's eyes on her while she talked. Jess wanted to shout: *You aren't the one who should be ashamed!* But Marie-Laure hadn't yet finished.

'When the last one was nearly done, the others left the room. They came back with my mother. And they made me watch.'

Jess's eyes burned with useless tears.

'The next day, they returned.' Marie-Laure lit another cigarette. 'My mother hadn't been able to leave her bed since they'd gone. My father was on the floor by the bed crying. The Boche took the pilot, and my father. It had all been for nothing.'

<hr/>

It had all been for nothing. The words rang in Jess's head as she drove back to Reims.

And Marie-Laure had said one last terrible thing to Jess before she left.

'Two weeks ago, some Americans were here. This time, I just took off my dress. It hurts less when you don't struggle.'

Jess knew that nobody would publish it if she wrote it into a story. Nobody wanted to read about American soldiers raping the women of a country that had been under German rule for years, behaving as everyone imagined the Germans did. Nobody wanted to see what lay beneath the resignation on Marie-Laure's face and the silence of her mother's mouth, which Jess had captured in a photograph of the two of them, sitting at the table before two thin slices of bread, gripping their cigarettes as if keeping hold of their sanity.

What to do? The question haunted Jess on the long, dark road home as she used every bit of strength and judgement to make her way without a navigator, praying there would be no Germans on the road, no bombs, no 88s, no shells, no reason to have to leap out of the jeep and into a ditch and lie in the shadows alone. She reached the chateau late, tired, filthy, every muscle taut.

It was quiet, many of the rooms unlit, some of the men in the tents still moving about, but she could see that a light still shone brightly in Dan's room, and in hers right at the top. She shook her head. Surely the men weren't stealing more souvenirs? She might as well just empty her bag on the lawn and tell them to take what they wanted. She was too tired to fight anymore.

She climbed the stairs, cameras digging into her shoulders, stomach growling at eating nothing but a K-ration all day. The door to her room was ajar and she stopped short at the sight of Sparrow and Jennings and several others in her room. So they *had* come to take everything that was left.

But then she realised that Sparrow had a broom in his hand. Jennings was tucking clean sheets onto her bed, another GI was putting a tray of food down on the table she used as a desk. On the bed were all her uniforms, washed and pressed and folded with military precision. She rubbed her eyes.

The men saw her and stood stiffly to attention. 'Captain May,' they said in unison.

'What are you doing?' she asked warily.

'Tidying your room, ma'am,' Jennings answered.

'I can see that. But why?'

The men looked sheepishly at one another and then Sparrow, face tinged red, replied. 'We're all done, Captain May. I hope it's satisfactory.'

'It's like heaven,' she said. 'But why?'

None of them answered. Instead they filed out, heads down, gazes fixed to the floor.

Jess's bag dropped to the ground and she placed her camera on the bed, wincing when she saw the dirty mark her hand left on the clean sheets. And that smear, for some reason, undid her. The tears she hadn't allowed herself to shed while she listened to Marie-Laure's terrible tale filled her eyes now and she stood still for a long moment, swallowing hard, the ache in her throat almost insupportable.

She knew why the men were in her room. And she knew there was at least one man in the chateau who saw past the smile and the face and the body to the things that really were inside her, who didn't think she was nothing. When the tightness in her throat eased, she walked down the stairs and knocked at Dan's door.

'Come in,' she heard him call, faintly, as if he wasn't quite in the room.

She pushed open the door but couldn't see him. A gentle swish of white drapes caught her attention. The door to the balcony stood open and she could see the back of his head, leaning against a sofa that had been dragged out there, taking up almost all the room.

'Dan?' she called from the door.

'You can come in, Jess.'

She left the door open for propriety, a gesture that almost made her laugh, and stepped outside, drawing in her breath as she did so. The room was at the back of the chateau, looking north towards Belgium and over the tents and the remaining snares of garden, which fell away to the canal, a black ribbon in the distance. The night sky draped softly around them like velvet, stars dotted over its surface. There were no clouds to obscure the points of light, just the delicate waft and plume of white phosphorus. At regular intervals a shell or a tracer arc lit up the sky beyond like an unearthly rainbow or a falling star. A comet, even. 'It's beautiful,' she breathed.

'I know,' Dan said.

She dropped onto the sofa beside him.

'You're just in time.' Dan held up a glass of cognac and passed it to her.

She sipped gratefully. 'Thanks.'

'You look like you've had a day and a half,' he said, studying her face.

'Topped off by my arrival in my room to find six men cleaning it. My uniforms are washed. My bed has clean sheets.'

'I asked for all the members of the J Club to assemble this afternoon,' he said cheerfully. 'I expect what they got wasn't quite what they anticipated. I told them I'd heard of the J Club and understood that the J stood for Janitor. Their janitorial services were required in your room, for as long as it took, until everything was spotless.'

'They'll hate me.'

Dan shook his head. 'No they won't. They'll know they did the wrong thing. Fine, find a way to let off some steam but not at the expense of somebody's character. If I didn't do anything about it, then that's as good as saying I think it's okay. It's not.' He paused, watching another tracer dance across the sky. 'You're back late.'

She passed the glass back to him. 'I'd heard whispers about soldiers raping women. And I found someone who spoke to me about it. I don't think I can ignore it, even though I know I'll never be able to publish it.'

He didn't reply and Jess clammed her mouth shut. She'd given him one too many confidences. How could he condone her doing something like this, actively slandering the organisation that he, as an officer, was sworn to uphold? But then he said, quietly, 'You should write it anyway.'

A faint smile drifted onto her face. If only the army was peopled with men like Dan, rather than men like Warren.

She turned the conversation back to the reason she was late, not wanting to tell him anything else; it wasn't fair to drop the burden of what she was doing onto him. 'The drive took forever,' she sighed. 'I didn't realise how much time you save when you have someone navigating and watching one half of the road for you.'

'I thought you went with Martha?' He sat up straight, alert.

'I took her to the hospital yesterday. She's ill.'

'You drove back alone at night? Yesterday as well?' Still that attentiveness, the attitude of his back like raised hackles.

'I was fine.'

'But you mightn't have been. Jesus, Jess, you should have stayed at the press camp for the night.'

She tried to interrupt, to protest that she didn't feel like sharing with a pack of correspondents, not when the day had been so gruelling, but Dan didn't let up.

'Anything could have happened,' he said. 'It's not safe enough yet to go driving at night alone. And it's as slick as an ice-rink out there.'

'Dan,' she said gently, staring at him until he stopped. 'If I'd been blown up it wouldn't have mattered a damn if I was with someone or not. I'm not your responsibility. You have a whole battalion to worry about. You don't have to worry about me too.'

'If you're not my responsibility then whose responsibility are you? SHAEF PR? They take such good care of you. Warren Stone? Damned if I'd leave you in his hands for more than a second.'

'I'm responsible for myself,' she stated. 'I knew that when I decided to come out here.'

'But you take that responsibility too lightly.'

He was glaring at her but she knew the anger came from concern. That what she'd said to him that morning – *I think of you as a friend first and the guy in charge second* – was true for him too.

She put her hand on his arm. 'I take that responsibility very seriously. As seriously as you take your responsibility to yourself. I was aware of the risks posed by both the Germans and the roads and I was hyper-alert on the way back. Which is why I'm so filthy and tired now,' she added ruefully. 'I know how I'd feel if anything happened to you. So I'm extra careful if I'm ever in a jeep by myself.'

Neither of them spoke for a long moment. Neither of them looked away. They stayed eye to eye, the sound of the shells falling far beyond like the subdued whimpers of a person trying not to cry. Then the anger relaxed from his face a little, but his eyes were still dark blue and unsmiling. 'Your face is so dirty right now all I can see are the whites of your eyes.'

She laughed and wiped a futile hand across her cheek. 'What a day to have a clean bed. Now I have to take a freezing shower and then spend the next two hours trying to get warm. What I wouldn't do for hot water.'

Dan raised his eyebrows. 'I have hot water.'

'What? Where?'

'I didn't know you didn't. Fuck,' he swore. 'Sometimes I think being an officer just means being ignorant of the way things really are. I'm ordering you to go and use the shower on this floor. I will personally stand guard to make sure nobody else uses the bathroom while you're in there.' He stood up. 'Let's go.'

She was marched to the bathroom where he pushed her in, along with a clean shirt of his that he'd grabbed on the way. She shut the door and could hear him, while she let the deliciously warm water run over her and the dirt wash away, redirecting anyone who wanted to use the bathroom, brooking no opposition.

Eventually, she heard a knock on the door and Dan's voice call out. 'Jess? Are you all right in there?'

She turned off the tap. 'Sorry!' she called back. 'I'll be out in a minute. It's just that I haven't felt hot water since Paris.' She dried quickly, slipped on Dan's shirt which was, she thought, perfectly decent, being longer than some of the playsuits she'd once modelled for *Vogue*, and stepped out of the bathroom.

'We'd better get you tucked safely away before anyone sees you in that,' he said.

She laughed. 'I'm sure that, after today, they'll all be staying well away or you'll be getting them to wash my jeep next. Can I just have one last look?'

'At what?' he asked, following her down the hall.

She pushed open the door to his room and crossed to the balcony. 'At this,' she said, pointing at the sky and sinking into the sofa.

He sat down too, stretching his arm along the back of the sofa. Jess leaned her head against his shoulder. And Dan didn't shift uncomfortably away or take it as an invitation to do anything else; he just reached over for the blanket folded on the arm of the sofa, draped it around her, dropped his arm to her shoulder and let her curl into his side while they passed the cognac glass back and forth and watched the electric sky erupt magnificently around them.

Minutes passed. 'Did you really mean what you said this morning?' Dan asked eventually.

Jess's mind cast back through the day to her dawn conversation with Dan and she smiled ruefully. 'About not having sex for more than twelve months? Yes.'

'You're worse off than I am, then,' he said, staring at the sky. 'I swore off it in Italy.'

'Why?' she asked.

'Because I was doing it to forget. But to lose yourself in someone so completely that you do actually forget is more intimate than any physical act. I didn't want to be that intimate with any of the women I knew.'

'Yes,' Jess breathed as she felt her eyelids drop sleepily over her eyes. 'That's it exactly.'

She woke with a jolt some time later. Dan's head was resting back, his eyes closed, face young and peaceful. She remembered their conversation and knew, without doubt, that falling asleep tucked into Dan's side was the most intimate thing she'd ever done and that she should leave now before she ruined it.

She leaned over and kissed his cheek. 'Thank you, Lieutenant Colonel Hallworth,' she whispered before she turned to walk away.

And she just heard the words, whispered faintly behind her, 'My pleasure, Captain May,' as she left his room.

～

The next day she woke to the sound of a knock and a note slipped under her door. It was from Dan. *You have the bathroom from 7.30 a.m.* She checked her watch. It was 7.25. She jumped out of bed, uncaring that she was in her pyjamas, gathered what she needed and raced down the stairs and along the hallway, passing Dan with a grin. At the bathroom, she discovered a sign on the door that read: *Reserved for Captain May from 7.30 a.m. to 7.45 a.m. every day.*

'Who the hell is Captain May and why does he get bathroom privileges,' she heard another officer say.

She turned on her model smile. 'I'm Captain May,' she said. 'I think I get bathroom privileges because Lieutenant Colonel Hallworth is worried that if I share the bathroom with you, I might set other parts of your anatomy aflutter than just your heart.'

The officer's mouth dropped open and he blushed crimson from his hairline all the way down his neck, struck absolutely speechless. Jess heard Dan explode with laughter behind them before she pushed open the bathroom door, took her shower and made sure to use no more than her allotted fifteen minutes.

~

It might have seemed a frivolous thing to do in the middle of a war but as the Germans pushed back into the Ardennes, Jess decided that everyone needed a party. How else would anyone have the energy to move into 1945, still fighting, still far from home, still without really knowing when it might all come to an end? And over everyone hung the knowledge that Dan's division would be called out of reserve very soon as the battle in the Ardennes pounded on.

The party would be held on Christmas Day, she decided, and she worked, huddled in front of the tiny camp heater she'd been carrying around since Italy, to make it happen. Jennings helped her; he'd sprained his wrist tripping over a guy rope and Dan had asked Jess to keep him as busy as she could so he'd at least make the year's end without further injury.

As much as the men groaned when she cajoled and persuaded them to help her get everything ready, she knew they were as excited as children about a birthday party. She'd put the J Club misadventures behind her; grudges caused wars whereas forgiveness stopped them and if she couldn't practise a little of that herself, how could she expect nations to?

But then came the orders from HQ; Dan's division would mobilise at dawn. So they moved Christmas forward by a few days, Jess promising Dan that she would go to Paris as soon as he left for the Ardennes so that somebody would be with Victorine. Then she commanded everyone to wash and meet her in the chateau's scullery, which she'd set up as the change room. Once the men were suitably clean, she told them to don their outfits, while she decorously stepped out to allow them privacy – although as Sparrow called out, they might all prefer it if she watched. He said it without meanness though, the J Club antics having ended all such innuendo.

'But imagine what it would do to my eyes,' she said teasingly.

The hum from the ballroom-turned-mess, a large and magnificent columned space with soft grey walls lined with *boiserie* – onto which had been painted scenes depicting a child charmed by the magical and aberrant beech trees – suggested that quite a gathering of people were waiting. The mess tables had been dragged to the sides and were now adorned with soldiers flirting with WACs and with nurses who'd been allowed out of the hospital for a few hours. Many correspondents, never wanting to miss a party, had travelled across from Paris or the press camps and were draped over benches, drinks in hand, chatting.

Jess nodded to Private Ronnie Page, a new recruit, to whom she'd assigned gramophone duties, and as the music lifted through the room, she sent out her first model – Sparrow in a dress Jess had fashioned from a couple of threadbare American flags. He was greeted by laughter and a resounding cheer, which rose louder and longer as another private followed, dressed in one of the Edwardian ballgowns she'd found in trunks in the attic. He executed a perfect twirl at the end of the area of floor designated as the runway and Jess grinned, sure now that she'd been right. That everyone did need a night that veered close to the ridiculous, a night that was certain to make even the hardiest soldier discover he was still capable of smiling.

After that she sent out Jennings; he'd found an old suit in the attic and she'd helped him affix onto it the black-and-white United States Army-issue chocolate bar packets, which stated that he should be consumed slowly or dissolved as a beverage. Howls of laughter followed him around the ballroom. When he managed – of course he managed; it was Jennings, the man who injured himself just getting out of bed – to slip and land on his backside, the hoots escalated and Jennings joined in.

Then there was a private in a coat made of bandages donated by the nurses, a shirt fashioned from camouflage netting, a hysterical hat made from ration boxes, and a handful of other outfits that the men had helped her to make with good humour. The merriment sewn into each costume was made manifest in the room and she could see that everyone had actually forgotten, for a moment, why they were all there. Her eyes, roaming the happy faces, caught Dan's and he smiled and gave her a thumbs-up.

She slipped back into the scullery and changed into her own gown; she'd stitched together whatever fragments of fabric she could find from ripped or threadbare or no longer usable US Army shirts and trousers and coats and jackets and made a patchwork of a khaki dress. But the dress was as close as her sewing skills would allow it to be to the one she wore in the photograph from *Vogue* that many of the men had pinned over their beds: the floor-sweeping Lelong princess gown with a full skirt, the bodice that left her back bare, her neck long, her arms fluid by her sides.

She'd washed her hair that day and now she brushed it to shining, not minding that it was cut shorter than ever, realising that she looked all the better for it, the features of her face – her dark brown eyes, her full lips, her strong cheekbones – accentuated, and she was startled for a moment into thinking that somebody else had stepped up to the mirror: the Jessica May of two years before who'd never looked anything other than nonpareil, a stark contrast to the often filthy woman in combat trousers she'd become.

She brushed powder over her face, swept mascara onto her lashes, rouged her cheeks and outlined her lips in red, then took her turn to parade through the ballroom as the finale of the show.

She expected the hooting and cheers, she expected the laughter as they realised she'd turned a picture of herself, a picture that so many of them revered, into a caricature. Instead what greeted her was silence. Only the gramophone played on, a ridiculously melo-dramatic turn-of-the-century operetta screeching into the room. But not a sound escaped from any of the men as she strolled in, her body easy and relaxed as it swung into the model's walk that came back to her as naturally as breathing, as she strode to the centre of the room, one hand on her hip, eyes sweeping the silent faces. Her smile, which had been bright and full, faded, then fell as she waited for something, anything that would rescue her from this awful silence.

After a very long moment, she put both hands on her hips. 'What?' she demanded. 'Is the back of my skirt tucked into my knickers or something equally jaw-dropping?'

Then the burst of laughter she'd been expecting rushed through the room and the cheers began, the clapping and roaring reaching a peak so great that Jess wondered if the applause could be heard all the way over in Germany.

She put her smile back on as she finished her turn about the room, but she still carried a knot in her stomach as she wondered what on earth she'd done, what rule she'd broken, to strike them all so dumb.

At the end she curtsied and summoned the other models over to take a bow, after which she expected they'd remove their ridiculous garb and change into their uniforms, but no one did. WACs and soldiers alike came over to examine each one, exclaiming over the chocolate wrappers, touching the ration boxes, commenting on Sparrow's hairy legs protruding from his patriotic frock of flags.

Jess moved around the room until she found Dan. She looked up at him quizzically. 'What the hell did I do this time? My skirt definitely wasn't tucked into my knickers so it can't have been that.'

Dan shook his head. 'No. It was just . . .'

He paused as if he really didn't want to tell her and she almost shook her head and said, *Don't bother*, not wanting this night to be ruined by hearing of some other wickedness wrongly attributed to her. He looked away as he spoke and Jess stared at the ground.

'I don't think anyone realised what had been right under our noses for so long,' Dan said eventually. 'You looked . . . stunning. As if you'd arrived from another world. A bewitching stranger. Someone more than worth fighting for.'

She dragged her eyes away from the floor to gape at him, speechless, until he continued.

'And then you opened your mouth and spoke to us just like Jess would,' Dan grinned, 'and we remembered that behind the apparition was someone we knew. Someone we're all glad to have here with us. Cheers.' He raised his glass and clinked it against hers, then moved away to clap Sparrow on the back, leaving Jess to recover her power of speech, to be reminded by Jennings that she was supposed to be taking photographs, to wonder why on earth Dan's words – *you looked stunning* – had unsettled her so much.

Once she'd snapped as many pictures as film allowed, the gramophone was put to full use, nobody caring that the dusty collection of records wasn't exactly up to jazz club standards.

For more than an hour she whirled around the ballroom floor with one or another of the men, surprised at how light she felt, the heaviness of war momentarily lifted by the glee in the room. It had become abnormal, she realised, for so many people to be so outwardly happy and that in itself was a reminder that they were all, every one of them, clinging to a kind of amnesia for as long as they could hold off the dawn and re-mobilisation.

At the end of every song, her partner changed, and each man ceded way graciously to the next – no arguing, no jealousy, no jeers – until she saw Dan tap her partner on the shoulder and say to her, 'Surely it's my turn now.'

She smiled. 'I think it must be.'

Private Page moved back, stammering, and she couldn't help kissing his cheek – which only made him stammer all the more – because he'd been as sweet as candy floss at a summer fair, talking to her about his kid sister, who ordinarily liked to follow him around at home and he'd wondered what she did now that he wasn't there to shadow. Page scrambled over to the gramophone to set down the next recording, which was the oh so slow and oh so treacly 'Smoke Gets in Your Eyes', sung by Irene Dunne.

'Oh dear,' Jess said wryly. 'I'm sure you'd prefer a nurse for this one.'

Dan shook his head. 'I think I'm safer with you.'

She laughed. 'And vice versa. I'm not sure Private Page would know what to do with himself if this had played while I was dancing with him.'

'Then let's show him.'

With that, Dan placed a hand on her back, on the skin left bare by her dress. One of Jess's hands reached up to his shoulder and their other hands clasped together.

For a long moment there was nothing beyond Dunne's operatic voice soaring through the room, the entire congregation of people suddenly silent for this one slow dance in a ballroom in a chateau in the midst of a war zone, somewhere in France.

Then the bubble of conversation began to rise once more.

Except for Jess and Dan.

When does friend become man? When is the touch of a hand transformed into a caress? When does amity turn instead to desire?

In a ballroom in a chateau in the midst of a war zone, somewhere in France.

As they danced, Dan's fingers uncurled so the flat of his palm rested against her bare back, and then she felt his thumb stroke her skin ever so lightly, a whisper that she could choose to ignore if it meant nothing to her. Instead, she shivered, her whole body reacting to his touch as it spread out like the aftershock of an explosion, everywhere.

She knew he'd noticed because he did it again and her response was the same: a shudder that she couldn't control, other than to step closer, her body against his. His hand at her back held her more tightly, drawing her in so that nothing separated them except the thin and seductive notes of the music.

She remembered the way she'd curled into him on the sofa on his balcony. She remembered opening the door to his room to find him shaving, bare-chested, and the image made her close her eyes and feel the press of that same chest, unbearably covered now, against hers. There had been so many times he could have taken advantage of her, and even now Dan was so careful not to trespass onto her body without being certain it was what she wanted. She felt her heart crack a little at the tenderness his restraint implied.

The song played irresistibly on. Jess was aware of nothing around them, nothing beyond Dan's thumb brushing up and down in minute movements on her back, and a longing to do the same to him: to feel his bare skin beneath her hand. She lifted her head so that her forehead brushed his cheek; he lowered his head in response and she whispered into his ear, 'Dan.'

At the same time, he said her name — 'Jess' — and his voice matched hers.

'It's my turn!'

Jess gasped as Jennings' eager words crashed over her like a grenade, making her and Dan jump apart, the moment fragmenting into dust around them.

She hadn't danced with Jennings and he had helped sew chocolate wrappers onto a suit so it was only fair that she say yes to him and, besides, the song had ended and she hadn't danced with any other man twice, so Dan stepped away.

Jess had no idea what song she and Jennings danced to, nor whom she danced with after that, unable to escape because she was a woman and a rarity and also the star of the show and they would all notice if she went missing; she only knew that what she'd been about to say to Dan was, 'Come upstairs with me. Now,' and that as her eyes searched the room desperately for him, he had gone.

Gone to the killing field of the Ardennes. And she hadn't had time to say to him, 'Make sure you come back alive.'

PART FOUR

D'Arcy

Sixteen

'So tell me what you do know,' Josh said, eyes following D'Arcy's to the ceiling of the attic room in which they sat, cognac in one hand, inconceivable photographs in the other.

'Not much,' D'Arcy admitted, gripping her glass. 'My mother, Victorine, was born in France. Her father died in the war, she told me, and she was raised by relatives, who put her into boarding school when she was a child; she rarely saw them after that. Once she finished school, she became a reporter, then editor for a magazine in Paris, worked her way up and ended up in Australia running the Asia-Pacific arm of World Media Group. I have no idea how she could be in this picture and I have no idea why your photographer might have it.'

She paused. 'Anyway, it's my problem, not yours. Your mother isn't the one mysteriously appearing in famous photographs.'

'If it concerns the photographer, then it is my business. So let's break it down,' Josh said, in his crisp, business-like voice which D'Arcy treasured at that moment because it made the problem seem impersonal, solvable, separate from her. 'How did your mother end up with the name Hallworth? It's not French. And how did she find her way to Australia; it's not an obvious leap from working on a magazine in France.'

'More cognac first.'

D'Arcy held out her glass, unsure which of Josh's questions to tackle first. She started with the story she knew best, although it was as full of tiny holes as a round of mimolette cheese. 'I always thought she came to Australia because of some sort of failed love affair. She never really said why but her move to Australia coincided with my birth, which is why I put it down to love gone wrong. And she was given the name Hallworth because her father was an American GI. Another love affair gone wrong: her mother fell pregnant with Victorine while unwed. Hence Victorine was put into boarding school and the family kept her at more than arm's-length. She was just one of the many illegitimate children borne by a Frenchwoman to a US soldier in a war zone. And as she never really knew her family, they didn't keep in touch once her schooling had finished.'

'And *your* father? Victorine didn't marry him or she just didn't take his name?'

D'Arcy hesitated, sipping the cognac. She hardly knew this man sitting beside her and he was asking her things she rarely talked about. Yes, she'd been happy to have sex with him but, somehow, that seemed far less intimate than this discussion. She kept it brief. 'Neither. I don't know too much about him. Like I said, I assumed my mother had her heart broken by him. She told me that she hadn't been able to tell my father about me because by the time she knew she was having a baby, he was no longer in France. Maybe he was a tourist passing through, and it was the seventies, so texts and emails didn't exist. I never knew him so I never missed him. My mother is redoubtable; she's more than enough of a parent to be both mother and father,' she finished firmly.

Josh shifted a little closer to her, putting down his glass, casting his eyes over the figure of the girl in the photograph who bore the same name as D'Arcy's mother. 'You don't seem like someone who's afraid to ask questions, nor like someone who has no natural curiosity. It all sounds like a made-up story. Did you never ask any more?'

'I didn't,' D'Arcy said quietly. And then the truth came out, a truth that was a thousand times more intimate than kissing. 'I adore my mother. But she looked so sad every time I asked her about it. More than sad; she looked as if I were tearing out her heart, piece by agonising piece. I didn't want to be the one to make her look like that. So I stopped asking.'

Then D'Arcy stood in one quick motion. She'd told him more about her mother, and also herself, than she'd ever said to anyone. It was making her eyes a little too damp. 'Sorry. You're not interested in my personal wallowing. You should go to bed. I'll be back to sawing in the morning.' Her voice sounded convincing, as if she really would just pick up her saw and get on with the job like none of this had happened.

He put out a hand to halt her. 'I'll talk to the photographer. Ask if she'll see you. Maybe she has some answers for you.'

'Thank you,' she said, before she hurried back to her room and sat on her balcony, staring unseeing at the resplendent gardens spotlit by the full moon, and the dark coil of canal that lay just beyond.

When she awoke the next morning, D'Arcy had to check the carriage clock on the bedside table several times before she would believe what it said. Nine o'clock! She couldn't remember the last time she'd slept until nine o'clock. She'd fallen into bed at dawn after sitting awake for hours, thinking about her mother, debating whether she should just call her. Victorine's always practical tone would offer up a simple explanation: Victorine wasn't the girl in the photograph. It was just a very big and very startling coincidence of names.

D'Arcy leapt out of bed and threw herself into the shower. She had work to do. Sleeping in until nine o'clock was taking the wallowing too far. She threw on a black 1950s sundress, a find from a vintage store; it had spaghetti straps, a fitted bodice and a full skirt made bell-shaped by polka-dot crinoline petticoats that peeped out at the hem.

Célie, who either had an intuition as to when her guests woke up, or simply heard the clanging of the water pipes, knocked and brought in the same delicious breakfast tray as yesterday.

'I really should just grab the croissant and the coffee and go downstairs and start work,' D'Arcy said regretfully.

Célie shook her head. 'Breakfast is meant to be enjoyed. Here is the paper. Sit outside and relax. You look tired. And Josh hasn't started work yet.'

It wasn't hard to be convinced. Once outside, she realised it was a warm day already, the sky clear blue and untroubled. It was the perfect day, in fact, to sit on the balcony of a chateau in France and sip coffee and read newspapers and do very little. But of course she wasn't on holiday.

She stared at her phone and thought again about calling her mother but the time difference wouldn't be right. Then she heard the low hum of voices and saw Josh and an elderly woman strolling back up from the canal.

The woman held onto Josh's arm and he walked slowly, keeping pace with her. She was tall, even though her shoulders were rounded a little with age, and her face was shielded by large Bardot-esque sunglasses. Her silver hair was cut into an elegant and classic bob, waving gently at the ends. She wore white trousers and a fun but modish update on the striped Breton top, with gauzy sleeves and a raw hem.

D'Arcy realised she was holding her breath, as if she thought that simply inhaling would make them realise she could see this woman who must be the photographer. Then the woman looked up at D'Arcy's balcony and smiled. D'Arcy froze, unable to smile or wave or do anything other than stare, stupidly, as the woman and Josh walked closer to the house where she could no longer see them.

After several long moments, D'Arcy roused herself, her mind whirling. Why had the photographer let D'Arcy see her? What was going on? And did it have anything to do with what she and Josh had found the night before?

Josh. D'Arcy remembered their kiss. What would he be like today? Embarrassed? Professional? Would he kiss her again? She shook her head. Josh was probably one distraction too many at the moment.

But she still found herself looking for him when she stepped into the *salon de grisailles.* He was already there, talking on the phone. She thought maybe his eyes flickered with something like gladness when he saw her so she risked a smile, picked up her tools and went out to the terrace to work where she wouldn't disturb him.

It was meditative and soothing, the push and pull of the saw through the wood, the hammering of nails into crates, ticking off each artwork on her list. As the sun ran warm fingers over her shoulders, she managed to forget all of her worries and fears and questions about her mother, forget everything except the artworks.

She reached for a set of images, her favourites of the photographer's works, a series showing children doing distinctly unchildlike things: two boys aged about ten, with curly blond heads and brightly coloured T-shirts, one smoking a cigarette, holding it in a way that suggested much practise, the boy beside him with his mouth wrapped around a lollipop; a boy lying on the ground, curled up in pain, holding his stomach, a girl in a white dress skipping away with a smug smile on her face; the child in the candy-striped dress, tights and patent Mary Jane shoes, head lost in the big seventies dome-shaped hairdryer, her mother beside her, oblivious, reading a magazine with a picture of the Queen on the cover; a group of adults at a protest march, bearing banners with uncensored slogans, the focus on the mouths of the adults, open in rage, screaming out their protest, and a child smiling beatifically beside them.

D'Arcy knew from her studies that the photographer had never
tried for the iconic shot, that she preferred to gather a series of images
that each spoke to the other, posing questions in one, answering them
in another, the theme emerging from the collection, not the single
image. She picked up the final photograph in this set: a homage
to Diane Arbus's iconic close-up of the sobbing child. It showed a
child the way one might expect to see them represented in a book of
fairytales: blonde curls, blue eyes, soft cheeks, but there was a look
of such potent concentration in the intense close-up of the child's
face that it was impossible to think of innocence and unworldliness
and naiveté. She looked as if she knew far too much and the effect
was visceral and unsettling, like a slap to the cheek.

D'Arcy started at the sound of a throat clearing. 'You look lost
in another world. I wasn't sure whether to disturb you,' Josh said,
leaning in the doorway, having made a concession to the weather by
rolling up the sleeves of his shirt, which perfectly matched his eyes.

And D'Arcy ruefully conceded that it hadn't been the wine or
the ambience of the evening before; he *was* a very sexy man and her
eyes couldn't help but be drawn to the lips that had kissed her. He,
on the other hand, was having a hard time looking at her and at first
D'Arcy thought he was being a dick again, pretending they'd shared
nothing more than a meal. Then, with a sudden flash of insight, she
wondered if, despite the air of confidence and coolness in his business dealings, he might be a little shy.

She held out the picture to see what he would do: remain in the
doorway where he had the upper hand, or come closer, where she
suspected he might feel decidedly less comfortable. He chose a position halfway, stopping to pour himself some water.

'I've only ever seen this reproduced in books,' she said of the
shot she was holding. 'It was powerful even then. But holding it
is,' she hesitated, 'violent almost. The girl's stare is so forceful
even though you know she had no intention of it being so. It's like
everything she's thinking is just there, and you catch a glimpse of

it, then it slips away.' She smiled. 'There I go being the lecturer again. I just mean that I almost don't want to pack this one. It's like the picture of the child we found last night.' She stopped. 'It's like the picture of the child we found last night,' she said again.

She stared at Josh, certain he'd think she was drawing a bow so long it would stretch all the way back to Sydney. She'd dismissed the thought last night as foolish, the effect of sitting in an attic near midnight drinking cognac and discussing the mysteries of the past. But now, in the light of day, she couldn't shake it. And nobody knew what had happened to Jessica May. So it was possible. 'Maybe your photographer has Jessica May's photographs because she *is* Jessica May.'

Josh nodded. 'I wondered that too. I spent hours googling her last night. I'd hardly heard of Jessica May, which seems crazy because her work is outstanding. I can't believe she was forgotten after the war, that everyone uses one of her photos but nobody remembers who took it.'

'Exactly!' D'Arcy cried. 'And she wasn't the only one. Which is why —'

'You wanted to make the documentary.' Josh finished her sentence for her. 'I wish you could find a way to do it. It's worth making.'

'Thanks,' D'Arcy said, touched by his understanding.

'And you're right,' he said. 'The photos are similar. But only if you're looking for similarities. Here.' He handed her an envelope, in which she saw negatives, square and oversized, that must have been taken on an old Rolleiflex camera.

'There's a lightbox in there.' Josh pointed to the salon.

D'Arcy walked through, snapping on the light, bending down with the loupe, scanning each one. They were all of the same man — Dan Hallworth — in US Army uniform. A couple more of the girl, Victorine, including some at what looked like a picnic, a stream of water behind her, as well as a peculiarly twisted tree, like the ones painted into the panels in the room. A tree that looked as if it were reaching out to D'Arcy, pleading to her. She stepped back from the lightbox.

'If you googled her,' she said suddenly, to cover her attack of the heebie-jeebies, 'then you must know if it *is* her. You would have seen pictures of her on the net. I know she's sixty years older now but if she is Jessica May, she must look similar.'

'She said she'd see you,' Josh said, not answering her question. 'But she's my client, D'Arcy. I have to look out for her. If you ask her something and she doesn't want to answer, you can't push her, okay?'

'You know, don't you?' D'Arcy felt a shiver prickle her skin, a mixture of both excitement and fear.

'It's not my place to tell you.'

'I think you might be the only man in the world who'd put his client's interests over making one of the biggest discoveries in the art world for years.'

Josh started to speak but she held up her hand. 'I meant it as a compliment,' she said. 'I can see why she has you as her agent.'

He studied her face. 'Are you going to ask her about your mother too?'

'Of course,' D'Arcy said breezily, as if that were of small concern in the light of the other revelation that might be made.

'She has a sitting room up there. Second door on the left.'

D'Arcy ascended the staircase, one half of her brain buzzing. What if the photographer really was Jessica May? What would D'Arcy do with that knowledge? Quiz her on the thinking behind every photograph from 1943 through to the present day at the very least. Ask her why she'd chosen to vanish. Tell her that the world needed to know she was still alive, needed to remember work that was so very important when it was taken, and was still important now, not just artistically, but in jolting the memory of a world that seemed too ready to fight at any provocation. The Photographer was a renowned artist; Jessica May could, once again, be similarly acclaimed.

D'Arcy stopped before the door to settle herself before she knocked, knowing it was most likely she would say none of that. Instead, she would probably stare open-mouthed and be too awed to speak. If it were true.

'Entrez!' a voice that was lighter and clearer than D'Arcy expected called out.

D'Arcy pushed open the door and came face to face with a woman who still held the trappings of a beautiful face in the cheekbones, only slightly attenuated by the lines age had etched into them, and in the large brown eyes. The woman smiled at D'Arcy from her chair, a warm smile, one that belonged in this place of beauty and exuberance.

'Thank you for taking such good care of my work,' the woman said in the voice that wasn't at all blurred or slowed by age. 'I'm sorry you expected more of it to have been packed. We did get someone in to begin the process but I found I couldn't trust him to handle it the way I prefer. By all accounts, you're doing a vastly better job.'

'Thank you,' D'Arcy said. 'It honestly doesn't feel much like work. Being so close to your photographs is what every art historian dreams of. I've been fed extremely well. The chateau is magnificent. And Josh has been very . . .' she felt herself blush a little, '. . . kind.'

The photographer nodded and D'Arcy noticed another smile settle on her lips. 'He is kind. People don't think so because he seems like such a serious person but sometimes you just have to be patient with people and let them reveal themselves to you. The same way you wouldn't rush past a photograph in an exhibition; you'd take time to consider it and study it from every angle before you made a decision.'

D'Arcy didn't know what to say in response. Was the photographer asking her to take her time before she did anything rash? Or saying that Josh was worthy of time? It didn't matter though; D'Arcy didn't have time because she was leaving at the end of next week. 'Josh said I could come to see you,' she said instead.

The photographer nodded. 'I want to photograph you.' She said it as if that were the subject of their meeting. 'I thought I needed to do it formally. But I've changed my mind. I might take some shots of you every now and again when you're working, or in the garden. If you don't mind.'

'But why . . . ?' D'Arcy began.

'Call it a whim. A beautiful young woman who's at the age when she has the whole world ahead of her, when the decisions she makes will either be the best or hardest to live with in the years to come.'

The words settled on D'Arcy like a fur coat in summer. 'That sounds ominous.'

'Only if you make the wrong decisions.'

'Did you?' D'Arcy couldn't stop herself asking.

The photographer nodded. 'They were both the worst and best decisions I could have made.'

It was the moment to ask. And the words came out in a rush. 'Are you Jessica May? The *Children* series has definite echoes of her work and –'

'I have an attic full of Jessica May's photographs. Of course I'm Jessica May.' She said it as though it had never been in question. 'But you can call me Jess.'

D'Arcy gaped, just as she'd worried she might, but it was more at the casual way the revelation had been disclosed. After taking so much trouble for so many years to hide who she was, Jessica May was, in just a couple of offhand sentences, giving up the secret of the photographer's identity. 'Wow,' D'Arcy managed at last. She shook her head. 'Sorry, it's just . . . incredible.'

'I doubt that many people would care. Not anymore.' The photographer – Jess – pulled herself out of her chair, gripping the arms for support, and walked carefully over to the window.

'Are you kidding? Of course people will care. *I* care.'

'That's very sweet of you.'

She spoke as if D'Arcy were being polite, or doing her a favour. Not as if D'Arcy was reacting with genuine excitement about meeting a woman who was a hero of the art world, if the art world could ever be thought of as having heroes. 'But why me?' D'Arcy blurted. 'And why now? Why would you choose a complete stranger to tell that to?'

'I told Josh this morning too. Of course, he'd worked it out for himself after a night spent searching for photographs of Jessica May in the 1940s.'

It was not an explanation, not at all. And there was still the question of the Victorine Hallworth in the photograph. So D'Arcy tried again. 'I don't understand why you would hide it. But there was also, among your war photographs —'

Jess interrupted. 'Yes, Josh tells me you know quite a bit about my war work. That you have an interest in it, even. He mentioned a documentary that you wanted to make.'

D'Arcy would kill Josh when she went downstairs. As if Jessica May would have any interest in D'Arcy's childish attempts at film-making. 'I can't make it now,' she said dismissively, as if it didn't matter. 'I didn't get the fellowship that I wanted. It was a fellowship named after you, actually. Another in a series of very strange coincidences.'

This time, D'Arcy waited for Jess to say something about Victorine: *I once knew your mother . . .* But she didn't. She appraised D'Arcy instead, as if weighing her up, seeing what she was made of. What would she find? Little of substance. Air, whimsy, fluff. All things light and fleeting.

And D'Arcy didn't know what came over her in that moment, a foolish desire to prove herself, to show Jessica May, photographer extraordinaire, that D'Arcy was worthy of the confidence she'd been gifted. 'Can I . . . can I . . .' D'Arcy almost clamped her mouth shut — Josh would kill *her* this time — but out it came. 'Can I film you? Even though the fellowship people didn't think so, I actually can make documentaries; I can give you my résumé if you like. My degree is

in art and media; media because of my mother, art because of me.
I took every unit in filmmaking that I could at uni and I used to
crew on documentaries occasionally and I loved it. I haven't made a
documentary for a very long time but I'd like to make one of you.
If you'll let me.'

D'Arcy expected the woman in front of her to laugh. How preposterous was it that D'Arcy, an amateur, would suggest making a
documentary about a woman who would have film crews the world
over salivating at the prospect? She'd done no research, no planning,
would be extremely limited by the little equipment she had with her
for sound and production quality. 'I'd love to ask you questions, to
tell your story,' D'Arcy finished falteringly. 'I bet it's worth telling.'

'It would mean revealing to the world who I am. I've rather
liked being someone else for the past sixty years.' Jess turned to face
D'Arcy, the expression on her face indecipherable.

D'Arcy almost smacked her palm to her forehead. Why did she
speak before thinking through all the issues? All she'd been focused
on was the filming and the putting together of a narrative. Not on
what would happen to it after she'd finished. 'I don't have to show it
to anyone if you'd prefer . . .' Her voice trailed lamely away. Then she
shook her head. 'This . . .' she waved her arm around to signify the
chateau and Jess's work and the larger truth of who Jess was '. . . and
you are extraordinary. *Why* wouldn't you want to tell everyone?'

There was a long silence, the buzz and hum of the garden below
them the only sound in the room. Jess eventually spoke. 'There are
some people I should speak to first.' Then Jessica May turned a smile
towards D'Arcy that was striking, but it also held a kind of sadness
that made D'Arcy move suddenly to her side and touch her hand. 'I
suppose I can't very well expect to photograph you if I won't return
the favour,' Jess finished, then she waited as if she expected D'Arcy
to say something, but D'Arcy didn't speak.

'You're supposed to say, *Oh, you don't have to if you'd rather not,*' Jess
said, smiling more naturally this time. 'But I can tell that you don't

do false politeness. So yes, you can film a documentary. But, as I said, there are others I would need to talk to before you could show it to anyone. Would you give me some time?'

'Of course.' D'Arcy grinned at last and tried not to bounce up and down like a child. 'If I say this is the most exciting thing that's ever happened to me would you think I was completely ridiculous?'

Jess laughed. 'I would be very flattered. Thank you for coming to see me. If you do notice me around with my camera, try to ignore me. And come back when you want to interview me. You have free rein to film anything you choose in the meantime.'

She was dismissed. Which was just as well because she wasn't sure how much longer she could be so demure in the face of something so incredible. As D'Arcy walked out of the room, her eye caught a photograph propped on a table, directly in Jess's line of sight. Two people, the moment before they kissed, love for one another caught as recognisably on their faces as the fact that they had eyelashes or noses. It was an imperfect photograph of an intensely private moment, real beyond anything D'Arcy had ever seen in all of the posed and photoshopped and cropped pictures that dominated contemporary life. It was the kind of picture that made D'Arcy want to reach into the frame and extract the two people so that they could have the kiss the photographer had forever prevented them from sharing. At the same time, she wanted the draught from the door to tip the frame over so it would fall face down and D'Arcy would no longer be able to see it – the man was the same one from the photograph with Victorine. Dan Hallworth. And the woman was Jessica May.

D'Arcy walked back down the stairs slowly, exhilaration flooding out of her like a waterfall. There, in front of her eyes, where there had been the photograph of moments before, was the question Jess had so carefully not answered: why, after all this time, would Jessica May reveal herself to D'Arcy? And the realisation – that D'Arcy hadn't actually asked about Victorine – carried like deceit in her stomach.

D'Arcy stopped walking and held on to the banister. There was something linking D'Arcy to Jess, a link that began in that photograph of D'Arcy's mother and continued on to Dan Hallworth. She knew it as surely as she knew that Jessica had somehow bewitched her – with discussions about being photographed, with permission to film documentaries – into not asking about Victorine. And she also knew that her mother had once had a black-and-white photograph on her dresser of a woman wearing a khaki uniform, arms heaped with flowers, the city of Paris just discernible in the background. The photograph had mysteriously vanished one day after D'Arcy had asked her mother about it but D'Arcy now knew that the woman sitting atop Victorine's dresser had been Jessica May.

D'Arcy felt as if she were being lured little by little into a forest, as if a trail had been laid for her the moment she stepped foot into the chateau and she could do nothing but continue inexorably on into the gloaming. It was impossible for her to see the image of Dan Hallworth and Victorine Hallworth embracing as depicting anything other than the closeness of a father and daughter. And the photograph on Jess's dresser showed that same Dan Hallworth with Jessica May, both clearly in love. Were they Victorine's parents? And why would Victorine have kept it a secret, why would she have become so estranged from her own parents?

D'Arcy shivered and opened her eyes. She would work some more, and she would think. And then she would make a decision, one way or another, about what, if anything, she should ask her mother.

Seventeen

Working and thinking consisted of not doing any actual work or any thinking at all. Instead, she studied the *Children* series once more until Josh walked outside and caught her. It was the first time she'd seen him since her meeting with Jess and she didn't know what to say. So she prevaricated. 'I suppose I should apologise for slacking off,' she said, 'but I could honestly sit and look at these all day and continue to find something new. Aren't you ever tempted to do that?'

He came to stand beside her, eyes resting on the photographs. 'I guess I've made the mistake of taking this all for granted,' he said. 'Of getting the business done because the emails and the phone calls always seem to be the most urgent. I can't honestly remember the last time I stopped to look at any of the pictures for more than a minute.'

'You know that's sacrilege and therefore punishable by having to spend the whole of tomorrow in a T-shirt and shorts instead of a business shirt and trousers,' she teased, trying to lighten the load she felt pressing on her heart from her conversation with Jess. 'Or do you not own anything else?'

'I'm pretty sure that sawing wood while wearing a dress like yours isn't exactly normal,' he said, his tone a statement rather than a jest.

'So I'm not sure that my wardrobe choices should be the only ones coming under scrutiny.'

'Oh, this old thing?' she said, flipping the skirt a little to show off more of the amazing polka-dot petticoats underneath. 'It's at least fifty years old so if it hasn't given up the ghost by now, I don't think a little sawing is going to harm it.'

But it wasn't Josh's style to let her get away with flirty evasions. 'So,' he said. And she knew he meant: *So, you know that the photographer is Jessica May.*

'So,' she repeated.

Then Célie appeared with a picnic basket. 'Everything you need should be in here,' she said, smiling at Josh.

'Who are you picnicking with?' D'Arcy asked, voice light as if she didn't care. Maybe he had a girlfriend? Someone coming to the chateau to picnic with him and spend the night. It would be the most romantic place to spend a dirty weekend. No wonder he hadn't wanted to kiss her. D'Arcy felt her heart twist with what she was almost sure, even though she'd never felt it before, was jealousy.

'I'm picnicking with you, I hope,' he said. 'Unless you'd prefer to saw. I'll even get changed.' He actually smiled.

D'Arcy's stomach contracted in response.

~

D'Arcy agreed to meet Josh in half an hour, which gave her enough time to find a hat from Célie and send her mother a text to say she was busy and would call later. Because she still had no idea what to ask her, what to say. Staring at photographs all morning hadn't made anything any clearer.

When she met Josh downstairs, he was indeed much more casually dressed. 'There's a nice spot close to the canal,' he said to her. 'It's only a short walk.'

'I feel like a child skipping school,' she said as they started out on the gravel path. 'As if someone from the museum is going to ring at any moment and catch me sipping wine under a chestnut tree rather than crating fragile photographs and talking to customs agents.'

'They'll be asleep. Besides, it's siesta time. We'll work late tonight.'

Work. What if he was just being polite, would rather be writing up contracts but felt as if he had to show the Australian art handler around and be hospitable? 'We don't have to picnic if you're busy,' she said.

'I know. I never do things I don't want to do,' he said.

D'Arcy couldn't resist. 'Including having sex with women in mini-dresses when they throw themselves at you?'

Her reward was a laugh, like the one she'd heard the first day when she'd called him dashing. 'Do you have a single shy bone in your body?' he asked.

'I don't think I do,' D'Arcy replied honestly as they passed a row of Judas trees in lavishly pink flower. The busy sound of woodpeckers contrasted with the lazy circling of a lone hawk, and the brusque quacking of distant ducks. The air smelled better than the Buly 1803 shop ever could, a melange of pollens so heavy and diffuse it was impossible to separate the individual scents, more dangerously heady than cognac at midnight. They passed an elfin tree, dressed in a canopy of green as rounded as a crinoline skirt, but beneath the foliage D'Arcy could see the crone-like branches whorling and winding into grotesquely beautiful shapes.

'What are those?' she asked, recognising that the panels in the salon and the tree in the negative they'd looked at that morning were of the same type.

'Les Faux de Verzy,' Josh replied. 'Part of a forest of dwarf beech trees. Nobody really knows why they've grown like that. Some people say it's witchcraft or magic.' He shrugged as if he didn't believe it.

D'Arcy found she couldn't tear her eyes away from the tree. She had that same sense that it was beckoning her closer, as if it had a secret to tell her, should she chance to seek shelter beneath its draped and elegant boughs. What was happening to her? Her imagination was soaring more spectacularly than the hawk above, conjuring spells and fairytales and hexed trees when all there was before her was a chateau with a magical name, a man with a picnic basket, an old woman with photographs and her mother with — what? Lies?

D'Arcy talked on as if her words might break the enchantment she felt encircling her. 'It's my mother's fault I'm not shy,' she said. 'She taught me to question everything, to say what I thought because sometimes, if you didn't, people died. I know that sounds like a brutal lesson for a child but she'd talk about the way the Germans and even some of the French people had never said anything about what was happening during the war but that if every voice had spoken aloud, perhaps it would have ended sooner, or with a lower body count. She believed holding back was a dangerous thing that could end in sadness. Which obviously doesn't tally with your personal code of conduct,' she finished lightly.

'Hey, I invited you to a picnic. That was daring.'

'My God, what might you do by the end of the day? Hold my hand?'

She felt the brush of warm skin against her fingers as he threaded his hand into hers.

'I'm living dangerously,' he grinned, no longer inscrutable but exceptionally charming.

D'Arcy's insides flipped with joy at making him both laugh and smile in the space of two minutes.

When they reached the waterside and he let go of her hand to lay out the food, she found that she missed his touch. She wandered over to the canal, stopping at a cluster of deliciously cool and viridescent ferns beneath the regiment of plane trees lining the banks. It was hot, the sun burning down, but the shade beneath the foliage was lovely. She realised she was standing beside another of those strange dwarf trees but that this time, rather than coaxing her, its graceful arms were merely extending an invitation that she could ignore should she wish.

So she shucked off her shoes, lifted her skirts a little and waded into the water, revelling in the chill against her legs. She stood still for a few minutes, before tossing her hat onto the bank and turning her face up to the sun, her body softening in the warmth, as if she could so easily bleed into this place and never leave.

It shocked her a little, this sense of how simple it would be to allow her feet to sink into the mud like the roots of water lilies and remain there. Never before in her twenty-nine years had she felt any kind of urge for permanency or stability. After university in Paris and her stint at the gallery there, she'd travelled through Europe for two years, living off her wits, travel articles that she sent back to an editor of her mother's magazines, and occasional poorly paid stints on low budget arthouse films. She'd taken a dogsbody job over summer to show tourist groups through an art museum in Rome and had an affair with a much older Italian art handler, which had given her the idea that art handling would be the perfect job for somebody like her.

When her money had run out, she'd returned to Australia. She took up a position as an art consultant for a new hotel chain that wanted art to be its point of difference, then hopped to an art auction house, which brought her into contact with galleries, before finally landing an assistant curatorship. After a year, they trusted her enough to start doing the art handling. After another year in a permanent role combining curating and handling, she quit to freelance. Sometimes she had to worry for a day or two about where her next pay cheque might come from but she'd always been able to fill any gaps between art handling or curating contracts with freelance writing. It meant she could take off to Europe whenever she wanted and she was beholden to no one. She loved waking up every morning knowing she could do whatever she wanted.

Just as she loved standing in the river right now, and she knew it was only because she'd pursued freedom with such zeal that she was here in France, in bliss. An art handler or curator with a permanent position at a gallery would have to rush back, whereas she could enjoy the sunshine.

Her eyes snapped open with the sudden, curious sensation that someone was watching her and she whirled around. Nobody was there. But the *faux* – the eccentric trees – around her now appeared to be impenetrable, as if they were cradling something precious beneath their canopies.

A minute later, Josh appeared.

'I bet you've never waded in the canal,' she called out.

'You're right,' he said.

She bent down and scooped up a palmful of water, which she flicked at him. 'You said you were being a daredevil . . .'

He was in the water before she could finish her sentence, scooping up an even larger handful of water and pouring it down her back.

She gasped and let go of her skirt, which tumbled into the water. She looked down at it ruefully. 'Luckily it's a warm day so I won't have to take it off and drape it over a bush to dry.'

He actually laughed. 'That *is* lucky,' he said dryly. Then he put his hands lightly on her waist and spun her around to face the bank, propelling her forwards. 'Besides, wearing a damp dress will cool you down, which it sounds like you need. Let's eat.'

She followed him over to the picnic blanket, where she found herself speechless.

Champagne bubbled in glasses. Baguettes piled high with brie sat beside fresh tomatoes and greens so crisp they looked as if they had just walked out of the garden. A bowl of imperfectly shaped berries shone red and purple. A plate filled with luscious chocolate tarts, macarons, palmiers and slices of cherry clafoutis sat in the centre of it all.

'If this is what you do when you're not trying to seduce someone, then I don't think you should ever show me what you do when you *are* trying to get someone into your bed. I don't think I'd survive,' she said, sinking onto the rug.

'See, that's why I said no last night. I didn't think you'd be up to it.'

The laugh bubbled out of her like the champagne. 'I would call that flirting,' she replied. 'Which isn't allowed during business hours.'

'But proposing to remove your dress is perfectly suitable for business hours.' He sat on the blanket and she liked the way the sun fell on his face out here; she could see now that he was teasing, even though his voice was deadpan.

'I was being practical, not flirty,' she said. 'Do you think it's bad if I start with a chocolate tart?' Before he could answer, she picked one up and bit into it. 'That is *so* good,' she said through a mouthful of chocolate. 'How can you not want to spend every day here just eating? No wonder you run. If I keep eating like this, I'll need to run all the way back to Australia.'

He smiled. 'Running means I get to spend time in the gardens. I hardly ever go outside when I'm in Paris.' He picked up a chocolate tart too and she smiled back.

Then he said, wonder in his voice, the same wonder she knew was inside her too, buried below all the questions, 'So she *is* Jessica May.'

'I'm glad you're impressed,' she said. 'That I'm not the only one who thinks she was a real artist.'

'I read a lot of stuff about her last night and today, filling in the gaps around what you'd said. I always knew she was a formidable woman but I had no idea just how formidable, and why. Ask anyone if they could name any photographers from the war and they might say Robert Capa. Joe Rosenthal, perhaps, although he's more known for that one photograph than a body of work. But she should be one of the names people remember.'

'She should.' D'Arcy felt another moment of affinity settle between them and it made her feel that she could ask: 'Before all this, who did she tell you she was?'

'She always told me that anonymity was something she prized more than fame or money. And the way she said it . . .' He paused. 'She sounded almost desperate, as if she would sacrifice anything and everything for the right to remain unidentified. It, I don't know, touched me, I guess. It was a condition of me becoming her agent that I never try to discover anything about her. And because of the way she'd made me feel when she asked, I never did. To do so would have been akin to killing her. Which sounds overly dramatic but . . .' He shrugged.

'If there's one thing I've learned about you over the past twenty-four hours, it's that you're not prone to dramatics. She chose her agent well. I don't know too many others who would never even have one sneaky google to see what they could find.' D'Arcy caught his eye and saw the integrity that Jess must also have recognised. It was tempting to end the conversation on that amicable note but there was still the most important question hanging over them as weightily as the draped tree branches around them. 'Do you know why she's chosen to tell you now? And why she's chosen to tell me? I tried to ask her but I didn't get very far.'

'All she said was that it's time. She reminded me how old she is, which I always like to ignore because as well as being my client, she's someone I respect and look forward to seeing each week. It's hard to imagine that she might, one day soon, not be here anymore.' He sighed. 'Now I'm turning the picnic into something maudlin.'

D'Arcy reached out for his hand. 'You know, most agents in your position would be crowing over the fact that their client had such a newsworthy backstory, not worrying about them dying.'

'She's too precious to throw to the publicity wolves,' he said quietly.

'She is.' D'Arcy paused, then said, 'Of all the women who might end up alone and reclusive, it's hard to imagine Jessica May as one of them. I mean, she was a model; she was stunning. But she was obviously smart too. Her journalism is excellent and her photographs extraordinary. Why would she vanish from the world? Why wouldn't someone fall in love with her and share this place with her?'

'Did you ask her about the photograph of Victorine and Dan Hallworth? It's not the Dan Hallworth who owns World Media Group, is it?'

'I'm not sure.' D'Arcy let go of Josh's hand and chose a baguette. She bit into it, chewed and swallowed before she replied. 'He's the only Dan Hallworth I know of. My mother runs the Asia-Pacific arm of World Media out of Sydney. Everyone always teases her about having the same surname as the man who owns the business and she always laughs in response like it's a joke. But what if it isn't? What if she actually *is* related to him? Why would she never tell me that?'

'Didn't want to be accused of nepotism?' Josh guessed.

'It's a fairly dramatic way to avoid accusations of nepotism: not even telling me about my – what, grandfather? I suppose the connection mightn't be that immediate; perhaps he could be a great-uncle or distant relation but the way they were holding one another in that photograph . . .' The words tumbled out, unstoppable because it wasn't just her imagination or the lure of the trees or the captivating smile of Jessica May. It was near fact, written in black ink on a set of old photographs.

'I've lived my whole life thinking my only relation is my mother.' D'Arcy studied her baguette as she spoke. 'But don't you think it's much too coincidental that, when I'm here, I happen to find a box of photographs containing a picture of a woman with the same name as my mother, and a man with the same name as her boss? I keep trying to tell myself that there are probably lots of Dan Hallworths in the world, that the one in the photograph is not the same one my mother works for. But I'm not sure I've convinced myself. And the only mystery I've managed to solve is one that's the least important to me personally – although it's the most significant to you and the rest of the world.'

D'Arcy put the baguette down, lay on her back and closed her eyes before she offered up her next confession, one she was sure, as Jess's agent, he'd be unhappy about. 'Jess wants to photograph me. Does she ordinarily photograph visitors to the chateau?'

'Never,' he said flatly.

'Isn't that a little strange, then? Compared to everything else she's photographed, I'm hardly a worthy subject.'

'You're beautiful, D'Arcy.'

She rolled her head to the side to look at him and, as she did so, he stretched out a finger and traced a line from her forehead down to her cheek and then to her jaw. 'So beautiful,' he repeated, bending his head to kiss her, not softly or gently but hungrily and exactly like she'd wanted him to kiss her the night before.

He lay beside her, and she rolled into him, thanking God she'd asked him to wear a T-shirt because she could feel his body all the better beneath the soft fabric. She concentrated on the feel of his mouth on hers, on his hand slowly moving away from her face and lightly caressing the bare skin of her neck, the tops of her shoulders, sliding the strap of her dress down a little, his palm splayed against her collarbones.

She tried her hardest not to do anything that might scare him away, felt her breath coming fast against his hand, tried to tell him with her lips pressing against his that she wanted him to slide his hand down further. The waiting was like torture and restraint almost impossible so, before long, her fingers crept up slowly beneath his T-shirt and she heard herself sigh as her hands met the bare skin of his back. She bent her leg to move into him even more closely and was both surprised and entranced to feel him tighten his hold and shift his weight.

Her breath caught and held and she almost forgot to return his kisses when his hand began at last to move down her side. He reached her hip and she reminded herself to breathe until he whispered against her lips, 'You've gone awfully still. Are you okay?' to which she replied, 'Okay isn't quite the word I would use.'

She felt him smile against her lips and that, somehow, was the most sensual moment of all. He kissed her jawline and her neck, paying special attention to her pulse point, before he drew back his head to look at her.

'As much as I don't want to, I'm going to make myself stop,' he said. 'I'm hoping one day soon we won't stop and you'll maybe see why it was better not to fall straight into bed last night or today.'

D'Arcy reluctantly withdrew her hands from his shirt. Her mind was screaming at her: One *day. I don't have* one *day. I'm only here for two weeks.* But she only said playfully, 'It feels as if you have everything in good working order down there so that can't be why you don't want to.'

He smiled and rolled off her, onto his back, lying next to her, hand reaching out to take hers.

'Will you tell me?' she pushed, wanting to know why this man was so delightfully old-fashioned when it came to sex.

He sighed. 'See, this is where you don't necessarily need to say everything that's on your mind.'

'You don't have to tell me if you don't want to,' she lied. Then she came clean. 'But I'd really like to know. I have no idea if I terrify you or if I turn you on or if I annoy you or . . .'

He kissed her knuckles. 'Definitely the first two. Occasionally the third.'

D'Arcy felt a pang of something unfamiliar – something like tenderness – at his words, which confirmed her suspicion that he was a little shy. That she was his polar opposite. But that he was still here anyway. So she waited, not wanting to press him again, hoping he would trust her enough with whatever he wanted to say.

'Basically I used to be an asshole,' he said eventually. 'It started at college and got worse when I was a lawyer; associates fresh out of university work hard, play hard and drink hard, and I was one of that pack. It was too easy for all of us to get girls; we had money and prestige and so one-night stands became a way of life. I never dated anyone properly and I was an arrogant prick. I hated myself for it but it became like this horrific game that I was trapped in. I didn't know what I'd be if I didn't keep doing it. Until . . .'

He stopped and D'Arcy very carefully made herself stare at the sky and not look at him because she sensed it was hard enough for him to say all of this, let alone with her gawping at him while he did. 'I'm listening,' she said quietly, squeezing his hand a little tighter.

'Until one of the girls went a little crazy. Which I deserved. I always used to go back to their houses; I never wanted anyone to know where I lived. I never gave out my phone number. But I told them all I was a lawyer because it was impressive and one girl tracked me down to the law firm where I worked and she turned up there. I spoke to her harshly; it was inappropriate of her to come to my workplace but I hadn't been a saint so I could hardly blame her for behaving likewise. She turned up every day for a fortnight until I got one of the secretaries to catch the elevator down with me to where the girl was waiting and I kissed the secretary right in front of her. The next day the girl slashed her wrists in reception.'

What to say to that? Nothing. She rolled onto her side and laid her head against his chest.

He played absently with her hair. 'I was lucky she didn't cut deep enough to do any serious damage. But I quit law. I realised that I was characterless; all I had to say for myself since leaving college was that I was a lawyer who'd slept around. There was nothing more to me than that. I hadn't looked at a painting in years and had all but forgotten having studied art. So I came to Europe and travelled and gorged on art like I'd always promised myself I'd do but had never made time for. I went back to New York after a year, once I'd real-ised that, while I was to blame, it wasn't totally my fault. I talked my way into a job with the agency. They wanted someone who could do the contracts with galleries and all the legal stuff, not necessarily someone who would find work for their clients. And, ever since, I've tried to live a slower life where I appreciate things a little bit more. But I've realised this week that I haven't been especially good at that lately; too busy with the office. Like I said, I haven't even stopped to look at the art on the walls in there for months.'

She knew as he finished speaking that the man he'd told her about was someone completely removed from who he was now – other than the consequences had made him an unusual and, she had to admit, rather beguiling man. 'Thank you for telling me. I'll stop behaving like a teenager who's just discovered sex,' she said apologetically.

He propped himself on his elbow so he could look at her. 'You shouldn't change anything. You're candid and unafraid and happy to ask for what you want and that's great. I'm pretty sure I've never talked about sex with anyone as much as I've talked about it with you in just two days.'

It was a gamble, asking the next question. But, as she'd said to Josh, life generally worked better when spiced with a little risk. 'Is that why you're so abrupt on first encounters? Not wanting to lead anyone on? Not wanting to be who you used to be?'

Josh's cheeks pinked. 'Was I abrupt?' He glanced across at her. 'What? You're staring at me.'

It was her turn to laugh. 'I was actually thinking you were rather gorgeous.' He blushed even more and D'Arcy added, 'You were probably no more abrupt than I was tired and grumpy.'

'But we still had the best debate about photography that I've had in ages.'

'We did,' she said, smiling.

'See?' He returned the smile. 'You be you and I'll be me and, I don't know, maybe we'll –'

D'Arcy's phone rang, startling them both. It was her mother. She frowned.

'Your mom?' he asked.

'Yes.'

He reached over and pressed the call answer button for her. 'You should talk to her.' He stood up. 'I'm going back to the house. I'll collect everything when you're finished.'

Just like that he was gone, leaving her to talk to Victorine.

'Hello, darling. I know you're working. But I miss you.'

The familiar voice, a French accent altered only slightly by her years in Australia, the words soaked through with love, made D'Arcy's eyes fill with tears.

'I miss you too,' D'Arcy said. 'I wish you were here with me. You'd love it. You really would. It'd be impossible to have bad memories in a place like this. And, for an added bonus, there's a rather handsome man here too.'

Victorine laughed. 'Don't tell me France's romantic powers are working on my determinedly single daughter? I don't believe it!'

D'Arcy laughed too. 'I said he was handsome, not that I want to marry him.'

'But you don't normally tell me about the handsome men you meet overseas until after the fact, once you're safely home and out of their reach.'

D'Arcy knew her mother was right, but this time she really wanted to talk about Josh. She hesitated, before the words rushed out. 'He's different to anyone I've met. He's . . .' D'Arcy searched for the right word '. . . unhurried. Steady. I don't know; those aren't attributes I'd ordinarily find appealing. In him, they are. But he lives in France. So I'll spend a week or so admiring his looks and then come back to Australia and that will be that.'

'Or you could let yourself see what happens if you stop thinking about the reasons you want it to be impossible.' Her mother's voice was gentle.

Just as she'd told Josh, for her whole life it had only been D'Arcy and her mother; they understood everything the other was thinking and feeling with just a glance. And D'Arcy thought that, right now, her mother was telling her daughter to choose a different life to the one Victorine had chosen, that even though her mother had never seemed interested in taking up anything serious with a man – she dated occasionally and distractedly, she loved her work and her daughter – and she constantly told D'Arcy she was happy, D'Arcy no longer believed her.

D'Arcy knew then that she would take great care with her next words. If Victorine said nothing, D'Arcy would look for more answers without involving her mother. Because it might all be easily explained away, somehow, and she would never do anything to deliberately cause Victorine pain.

'You were so busy before I left that I didn't get a chance to tell you what I was coming to France for,' D'Arcy said slowly. 'The gallery is exhibiting the works of The Photographer. It's the first time they've ever been in Australia and it's such a coup to get them. I'm doing the art handling so I get to touch them. They're amazing. It's the photographer's chateau I'm staying at, *Lieu de Rêves*.' D'Arcy lay back and closed her eyes, sun dancing over her face, expecting Victorine to say – which the picture of her mother picnicking before one of the enchanted trees proved – *I went there when I was a child*.

Complete silence met D'Arcy's words. At last her mother said, 'Sorry, someone just brought in some papers for me to sign. I should go. You're not there much longer, are you?'

'Home next week.'

'Wonderful. I'll see you then.'

As she hung up the phone, D'Arcy's mind circled around her mother's omission. The silence. The rush to get off the phone. Of course she might actually be busy. Why then had she called?

D'Arcy jumped to her feet and began to pace. What were her options? To ask Victorine. But it was clear Victorine was not going to, willingly, reveal anything about her connection to Jess or the chateau. She could always ask Jess directly, but Jess had cut her off that morning when she'd tried and D'Arcy didn't think it was accidental. Besides, if Jess knew everything and D'Arcy knew nothing, it put D'Arcy at the disadvantage of simply having to believe what Jess told her. She didn't know Jess well enough to be able to ascertain if she might omit details or present a biased version of events. If D'Arcy had more information, then she would be better equipped to decide who to ask and what to ask them. Which meant she'd have to find out more from another source. But what source?

A crazy idea started to form, one she hardly knew how to put into practice, but one she felt she had to, nonetheless. She hurried back to the chateau and threw some things into an overnight bag.

She found Josh in his office, talking on the phone, his voice so different to how it had been when he'd told her about his past, now rushed and clipped as if he was under pressure and didn't like it. She waited for him to finish his call, then indicated her bag. 'I need to take the train to Paris.'

He frowned and she hastened to reassure him that she wasn't doing a runner. 'I need to go there just for the night. It means I'll miss a day of work but I'm confident I can catch up. I'll work late tomorrow. I won't miss any deadlines.'

'Why are you going to Paris?' he asked.

'I want to . . .' She hesitated, aware it would sound strange. 'I want to visit the school my mother attended. It's the one place I'll be able to find out more about her childhood.'

And rather than remind her that she was in France to work, not to run off on wild goose chases, Josh just nodded and said, 'I'll give you a ride to the station.'

Eighteen

*A*t her favourite hotel in the Marais that night, D'Arcy opened her web browser and typed: *Victorine Hallworth and Dan Hallworth*.

Everything she expected to find came up. Their jobs, the World Media business, their distinguished reporting and management careers, nothing she didn't already know and nothing proving that there was any kind of connection beyond the fact that Victorine worked for Dan.

Then she typed in the name Jessica May and again found what she expected to find: information about May's shift from model to photographer, mentions of her work as a photojournalist in World War II, the iconic images she'd shot, her mysterious disappearance after the war.

It was only as she scrolled down further, to oblique references and articles that had no bearing on the Jessica May she was interested in, that she found one that caught her attention. It was a piece about women in journalism, and it put forward a theory that a writer reporting on the Nuremberg Trials in 1946, and who had been tipped to win a Pulitzer, was actually Jessica May using a male pseudonym. It was also the year, the article said, that Dan Hallworth won a Pulitzer. The author suggested that May had lost because somebody had found out she was a woman. In its final paragraph, she saw the words: *The night of his Pulitzer win, Dan Hallworth established the Jessica May Foundation, designed to encourage women artists to pursue their calling despite the myriad obstacles.*

Dan Hallworth had established the Jessica May Foundation? D'Arcy heard her surprised 'Oh,' echo through the room. She navigated to the Foundation's website and read through the history of the fellowships. Yes, Dan Hallworth had indeed set up the Foundation in 1946 *in honour of a woman I met in Europe who was lion-hearted.* That short extract from the speech he gave on the night the Foundation was established made her shiver.

It forged yet another link between Dan Hallworth and Jessica May. But the missing link was still Victorine, D'Arcy's mother.

She decided to tackle Dan Hallworth's name alone next, something she'd been delaying out of fear, she knew, of what she might find. His bio details confirmed his war service, which made it seem even more likely that her mother's boss and the man she was embracing in the famous photograph were one and the same.

The rest of the information was less relevant to her search, being only a long list of his newspaper holdings, estimates of his wealth, a précis of his family background, which included marriage to an Englishwoman named Amelia in 1945, a son from that marriage, and a subsequent divorce. She was about to give up when she found a very old and out of copyright biography of America's news-papermen reproduced in full, with an entry on Dan Hallworth. She sat up straight and almost knocked over her coffee cup when she read the information it contained about his family background. It was different to everything else that had been published later. Two children, this one said: a daughter Victorine Hallworth, born 1940 – her mother's birth year – and a son, James Hallworth, born 1946. D'Arcy snapped her laptop shut.

Was it possible that D'Arcy had a grandfather she'd never known?

D'Arcy's preparations for visiting Victorine's boarding school were aided somewhat by the cognac she'd drunk in order to forget what she'd read on the internet. Her eyes were bloodshot from lack of sleep and her skin was much too pale for an Australian who spent so much time outside. It gave her the appearance of someone who was suffering, which was the effect she'd thought she'd wanted, but now that the suffering was real, she wished she could think of another plan. She stepped gingerly, as if her pain were physical, into the most demure things she owned, a black velvet YSL blazer she'd picked up for a steal at a charity shop in Sydney, and a pair of slim black capri trousers. She assembled her face to look distraught, which wasn't all that hard, and then she walked through the doors of the Parisian boarding school her mother had once attended.

'May I help you?' the lady at the front desk asked.

D'Arcy fumbled in her handbag for a tissue, which she dabbed to her nose. 'Excuse me,' she said in a thin voice. 'I'd hoped to be able to get through this without tears but it's become a struggle to get through even an hour without crying.'

The receptionist stepped out from behind the desk and offered her a box of tissues, from which D'Arcy gratefully extracted a handful. 'Please, sit down,' the woman said, ushering D'Arcy to a chair.

Once D'Arcy was seated, she began. 'It's my mother. She ...' D'Arcy had planned to pause here for another dab of the tissue onto her face but she felt a real tear leak from the corner of each eye. Then she told the lie. 'My mother recently ... died.'

The woman mumbled something sympathetic and volunteered to find D'Arcy a glass of water.

D'Arcy shook her head. Then she began to tell the lady about her mother, Victorine Hallworth, who attended the boarding school from a young age and who had been unexpectedly taken from D'Arcy's life. 'We were estranged, you see,' D'Arcy said, her voice strangled with the fear of this ever happening, but how could it not given what Victorine had most likely hidden from her? 'Now I can see that everything I thought about her was wrong.' Another truth amidst the lies. 'I have to make it up to her, or I think I might go mad. Do you understand?'

The woman nodded, clearly far from understanding where this was all going.

'I've been trying to gather as much information about my mother as I can; I want to get to know her properly at last. I want to start at the beginning of her life, from when she was a child, and I hoped that perhaps the school might have records of her time here and that you might let me look over them. It would mean the world to me.'

D'Arcy wasn't sure if her tale was convincing, or her tears, but she found herself being ushered into a quiet meeting room, a couple of folders placed before her, and then she was left in peace to read about her mother's life. She opened the first folder.

On top was a letter, dated early November 1944. It was an enquiry about whether a place could be found at the boarding school for a little girl called Victorine Hallworth. The writer explained that he was fighting with the American army and that he wanted to be sure his daughter would be looked after while he carried out his duties. The name typed at the bottom was, of course, Dan Hallworth. Unarguable proof that the famous photograph of the man embracing the little girl was a photograph of D'Arcy's mother and grandfather.

D'Arcy pushed the folder away. Why was she doing this to herself? She didn't need to know any of this. She'd been perfectly happy, her mother had been perfectly happy, until now. There was no point in ruining that happiness for a search into a past that had happened so long ago it no longer mattered. But what if it did matter? What if D'Arcy wanted a grandfather?

She buried her face in her hands and rubbed her forehead. She was so bloody selfish. Her mother had always been enough, just as she'd told Josh. She didn't *need* a grandfather. And what if Dan Hallworth wasn't the ideal clichéd grandfather: soft and warm and endearingly grey-haired and always losing his glasses. There had to be a reason why Victorine had disowned him.

D'Arcy's hand betrayed her. It crept back to the folder and sifted through the papers. There were several letters from Dan Hallworth to the school, confirming Victorine's placement there in 1944. There was a list of approved visitors for the child, which comprised a few soldiers – privates Sparrow and Jennings – and the name of one woman: Jessica May. But nowhere was there any correspondence from Victorine's mother, nor any mention that Jessica May was the mother.

D'Arcy opened the next folder with a feeling of trepidation. It bore dates later than the first, and would account for Victorine from age ten to sixteen. But there were only copies of school reports, plus more correspondence from Dan Hallworth, this time typed on a letterhead for the *New York Courier* and then World Media Group.

Then one final, catastrophic letter. It looked benign, black letters on white, correspondence from a Parisian hospital. Victorine had had an appendectomy when she was sixteen. D'Arcy almost didn't bother to read past the opening paragraph because what could a record of an operation tell her about her mother?

But the letter said that the child had not complained about the pain in her stomach for several days and that, by the time the pain became so acute it couldn't help but be noticed, Victorine's appendix had perforated, sending infection out into her body. She'd been deathly ill in hospital for weeks, had undergone several operations to clean up the mess, had multiple abscesses from the infection.

It was the penultimate paragraph, before the polite closing, that D'Arcy wished never to have read. It said that the scarring from the subsequent infections had blocked Victorine Hallworth's fallopian tubes so badly that she would be unable to bear children.

Unable to bear children. D'Arcy stood up, the words shuttering before her every time she blinked, like a relentless slideshow. She stared at the wall, eyes stretched open but she saw the words flash there too, filmic and devastating in their scope, casting everything that she had thought to be true into the black and stygian realms of falsehood.

PART FIVE
Jess

When I looked at those photographs, something broke. Some limit had been reached, and not only that of horror; I felt irrevocably grieved, wounded, but a part of my feeling started to tighten; something went dead; something is still crying.

— Susan Sontag

Love is like war: easy to begin but very hard to stop.

— H.L. Mencken

Nineteen

As Jess drove into Bastogne with Martha, they passed tanks that had been torn apart, trucks pulverised into the ground, and lorries dragging trailers with neat stacks of dead bodies that looked, from a distance, like firewood. The siege of Bastogne had lasted for a week and, from what Jess could glean, the siege meant that Dan's division had been encircled and ceaselessly bombed and shelled and shot at by the Germans who had four times the number of soldiers. It meant that the men, against all the odds and sustained only by prayers and a stubborn implacableness of spirit, fought their way out and the Germans fell back and Bastogne, a stew of blood and bodies, surrounded by snow stained pink with the life-force of Americans and Germans alike, was back in Allied hands and the press were allowed to return.

But what were they returning to? *Make sure you come back alive.* Jess had repeated those words to herself every day since the party at the chateau and now she was to find out if they had come true. That was if they ever found the battalion headquarters. When at last they did, Jess's legs almost ceased to function. Because in that building with only two walls and half a roof was Dan, alive. Thank God!

He was standing beside a wall map scribbled with red and blue marks signifying areas of heavy mortar, or panzers, or ferocious small arms fire, and relaying orders on the phone to his men out in the field. She watched him ask a team of engineers to signpost and clear a road studded with mines, heard him say in a soothing voice to someone on a field phone that Company B were on their way in to help, and at last she smiled.

Every man who conferred with Dan did what Dan asked of him willingly. Every man spoke to Dan with respect, even a little hero-worship. *That* was what had kept Bastogne in Allied hands: the leadership of men like Dan, who knew not just how to manoeuvre companies and battalions, but how to make men believe that what they were doing meant something when, all around, the evidence of obliteration suggested otherwise.

Marty waltzed over and kissed his cheeks. 'I know someone who'll be glad to see that you made it,' she said, indicating Jess, who hung back awkwardly, fiddling with her cameras as if they needed her attention, unable to follow Martha's lead and kiss him too even though it was all she wanted to do.

'Sir.' Sparrow appeared from behind them and claimed Dan's attention before he'd had time to offer Jess more than a smile. 'You're needed out there.'

'Coming?' Dan asked Marty and Jess, who both nodded eagerly, knowing they couldn't venture out to the front without someone who knew exactly where the front was and how hot the hotspots were.

'Jess!' Jennings' voice broke into the conversation and Jess turned to find her cheek kissed by the perennially smiling Jennings, wearing new insignia – now adjutant, Dan's administrative assistant.

Jess's eyes met Dan's at last and she knew he'd found a more permanent solution to his personal mission to keep Jennings alive and her heart hurt as if it wasn't quite big enough to contain everything she felt in that moment. Now she wished she had kissed his cheek because Dan deserved at least that much.

'This way, Sir.' Sparrow led the way to the jeep, more serious than Jess had ever seen him, more corporal now than joker – a promotion he'd gained since Bastogne too, as well as landing the job of Dan's driver. Which only served to underscore just how many had died and how lucky Jess was to find these three men had dodged, not just a bullet, but some pretty heavy damn artillery.

'Where are we off to?' Martha asked Jennings as they pulled onto the road, following Dan and Sparrow's jeep.

'Something I thought our CO would want to deal with,' Jennings said quietly.

But how could anyone deal with what they found?

In the forest, surrounded by shell craters, trees splintered like matchsticks or disfigured with bullet holes, and foxholes lined with snow in which men had been living in groups of three of four for warmth for weeks, was an injured man. He'd been lying in the snow for three days after stepping on a mine. He'd been lucky, Jennings said grimly as they drew near; if you stood on a mine in a particular way, it pushed the veins and arteries up into the leg, closing them off somewhat, staunching the bleeding from the severed foot.

'The medics tried to get to him,' Sparrow added as they walked closer, 'but they got shot at every time. The Krauts have pulled back now so we can reach him.'

Jess could see that the injured GI was still, somehow, through losing a foot and lying in the snow between two opposing sides for three days, conscious. His lips were moving. Dan dropped down beside him.

Jess took a picture of Dan, sitting in the snow and lighting a cigarette for the injured man who was telling Dan that he'd been set upon by Germans under cover of darkness on the first night. The Germans had booby-trapped him, rigging up a device under his back that would explode the moment he was lifted up by the medics or someone like Jennings from his platoon, killing them all.

Thank God he was still conscious, Jess thought now. Thank God he'd been able to tell them.

While Dan smoked a cigarette with the man, more the leader right now than he'd ever been as he saluted the courage it had taken to not succumb to blackness in order to save a life or two, while an engineer worked to cut the wires leading to the explosives, all Jess could do was record with her camera, honour this man in black and white for an act that would never win a war, but that meant Jennings' parents or Sparrow's parents or somebody else's parents would still have sons to pray for.

The costly battle of the Ardennes meant that Jess hardly spoke to Dan for the next month. To even want to take his attention away from the things he had to do would be pure selfishness. But, every time she saw him, she remembered the caress of his thumb, which meant that the quick dozen words and smiles they occasionally exchanged weren't enough.

Soon, like every other fight, the Ardennes was over but Dan was with the advance troops as they pushed down to Cologne. Jess and the other correspondents ferried back and forth to Spa from the front each day, a situation that wouldn't change until they'd secured a base in Germany. All the travelling meant even less chance to see Dan, and that she rolled a jeep in the ice, which was a common problem among correspondents in the late winter weather. Dan visited her, fuming, in March at the hospital where she'd been sent to have two broken ribs bandaged.

'Lee Carson rolled four jeeps in a week,' she said to him weakly, trying to smile over her sore ribs.

'I don't give a shit about Lee Carson,' he said. He stepped closer to the bed, furious in a way she'd never seen before.

What had happened to them? Jess almost wished they'd never danced together but at the same time she wished they'd danced for longer, anything to relax the strain that seemed ever present between them now. And she vowed then that she would never ask him about what had happened in the ballroom because it had only made things awkward.

Before she could reply, Lee Carson herself, along with Martha, appeared.

'They told me to tell you they're running out of jeeps,' Marty said, planting a kiss on her cheek.

'Which is more your fault than mine,' Jess said lightly to Lee, who grinned.

Dan didn't smile. Instead he gave everyone a curt goodbye and left, after practically yelling at Jess to be more careful.

'What's up with the gorgeous Lieutenant Colonel?' Lee drawled, helping herself to Jess's cigarettes.

'I don't know,' Jess replied honestly.

By the time Jess was out of hospital, Cologne was secured, and then the Rhine was crossed. After that it was impossible for anyone to enforce the rule of women not going near the front because the front was everywhere. Nobody cared anymore about Martha's lack of accreditation papers; the quality of her reporting for *Collier's*, in spite of the impediments, was all the proof anyone needed. In fact, the women correspondents were encouraged to use the press camps for the first time ever because it was the only way to stay safe. Which meant Jess having to use all her skills to avoid Warren Stone. She was getting better at that though, and he was so busy actually working that he left her alone more often than not.

At the press camp in Schweinfurt, news came in that President Roosevelt was dead. Following in its wake, GIs poured in, wanting to find out if the reports were accurate, wanting just to sit and talk.

Jess walked out of the censor's office after a particularly bruising row with Warren about whether there really were camps all over Germany holding people the Nazis considered undesirable – of course Warren found her belief in the rumours laughable – and saw

Dan standing a few feet away. It was the first time she'd seen him this close since the hospital, and he smiled at her. She walked over to say hello, resisting the urge to wrap her arms around him.

'So it's true,' he said when he saw her face.

She nodded. 'Come and sit down. I'll find some schnapps.'

He raised his eyebrows.

'We drink whatever's available. Calvados in Normandy, champagne in Paris, schnapps in Germany. It's the only thing I miss about Paris.'

Dan laughed and suddenly it felt normal again: Jess and Dan sharing a drink and a joke the way they'd always done. Thank God! She knew her smile was too bright for a day of mourning but she was so relieved to have restored her friendship with Dan that she couldn't wipe it away. She led Dan into the mess where she saw soldiers and correspondents all doing the same thing, drinking and talking, the death of one man like a blow that almost could not be borne.

Jess poured the schnapps and sat across from Dan. 'To Roosevelt,' she said, lifting her glass.

He clinked his glass against hers. 'We've seen so many dead men over the past two years and here we all are, brought to our knees by a death we haven't even seen.'

'I know,' was all she could say, because she did know. War made one irrational; sights that were incomprehensible failed to pierce one's consciousness, yet seemingly small moments became the incidents that must be talked over, that could never be forgotten.

'How are your ribs?' Dan asked. 'And how many more jeeps have you slid off the road?'

'Ribs are fine. And while at least a dozen correspondents have rolled jeeps lately, I haven't been one of them. I used to dream about being killed by a shell; now we all dream of being killed in a jeep accident,' she said wryly. 'It's April though, so that should stop soon.'

'It's not funny, Jess.'

'Nor is watching you walk out of here and not knowing when I'll see you again,' she said quietly. It was close to what she meant but still skated on the edge of friendship.

Dan stretched out his arm, as if he intended to take Jess's hand across the table. But then he stopped as the seats around them began to fill with too many people for privacy.

'Shift over.' Martha, bearing more schnapps, bumped Jess's shoulder and slid in next to her as Lee Carson sat beside Dan.

'It's interesting, isn't it,' Marty said. 'How it's impossible to find any Nazis in Germany. Nobody was ever a Nazi; somebody else was to blame. Amazing that an entire country could have been so ignorant.'

'When will we get to the camps everyone's talking about?' Lee batted her eyelashes at Dan, just as Jess had seen her do at the Hotel Scribe with Major Mayborn.

'Getting your story the usual way, Lee?' Warren Stone jibed as he walked past. 'You're taking lessons from the best, aren't you?' He smiled at Jess as if he'd meant to compliment her.

Dan stood up. 'I'd better get back. Before I punch someone,' he muttered under his breath but Warren had moved on, as always doing enough just to irritate but never enough to justify drawing real fire.

'I'll walk you out.' Jess stood up too and felt Lee's eyes on her, watching her accompany Dan out of the mess. Warren's eyes too, most likely.

And that was the problem. There were eyes and people all around. No possibility of a quiet moment, an actual conversation. Even here, by the entrance, people flowed in and out, nodding at Jess or at Dan or at both.

'Do you think there are camps?' Jess asked as they reached Dan's jeep. 'Some of the correspondents say there aren't and I was just told in no uncertain terms by the delightful Warren Stone that I was being fanciful and I wasn't to report anything on the speculation. But . . .'

Dan sighed. 'I think Warren's wrong. We won't know until we find the first one though.'

'How does a world become so evil?' Jess said, staring out at what she could see of Germany. 'That's why I think people say it can't be true. Because they can't imagine there are worse things. But every time we think that, we find evidence of something worse than the worst possible thing.'

'Do you want to come when we do? You don't have to. Nobody would think any less of you.' Dan's voice was gentle, his eyes like soft fingers stroking her face.

'*I* would think less of me. I already have one piece I'm too scared to write.'

'Your piece about the rapes?'

Jess nodded. 'I keep telling myself it's not the right time, that now, when Germany must surely be close to surrendering, I shouldn't do anything to hurt morale. But what if it means that every week I delay, another woman is raped? Doesn't that make me responsible? Doesn't that make me a coward? I assume it's why the edict about fraternising with the locals came down – because the powers that be have got wind of what's happening too. But how do you square that with the prevailing view – which I've heard is General Patton's own – that fornication without conversation is not fraternisation? So if you club a German woman over the head and make sure she can't speak, then you can do whatever the hell you like to her?'

'You're not a coward, Jess. In fact, you're the bravest woman I know.'

Their eyes locked just like they had on the balcony that night at the chateau; honesty, care and concern all caught there – but something more too, the shadow of what had happened in the ballroom.

'Hey Jess.' Jennings had come to fetch his CO, making Jess and Dan start.

'Goddammit,' Dan said through gritted teeth. 'I have to go. I'm sorry I've been absent. But I'll come and get you if I hear anything about a camp. I promise.'

With that he hopped into the jeep and Jess returned to the mess where she had to field Lee's questions about Dan and avoid Martha's knowing eyes when Jess found that every time she said Dan's name, her cheeks flushed in a manner entirely unlike that of the worldly Jessica May.

Only a night passed before Dan returned to the press camp in the early morning to collect her. Luckily she was up and about and had spotted him pulling in before anyone else asked for a ride too. 'Where are we going?' she asked after she'd raced outside to meet the jeep.

'The scouts came back with a report that nobody can quite reconcile. I think it'll be gruesome,' Dan said soberly.

'Just like the past two years then,' she replied, more lightly than she felt, even as her stomach lurched.

'Yep.'

The passenger seat of the jeep was occupied by Sparrow, who seemed lost in a trance.

'Sparrow was one of the scouts,' Dan said as if that explained it.

But it didn't. Something was up. And she could smell it now as they drove onwards, the scent of anguish in the air, a miasma of ash and marshy earth and salted tears.

'Pull over,' came Sparrow's voice.

Dan drew as close to the shoulder of the road as was safe and Sparrow leapt out, trying for the sake of propriety to make it behind the scrub but instead heaving the contents of his stomach onto the ground not far from the vehicle.

Jess and Dan both jumped out but Dan shook his head at Jess, so she stayed where she was, watching Dan stride over to Sparrow and say, 'I'll take you back.'

And Sparrow, shaking his head and pushing away the hand Dan placed on his back. 'No. If she can stomach it, then so can I.'

Jess's gut contracted again.

After an hour they reached the abyss. At first it seemed almost pleasant, a great square, surrounded by immaculate lawns. Bright red flowers, the colour of love and hope, bloomed from well-kept beds. Two rows of wooden barracks stood on either side of a raked and tended street lined with trees, a road that swept forward grandly in a manner reminiscent of manorial gardens.

But then there was the stench. Not an odour or a smell. A pervasive and choking fetor that had Sparrow leaping from the jeep again, dry retching. Belying the reek and the fortifications, the impression of having chanced upon an estate was reinforced by the large cage of resplendent peacocks, the monkeys swinging on trees, and a parrot coloured like a rainbow screeching 'Mama!'.

Jess almost didn't wait for the jeep to stop before she climbed out and began to shoot pictures of this paradise, knowing this was what she had come here to do. To document the indescribable. The malodour clung to her and she knew that somewhere beyond lay the inferno.

Then Jess saw what looked like human figures, scorched, spread along the barbed wire fence, frozen in poses that indicated they'd been running. Desperate to risk death in order to flee what they'd faced inside the camp walls. But that wasn't where the smell came from. It rose like an inescapable fog from the more than a dozen boxcars to the side of the camp, filled with the remnants of human beings, all dignity taken from them, their lives deemed worthless as they were left in the sun to ebb into the German soil.

For the first time, Jess realised there were degrees of death. That these once human beings were radically and starkly dead in a way that a person in New York who'd been placed carefully in a coffin, dressed, hands folded, awarded a tombstone and flowers, would never be.

Suddenly the women appeared. Or what were once women. These creatures had been pushed beyond the limits of what was human. Cadaverous, some crawling, or not even crawling; dragging their bodies along the ground with the last remnant of strength left in their arms. They were nothing but enormous eyes, bone, nostrils, and open mouths.

A movement above made Jess look up to the watchtower looming over her. The guard inside trained a gun on her. 'We're Americans!' she screamed in German. 'Get the hell out of there!'

She was barely conscious of Dan and the others moving in front of her, weapons ready, of the rest of the jeeps in the convoy drawing up. She kept shooting pictures as Dan shouted at her, 'Move!'

But she didn't.

'Goddammit Jessica! He's got a gun. Move!' Dan yelled again, pushing her behind him.

She was barely conscious of the fact that Dan was so incensed that he'd called her Jessica, barely conscious of the moment the guard in the watchtower dropped his gun and Dan released his iron grip on her arm.

She entered the camp with the men of the United States Army and she knew the moment she caught it that it was the image that would show America what war had become. Not a gallant and heroic jousting for glory but a savage and bestial destruction of humankind.

Her camera foregrounded fat peacocks, plumage bright as a summer sky. The red flowers dancing strong and bright, reaching up to the sun shining above them. And behind that, the women. Tissue-paper skin barely covering bones; it was almost possible to see inside them. And their faces. Bereft of emotion. Dead, but given the sentence of living.

The guard in the tower stood down, as did the handful of other guards left to face the consequences. The skeletal women didn't cry. They barely reacted to Dan and Jennings and Sparrow and the vehicles following behind. Didn't respond to the medics laying them on stretchers; flinched in fact, as if they would rather be left alone. And Jess knew that meant their sufferings were beyond imagining; to wish for the hell they already knew rather than the terror of the unknown was a fear too stark to contemplate.

Jess found a female camp guard who, now that she'd been taken into custody, was willing to tell them everything.

'We had too many women to look after them properly,' the guard said to Jess in German and Jess translated for Dan. 'Each building was meant for five hundred but was filled with more than two thousand. One bunk for four women; they slept head to feet. And every day fifty died but two hundred arrived. What was I supposed to do?'

The guard looked at them as if she expected their pity. Jess blanched but made herself ask, 'Why are the women here?'

'Some are Jews. Most are resisters,' the guard replied and Jess repeated the words to Dan as best she could through a throat tight with tears.

'Every morning the beds were filled with dead bodies,' the guard went on, eager to have it all out now. 'We woke the ones still alive at three in the morning and did the roll call to see how many we had left. It took two hours to call each name and every morning someone would fall or faint or die but even if it happened beside them, the women were not allowed to move. If they did, they would be beaten with the wooden stick.'

They would be beaten. Not: *I would beat them.* The guard had devolved responsibility, just like Martha had said.

Jess moved back outside. General Collins had been to the town on whose doorstep this abomination lay and he'd brought back with him a group of German civilians. He now made them walk through the camp, which they did, staring directly in front, seeing as little as possible. Refusing to bear witness to what had happened right beneath their unseeing gazes.

'The Germans did not do this,' one of the civilians protested. 'Our Führer would not let this happen.'

What was there to say to such ignorance, when the evidence, so much terrible evidence, was right there? General Collins told the civilians they must bury the dead with their own hands. Two thousand bodies. Two thousand forgotten people buried by those who'd ignored their plight, watched over by a company of American soldiers and Jess, trying to find prayers that might bless the unblessed.

How can we pray, Jess wondered, when it is our fault too? We'd heard there were camps. Why were we so slow, so unseeing, so obtuse as to not come straight to these places and free those who needed it most?

Before they left, they learned that the people they'd found were genuinely the living dead. Unable to work or to move. More than twenty thousand women who had still been able to crawl or stumble or trudge had been sent on a death march from the camp before the Americans arrived to free them. They were the vanished, the *Nacht und Nebel* – the Night and Fog – mostly resistance fighters the German army had wished to render invisible. And they'd all but succeeded.

The journey back to headquarters was long and silent.

'I'll sit next to Sparrow,' Jess said when they reached the jeep.

Even though Sparrow hadn't been sick again, he'd withdrawn far inside himself, face pale, smile gone, eyes dull. She took his hand in hers and held it, limp and spiritless.

For the rest of the drive, Jess wondered what she would say to Bel. How she would make her believe that her camera hadn't created the pictures, that she hadn't zoomed in too narrowly or composed the image in such a way that it seemed worse than it actually was. That the savagery was real.

I implore you to believe this, was how she would begin, begging Bel to let the women of the camp speak, to declare to the world that their lives had, after all, not been for nought.

Night had cast a shroud over them well before they reached Dan's HQ. Then it was another long drive back to the press camp, a drive Jess wasn't sure she was up to. She was hugely grateful when Dan said, 'Stay here tonight. There are some female translators and WACs around. I'm sure you can bunk in with them.'

She nodded. 'Thanks.'

They were the only words exchanged. Dan spoke briefly to a woman exiting the mess to secure a bed for Jess. The woman smiled so brightly that Jess wanted to hold up a hand to ward her off. She told Jess to follow her and soon she was found a tent and a bedroll. But she knew she needed to shower. She had to sluice off the smell that clung to her, had to wipe away all the physical remains of the day in a way she could never erase the images and stories from her mind.

As she set off for the ablutions, she heard a strange noise, a rending of the pall of night with a sound that was at once incendiary and keening. She kept walking, flashlight on, until the familiar smell of latrines told her she was going the right way and she found the fabric flaps that screened off a shower.

She pushed open the flaps and the smell assaulted her first: base and foreboding. And then she saw. She dropped the flashlight instinctively, knowing she couldn't face any more brutality.

The sound came as she dropped to her knees – a cry so loud and so long and so excruciating that she thought at first it must have come from the man slumped in the shower stall, gun drowning in the pool of blood at his side, face smashed through by the bullet, but still unmistakable as Sparrow.

Twenty

As dawn touched the sky the morning after Sparrow killed himself, Jess took a jeep, stopped at the press camp to write her story and parcel up her film, and then Marty drove her to Paris. On the way, her mind played ceaselessly over the peacock, the guard, the bodies in the boxcar, the women's eyes, and Sparrow, resplendent in his patriotic dress the night of the party in Reims. Sparrow, his bloodied head in her lap when Dan and a group of others heard her God-awful cries and found her. Dan ordering someone to lift her up and take her away. A glimpse of Dan sitting where she had sat, cradling Sparrow like a brother.

What time I am afraid, I shall trust in Thee. The words, one of many prayers from the *US Army Prayer Book*, words that were supposed to provide comfort to a man like Sparrow when he most needed it, echoed mercilessly in her head. Where had God been when Sparrow had needed him, when he'd made his way to the shower, when he'd felt more frightened of living than of anything else? Jess shut her eyes but the tears pressed mercilessly through her lids.

One day and one unsleeping night back in the Hotel Scribe was enough to convince her that she couldn't go on that way. Marty suggested a party and in her voice Jess heard the same fatigue, the same enervation, the same fracturing sound of a person pushed so close to their breaking point that anything, even a mistimed smile, might cause them to snap.

So a party they would have the following night. She made sure the word was spread out to the hotels used by the GIs – everyone who'd been at the camp had been given several days' leave and most had come to Paris.

When it was time to dress, she dismissed her pinks. She was going to wear a damn normal dress – no Chanel, no Schiaparelli; she refused to wear anyone who'd run from the war. She'd wear the dress she'd been carrying in the bottom of her bag since she'd arrived in Europe, the dress she'd left in London and then in Paris for safekeeping. The dress she'd had Estella Bissette make for her before she'd left America, before she understood that war was not a noun but a wretchedness imprisoned inside a smiling face.

She opened the wardrobe and took it out, running her hand along the skirt out of habit, the black satin pooling in her fingers. She put it on, the white bodice covered with delicate and lovely lace, the scooped back reminding her of the Jessica May in the magazine photos she'd once been, the nipped-in waist underscoring the fact that rations were not enough to subsist on for very long, the skirt dropping like midnight into a long train that would most likely be crushed and torn by the boots of the GIs who came to the party.

She would wear it anyway and she would smile and behind the lipstick she would hide the fact that every night when she lay down, she had to first drink enough whiskey so that the images before her eyes blurred into indistinction.

Hemingway came, along with all the correspondents in Paris. He took up a place on the balcony among the jerry cans of fuel and waited with a bottle of whiskey for everyone to pay homage to him, which Mary Welsh was still doing. Marty rolled her eyes at Hemingway and danced with James Gavin, the divisional commander who'd caught more than her eye. Picasso and Simone de Beauvoir strolled in; Jess's currency as a model and her past relationship with Emile – who'd thankfully given up his accreditation pass and, even though he was now living in Paris, knew well enough not to come – was enough to make sure that if she was having a party, most of one slice of Paris would hear about it and come along.

Then came the GIs, not just from Dan's battalion but others she and Martha had met over the past eighteen months. The tiny room was thick with bodies and she could see that was all part of the appeal, the press of flesh to flesh, a dance and a kiss and who knew where it might lead. Because they all had a reason to seek oblivion, to erase, for just one night, the awful press of knowledge that Allied victories didn't erase the abominable things that had already been done.

To help the mood, the gramophone played French jazz, the lights were off, the room was lit by candles, and Jess had found some vermouth, which she'd used to make a Manhattan; a Manhattan wasn't champagne and it wasn't schnapps and therefore it couldn't remind her of war. But as for everything else . . .

She leaned her back against the door, holding the almost empty Manhattan by the rim, the glass resting against her leg. The door behind her opened suddenly, propelling her forward, knocking the remaining liquid from her glass.

She turned around and saw Dan.

'Oh, it's only you,' he said, then shook his head. 'I didn't mean that the way it sounded. I just meant . . .'

'That you're glad it's not someone who'll make a fuss about being knocked over by a door and having vermouth spilt on her one fine dress.'

'You've never made a fuss about anything even though you've had more cause than most.' There it was, a veiled reference to what they'd seen and he smiled at her but she could see it was an action rather than a sentiment. That he'd forgotten how to be happy.

He joined her, his back against the wall too, staring at Picasso who was asleep in the chair before Jess's typewriter, at Hemingway and his band of admirers, at Jennings slavering over a woman who was equally slavering over him and Jess saw in his desperation that Jennings was no longer the young boy who'd managed to injure himself everywhere except the battlefield; he was now a man with a bruised soul.

'You don't have a drink,' she said to Dan.

'Is it helping?' he asked, nodding at the now empty glass in her hand.

'No.'

'Is any of it helping?' He gestured to the room.

She shook her head, then slipped her hand into his. She didn't expect to find comfort there; knew that comfort was impossible but he squeezed her hand in return and didn't take his eyes off her face. For the smallest fraction of time – a second split in two – they stood with hands clasped, eyes locked, the music scattering crotchets around them, the candles bathing their skin gold.

Then her other hand reached out to run one finger ever so lightly along the line of his jaw, to feel the stubble there, stubble she'd seen most days since she'd been in Europe, stubble she'd never really noticed because everything was about the war and the fighting and the dying. Nothing was ever about them. But this moment was. Two people, hearts flayed by the cruelties they'd seen, stopped in a moment of rare beauty.

He leaned down and whispered in her ear, his breath hot against her skin, 'Can we ask them to leave?'

'Yes,' she said.

She clapped her hands and declared that the party was over, that they should all retire to the bar downstairs so she could get her beauty sleep. Nobody except Martha noticed that Dan didn't leave with the rest of them.

Once the last person had gone and the door was shut, Jess and Dan remained where they were, backs against the wall, hands no longer joined because she'd had to let go of him to kiss everyone goodbye. The candles flickered in the breeze wafting in from the balcony, then Dan turned to her.

This time, it was his finger that reached out and traced a line down her neck, over her right collarbone and then her left. She could hear the sound of her breath, anything but calm now, and saw the pulse in his throat beat faster.

She stepped closer, the air between them alight with everything that hadn't happened since they'd last stood this close together in a ballroom, when he'd told her, with the touch of his thumb, that he wanted her.

'Are you sure about this?' he asked softly.

'Yes,' she said. 'Don't you feel a need to make the pictures stop, just for an hour or two?'

'Yes,' he said too, cupping her cheeks and drawing her in.

And Jess at last kissed Dan.

They kissed and they kissed, his hands sliding up her back, hers wrapped around his neck. After a long and luxurious time in which they both revelled in the sensation of finally doing what they'd wanted to do in the ballroom at *Lieu de Rêves*, Dan moved his lips to her throat, tasting the skin with the tip of his tongue, kissing the hollow between her collarbones, then the sharp points of her shoulders and she could feel the apologies and regrets over everything that hadn't been his fault but that he wished her never to have seen – and him too – over the past two years press into her skin. Her arms tightened.

'We need a bed,' she said and he nodded and took her hand and followed her across the room.

They didn't quite make it to the bed, though, because one of the candles illuminated Dan's face, catching it unarmed and she had to stop and stroke his cheek, to try to, with the tips of her fingers, redraw it into the face of a young man who knew only hopes and dreams and joy. She kept her eyes on him as she unbuttoned his shirt and he smiled at her and this time she saw the emotion that should always accompany the action and she was glad.

Then she let her fingers roam across the hard muscles of his chest, let her lips taste the skin there. She felt his heart beating hard against her mouth, his dog tags shiver, heard the quick gasp of breath as her fingers found the top of his hipbones.

She turned around so he could unfasten her dress. Once he'd done so, he slipped his hands into the open back and ran them down her spine, touching her skin so gently, so lightly that she closed her eyes, adoring the sensation of being held in a reverent way.

At last, he moved the dress over her hips, where it fell to the floor. He brought his hands around to drift over her stomach, travelling up to her breasts in a slow and glorious dance. Finally he touched one nipple and then the other, lingering, touch firmer now, taking his time. Then he began to kiss her neck, her shoulder, the top of her back and she spun around because she couldn't stand it anymore.

Her mouth found his and he moved his hands down to her knickers, slipping them off, before lifting her, legs wrapped around him, and carrying her to the bed where he lay her down.

'You have too many clothes on,' she whispered.

'I can fix that,' he whispered back, shucking everything off.

The candles still shone and she hadn't drawn the drapes so she could see by the moonlight that he was as aroused as she. She reached out for him, wanting him beside her, wanting her hands and mouth on him. She kissed his chest; she could lie there and kiss that chest forever, she thought, but he had other ideas and he slipped a hand between her legs, which made her inhale sharply and say, 'Mmmm, you can do that again.'

He smiled again and he almost sounded like the old Dan when he said, 'Good to see you're as unabashed in bed as you are everywhere else.'

She laughed. 'Would you prefer I didn't tell you what feels good?'

'No. Tell me. Because this is all about feeling good.' His fingers found her breast again.

'Well, perhaps your mouth could follow where your hand is leading,' she said.

'Jess.' He spoke her name in a voice thick with desire and that was it; as if they both agreed they couldn't wait any longer.

She straddled him, sliding him inside her, leaning forward to kiss him and she heard him say her name again, urgently, and then she couldn't think anymore as she moved against him, gasping as a kind of pleasure she'd never known slid through her entire body.

Afterwards, Dan lay on his back, head on the pillow, and Jess lay across the bed, head resting against his chest. He lit two cigarettes, passing one to her. She exhaled blue smoke into the room, which caught the light from the street.

'Doesn't it seem like night-time is too bright in the city now?' she asked. 'I've become so used to blackout curtains and no street-lighting, to the dark of being out in the field, that this feels like some kind of strange eternal day.'

'It's the first time I've been here since the blackout was lifted,' Dan said. 'And last night I couldn't sleep. I couldn't work out why at first. I thought it might be the noise.'

'It's hardly quiet out in the field.'

'I know. It was the light. And you're right; it feels like everything outside is on fire. Or else as if . . .'

'We really are in hell.' She breathed in smoke again, blew out, watching the thin stream sparkle in a way it wouldn't in her quarters in Germany.

'I think we discovered that a long time ago,' Dan whispered.

Neither spoke for a long moment. Jess rolled onto her side, so she could look up at him. 'Talking like this isn't making the pictures stop.'

'It's not.' He reached down and took the butt of her cigarette from her, stubbed it out in the ashtray on the bedside table, then stroked a finger lightly through her hair. 'I know everyone ribs you about your short hair and your predilection for trousers but I have to say that, even though I've always thought you were beautiful, I wasn't expecting to find such an incredible body hiding beneath the uniform.' His finger trailed down to the top of her breast.

'Yours isn't so bad either,' she smiled. 'And you don't need to flatter me. I know half the men have pages from *Vogue* of me in my modelling days. I'm sure you've seen more of my body before today than you're admitting.'

'I never look at that stuff, Jess. From that day in the foxhole in Italy, you became one of us. So, like I said, it's impossible not to see you as beautiful but I saw it in the same way that you know Jennings has freckles. A fact, not a feeling. And I let the men keep their posters because it gives them hope. But you're one of my men. *Were* one of my men,' he corrected himself with a grin. 'Now I don't know what the hell you are.'

She laughed. 'I don't know either.' She propped her elbow on his chest, rested her head in her hand. 'Do you think that we'll ever, once we're back in America after this is all over, be able to forget? Not forget this,' she added, touching his cheek, 'but everything else?'

'It'll fade.' Dan threaded his fingers into hers. 'It might linger for a bit but then, finally, it'll disappear, like cigarette smoke. Everything does.'

'Do you think so? And doesn't Sparrow deserve more than that?'

'He does.'

Neither spoke for a long time. Jess lay her head down again, her ear filled with the sound of Dan's heartbeat, slow and steady and inexorable. She ran her hand along his chest and he curved an arm around her, warm and strong, and little by little, in that tranquil and private moment, she felt her limbs relax and the pictures fade once more.

It was late when they at last fell asleep and early when Jess woke, listening to a Paris that sounded almost the same as the city she'd left in 1939: the elegance of the language rolling up from the streets below, the clatter of chairs placed on the pavements for those who had time to linger over coffee, the occasional horn blasting its way through pedestrians who'd forgotten, over the long years of hardly any cars on the streets, that they now had to cede way.

She stepped lightly out of the bed, smiling at the way Dan looked when sleeping – on his back, one arm flung over his head, black lashes curving upwards from his closed eyes, eminently kissable. Her eyes ran over the dark hair, the line of black stubble along his jaw, the dog tags sitting on the muscles of his chest, which rose and fell as he breathed. She reluctantly moved over to the window, knowing that if she stared at him for longer she'd want to at least kiss him, if not trail her hands over his body. But he deserved to sleep.

Instead she gazed out the window at the people moving below, at the shops still clogged with queues, at the lack, the lovely lack of German uniforms. At the British uniforms, the American, the French. At the undiminished presence of the Opéra to her right. At the streets to her left that led down to the elegance of the Place Vendôme, and then the Seine. She felt the wonder of not instinctively ducking or crouching or diving each time she heard a sudden noise, of not having to keep her head down, of not being always on the alert.

But she also saw the absences: the Jewish people who might once have held businesses in this area, the men who should be rushing to work, the joy that a spring morning in Paris, with the air perfumed by lilies and rose and chestnut, should bring. And if she listened hard, she could still hear, beneath everything, the guns, the bombs, the screams, the sirens, the sobs.

A rustle from the bed made her whip around. Dan had rolled over, had stretched out his arm, searching for her, had shifted his body across to her side of the bed when his arm didn't find her. The gesture, that he remembered she was supposed to be lying beside him, that he would scour the bed for her, made her eyes fill with tears. Before she could stop it, one of them rolled down her cheek.

Dan's eyes opened. 'Jess?' he mumbled.

'Here I am,' she said, wiping her cheeks and slipping back beneath the sheets, letting herself be drawn into his arms.

She kissed him, not wanting him to see her face but he must have felt it, that something had shifted, and he drew back and said again, 'Jess?'

He studied her face and she knew her eyes were too damp to pretend she'd been doing anything other than crying. 'Are you all right?' he asked. 'You don't regret . . .'

'No.' She shook her head firmly. Their night together was the one beautiful thing in the whole damn mess of war.

He kissed her gently, so gently she almost couldn't feel it. He continued to kiss her that way, lightly, softly, his lips a breath on the skin of her cheek, her neck. His fingers light too, tormentingly so, following his lips down her body. She could do nothing other than lie back, eyes closed, breath coming faster and faster as he made a slow and reverent path over every inch of her skin, from her toes to her calves, to her knees, to her thighs, then up to her belly. Then her breasts, taking an agonisingly long time over her nipples, then back along her stomach.

He reached her hips and she shivered, unable to stop herself tilting her pelvis towards him. His hand moved first between her legs and then his mouth and the moment she felt him kiss her, she cried out his name, feeling nothing other than the sensation of being, for once, truly adored.

~

'We should go out,' she whispered a while later when they had both recovered and were lying wrapped in one another's arms.

'Or we could just stay here.' Dan grinned lazily at her.

'I have to admit it's tempting.' Jess smiled too. 'But I feel as if I need to see what life is like out there. To find something that says it really will be okay.'

'Where should we go?' he asked.

She hesitated, knowing where she wanted to go but feeling foolish for such a fanciful wish.

'Tell me. Please?' he said.

'I imagine it's impossible but I'd like to go back to *Lieu de Rêves*.'

'Nothing's impossible. You have a jeep.'

'And a balcony full of fuel.'

He laughed. 'I forgot about that. Let's do it. Let's just do something crazy and not about the war and that might even be fun.'

'Fun?' Jess mock-gasped. 'I'd forgotten such a thing existed.'

'You mean last night wasn't fun?' He shifted his chest over hers, smiling.

She laughed. 'It was terrible. We definitely need more practice.'

He leaned down to kiss her expertly, in no need of practice. 'So are we practising or going to a castle?'

'As tempting as it is to stay here, I think we should go. Besides,' she said, sliding out from underneath him and hopping out of bed, 'we can practise when we get back. This way, we get to spend the whole day thinking about how much fun we can have tonight.'

Dan groaned and lay on his back, watching her walk, naked, across to the bathroom. 'I hope you don't expect me to concentrate on anything today.'

'Just on me,' she called over her shoulder before she shut the door and ran the bath.

Twenty-one

As Jess drove off in the jeep, Dan raised an eyebrow at her. 'You're going the wrong way.'

'We have to make one stop,' she said.

'Okay,' he smiled. 'I'm in your hands.'

'Don't tempt me,' she said and he laughed.

His laugh turned to silence and she became aware of the tight clenching of his jaw when she pulled up outside Victorine's school.

'Are you sure?' he asked. 'I saw her yesterday afternoon. I can come back and see her later.'

'I'm sure.' She didn't elaborate, didn't explain that she knew how much he missed the girl, that she knew he wrote to her twice a week and that he constantly questioned whether he'd done the right thing in putting her into boarding school so young. She didn't say that she knew he would ordinarily be spending the day with Victorine and that, after the night they'd had, the joy they'd found in one another's arms, it didn't seem fair to keep that joy to themselves.

But she knew he understood when he leaned over and kissed her. 'Thank you,' he said.

He jumped out of the jeep and returned a few minutes later with Victorine, who had her arms wrapped around his neck as if she would never let him go.

'Jess!' she cried, wriggling out of his arms and scampering over to the car to wrap her arms around Jess's neck as well. 'You *both* came!'

'We did,' Jess smiled and knew she'd done the right thing.

'A whole day with you and Papa!' Victorine beamed.

Jess's throat hurt and Dan caught her eye. 'She's been calling me that since she came to Paris,' Dan said, voice husky. 'The teachers say it's because she's with lots of other girls who talk about their papas.'

'And because you're more like a father to her than anyone else,' Jess said, squeezing his hand and taking the opportunity, while Dan settled Victorine on his lap in the front of the jeep, to wipe her eyes.

There were few vehicles on the road and it took only a couple of hours to reach the chateau. They never once ran out of things to say, especially Victorine, who filled them in on every minute detail of each day that had passed since she'd started at school.

'With a memory like that and such attention to the particulars, she'll be following in your footsteps before you know it,' Dan said to Jess. 'Then I'll have two reporters to contend with.'

'And you'll love every minute of it,' Jess said with a grin and if Victorine hadn't been in the car, she would have pulled over and kissed him, such was the way he looked at her.

At *Lieu de Rêves*, they bumped along the once sweeping drive. It was overgrown, as it had been last year, with angelica and soapwort, wild pansies and wild orchids painting colour into the landscape. The typical formality of a chateau garden had been lost through wartime misuse and neglect but Jess liked it all the more for the profusion of wildflowers and the wild plum and white mulberry trees, the oaks and sweet chestnuts that had been allowed to flourish untamed.

She pulled over and, as she cut the engine, the song of a nightingale could plainly be heard, its trill echoing on without the force of a shell or an ack-ack bomber, simple and rhapsodic. It made them all stop, the sound of a bird now something remarkable and worth their tribute.

'You were right,' Dan said to Jess. 'Coming here is just what we all needed.' He put his arm around her and kissed the top of her head, and if Victorine thought there was anything strange about these signs of affection, she didn't say so.

They climbed out of the jeep. Without the expanse of olive drab tents and vehicles and soldiers to mask it, the chateau rose into view from behind a screen of plane trees as if they were meant to come upon it suddenly and be astonished. All three of them said a wondrous 'Oh,' at the same time.

Victorine ran forward to the fairytale castle before them. Medieval in style, it had a keep, a drawbridge and round towers at each corner with slit windows from which archers must once have shot their arrows. Red and green ivy crawled unchecked over the stone walls. It looked so different to the place they had stayed with an entire division in the month before Christmas 1944, although the fields to one side were still marked with the ashy remains of wood fires and the rutted tracks of jeeps and heavy vehicles.

'Look, there's a butterfly!' Jess said to Victorine, who dashed off after it.

That afternoon, they lazed on a blanket, watching magnificent Queen of Spain butterflies, the nacre on the underside of their wings flash lunar in the sun, the rows of black spots on the other side of the wings as smooth and soft as velvet. The day was pleasantly noisy, filled with the chirrups of field crickets, the hum of damselflies, and the cries of the plovers and kingfishers, punctuated occasionally by the hoots of mallard ducks on the canal beyond. They lay almost hidden by the swathe of orchids grown up all around – spider orchids, monkey orchids, lady orchids – which gave way to a mass of ferns closer to the canal. Black beetles scurried busily around, rosemary perfumed the air and Jess found some early wild strawberries and wild currants for Victorine to eat.

In between, they laughed at Victorine's stories and Jess took photographs: of Victorine's face haloed by flowers; of Dan lying on his back, awake but unmoving because Victorine was sleeping on his chest; of the Wood White butterfly, like an angel or a ghost, come to rest for the briefest moment on Victorine's shoulder and Victorine calling out, 'Look Papa!'; of the crown of yellow water primrose that Victorine made for Dan, transforming the flower that most thought was invasive and alien into something fleetingly beautiful.

Victorine took some photographs too, of the plump strawberries, of the castle towers, of the serenading nightingale that flew out to bid them good day before taking its song elsewhere. She was especially fascinated by the dwarf beech trees and she named them all: the teacher was the one that looked, according to Victorine, wise, its head bent over its raised boughs; the little girl was the one that looked as if it might pick up its skirt of leaves and dance down to the water; the mother was the one whose crossed branches formed a cradle in which sat a richness of greenery.

And one final photograph of Dan leaning over to kiss Jess, the look on his face so tender and fierce that Jess's breath caught, and she wondered if Victorine had managed to freeze that moment on film, or whether Jess would only be able to recall the sense of it later, blurred by passing time, but still precious.

At long last Victorine began to yawn and the sky to lose its brilliance, discoloured by dusk. Reluctantly, without saying they were leaving, Jess collected their things and Dan picked up Victorine, lying her across the back seat where she sleepily protested that she wasn't tired, only to fall instantly into slumber. Before he climbed into the jeep, Dan pulled Jess towards him and began to kiss her with promise, all her senses stirred at the touch of his lips on hers.

'I cannot concentrate on anything, least of all driving, if you do that,' she murmured. 'Let's get back to Paris, drop Victorine at school and then . . .'

She stopped because the longing in Dan's eyes was too much.

He leaned his forehead against hers until his breath steadied. 'You're right,' he said. 'Let's go.'

A sleepy Victorine kissed Jess goodbye once they reached the school and seemed happy enough to let Dan go, the unexpected joy of spending an entire day with him enough to satisfy her for a time. Jess's heart ached for the little girl whose life was so far from normal, and to whom the gift of a few hours with the man she now called Papa was all she wished for – not Christmas presents or candy or a puppy or any of the other things a girl her age might ordinarily dream of.

'So, my place or yours?' Jess asked when Dan returned. 'Who are the biggest gossips, GIs or journalists?'

'GIs,' they both said at the same time, laughing.

'It's not that I'm ashamed of this,' Jess hastened to add. 'I just like that nobody else knows, so they can't give us their commentary or analysis on what we're doing and why we're doing it and –'

'I know,' Dan said, leaning across to kiss her again, even more intensely than before and desire swept through her so fiercely that she could do nothing other than return the kiss and wish they could click their fingers and be alone together in her room at the Scribe.

'I thought I told you to stop that,' she said against his lips. 'Perhaps we should talk about how exactly I'm going to get you through the lobby without anyone noticing. That might make you behave for a minute.'

He smiled. 'Maybe for a minute. Why don't we just have a drink at the bar – everyone knows we're friends so no one will think that's strange – and then I'll sneak up to your room first under the pretext of talking to one of the SHAEF PROs and you can come up after me when it's safe.'

'But that means I have to sit through an entire drink with you when all I want to do is –'

Dan touched a finger to her lips. 'Stop talking. The quicker we get there, the quicker I can take you back to bed.'

Jess used all her willpower to resist the urge to kiss his finger. Instead, she drove, not daring to look at Dan until they reached the hotel, which was buzzing more than usual.

'Something's going on,' Jess said and Dan nodded before they both heard someone call, 'Sir!'

Jennings leapt on them. 'Thought you'd be here, Sir.' Then he blushed and stammered, 'I just meant . . .'

So Jennings had figured it out. Jess stiffened, unwilling to allow whatever was between her and Dan to be subjected to the ribald commentary of the army.

'Spit it out,' Dan said to Jennings, obviously as annoyed as she was although she knew it wasn't Jennings' fault that he'd shown, for once, such perspicacity.

'We've been recalled,' Jennings said. 'We're going into Munich. They're saying it's almost over. And we have to leave in half an hour if we're going to make it to the muster point on time. That should give you time to . . . ummm.' Jennings blushed again.

Half an hour. No time to worry about gossip and scuttlebutt, then. 'I promise I'll return him in half an hour,' Jess said, which made Jennings flush so extravagantly it was impossible to tell he had freckles anymore.

Jess took Dan's hand and they hurried to the elevator, mostly unnoticed in the general hubbub about Munich. They restrained themselves until they reached the door of Jess's room where, once safely inside, they turned to each other at the same time. As their mouths met, their hands worked furiously at clothes, she unbuttoning his trousers, him lifting her skirt and pulling down her knickers, both so ready that the instant she could, she wrapped her leg around him and he lifted her up, pressing her back into the wall.

He slid into her, moving so quickly that she gasped at the overwhelming rush of sensation and she shook her head vigorously when he misunderstood her gasp and he said, 'Sorry, I'll slow down.'

'No,' she could barely say the words. 'Please don't.'

After they'd recovered enough to be capable of speech, they both laughed.

'We're worse than sophomores at a frat house party,' he said.

'We are,' she agreed. 'I blame you entirely.'

'Yes,' he grinned. 'My fault of course.'

He lowered her to the ground and kissed her, then moved off to the bathroom to sort out the rubber and the smile fell off Jess's face. He had to go. And she'd miss him, of that she was certain.

She pulled down her skirt and put her knickers back on, only to have him say, when he re-emerged from the bathroom, 'Can I take off all of your clothes?'

'Surely you're not capable of doing that again already?' she asked incredulously.

He laughed. 'No, you've finally worn me out. But we still have fifteen minutes and I want to lie down beside you for all of those minutes.'

He drew her in, not kissing her now, undoing her blouse and her skirt, slipping off her underclothes. Then he lay her on the bed, removed all of his clothes and held her as close as he could, as if he wanted to sweep her inside him, one of her legs threaded between his, one of his arms wrapped over her and one wrapped under her, braided together.

'Dan,' she said hesitantly, shy in a way she'd never been before, because there seemed, in this moment, to be so much at stake. 'That night in the ballroom . . .' Her voice trailed off.

He kissed her and repeated her words. 'That night in the ballroom . . .' It was his turn to pause. 'I don't want you to take this the wrong way but I'd always just assumed the rumours I'd heard of you sleeping with this man and that were true. I didn't think any less of you for it,' he hastened to add as she pulled away, his arms firm, not letting her withdraw from the embrace.

'You're a gorgeous woman,' he said, eyes searching out hers and holding them while he spoke. 'God knows we all need to feel good from time to time but it made me think there was this divide: the men you would sleep with, and then me, who you'd never shown any interest in beyond friendship. Which was fine, because I valued our friendship more than one night of infatuation. But when you told me none of it was true, that you hadn't been with anyone, the divide disappeared. That night in the ballroom, I couldn't think about anything else but you, a woman I'd known as a friend, a woman who was the most beautiful thing from the inside out. When we danced,' he whispered into her ear, 'and I touched your back, it was like walking into a fire and all I could do was curse myself for ruining our friendship because I knew, after feeling that, it would be impossible just to sit next to you on a sofa on a balcony ever again.'

God, he was going to make her cry and she didn't want to spend the last five minutes with him sobbing. 'Why didn't you say something?' she asked, voice husky with emotion.

'Jess,' he said, and his voice had changed.

It was as if he was preparing her. She was used to that certain inflection; she'd heard it throughout the war as officers told the men which of their number had died, or what suicidal target they were to attack next, or any other of the myriad pieces of news one didn't want to hear.

No, no, no, she thought, unable to stop her eyes from filling with tears now. What had he said? *A night of infatuation*. That's all it could be in France in April 1945 with the war still firing on. He was going to tell her that it was time to go back to being friends. But that was unthinkable.

Then he kissed her, lips brushing hers. 'There are three words I want so much to say to you, Jess. But in my experience, every time someone over here says those words, something terrible happens to one of them not long after.' He drew back and studied her face.

It hurt just looking at him, hurt to see what he felt, which she recognised because she felt it too; she knew he was right and that if either of them said it, they'd be cursed by the words. They'd seen too many young lovers – nurses and soldiers, WACs and soldiers, Frenchwomen and soldiers – declare their love for one another and then wake up the next morning to find their love was as ill-fated as Romeo and Juliet's, a tragedy playing out off the stage and on the battlefields of the European Theatre.

She swallowed and blinked. 'Then don't say it.' She laid her palm along his cheek. 'Instead I'm going to say . . .' She hesitated, searching for something, some alternative that could possibly express what had happened between them. 'I know you,' she said at last. 'Because I do. Better than anything or anyone.'

He kissed her again, long and searchingly, then whispered the same words – *I know you* – in her ear.

When he broke off she saw that his eyes shone as brightly as hers with the knowledge that they had both exposed their already fragile hearts to a brutality of the kind they had, despite every savage act they'd witnessed, never imagined.

He jumped out of bed, threw on his clothes and only said, 'I can't say goodbye,' before he left the room and she grabbed hold of his pillow and held it against her body, breathing in the faintest scent of him, barely able to catch her breath between sobs.

$\mathcal{T}$wenty-two

$\mathcal{J}$ess rolled into Munich in her jeep just after Dan's division did. The city was synonymous with Hitler; it was well known to be his preferred headquarters, and the mood among the troops was buoyant. Surely if they were in Hitler's city, the war would be over soon. Surely nobody else would die now.

The irony of dying so near the end was uppermost in everyone's minds – all the more reason, Jess thought, to not say those words to Dan and to not let him say them to her.

As she followed Dan's jeep to Prinzregentenplatz 16, Hitler's apartment, anger surged through her. How dare Hitler run away to Berchtesgarten? How dare he not step into the street and see what he'd done? The women at the camp, the graves spread across Europe as thickly as blades of grass? How dare he be so craven? How could there be any justice, if justice was at all possible now?

She pulled up at the apartment and stepped inside with Dan. Her eyes saw but her mind barely registered the SS guards' quarters on the first floor, the bomb shelters in the basement, the library, the small conference room in which everyone from Churchill to Franco to Mussolini had once sat. The plaster cast of Hitler's hands, which Jennings bumped into and let smash onto the floor.

Most of the troops filtered out after a short time, hands full of crystal and cutlery engraved with the letters *AH*, linens and silver too; sweethearts across America destined to eat for the rest of their lives using Adolf Hitler's spoon, or sleeping on Adolf Hitler's sheets. Dan began setting the battalion to task, turning the place into their HQ. Maps were spread out on Hitler's desk, someone sat in the chair once occupied by Hitler's ass and a chorus of laughter ensued.

Jess pushed on, upstairs, past the out-of-tune piano on which a GI was playing a bastardised version of 'Königgrätzer Marsch', past the switchboard that had a direct line to Berchtesgarten; Jennings tried it but nobody answered. She walked through Hitler's almost girlish chintz bedroom and into the pristine bathroom. Everything was spotless, tiles polished, no black spots of mould, the towels and bathmat a plush white, a colour Jess couldn't remember seeing for the longest time because who had the time or the soap or the bleach required to bring things to such a state of purity? The anger roiled stronger than ever.

She walked back out into the bedroom and picked up a framed photograph of the Führer. She took this into the bathroom, propping it up against the wall on the far side of the bathtub rim. Then she stood with her filthy paratroop boots on the white bathmat, marking it brown and muddy and soiled.

She set her camera down on the vanity and was undoing the buttons of her shirt, water splashing warm and clean into the bath, when Dan came in.

'What are you doing?' he asked as she slipped off her shirt.

'Using Hitler's bath,' she said calmly. 'And you're just in time to photograph it. You don't need to shut the door. I don't care who sees me.'

None of this was about her naked body, which felt, right then, asexual. It was about making a statement to the world.

She took off the rest of her clothes and dumped them on the stool. She left her boots, cloddish and stout, on the delicate bathmat.

Then she sank into the water, only her bare shoulders and grimy face visible above the rim.

'The Rollei's there,' she said to Dan. 'You know how to use it. Make sure you get him,' she pointed to the photograph of Hitler, 'in the shot. And me. And my boots. And the dirt I've left on his heretofore undefiled room.'

She picked up a washcloth and rubbed it across her shoulderblades, watching muck bleed into the white cloth. And Dan did as she asked him, taking a series of shots that didn't diminish her anger, but perhaps showed the world something of how she, and everyone else, must feel.

The photograph caused a sensation. It was reproduced everywhere, featuring in all her fellow correspondents' newspapers. And this time, nobody accused her of using her feminine wiles to get the shot. Who would want to see a haggard male journalist in a bathtub? She'd used her looks and her body, she knew – even though all that was visible was her naked back and shoulders – to say, on behalf of all those who could not, *We are the victors*. To give Hitler the finger, preserved in an image for all time, inescapable. And when Warren Stone bawled her out in front of the entire press camp, stopping just short of calling her a slut, every person there leapt to her defence. Which didn't endear her to Warren, as she well knew.

His parting shot, delivered with that omnipresent and awful smile, was to say, 'For those of you wondering how to gain access to the best stories, just be sure to slip a Lieutenant Colonel into your trousers.'

He couldn't know. If Warren Stone ever found out how she felt about Dan and how Dan felt about her, then . . . She didn't want to contemplate the end to that sentence. Still, Warren didn't ascribe to her any feelings beyond that of a courtesan's so perhaps she and Dan were safe. Of course letting Dan photograph her naked was, to anyone with a brain, close to a confession.

But the worry over how much Warren knew was forgotten amidst the sudden whooping cheer that drowned out the sounds of the typewriters clacking, the poker game, and the correspondents' chatter.

'Hitler's dead!' came the shout from a PRO on the telephone. 'Topped himself, alongside Eva Braun.'

'About bloody time,' Lee Carson muttered and the laughter following that understatement was uproarious, an intense rush of relief that rebounded through every person gathered there. Except that, inconceivably, Grand Admiral Karl Donitz had exhorted the German Army to continue to do their duty at their posts.

'It's not over yet,' the PRO concluded.

But the party started anyway. Every typewriter in the copy room was put away. Every map was rolled up. Someone thought to stick lilac boughs in water jugs, the correspondents with the best connections provided the cognac and schnapps, and everyone put on their best and cleanest uniforms.

It wasn't long before General Collins filed in, along with his staff, the intelligence officers; even the censors joined in the fun. Jess watched, alert, as the officers came too, looking for Dan but not finding him. She was just walking back to the party from the ablution facilities when she felt a hand on her arm and someone dragged her into one of the many dark hallways. The hand belonged to a scent she'd know anywhere, a combination of army soap, and the slightest hint of cologne – sandalwood and citrus. And the arms, arms she'd most definitely kissed, circled around her and drew her close.

Dan's voice murmured in her ear, 'Sorry about the ambush.'

He kissed her, long and deeply, the kind of kiss that made her stomach clench and her skin flush. She worked her hands under his shirt and felt his intake of breath when her fingers trailed unrelentingly up his body. He dived his hand down to the hem of her skirt, found his way underneath and was tracing a path up her thigh when they both heard, very close by, 'Sir!'

Neither moved, Jess's hands still resting on his chest, his fingers still touching her thigh, both of them hoping it was a different 'Sir' being sought, not Dan.

'Lieutenant Colonel Hallworth!' The sound came again and they both looked at one another.

'You're going to have to move your hands or I'll never be able to leave,' he whispered.

'Move them here?' Jess whispered back, shifting her hands down his chest to the waistband of his trousers where she slipped the tips of her fingers inside.

He couldn't stop the surprised yelp of a laugh, which was loud, definitely loud enough to give them away.

'That you, Sir?' Jennings' voice was close, just around the corner.

Dan ripped himself away and walked back in the direction of the party, while Jess waited for a few seconds, long enough to hear Jennings' voice say, 'You all right, Sir? You look flushed,' at which she grinned, but then sobered up, realising there was another man in the hallway now.

He lit a cigarette and blew smoke in Jess's direction.

Warren Stone. How much had he seen?

He answered her unspoken question.

'Last time,' he drawled, 'I accused you of sleeping with the Lieutenant Colonel, you made me look like a fool. But who's the fool now? Won't you hate it, now the press camp has mostly forgiven you for being a woman, if they find out you really have parlayed your sexual favours to get every single one of your pictures and your stories?'

What could she say? Because of the way the system worked, some women – Martha, Iris, Lee, perhaps herself – *were* able to transmit more newsworthy stories than the other women as their relationships came with a side-serve of access. But that wasn't *why* they had those relationships. If she had something to throw at Warren, she would.

But besides praying that his cigarette butt might catch alight and singe his always polished shoes, Jess had no ammunition.

He handed her a sheet of paper. She took it from him reluctantly before she realised it was hers, that it was a page of notes she'd transcribed from the conversation she'd had with Marie-Laure and her mother. 'Where did you get this?' she asked coldly.

'When the table was cleared for the party, this ended up on the floor,' Warren replied. 'Lucky I found it. I didn't realise you were so *interested* in rape.'

Jess shivered. She wanted to walk away but turning her back on Warren Stone right now took more courage than she possessed.

Thank God for Marty, who must have spotted Warren heading the same way as Jess and Dan and come to warn her. 'Your drink's getting warm,' she said to Jess when she came upon her. Then she rounded on Warren. 'For God's sake, leave her alone. The war's nearly over. You won't have to look at her for much longer. Or maybe that's the problem?'

'Let's just go,' Jess said to Martha, not wanting to hear what Warren might say in reply.

The day after the party, desperate to get out of the press camp and away from Warren, Jess went looking for a story. She drove to the outskirts of the city, where she met a young woman who rent her heart a little more. Jess had stopped to refill her water canteen at the woman's house, which the woman allowed, but she was most insistent that Jess not have anything more.

'I have a special pass,' the woman said in German. 'I have already provided food and shelter to the American soldiers and they gave me a pass to prove I have done what I needed to. They said I should show it to other soldiers who stop here.'

'A pass?' Jess asked, brow furrowed. 'Can you show me?' No such pass existed, as far as she knew.

The woman, who was pretty – blonde, blue-eyed, shapely, about sixteen – went off to get her pass. She held it out to Jess.

As Jess read the words, she wanted to be sick. *To whom it may concern, you are now looking at the best piece in Germany.*

The girl didn't have a word of English and she obviously had no idea what it said or that any American soldier she showed it to might well do . . . what?

'Did the man who gave you this . . .' Jess faltered. 'Was he kind? Or did he hurt you?'

'The Americans saved us,' the girl said simply.

They can take anything they want. The unsaid words sparked like a flashbulb providing an illumination neither Jess nor the girl desired.

What to do except photograph both the girl and the note, to write it all down, to save it for the piece Jess still hadn't written. The piece that taunted Jess for her cowardice. The piece that made her as craven as any Nazi.

She drove furiously back into Munich, stopping at headquarters on Prinzregentenplatz, where Jennings let her have a desk and didn't ask her why she wanted to write the story there instead of at the press camp. Dan found her just as she'd finished. She showed him what she'd written.

Dan sighed as he read her words. 'A woman came to headquarters this morning and asked me if she had the right to refuse a soldier who wanted her daughters.'

Jess's mouth fell open.

'I told her that of course she had the right,' Dan continued. 'So she asked to have her complaint recorded: two soldiers entered her apartment last night and told her they were going to amuse themselves with her daughters. She wanted to throw them out but they had guns and she didn't know if it was perhaps a new rule, that the soldiers could do what they wanted. I took down what she said and passed the complaint on to Major Thompson, CO of the company I thought the men were from.'

'And?' Jess whispered, fearing what he would say next.

'Major Thompson handed it back to me. He's not in my battalion and therefore not my subordinate, so there was nothing more I could do. Of course I told his CO as well but I expect Thompson has picked up his habits from his commanding officer.'

They stared at one another, words having become meaningless in this exchange of horrors about which nothing could be done. Dan stroked her cheek. 'Let's get something to eat,' he said.

On the way into town, Jess had to slow down for a group of British Auxiliary Territorial Service girls, most likely newly arrived given the way they were standing on the street, pointing at the Frauenkirche as if they were tourists on a holiday. Jess envied their laughter; that Munich had an air of spectacle about it, that they did not understand what lay beneath the smoking ruins.

The women were oblivious to everything around them and Dan reached over for the horn. 'Glad somebody thinks it's a day for sightseeing,' he said tetchily.

At the blare of the horn, the women turned and Jess gasped. She pressed her foot to the brake much too quickly and Dan looked across at her quizzically as he was jolted forward. 'Jesus, Jess. That's the kind of thing Jennings would do.'

'Amelia?' Jess called to one of the women who stared at Jess in her helmet, goggles and army uniform and Jess realised where the confusion must lie. She took off her helmet, took off her googles, raked a hand through her hair and smiled. 'It's Jess.'

'Jessica May! I don't believe it,' Amelia gasped. 'Look at you. What are you doing riding around in jeeps with . . .' She paused and looked over at Dan and simpered in a way Jess remembered from boarding school. 'Handsome men.'

The stony look on Dan's face at the women who were treating Munich like a vacation didn't soften in the light of Amelia's smile.

Jess jumped out of the jeep and embraced Amelia, who was wearing stockings of all things, immaculate stockings, unladdered stockings and Jess couldn't remember the last time she'd seen a pair of legs clad like that in silk. Amelia's brown hair sat in curls around her shoulders and her ATS hat was perched on top of an enormous and probably stylish, Jess thought wryly – it had been so long since she'd considered style that she really had no idea – Victory roll.

'When did you arrive?' Jess asked. 'And since when are you in the ATS?'

'A few days ago,' Amelia said airily. 'I wanted to come earlier but thought it best to wait until the danger had all but cleared.'

Jess didn't have to look behind her to know that Dan was rolling his eyes. She turned to him and said, 'Sorry, I'm being rude. Amelia Cosgrove, this is Lieutenant Colonel Dan Hallworth with the US Army.'

Amelia's smile was beautiful and lipsticked with red and Jess felt another twinge of envy that stockings and cosmetics had become things she barely remembered, that dirt and blood were more her style of decoration and that Amelia was looking at Dan as if she'd like to eat him up.

'Hallworth,' Amelia mused. 'Not related to Walter Hallworth by any chance?'

Dan grimaced. 'He's my father.'

It was Jess's turn to gasp. 'You're Walter Hallworth's son?' she said incredulously. 'You never told me.'

'You never asked. Besides,' he said more quietly, 'I liked that you didn't know.'

Jess could do nothing but stare at him. Walter Hallworth owned one of the largest newspaper companies in Manhattan. And Dan had never once let on, in all the stream of articles and photographs and correspondents he'd seen and met, that he could have been doing something like it too, something safer, rather than putting his body into battle and doing his best to protect his men each and every day.

Amelia laughed. 'You're still as unworldly as ever, Jess. You know,' she said to Dan, 'on our morning promenades at boarding school,

Jess would walk right past a Rothschild but wink at the impoverished pianist from the jazz club.'

Jess interrupted. 'What happened to your husband?' she asked, noticing Amelia wasn't wearing a wedding band.

'He died.' Amelia sniffed dramatically and without any real emotion. 'Somewhere in the Mediterranean. Didn't I write you that?'

'No,' Jess said, both exasperated by Amelia's usual lack of sentiment and pleased to see a familiar face. 'You didn't. I think I'd remember that.'

Jess saw Dan shifting with impatience in the jeep; he'd moved across to the driver's side, obviously keen to go. 'You take the jeep,' Jess said to him, really wanting to keep to her plans with Dan but knowing she should catch up with Amelia while she had the chance. 'I'll get a ride back with someone later.'

'Why doesn't Amelia go back with you now to the press camp and you can talk there?' he said. 'Drop me at Prinzregentenplatz. I'll come and get the jeep later. Then I don't have to worry about who you're hitching a ride with.'

'How sweet of you,' Amelia said, behaving as if his solicitude was all for her. She opened the door of the front passenger seat, waving her ATS companions off with a cheery, 'Bye!'

'Jess is navigating so she needs to sit there,' Dan said to Amelia.

'I'm sure I can navigate,' Amelia protested.

'You know what unexploded ordnance looks like?' he asked.

'I don't think I want to,' Amelia replied primly as Jess, trying not to smile, hopped in beside Dan, knowing he didn't need her to navigate through the city streets but glad that he wanted her beside him and not Amelia, despite Amelia's beauty and silk stockings and clean face.

⁓

'Is he single?' were Amelia's first words when they arrived at the mess and Jess poured out the schnapps.

Jess could feel her face burning. Amelia looked at her appraisingly.

Lee Carson walked past at that moment and took a seat on the other side of Jess. 'How's your Lieutenant Colonel?' Lee asked Jess, thankfully with teasing rather than malice, which perhaps meant that Warren hadn't yet told the world about Dan and Jess.

Amelia smirked and held out her hand. 'I'm Amelia and I was just asking Jess the same question. Perhaps you'll be more forthcoming with the details.'

'Lee Carson, and it's useless asking her anything.' Lee tipped her head at Jess. 'She and Lieutenant Colonel Hallworth are the tightest of buddies and they never gossip about each other. Believe me, I've tried more than once to prise info out of Jess about the oh so hand-some Dan and I've tried even harder to prise something out of him but . . .' She spread her hands out, palms up. 'Empty handed, as you can see.'

'Isn't it your duty to keep our spirits up by sharing what you know?' Amelia said to Jess.

Jess knew they were teasing her, knew that if nothing had happened in Paris with Dan, she'd laugh and move the conversation on to something else, that she wouldn't feel the horrible fist in her stomach as she lied. 'Dan is my friend, and Lee's right. I don't gossip about him. In fact,' she said to Amelia, although it hurt a little to say it, 'You seem to know more about some parts of his life than I do. I had no idea he was Walter Hallworth's son.'

'He kept that one a closely guarded secret,' Lee said, helping herself to the schnapps. 'Wonder why he didn't just join the press?' She sighed. 'So he's rich *and* handsome. Guess I'll have to try harder with the prising next time.'

'You might have more competition now,' Amelia said with a grin that clearly indicated her own interest.

'Aren't you in mourning for your husband?' Jess asked.

'Mourning,' Amelia scoffed. 'Nobody mourns anymore. We'd never do anything else given how often people die lately.'

Jess flinched but it was true. Mourning had become an outdated custom when, every second of every day, there was a dead body to weep for.

'I just have to work out when I can see him again,' Amelia continued. 'You won't mind helping me, will you, Jess? Seeing's how you and he are just friends.'

Amelia eyed Jess as if daring her to contradict her words. And Jess knew she couldn't, because what if to admit out loud that she and Dan were . . . She cut off the thought.

Thankfully, Lee saved her by pointing to the doorway. 'Your puppy dog's here,' she said.

Jess turned to see Jennings gesturing to her. 'I've got to run,' she said, leaping up gratefully.

The note Jennings passed her was cryptic but she dashed off, showered and changed into her pinks. Then Jennings drove her to a house she wasn't familiar with, near Prinzregentenplatz.

'You're needed in there,' he said, indicating the house, the flush on his face betraying just who was inside.

'Thank you,' Jess said, squeezing his hand. 'I know it's not your job to escort your CO's girlfriend to secret trysts.'

'He deserves it,' Jennings said shyly, hero worship for Dan as plain in his eyes as the freckles on his face.

As Jennings drove off, Jess pulled open the door and drew in a breath. It was magical. Dan had somehow found old hurricane lamps to soften the air of abandonment in the house, and he looked up from lighting the last of them to smile at her. The minute he did, she leapt into his arms, kissing him, then tearing at his clothes, wanting to feel him beneath her palms, and he tugged at the buttons on her blouse too, undid her skirt, unhooked her bra and when at last they were naked, he placed both his hands on her breasts and began to circle his palms against her nipples, while her hands travelled down over his belly.

'Jess,' he said, moving his hands away and taking hold of hers, his breath ragged like hers, skin warm, eyes glittering with desire. 'Stop for a moment.'

'Why?' she whispered, wanting to kiss him again but he placed a finger on her lips.

'Because I want this night to last forever,' he said. 'The last couple of days have been quiet but my men are going out on patrol tomorrow and I don't know when I'll see you again. It feels so good every time I'm with you that I just want to lose myself in it but let's make it feel that good for as long as we have.'

Then he knelt down to kiss her belly, her whole body burning from both his words and his mouth.

For the next hour, he concentrated on precise areas of her skin: first her stomach, then he lay her down and kissed her breasts, tongue relentless, until she was right at the brink. The moment she arched backwards, calling his name, he moved away and concentrated on her earlobes and then her neck, which almost drove her wild too. After a time, he played lightly between her legs, taking her almost to the precipice again before he rolled her onto her stomach and kissed the tops of her shoulders and the length of her spine.

She did the same. For a while she paid careful attention to his glorious chest with her mouth. Eventually, her hands crept down to wrap around him until he said her name in a voice so bathed in hunger that she stopped and concentrated on the soft skin on the underside of his forearms. When his breathing had settled a little, she took her mouth to his thighs and worked her way up, stopping again when his fists clenched.

At last she was lying on her back, arms stretched above her head, every inch of her skin flushed, eyes fixed to his, her whole body ready for him and this time when he touched her, she jolted and she cried out, 'I can't wait anymore.'

He slid into her and whispered in her ear, 'Thank God. Because nor can I.'

As he rocked inside her, the strongest and most powerful feeling swept through her, as if she were truly inside him, inside his mind, seeing into his thoughts, feeling everything that he felt for her. The sensation was so visceral that she could do nothing other than look into his eyes as he looked into hers, joined by more than just flesh — souls entwined like those of lovers cast forever in marble, unable to be torn asunder.

At the end, her whole body shook and his too, and it was a long time before she thought she could speak. 'Did you feel that?' she whispered against his cheek, because the way he'd looked at her made her believe that perhaps he had.

He threaded his fingers through hers and clasped her hand tightly. 'I did.'

'What was that?' she asked in wonder.

'I don't know,' he said. 'It felt like . . .' He hesitated. 'That word I'm not going to say because I never want to jinx this. It felt like I knew you from the inside out, more intensely than I thought possible.' He rolled onto his side and drew her in, wrapping one leg over hers, arms around her, just as they had been in Paris before he'd had to leave, so close that even a feather couldn't have slipped between them, both having given themselves to the other entirely in a way Jess had never experienced or thought she was capable of. What was the use in holding back when they knew how short and how precarious life could be?

'I still can't believe I'm lying here next to you, naked, having just done that,' he murmured, kissing her softly, tongue still exploring her mouth as if he couldn't possibly ever have enough of her, as if he still wasn't sated.

'Remember when I first met you in Italy?' she said, smiling at him. 'And you yelled at me. Then when you came to London, Martha thought you were gorgeous and I said that I wasn't ever going to think of you like that because you'd just proved yourself a friend.'

'And now?' he teased. 'What do you think now?'

'That you're the most incredible man I've ever met,' she answered honestly. 'That I can't bear the thought of stepping outside this house, away from you. That I would rather die myself than know you had.'

⁓

Not long after, they both fell asleep, the fatigue of the long years of war finally dragging them down into a slumber so absolute that there was no space even to dream. Every time she woke, there was Dan, gathering her into his arms, cradling her back to sleep.

Once they'd had a few restful hours, more tranquil than any other night either of them had spent in Europe, their lips touched once more and again their lovemaking was slow and gloriously prolonged, their hands speaking the promises that their mouths were too frightened to say. They made love as though they had all the time in the world and Jess even started to believe it. When they had finished and they lay drowsily spent, Dan stopped kissing her for just long enough to say, 'I'm sorry I didn't tell you about being . . .' He stopped.

'Walter Hallworth's son?' she asked. 'I guess it doesn't really matter, except I feel like an idiot for carrying on about my photos and my stories all the time when you probably know more about it than anyone.'

'I didn't want to be another man telling you that he was better or more experienced than you,' Dan said. 'Because I'm not. Definitely not at taking pictures like you do or at reporting a war. I worked at the *New York Courier* every summer since I was twelve, going out with the reporters on police beats, sitting in on news meetings, and finally writing my own stuff when I was at college. I'm supposed to take over the business when I get back but, over here, it's nice not to be thought of as the boss's son for once.'

Jess smiled. 'Dan, you're a leader like I've hardly seen anywhere in Europe. Your men will do anything for you. Your battalion has one of the lowest mortality rates, not because you haven't seen danger – you've seen more than most – but because of you. If the way you are here is the way you are in New York, then I doubt that anyone would ever think of you only as the boss's son.'

He kissed her and she sighed theatrically. 'So you'll be Editor in Chief of the *New York Courier* when we return to America and I'll be . . . what? *Vogue* won't need war reports once there isn't a war.'

'Jess, your photographs are famous. Anybody would want to work with you. I want to work with you. And be with you. Always. In fact . . .' He paused and studied her, as if unsure whether to continue. 'I don't have a ring or an extravagant dinner or anything else to persuade you, and I need to let you know that as Victorine's guardian, she's my responsibility and it's one I intend to honour, and it's probably not the way you might want it to be but, Jessica May, when we get back to New York, will you marry me?'

Jess froze, her body and her mind aching to just shout *Yes, of course I'll marry you!* But her caution and her awareness that being so close to the end of the war was not the time to die made her pause. 'What if, by saying yes . . .' Her voice trailed off.

'It won't happen. Not now. We're safe. I promise.'

I promise. She believed him. There wasn't a thing in the world he could say that she wouldn't believe. So she smiled. 'If you're brave enough to ask, then I should be brave enough to say yes. A thousand times yes.'

PART SIX

D'Arcy

Twenty-three

*F*or the entirety of the train ride back to Reims from Paris, D'Arcy felt herself sucking in air; her lungs wouldn't function and a thing she'd done for years without thought – breathing – became suddenly impossible. She struggled off the train and onto the platform, barely able to comprehend how she might get a taxi, when she saw Josh waiting for her.

All she wanted was to rush over to him and rest her head against his chest and have him hold her. But if she did that she would cry – again. The last thing he'd want was the art handler looking after his client's most precious works falling to pieces.

Which she was, like a negative never placed in a stop bath, overdeveloped, all the light blown out. Ever since she'd read the letter from the hospital, she had felt sobs rising from somewhere buried so deep inside her that she hadn't really known it was there – a place she'd hidden from her own self because there was nothing, she'd thought, that could be done about it. Everyone else had families, hordes of people who loved them unconditionally. D'Arcy had only ever had Victorine.

Which meant she had so little experience of the kind of love that came with family that she'd never wanted to push Victorine, to hurt

Victorine, to question Victorine – D'Arcy couldn't afford to lose the only family she had. That uncertainty had carried over into every other kind of human connection D'Arcy had formed; she'd been quick to look towards the end, wanting only the momentary balm of lust misconstrued as affection. And now, suddenly and swiftly, D'Arcy realised she'd never wanted to fall in love because she was afraid that her illiteracy in that emotion meant she'd ruin any such relationship.

But here was Josh, the kind of man who'd wait at a station – for how long? All morning, watching trains pass through until hers arrived? – so he could drive her home, the kind of man who just wanted to kiss her, to know her, the kind of man she wanted to hold her when she was hurting, the kind of man she didn't want to let herself love because she had no idea how to. Not when she'd be gone next week and would never see him again.

'Why are you here?' she asked tiredly, trying to hide every confronting and wretched thought that had just swept through her mind. 'I'm the kind of person who was going to do what you used to do: sleep with you and forget about you.' It was meant to show him the negative of D'Arcy, the darkness that lay beneath the smile and the bright dresses, meant to rend whatever fragile connection they'd forged at the picnic.

But he already knew. 'That's why I said no,' he said. He paused but she couldn't reply; opening her mouth was too great a risk when she could still feel the desolation pressing against the back of her throat.

'Thank you for coming to get me,' she managed.

'Do you want to talk about it?'

'No.' Then she added, inexplicably, because she'd made up her mind not to tell him anything, 'Not yet.'

'Let's go home,' he said, holding out his hand.

Home. Where was home? Not with Victorine, the woman who couldn't be D'Arcy's mother. Not in France, a country to which she'd thought she was linked by blood. Nowhere. Home had been mercilessly taken from her.

Still, she took Josh's hand, the feel of it so warm and gentle that it was difficult to relinquish it when they reached the car. They rode back to the chateau in silence, Josh glancing at her every now and again but she stared out the window and pretended not to notice.

⁓

Even though she was exhausted, D'Arcy spent the morning organising the transport to the airport for the crates, speaking in furious French to the company she normally trusted with the job who'd seen fit to tell her, in a jocular manner, that a forklift had punched a hole through a crate from the Musée D'Orsay just last week. After five minutes of her wrath, they became suitably contrite for her to believe that none of the inherent dangers of moving artworks – forklifts, fire sprinklers or simply being dropped – would be permitted to happen to her consignment.

She double-checked the booking on the cargo plane from Hong Kong, then finished the time-consuming insurance papers. Josh remained mysteriously and thankfully absent, or perhaps her silence in the car had told him she preferred to be alone. Célie quietly came and went with food, appearing just as D'Arcy's stomach began to growl, and D'Arcy ate as she worked. In the afternoon, D'Arcy collected her cameras, the mics, the LED light kit and the light-stand that she'd bought in Paris and knocked on the door of Jessica May's room.

Jess sat in a chair on the balcony with a pot of tea and two cups. 'I've been expecting you,' she said.

'I'll get set up,' D'Arcy said, assembling one camera on a tripod, positioned to fit both chairs into the frame, and one camera ready for close-up shots. She studied the scene through the lens, saw that the light was good, that there was no distracting ambient noise, and leaned down to pin a lapel mic to Jess's shirt. Jess smiled at her as she did so.

'I can see why you were a model,' D'Arcy said as she straightened.

'Oh?'

'Your smile.' D'Arcy searched for the right way to express herself. 'It makes a person feel as if they're the only one ever to have been smiled upon, that the gesture has just been invented by Jessica May, exclusively for them.'

'That's a lovely thing to say. You have a way with words.'

Beyond, D'Arcy could see all the way down to the crazy trees and she tried not to be ensnared by them again. But one caught her eye; it stood apart from the rest, boughs curled back in on themselves like the arms of a mother empty of child. D'Arcy was reminded of the panels in the salon downstairs, of the child depicted there: was it as lost as D'Arcy or was it found?

She sat abruptly in a chair opposite Jess. 'I don't have anything formal prepared,' she said. 'I normally would, but I tried to write down some questions and it didn't work. Sometimes it's best not to force it and this whole thing is a bit strange so . . .' She shrugged. 'I thought I'd wing it. Which mightn't sound professional, but there it is.' She knew her voice had a defiant ring to it, that she was being childishly provoking because of her suspicion that everything she'd found out in Paris could somehow be traced back to Jess, which made Jess the one to blame.

But Jess simply nodded. 'I winged it the entire way through the war. And it didn't make my photographs any less newsworthy.' She folded her hands in her lap, as if to indicate she was ready.

Where to start? *Why are you telling the world who you are now? Why did you hide who you were? Why did you tell me? Who are you to me?* Trite questions, the facile investigations of a petty teenager. 'Which of your reports from the war are you most proud of?' D'Arcy asked.

Jess hesitated, as if surprised by the question, which had also surprised D'Arcy. It was clear that the older woman was considering how to respond. Then Jess stood up. 'Perhaps if I fetch it for you. Will the cord reach?'

It was the kind of thing that would have any other documentary producer leaping up and stopping the recording, an old woman standing in the middle of the interview and pointing out the artifice of the microphone cords.

But D'Arcy liked it, the fleeting glimpse of uncertainty, so different to the artificial way everyone now saw the world, arranged just so by stylist-directed photographs. It was why she'd gone into film in the first place, rather than photography; film caught stretches of time, rather than just the one moment, so it was sometimes possible to catch the actual truth, instead of the ideal truth that had been frozen and downsized and trapped into a split second.

'It'll reach,' D'Arcy said.

Jess returned with, surprisingly, a newspaper. D'Arcy had been expecting a copy of *Vogue*. She picked up the other camera and moved the lens over the yellowed pages of a 1946 copy of the *New York Courier*, one of the papers owned by World Media Group, and an article titled, 'I've Got A Pistol and There Ain't Nobody Going to Stop Me Having Her'.

The article detailed rapes by US Army soldiers throughout World War II. It included photographs, grainy now with age, of sober women, eyes lightless, passive, as if anything they had would be gifted with resignation because they'd learned it was easier that way. D'Arcy read about a woman who'd been given what she'd thought was a pass excusing her from providing the US Army with more food and shelter because she'd done her share, but that the note, written in English and not understood by the German woman, essentially exhorted the next soldier to take from the woman what the first man had also stolen. At the next paragraph, D'Arcy stopped.

'Will you read this aloud?' D'Arcy asked, passing Jess the newspaper and focusing on Jess's face in close-up with the camera.

Jess didn't respond immediately, watching D'Arcy, who hoped the camera would record exactly what she could see: a frightened woman whom age had made more arresting because her huge eyes were overcast with tragedy. Why did pathos render something more beautiful? D'Arcy wondered now.

Finally, Jess nodded and began to read. '*A girl's screams came from behind a locked door and an American voice ordered, "Stop clawing, you little bitch, or I'm gonna break your bloody neck." Banging and kicking, I bellowed, "Hey, quit that and open the door!" The door opened — just a chink — as a man peered out to demand, "What the hell do you mean, squawking orders at me." With matter-of-fact brutality, he told me, "I've got a pistol and there ain't nobody going to stop me having her or any other German gal I want. We won 'em, didn't we?" Then he slammed the door.*'

D'Arcy put down her camera and let the silence suspend itself around them, knowing she would cut to the wide shot in the edit to take in the two of them sitting among the echo of Jess's words, which spoke more powerfully than any narrative or voiceover would.

'What was the reaction to the article?' D'Arcy asked at last.

'Outrage, of course. But not for the girl being raped.' Jess's voice was stark. 'Everyone was outraged that I'd dared to report any such thing about our victorious and honourable army.'

'What you did, reporting this when you must have known what the reaction would be, was extraordinary.' It *was* extraordinary. Taking on a sacred institution like the army when victory was still so fresh in everyone's minds in order to tell a truth that would not otherwise have been heard. A truth that must have been buried so deeply by the subsequent indignation that this was the first D'Arcy had seen of these photographs as part of Jessica's body of work.

'What I did during the war was also cowardly,' Jess said tiredly. 'It's difficult to celebrate one without remembering the other.'

D'Arcy knew her meaning stretched deeper, into the void gouged out by D'Arcy's visit to Paris. The defiance returned. 'I think I've had enough of riddles.'

'Have you?' Jess trapped D'Arcy's eyes in hers and D'Arcy blanched. No, she hadn't. She wanted to stay on the safe ground of Jessica May, the photojournalist, and not dig into the personal. She hadn't the resources of energy to deal with any more revelations right now.

'Which is your favourite picture from the war?' D'Arcy asked abruptly.

Jess gave out that same disarming smile and D'Arcy suddenly felt that she'd missed the point. There was something more within that article than D'Arcy had grasped, some reason why Jess had chosen it, of all the reports, to read.

'My favourite picture is that one, of course.' Jess indicated the wall behind her, on which hung Victorine Hallworth and Dan Hallworth. It wasn't the ubiquitous image that IKEA and advertising agencies had desecrated but the other photograph D'Arcy had found in the archives in which the man was lifting the girl high into the air, the love between the two caught on their faces in touching relief to the vista of wounded men behind. 'That one too.' Jess pointed to the picture on the dresser, the one in which she was about to fall into a kiss with Dan Hallworth. 'I didn't take it, though. But it turned out to be a prophecy – that those two people, for the rest of time, would have only the echo of that stopped kiss.'

Before D'Arcy could ask why, Jess turned the conversation. 'You've been in Paris,' she said.

'I visited my moth— Victorine's boarding school.'

'I see.' Jess stood up, moving across to the balcony railing, looking at the same tree that had caught D'Arcy's attention earlier. 'I didn't mean for any of this to happen,' she said, as if apologising to someone who wasn't in the room.

'Any of what?'

'I'm winging it again.' Jess turned back to D'Arcy. 'I only wanted to look at you. To know you, for just one brief snapshot in your life. I never expected you to know so much about war photography, and thus about me, couldn't believe there was anyone still alive who cared about Jessica May and now . . .' Her voice shook, and trailed off, and D'Arcy's stomach heaved. Jess looked terrified, which terrified D'Arcy in turn. *What* had happened?

'Dan Hallworth was the love of my life,' Jess finally said. 'He published the article about the rapes, which was an act of bravery in itself. I sent it to him, not really expecting he would. But he was always, above and beyond everything else, a man who did the right thing, no matter how hard, no matter the fallout. I've tried to learn that from him but I'm not sure I've succeeded.'

D'Arcy stared at the picture on the wall. Only someone who cared very deeply would take such a photo. It was a devotion apparent in each of Jess's photographs; it was what lifted them above the work of others and why they resonated with so many people, which was what she'd argued with Josh the first day she arrived at the chateau, eager to prove that the photographer was a woman. But what she apprehended now was that the quality of empathy she'd always admired could only have been caught by someone who knew suffering. Unbidden, Dorothea Lange's insistence that every photograph should become a self-portrait came to mind and D'Arcy wondered what she might discover about Jess if she were to re-see each photograph with that in mind, or what she might discover about herself if she were to watch the footage she was now recording, choosing to focus on herself rather than Jess.

'What happened?' D'Arcy asked tremulously, because she was becoming more certain that the past of everyone – Jess, Victorine, perhaps Dan Hallworth, and maybe even, unknown to her, D'Arcy – had been ruined somehow by acts for which they were partially responsible, but which had also happened regardless of what they had wished for instead. Words she had read not long ago suddenly scrolled across her mind: '*the landscape of devastation is still a landscape. There is beauty in ruins.*' At the time, her academic brain had nodded but now she understood. Something had ruined Jess, but here she was, still alive. Perhaps pathos made you grasp the wonder of endurance, that you could suffer all things but the spirit still held on. First, though, you had to look that suffering in the eye, be the spectator rather than the coward who turned away, unable to watch. Which was D'Arcy?

'I can only tell you part of it,' Jess said thinly. 'You need to . . .' Again that pause, that haunted expression. 'You need to ask your mother about the rest.'

Your mother. Did that mean Jess didn't know what D'Arcy had discovered in Paris? Why then the subtle apology when D'Arcy told her she'd visited Victorine's school?

Then Jess began to speak, telling D'Arcy how she'd met Dan on a battlefield in Italy, about Victorine's tumultuous early years, about the fact that Victorine was nobody's child and so she had become Dan's and, for a short time, Jess's.

Nobody's child. Just like D'Arcy was right now. 'Why just a short time?' she asked.

A knock on the door made D'Arcy jump. She stood up when Josh appeared.

'Sorry,' he said, the surprise visible on his face when he saw D'Arcy. 'I can come back later. I have some papers for you to sign,' he said to Jess.

But, rather than repeating her question, D'Arcy was already slipping past Josh and out the door. Which made her the coward, she knew.

~

That night, D'Arcy sat in her room and, after waiting hours for it to load onto her computer, she watched the footage she'd recorded earlier. She didn't edit it or cut it or adjust the sound or the brightness. Her hand hovered, uncertain, over the mouse, wanting to craft a film in the cinéma vérité style, to be unbiased, to let whatever truth Jess was moving towards gently and expressively declare itself on the screen. D'Arcy's impulse to be unscripted, to have no questions prepared, to simply converse, had been the right one, she saw. Otherwise she would only be fighting against the story that wanted to tell itself, trying to impose a narrative on what was, she suspected, unnarratable.

She rubbed her hand tiredly on her forehead. What was she thinking? That she, an amateur, could make any kind of film about Jess, let alone one that aimed for truth. Her postmodern arty friends would all be rolling their eyes at her, telling her to forget it; that whatever Jess had to say wasn't truth, merely her own agenda. That D'Arcy was being naive, or manipulated into believing that there was something to be revealed when there was only a whimsical old woman who'd chosen to hide her identity for reasons that belonged in the past.

D'Arcy stretched, letting the film play across her computer screen, and walked out onto the balcony, the cooler night air and the ever-present scent of the garden like a calm hand placed on her shoulders, loosening them, easing the stiffness in her neck.

What I did during the war was also cowardly. Jess's voice cut into the night and D'Arcy once again felt the certainty that she herself was the coward. Too afraid to do anything with the footage she'd recorded. Too afraid to have written a proper proposal to the Jessica May foundation. Too afraid to talk to Josh. Too afraid to speak to Victorine.

But fear was not a word D'Arcy had ever associated with herself. She was bold, adventuring around the world, unshrinking when it came to asking for what she wanted both from her work and the men she amused herself with.

She turned around, marched over to the desk, sat down in the chair and fixed her hand on her mouse. She might never be able to make herself talk to Josh; he would want her to confide in him, like he had done with her, but even thinking about what she'd discovered at the school hurt so much that she couldn't imagine talking about it, ever. And there was only a vacancy, an emptiness before her when she contemplated telling Victorine what she'd discovered. So yes, she was fearful. In that, but not in everything. She would make this film.

Every afternoon, she would spend time with Jess. And every night, D'Arcy would come to her room and she would edit the truth into being. What she would do with the film once it was finished she had no idea; it was preposterous to imagine that anyone might want to watch something made by her, a mere trifler. But she would make it anyway. Even if it only sat on her computer for eternity, unwatched by anyone except D'Arcy, it was worth doing.

Her phone rang then. Victorine. D'Arcy declined the call.

Twenty-four

Two days passed. Days in which D'Arcy continued to ignore Victorine's calls. Days in which she picked up her phone and had pretend conversations whenever Josh was nearby, or drilled or sawed at top volume to discourage conversation. Days in which she spoke to Jess most afternoons, filming her, then working every night on the documentary in the sanctuary of her room. Sometimes she was confident that her work was good, but mostly she felt certain she was wasting her time on a film that would show only her lack of expertise. She made herself so tired that her eyes burned but she couldn't sleep.

She pretended to Jess and to herself that she was simply waiting until Jess had finished telling her story about Dan Hallworth and Victorine's childhood and the war before she called Victorine back. It was such a nice deception, compared to the arid truth, that she sometimes almost forgot the real reason she was sad and would then be jolted into hideous consciousness by an anecdote Jess might share about Victorine.

One evening, when she realised she was far too intimately acquainted with every small crack and crevice on the ceiling of her room from the long hours of staring up at it, she threw on the black

300

dress she'd worn at the picnic and went downstairs to make herself some chamomile tea. Earlier, she'd seen that Célie had dried and placed some fresh buds in a tin in the library, a room adjacent to the *salon de grisailles*, but cosier, its walls covered in old fabric and leather-bound books. In the library she would be safe; there, she wouldn't be able to see the *boiserie* paintings of the salon, wouldn't feel compelled to try to discover whether the child was running towards or running from the ancient and gnarled trees of the chateau.

She sank onto the sofa, grateful for the way that, here, everything you wanted appeared just as you needed it. Tonight was no exception; a teapot of hot water sat next to the chamomile leaves and two china cups. She sipped, then closed her eyes.

'Mind if I join you?'

Her eyes flew open. *Josh.* She shrugged. 'Sure.'

He poured himself a tea and sat next to her, doing just as she had done, sipping and closing his eyes and resting his head back.

'We look like poster children for noughties' over-scheduled lives,' she said ruefully.

His eyes flicked open and he smiled. 'Except I think your exhaustion might be to do with something more than busyness. I'm happy to listen if you decide it's better not to bottle it up.'

'I wouldn't know what to say,' she said honestly.

'What's that?' he asked, pointing to the folded scarf on her lap.

D'Arcy flushed. Why had she brought it downstairs with her? As a peace offering? Or an inducement? 'It's a 1950s Hermès silk and angora scarf,' she said, handing it to him. 'It reminded me of your eyes.'

The afternoon she'd arrived in Paris, before that awful visit to the school, she'd stopped at one of her favourite vintage clothing stores, had seen the scarf and bought it without hesitation, knowing it belonged to no one other than Josh. She'd bought one for Célie too – a 1940s Stella Designs scarf in pale greys and soft blues, colours that reminded D'Arcy of the chateau and the people in it.

While she'd already given Célie her gift, she'd kept Josh's hidden for the past two days because D'Arcy didn't ordinarily buy presents for anyone; they were tokens of commitment. Even she and her mother mostly indulged in something transitory – a fabulous dinner and champagne – for Christmas rather than well-chosen gifts. But being in the chateau was somehow changing D'Arcy.

'Thank you.' His fingers ran slowly over the scarf. 'I might need scarf-tying lessons to do it justice though.'

'I think you could probably just toss it around your neck any old way and it will look . . .' *Devastatingly handsome*, she didn't say. 'Dan Hallworth is Victorine's father,' were the words that came out instead. 'This man, who used to be just the name of the person who owned the company my mother works for, is actually her family. And she never told me any of it.'

'You look so sad, D'Arcy.'

At Josh's words, a simple statement of truth rather than the meaningless *I'm sorry* she'd expected, or a jollying attempt to make her feel better, she felt her breath falter, her heart convulse, her eyes scald with white-hot tears. She pressed her lips together, the ability to speak, to tell him about the most brutal discovery, snatched away by his compassion.

He studied her face and shifted back into the sofa. 'Come here. I'm an expert in giving a neck rub in such a way that it will make you fall asleep.'

She looked at him warily and he smiled. 'I promise it will be very chaste and proper,' he said. 'Although this is a turn-up for the books; you eyeing me like I'm about to jump on you rather than the other way around.'

He made her smile so she stood up and perched on the edge of the sofa, between his legs, and he began to rub her neck the same way he did everything: lightly, softly, gently. As he massaged her neck and shoulders, he talked about Paris, about his favourite café in the city, about small and inconsequential things, which were the perfect things, because she could manage the small and inconsequential much better than the large and devastating.

Long minutes passed, minutes of feeling her shoulders drop down from around her neck, of feeling sleepy rather than exhausted, of the sound of his voice near her ear. She should probably stand up and go to bed. He'd been rubbing her neck for at least half an hour and he must have better things to do, like getting some sleep himself.

Then his voice trailed off. It took only a few minutes until somehow, in the silence, the heat generated by his hands intensified. The throb of whatever it was between them found expression in his fingers and even though he moved them the same way on her skin, it no longer felt like a decorous massage. His hands felt heavier, her skin almost unbearably warm. She shivered, heart skidding into a faster beat, the sound of Josh's breath obvious in the silent room.

She shifted a little, back into him, and his lips brushed against her hair, teasing her flesh into goosebumps. Then his mouth moved down the side of her neck and more long and lovely minutes passed as his lips fanned the fire that his hands had started. She closed her eyes when his hands ran down her arms, then all the way down to her waist, meandering, exploring her body and when at last he stroked her breasts, D'Arcy couldn't bear it any more.

She spun around to face him, straddling his lap, reaching behind to her zipper, letting her dress puddle at her waist so he could touch her without a screen of fabric between them.

And he did touch her, did bring his hands back to her breasts, running his fingers over her naked skin, tracing a line down from her shoulders before coming to rest on her nipples. She shuddered as his fingers caressed her gently, then harder, and she kissed him to stop herself from crying out at the rush of sensation that was taking over her whole body.

Their kiss deepened to match the intensity of what his hands on her breasts were doing to both of them and he shifted his weight and lay her back on the sofa. He took his mouth away from hers for just a moment to search out her eyes. The way he looked at her made her want to turn her head away, to reach down and pull up her dress to cover herself because she'd never before felt so vulnerable beneath everything that he told her in his gaze.

Which was crazy because just a minute ago she'd been prepared to give him everything. No, that was a lie. She'd been prepared to give him her body. That was all. But she could see in his eyes that he only wanted her body if she was prepared to give him the rest of her: her heart, her mind, her soul.

She had no idea how he read what she was thinking but after just a moment of eye meeting eye, he did what she'd wanted to: reached down and pulled up her dress. He brushed his lips against her forehead, then stood.

'Goodnight, D'Arcy,' he said and in his voice she heard hurt or disappointment – she couldn't be sure – and she knew it was because she'd just proven herself to be less than he'd hoped she was.

PART SEVEN
Jess

It is awful to die at the end of summer when you are young and have fought a long time and when you know that the war is over anyhow.

– Martha Gellhorn

Twenty-five

*T*he next day the war floundered on, Dan hurrying back to his men at dawn, cursing at having to send them out on a patrol that none of them wanted to make. It would take just one sniper and the end of the war, so close, would become something unreachable; they'd be in heaven or hell instead.

Jess returned to the press camp, keeping the incredible secret of her engagement to Dan more closely guarded than the papers in the Reichstag. She was unable to concentrate on anything, so she set out with Marty, driving through nearby towns, purposeless except that sometimes, they both knew, the best stories came from the most unexpected places.

In one tiny town, a German woman raced over to their jeep, calling out, 'Soldier women! Help me! Please!'

Jess stopped the jeep and both she and Martha jumped out. 'Is someone hurt?' Jess asked, thinking they'd need an ambulance, or a medic, wondering how far they were from the nearest hospital.

Then the sound of terrified screaming tore through Jess's ears and the woman pointed desperately at a locked door. Behind the door, a sharp American voice commanded, 'Stop clawing, you little bitch, or I'm gonna break your bloody neck.'

Jess and Martha banged on the door in unison, their cries matching the intensity of those coming from behind the door. It flew open and a GI peered out, gun raised, a girl sobbing in the bed behind him.

'I've got a pistol and there ain't nobody going to stop me having her or any other German gal I want.' He continued to rant, claiming the girl was simply the spoils of victory and Jess knew that she didn't have the stomach to photograph his foul mouth or his splenetic, hostile face because there was no humanity whatsoever in this moment and therefore nobody would ever be able to look upon it.

What had seemed so momentous in Paris in August last year had become a pyrrhic victory as the victors proved every day that their morals were often little better than those they had defeated.

The GI slammed the door shut.

'You stay there,' Jess said to Martha. She sprinted back to the jeep, speeding on until she found an officer. She filled him in through her panting breath, pointing to where he should go to stop what was happening.

He stared at her for a long moment, long enough for Jess to start shouting, as if he were deaf and hadn't heard her. The noise attracted a crowd and that was the only thing that seemed to make the major react. He called for a jeep but before he climbed in, he leaned down close to Jess and said viciously, 'The most stinking part of this whole stinking war business is that there should be women anywhere near it.'

He drove off in the right direction, Jess screaming after him, 'Damn you! It's not the women who are the problem!'

'Are you okay, ma'am?' one of the nearby soldiers asked.

She shook her head. 'What's his name?' She pointed in the direction of the officer's jeep.

'That's Major Thompson.'

Major Thompson. The same man who'd thrown away the note Dan had given him about his soldiers helping themselves to what they thought they had a right to. She jumped into her own jeep and tore off after him, arriving in time to see the soldier, not looking at all chastised, hopping into the car with the major and pulling away without a backward glance.

Martha appeared, cursing. 'They won't do a damn thing to him. Meanwhile that poor woman . . .'

That poor woman. Who could be pregnant, injured, mentally ruined by a man with a gun and the terrible power conferred on him by victory.

'What does it make us if we don't write about it?' Jess asked in a whisper.

'Smart,' Martha said firmly. 'Damn smart.'

'I need a drink,' Martha said when they arrived back at the press camp.

'I do too,' Jess said feelingly, hating herself for it. As if a drink would ever make that woman feel better. Jess had the power – not of justice, but of revelation – in her hands and she wasn't using it. She was blaming Warren Stone and the censors and everyone but herself. 'I'm supposed to be meeting Dan though. Will you be okay?' she asked, squeezing her friend's hand.

'I'll find Lee and a bottle of whiskey and I won't remember any of it. Until tomorrow.' Martha grimaced.

'I'll stay with you.'

'No. Go enjoy the one good thing there is. And don't you dare feel guilty about it.' Martha embraced Jess, which she supposed was Martha's way of telling Jess she knew what was going on with Dan and Jess blinked, hard.

'Thank you,' she whispered.

On her way out, Meg, the WAC coming off telephone duty, jumped up. 'Say, are you going into town? I need a ride.'

'Sure,' Jess said. 'I'm having a drink with Dan – Lieutenant Colonel Hallworth.' She tried to lighten her own mood by adding, 'I can't quite believe it's possible to do something so normal in Munich.'

Meg laughed. 'I'm meeting someone as well. Who knows, maybe we'll all go back to dating sometime soon rather than . . .' Her voice broke off as she searched for the right words to describe the way relationships developed in the cut and thrust of war.

As they climbed into the jeep, Meg said, 'Lieutenant Colonel Hallworth sure is popular. Someone else called looking for him earlier. I told her she should join the queue behind you but she didn't see the joke. She was very insistent about finding him so I put her through to HQ and told her this was a press camp, not a command post. Sorry,' Meg said, genuinely contrite when she caught Jess's stare. 'I didn't mean anything . . .'

'It's fine,' Jess said, pulling the jeep onto the road. Everyone seemed to know that she and Dan were some kind of item. Maybe that was okay. It took the power away from Warren; his revelation about Jess and Dan would be very anti-climactic if it was already accepted rumour. Maybe that was why he hadn't said anything, why he'd left her alone lately. He'd run out of ammunition at last.

Jess pulled up near the bar she and Dan had chosen because it was small and quiet and not frequented by press hounds. She said goodbye to Meg, went inside and ordered a drink while she waited. Half an hour later she ordered another one, and some food, unperturbed because arrangements in wartime were as flexible as elastic. After two more hours she gave up, knowing something had happened and he'd come to see her whenever he could.

She arrived back at the press camp a little subdued, only to run into Meg, also returned. 'Your night didn't work out either, I take it?' Jess said ruefully.

Meg shook her head. 'He was a jerk. And I know why yours didn't work out.' She passed Jess a scribbled note which read, *Message for Jessica May: Lieutenant Colonel Hallworth in hospital. Jeep accident.*

The note fell to the floor, swaying gently down as Jess turned and ran back outside, cursing herself. She never should have said yes to Dan. This was what happened in a war zone when you made someone a promise.

Twenty-six

She'd never been more relieved in her life than when she saw Dan on his feet at the main desk of the hospital.

'Dan!' Her cry echoed loudly and he whipped around, revealing a black eye with a bandage above, most likely obscuring a nasty cut, and minor scratches on his face and arms, but nothing more as far as she could see.

All her desire of concealment fled as she ran to him and he folded her in his arms, holding her so tightly she could barely breathe. After a moment he bent his head down to kiss her and Jess vaguely heard Anne's voice behind them say, 'About time.' Heard a GI's voice say, 'Well done, Sir,' and another say, 'Ten bucks is mine.'

Jess drew back a little, unable yet to smile at the jesting around them until she'd made certain of one thing. 'You're all right?'

He nodded. 'I am. But . . .'

His voice trailed off and Jess's stomach squeezed with dread. Not Jennings. Not now.

'Your friend Amelia . . .' He began to talk and the dread inside her twisted into foreboding.

Dan spoke haltingly about spending the afternoon clearing out a village where there'd been reports of sniper fire, of a band of rebels still fighting for their now dead Führer. Amelia had been there too; somehow the Major General had got it into his head that she was a fluent German speaker and she'd come to translate but they'd all discovered very quickly that the few German words Dan and his men had picked up in the last month made them better speakers of the language than Amelia.

The Major General had been disgusted, Amelia's legs and smile not being enough to placate him, and he'd roared off soon after they'd discovered that the reports of sniper fire were false and the whole mission had been a waste of everyone's time. But the Major General had brought Amelia with him to the village, which left her without a ride back to the ATS lodgings. Dan had been in his jeep with Jennings, about to drive off, when Amelia appeared, simpered at Jennings, and asked if he would give up his seat for her and squeeze into another jeep instead. Of course Jennings, being Jennings, had stuttered, blushed and jumped out of the jeep before Dan could stop him.

Dan knew he was going to be late to meet Jess, and the ATS camp where Amelia was staying was out of his way. So he'd taken a shortcut.

'If you'd been in the jeep with me, Jess, there's no way I would have taken that shortcut,' he said. 'But I just wanted to see you. I wanted to hold your hand and ask you if you'd really said yes or if it had all been a dream. I thought I knew the road well enough to avoid anything . . .'

He'd had his helmet and goggles on and had refused to leave until Amelia put hers on, even though she'd complained bitterly about the effect on her hair. What he hadn't realised, because his thoughts were on Jess, was that Amelia had slipped off the protective equipment sometime after they departed, most likely when he'd been distracted by the demands of navigating and keeping alert to any danger outside the vehicle. And the Germans, as so many times before, had strung a wire from tree to tree across the road, a wire that was almost impossible to see in the dusk and without an experienced navigator beside him like Jennings or Jess.

Dan saw it at the last minute, had yelled out to duck, which anyone else would have done without question but Amelia didn't know that when a Lieutenant Colonel yelled duck, you ducked. He'd swerved, with his head down, meaning his neck had avoided the wire. But the jeep had hit a tree. He didn't know how badly Amelia was hurt, but suspected it wasn't a matter of cuts and scrapes. That the wire, the God-awful wire might have . . .

'It's not your fault,' Jess said, squeezing his hand, trying not to think about the stories of guillotined bodies left by the Germans' infernal wires. 'She shouldn't have been out there in the first place, let alone without a helmet. The Major General shouldn't have left her behind. And you would never have taken a road that you thought was unsafe.'

'But I did,' he said, his face stricken and she led him to a chair and sat him down and kept her arms around him while they waited to find out what had happened to Amelia.

⁓

Hours later, Anne called them over. 'She's resting now. They had to . . .' she paused.

'Tell me,' Dan said grimly.

'They had to amputate her arm. It was crushed when the jeep crashed.' Anne paused and Jess knew there was more, that the amputation was the best news. Her heart skidded and she felt like cramming her hands over her ears but she kept her arms around Dan.

'Tell us,' she said to Anne.

'The wire sliced into her face,' Anne said. 'She'll have scars, bad ones, for the rest of her life. I'm sorry.' Anne gave Dan a sympathetic look and moved away.

'What have I done?' Dan said, face dropping into his hands.

'You've done nothing,' Jess insisted. 'Let's go see her. She'll say the same.'

But Amelia didn't say anything; she was sleeping. It was impossible to see how badly hurt she was but, judging by the size of the bandages swathed over her face, it was perhaps worse than they could imagine.

Jess stayed with Dan that night in his room in Hitler's apartment. If they were caught, there'd be trouble, but Jennings helped as usual; one look at Dan's face told him that Jess needed to be there for his CO.

Before dawn, she woke to find that Dan was already up and dressed and about to go back to the hospital to see Amelia.

'I'll come with you,' she said.

But he shook his head. 'I need to do this on my own. I need to make it right.'

So she let him go and, later, when Jennings asked her, 'Is he all right?' she shook her head too and said, 'I don't know.'

~

It was late afternoon when Dan came to find Jess in the clack and buzz of the press camp.

'She said I had to marry her,' Dan said faintly.

'What?' The word exploded from Jess's mouth.

'I've made her unmarriageable. The doctors say her face will be scarred for life. Horribly scarred. Impossible to hide. She only has one arm. Nobody will want her now, she says. It's the only way I can make amends.'

'What did you say?' Jess asked, incredulous that Amelia would propose something so preposterous.

'I told her I was engaged to you,' he said simply. 'That I'd do anything I could for her but I was marrying you and nobody else.'

'Dan . . .' Jess reached across the table and took his hand and the oafs at the other end whistled as if they'd never seen a man and a woman hold hands before. 'Let's go outside,' she said.

And there, beneath an optimistic blue sky, with Warren Stone – goddamn it, why was he always there? – watching on, Dan kissed her.

'I'll go and see Amelia tomorrow,' Jess said. 'I'm sure I can talk her round.'

But Amelia wasn't to be talked around.

'I have one arm, Jessica,' she spat. 'And scars where I once had a face. Part of my nose is gone.'

Jess flinched.

'If you're wincing at the mere thought of it, the sight of it will be a million times worse,' Amelia continued relentlessly. 'If I know one thing it's that there aren't enough men to go around, not now half of them are dead. Nobody will choose me over a smooth-skinned debutante with full use of her limbs. I came over here to find a husband – because God knows there are no men left in England – and Dan has made that impossible.'

'Love isn't about what you look like,' Jess said.

'Isn't it? So you weren't attracted to Dan's face? Or his body?'

'I was his friend for a long time before I was his lover, Amelia. I didn't think about his body or his face when I was his friend.'

'And you don't think about it now? Don't revel in running your hands over his naked flesh? Don't glance at him and catch your breath because he's so handsome? You were a model. You've traded on your looks and your body for years. Don't pretend it doesn't matter. Don't try to make out like I'm the unprincipled one. All's fair in love and war, didn't you know?' Amelia's eyes, between the bandages on her face, glared at Jess, a frosty, implacable blue.

Jess sat down. 'Wouldn't you rather marry someone you loved?' she asked gently. 'Someone who loved you?'

Amelia cut her off. 'Under the bandages, I now have a face only a mother could love. And you know as well as I do how much my mother loved me. Which means I have no one. So don't you sit there, secure in the knowledge that you've landed a handsome and wealthy man, and tell me to wait for love. I don't care about love. I never have. My parents cured me of that. I want my freedom.'

Amelia's voice lowered but it struck Jess harder than the forceful tone of a moment before. 'Marriage to the admiral gave me that freedom,' Amelia went on. 'He was away at sea and I had a house, parties, friends, fun. All for the bargain price of sex once in a blue moon and escort services at occasional dinners. As a single woman, I have *no* freedom. Nowhere to live, no money. Because I was childless, my husband's home and belongings have passed to his brother. But I also know that I won't have any freedom by marrying a man besotted with me.'

So Jess said it, hoping that because she wasn't saying it directly to Dan, it wouldn't have the consequences they'd feared. 'I love Dan. He loves me. What he and I have isn't a fleeing wartime romance. It's forever.'

'Hasn't everything you've seen over the past two years shown you that there is no forever? I learned that in boarding school – that even a daughter isn't forever. That's why there are boarding schools and husbands.'

For the first time, Jess felt how deeply Amelia's parents' abandonment of her at a Parisian boarding school in order to avoid the heavy lifting of caring for a child had hurt her. When they were fifteen, Jess and Amelia had turned the fact that their parents weren't concerned about them in the same way that most other parents seemed to be for their children into an amusing game: a competition to see whose parents would do the most neglectful thing that month. Amelia usually won.

'I don't believe in love,' Amelia reiterated. 'I've made my choice. Dan owes me.'

Jess stood up and whirled around, needing to leave. She crashed into a nurse who said, 'Pardon me,' in German.

The last thing Jess heard was Amelia shouting at the nurse, 'I don't speak your filthy goddamn language so don't use it in front of me!'

⁓

Jess drove straight to find Dan. 'I've made everything worse. I didn't mean to, and I know I can't possibly really know how you feel but, talking to her, I felt so guilty and you must feel a thousand times worse and I just wanted to help –'

'Jess.' He put his hands on her shoulders and made her stop. The light was back in his eyes and he looked determined, almost back to the Dan she knew. 'I can fix this. I feel better this morning. Plenty of jeeps use the road I took. I asked around. What happened was bad luck. So maybe I wouldn't have taken you that way but I've been down that road before. And yes, I was in a hurry to see you but I was concentrating on the road and I was being vigilant, like always. I owe her, that's for sure, but I don't owe her marriage.'

Relief coursed through Jess. She didn't know what she'd been thinking but Amelia's arguments had seemed unassailable, as if there really was no option other than Amelia being alone for the rest of her life. Jess knew Amelia well enough to know that was not something Amelia would tolerate and nor, she supposed, did Amelia deserve that. Still, Dan's last words haunted her. *I owe her.* They were so much like Amelia's words.

But maybe it wasn't true, Jess thought now. Maybe Amelia being out there *wasn't* an accident. *I don't speak your filthy goddamn language,* Amelia had screeched at the nurse.

Back at the press camp, she searched until she found Meg.

'Meg, you know you said a woman rang looking for Dan the other day?'

Meg looked momentarily puzzled, then nodded. 'Yes.'

'Was she American?'

Meg snorted. 'Hell no. She was as English as Henry the Eighth and just as snooty. Why?'

'No reason,' Jess said before she walked slowly away. Amelia had called the morning of the accident wanting to know where Dan would be that day. And lo and behold she'd turned up to the very same spot to translate German even though she didn't speak the language.

If Amelia hadn't lied to get herself to where Dan had been, none of this would have happened.

~

The whole next day ambled past without a word from Dan. When Jess found herself snapping at Martha, she took herself off in her jeep to Hitler's apartment, thinking Dan would be in the command room. But Jennings said, concern smudging his freckles together, that Dan was ill and had been in his room all afternoon. Jennings was happy to smuggle her upstairs when she said she had something important to tell Dan, something that might help.

Dan didn't answer her knock so she pushed the door open and found him sitting on the floor, back against the wall, eyes impossibly damp.

'What is it?' she cried, sinking to the floor, wrapping her arms around him and holding him to her.

He didn't speak for a long time. Then he said, 'Amelia's father is Lieutenant General Miles Gordon-Dempsey of the British Second Army.'

The words were enunciated slowly and clearly as if he was trying to understand them even as he spoke.

Jess shook her head, confused. 'What does that have to do with anything?'

'He was at the hospital when I went to see Amelia this morning. He's furious about what's happened to his daughter. He wants someone hung out to dry and he more than outranks me.'

'But Amelia shouldn't even have been there,' Jess began. 'She –'

Dan kept talking. 'Her father can make anything happen that he chooses.'

It was a bit late for parental concern now, Jess thought. Where had Amelia's father been all through boarding school? But amputation and severe facial scarring were probably traumatic enough to warm anyone's relationship.

'They'll court-martial me tomorrow unless I agree to what Amelia wants,' Dan said. 'A new CO will step in now, right at the end, not giving a shit about any of the men in my battalion. I've been with these men for two years and right now is the hardest time to keep them focused and motivated and unafraid because we all know the end is so goddamn near and nobody wants to be the one to die the day the Germans surrender like those unlucky bastards in the Great War. And even if it's over in Europe, they're still fighting in the Pacific. Right now, they're working out which divisions to send over there. It could easily be mine. And . . .' He clenched his fists and the look on his face was one of disbelief, as if he couldn't comprehend he was even saying these words.

'Major Thompson would be their new CO,' he finished.

'Oh no.' Jess's words were a moan. There was no way Dan would, or should, let a man like Major Thompson lead his men.

'I'm in charge of seven hundred and fifty men. I know almost all their names. I know that you can't put Grayson in the rear because he freezes if he sees what happens to everyone in front. I know that I have to let Kohn say all his prayers right before I give the order to move in otherwise Kohn won't shift until he's done and he'll be out in the open for anyone to shoot. Major Thompson won't know. He won't know that Jennings' mother still writes to me and asks me to keep her son safe. He won't know that, tomorrow, I'm supposed to get one of my platoons to clear the woods where there's a rogue Panzer and that nobody wants to go and I'm the only person who can get them to do it without force. As if all of that isn't bad enough, you and I both know what kind of man Thompson is.'

'So you told Amelia you'd marry her?' Jess's voice wobbled.

'No.' Dan shook his head hard. 'I told Amelia that the only woman I'd marry was you.'

Jess's choked-back sob was so loud it ricocheted off the walls like the crack of gunfire. Dan was here mourning his men, eyes soaked with tears because he wouldn't be able to see them safely through to the end of the war when she'd thought he was crying because he was about to tell her he couldn't marry her. He would sacrifice his honour, give up his good name, for her and their love. She was so goddamn selfish and he was so goddamn unselfish and the whole thing was so goddamn unfair.

She leaned into him, fingertips wiping his tears, one for Grayson, one for Kohn, one for Jennings, and one for every other man in his battalion who he'd trained and cajoled and protected and lead for two long years. He slid a hand along her jaw and drew her lips to his, kissing her in a haze of smothered sobs and falling tears.

'I love you, Jess,' he said, and it wasn't until after she'd left, after Jennings had smuggled her back out, that she realised he'd broken their promise.

PART EIGHT

D'Arcy

*T*wenty-seven

D'Arcy woke on the sofa the morning after Josh had walked away from her, not even remembering falling asleep, wishing she could forget Josh's kiss, Josh's hands on her, the way he made her feel – cherished – and the way she'd made herself feel at the end. She stood and climbed the stairs slowly, quietly, but still a door opened and Jess appeared.

'Will you walk with me?' Jess asked and D'Arcy nodded; anything to avoid facing Josh.

D'Arcy slipped her arm into the older woman's, returning downstairs and then outside, breathing in deeply because it was magical, a place apart from the world, except here, in this beautiful, deceptive oasis, she'd learned more about herself than she cared to know.

They walked down to the canal, to the very spot D'Arcy and Josh had picnicked at days before, as Jess continued her tale, telling D'Arcy about Dan's proposal, how she'd accepted, how her friend Amelia had used ruthless blackmail to try to force Dan to marry her instead. And that Dan had decided to give up everything – his honour, his men, his reputation – because his love for Jess was stronger than anything else.

'Could you help me to sit down?' Jess asked, breaking the flow of terrible words. 'I keep in reasonable working order by walking but getting up and down is much harder than it used to be. Beneath that tree would be perfect.'

D'Arcy hesitated. The tree Jess had indicated was one of *Les Faux*, the very one D'Arcy had thought might have secrets hoarded within its shadows. But of course it *was* the perfect place to sit; the drapery of the branches, falling like an elegant silk gown to the lawn beneath, would shelter them from the sun.

'It doesn't bite,' Jess said, indicating the tree. 'I once thought it was a sorceress but the only person who can change your future is yourself. Not a tree in the guise of an enchantress.'

So D'Arcy levered Jess down onto the bank of the canal under the trees. The older woman slipped off her shoes and dangled her feet in the water. It looked like such a good idea that D'Arcy did it too. For a moment, she could see them there as if through a camera: a younger woman and an older one, backdropped by a striking tree, in paradise, but neither of them truly happy. The weight of secrets and the past lay around them like the shell-torn debris of war, secrets and a past that were now being handed on to D'Arcy.

D'Arcy stared at the water. As far as she knew, it hadn't mattered how much Dan had loved Jess; the marriage had never taken place. And D'Arcy wasn't sure that, right now, she could face the end of this particular story if they were indeed marching straight on into heartbreak. 'Do you want to see the film?' she asked Jess suddenly.

Jess hesitated and D'Arcy felt her cheeks flush. Why would Jess want to see D'Arcy's efforts? Jess had photographed wars. Been published in *Vogue*. Had left a legacy. D'Arcy had made crates for artworks and had fashioned for herself a barren kind of life. Like Victorine's.

'Anyone else's film of me I could look at,' Jess said at last. 'But yours will be too honest for me, I fear.'

Jess began to stand and, somehow, as if he had a telepathic connection to Jess's needs, Josh appeared, ready to help her back to the house.

D'Arcy couldn't look at him. Instead, she stayed by the canal, feet wet, turning Jess's words over in her mind. Had she meant it as a compliment? And how did she know that, in choosing the cinéma vérité style, what D'Arcy had been searching for was honesty. Honesty of a kind Victorine had never seen fit to grant her. D'Arcy felt the boughs of the tree brush lightly against her back and she felt the untold stories, stories of which Jess, and perhaps now D'Arcy, were the custodians, begin to stir.

Inexplicably, Josh returned to the canal.

'I wanted to apologise,' he said, standing beside another of the crazy beech trees, the one that looked like a girl holding out her skirt of leaves, just as D'Arcy had done when she crossed the drawbridge that very first day, ready to dance away, laughing, before anybody could catch her.

'What for?' she asked warily. An apology from Josh was the last thing she expected.

'I promised you a chaste massage and it ended up being anything but. So I'm sorry. I know you have a lot on your mind and that you don't want to tell me about it and the last thing you need is me pushing myself on you. So I want you to know that I'll leave you in peace from now on.'

Please don't. But he'd gone before D'Arcy could say the words.

~

That night, D'Arcy asked Jess for the permission she'd been too afraid to seek before now. Jess granted it. Then D'Arcy rang the gallery and told them what she knew: that Jessica May was the photographer, that they should expand the exhibition to include her war photography, and that D'Arcy was making a documentary about

Jess. At the end, she made herself say, 'I think you should include the documentary in the exhibition. Otherwise it won't feel complete.'

And Esther, the curator, didn't laugh. She sounded excited. She'd been at university with D'Arcy and knew her well. 'When can you send me a rough cut?' she asked.

'By the end of the week,' D'Arcy promised, exhilaration and nerves making her smile crookedly. She'd given her work the opportunity to be judged. Maybe it wouldn't be adequate. And she would accept that and try harder and learn more. But maybe it would be more than adequate. Maybe it would be as honest as Jess had imagined.

Then, on the penultimate night of D'Arcy's stay, Jess asked D'Arcy if she would join her for dinner in the folly. It was hot outside so D'Arcy threw on the mini-dress she'd worn the night she had dinner with Josh but stopped short when she saw him sitting at the table with Jess, obviously having been asked to join them too.

He looked tired and the only chair available was the one beside him. She took it, thinking how easy it would be to lean across and into him, to feel the weight of his arm around her shoulders, to apologise to him. But then they would be back to where they were before, waiting for the next moment when D'Arcy would disappoint him. Waiting for D'Arcy to leave.

Jess began to speak. 'You think you don't want to hear the rest of it. But there are some things, the genesis of all this terrible aftermath, that would be better coming from me. Victorine wasn't there when some of it happened. I telephoned her a few days ago and told her that you were here, that you knew who I was and that was why you were ignoring her phone calls. She forgave my meddling, which I had never meant to go so far, or to have these consequences. She isn't to blame. I am. And if she, who has endured more than anyone, can forgive, then I think you can forgive her.'

'You spoke to Victorine?' D'Arcy said incredulously. 'When? And why does Josh need to be here?'

Jess forestalled her. 'I want you both to hear the story.' Then she began. 'Dan did marry Amelia. I . . .' Her eyes filled with tears, so many tears.

D'Arcy felt her own eyes fill too. All she wanted was for the story to be over; for the crying to stop. But what if the end of the story wasn't the end of the sadness? *Don't say any more*, she wanted to urge. *Stop now*.

And for a few seconds, D'Arcy thought that Jess had somehow heard her plea because nobody spoke. How lovely the night was, the gentle whisper of flower stems stretching and yawning and then curling in to slumber, the swish of the last bird's wings flying home to roost, the rustle of night creatures awakening. Lemon and chive-scented air. The taste of champagne grapes on her tongue.

'I fell pregnant,' Jess said. The fissuring of the calm. 'I couldn't be sure the child was Dan's. So I let him go with Amelia.'

Jess's eyes fell to stare blindly at her hands. D'Arcy had the overwhelming sense that Jess was ashamed – but of what? And why, if Jess had loved Dan so much, would she have been in a situation where she'd fallen pregnant to another man? It would be heartless to ask such a question, so D'Arcy did not.

'I suppose I chose heartbreak in an attempt not to hurt anybody else. Which seems to be a common thread in this narrative.' Jess finally looked at D'Arcy, quite pointedly.

'But the child might have been Dan's,' D'Arcy protested, as if she could undo the heartbreak, take everyone back in time, forge another path, one that wouldn't result in her sitting here, heart so heavy in her chest she wondered why her ribs weren't breaking.

'Might,' Jess repeated, her mouth quirking up ruefully. 'Such a simple but dangerous word. Like hope. The things we do for might and for hope.'

'Where is your son or daughter now?' Josh asked quietly, stealing the words from D'Arcy's mouth.

'She died in childbirth. Almost thirty years ago.'

'Oh no.' D'Arcy's words were stricken and the look on Josh's face expressed everything that she felt. 'The baby . . . ?' she whispered.

'Survived. The rest is for your mother to tell you,' Jess said, standing up. 'She'll be waiting for you when you return to Australia. Forgiving someone is the bravest thing you can ever do.' And then she made her way slowly back to the house before D'Arcy could ask the last question, the question Jess must want her to ask of Victorine: *But what has this to do with me?*

The moment Jess had gone, Josh stood too, as if eager to get away. 'You don't need to leave. I promise you're safe from me,' D'Arcy said, defaulting to a wisecrack to stop herself saying the thing she most wanted to: *Please stay. Help me work out what all of this means.*

The effect of her words on Josh was instantaneous. 'Am I?' Anger flashed in the blue-black of his eyes. 'That night on the sofa you would have had sex with me as a distraction. A short time off from thinking about whatever the hell is going on. I don't want to be somebody's distraction.'

What could she say to that? He was as stubborn as she was, and he was also right to hold fast to what he wanted, to not lose his scruples over a girl on a sofa who wanted something from him that he wasn't prepared to give in exchange for nothing. It was almost the inverse of how she'd seen the situation the night he'd massaged her shoulders on the sofa. While she thought about this, misinterpreting her silence, he walked away.

D'Arcy sat in the folly for a long time, the thick, pink scent of the Judas trees muddling her mind so she couldn't think at all. Eventually, she got up and returned to the chateau, almost jumping out of her dress when a shadow moved on the terrace.

'Can I ask you a question?' Jess said from the chair in which she'd been sitting, quite possibly watching the whole scene.

'I expect you will anyway,' D'Arcy replied with a half-smile.

Jess smiled too. 'You're right. Do you know Josh? Really know him? Because if you do, then you don't need hope.'

'I do,' D'Arcy replied unthinking. 'I *really* do,' she repeated, understanding at last the question.

She knew Josh's past; she knew he was a good man. She knew that he respected her; he'd listened to her talk about her dreams and aspirations in a way nobody ever had. Most of all, she knew now that he wasn't disappointed in her. Rather, she'd hurt him. Because he cared about her.

Everything she'd done since she'd arrived at the chateau ran in horrible slow-motion before her eyes. That she'd thought so much of herself and hardly ever about Josh. She may have bought him a scarf, but that was impulse rather than deliberate action. She *had* treated him like a distraction. She hadn't told him her deepest hurts and secrets the way he'd trusted her with his.

He didn't deserve her omissions. He deserved the gift of her trust, a gift he'd given her without hesitation. And Victorine deserved the same – for D'Arcy to have enough faith in her to allow her the chance to explain. To allow for the possibility of, as Jess had said, forgiveness.

Most of all, D'Arcy realised now, she cared for someone else besides her mother. She cared very much that she had hurt Josh. And her admiration for Jess as an artist had shifted; in working with Jess, in being taken into her confidence, D'Arcy now cared for Jess as a woman, as someone who had made mistakes and was hurting too.

D'Arcy stepped forward, without giving Jess any warning, and wrapped her arms around her, holding her. It took only a few seconds for Jess to sag into the embrace as if she'd been waiting for it for all her life.

And the strength of emotion in that embrace forced words to come together in D'Arcy's mind, Jess's words from earlier: *She died in childbirth. Almost thirty years ago. The rest is for your mother to tell you.*

D'Arcy was almost thirty years old. Victorine was not biologically D'Arcy's mother. Was that why Jess had told D'Arcy the story – was D'Arcy actually Jess's granddaughter?

PART NINE

Jess

War tears, rends. War rips open, eviscerates. War scorches. War dismembers. War ruins.

— Susan Sontag

And where do they go from here — the Servicewomen and all the others who, without the glamour of uniform, have queued and contrived and queued, and kept factories, homes and offices going? Their value is more than proven: their toughness where endurance was needed, their taciturnity when silence was demanded, their tact, good humour and public conscience; . . . how long before a grateful nation (or, anyhow, the men of the nation) forget what women accomplished when the country needed them? It is up to all women to see to it that there is no regression — that they go right on from here.

— Audrey Withers, *British Vogue*, 1945

Twenty-eight

FRANCE, MAY 1945

After Dan said those words – *I love you* – Jess left for Paris. She sent him a note, trying to explain the unexplainable. That she couldn't let him face a court martial, couldn't let the leaderless men in his battalion die in Europe or in the Pacific, governed by a man like Major Thompson, just so that he could marry her. She gave him her blessing to marry Amelia in order to keep his men safe. She told him he had to do the right thing. She ended the note by saying:

Remember how I once said that I didn't want to live if I knew that you had died? So I want your word that you will look after yourself. But I also don't want to live in the knowledge that you are heartbroken. One day, this will fade. You once told me that everything does. Why should this be any different?

A stupid tear dropped onto the notepaper as she wrote the last words, smudging the letters, betraying the fact that, while she might have written them, she did not for one minute believe them. It would never fade.

And she held onto the thought that, perhaps if she just absented herself, while Amelia might marry Dan, the marriage wouldn't last. Dan and Amelia would be married just long enough to save Dan. Despite her scars and her arm, Amelia would find her feet; she always did. Then a divorce could be arranged, leaving Dan and Jess free to be together.

'Jessica May. What a pleasure.' Warren Stone's smirking face greeted her as she pulled into the Hotel Scribe. 'I heard you were coming. And just when I'm in Paris too.'

'How the hell did you hear that?' Jess hauled her bags over her shoulder and marched up the steps.

Warren followed her. 'Correspondents love to gossip. I was on a call to the PRO in Munich yesterday and he filled me in on all the hot topics of conversation there.'

'Like the war?' Jess glowered. 'Isn't that hot enough for any of you?'

'All work and no play would make us a dull lot, as the saying goes. We have to take our amusements when we can. Which it seems you were more than willing to do with one Lieutenant Colonel Hallworth. Until he threw you over for an English girl. And you've come here to mend your broken heart.'

'Excuse me.' Jess stalked off to the elevator before she lost all of her dignity by crying in front of Warren Stone.

Her plan was to stay one night in Paris. Surely she could avoid Warren for one night? She'd spend tomorrow saying farewell to Victorine and then she'd get herself back to London, and on to New York. Easy.

And she wouldn't think about Dan. Which was the hardest thing of all.

She left early in the morning to collect Victorine, only to discover that her jeep was missing. The PRO told her that Warren Stone had borrowed it, leaving a message that Jess should take his instead.

'Why didn't he take his own?' she growled, knowing it wasn't the PRO's fault and the best thing for her to do was to quit grumbling and take the jeep so that Warren wouldn't find out he'd irked her, which was most likely his aim.

'I need to log where you're going,' the PRO replied, unperturbed.

'Verzy today, then London tomorrow. After that I never want to see another khaki-coloured jeep again,' she said petulantly.

Her mood hardly improved on seeing Victorine because the little girl would not accept the news that Dan was marrying a lovely lady, and that she would soon have a mommy.

'But you're my *maman*,' Victorine said sternly.

'Oh, darling, I'm not,' Jess protested, willing her goddamn eyes to stop leaking.

'Yes, you are,' Victorine said. 'I will not have another *maman*.'

Rather than discuss it, Jess drove them both to *Lieu de Rêves* for another picnic. They spent a sleepy and almost happy day, where they both behaved as if nothing had changed and oh, it was heaven. Jess almost began to believe it; that nothing *had* changed. Until just before they were about to leave and Victorine was inspecting the dwarf beech trees by the canal. Jess held her camera up, thinking to take a photograph, but the wind blew and one of the tree's gnarled and twisted branches reached towards the little girl, like a sorceress about to cast a spell.

'No!' Jess cried and Victorine looked at her, puzzled.

'The tree is lonely,' Victorine pronounced, in that way she had of seeming far too adult for her age. 'I was going to tell it we would be back soon.'

Back soon. Dan and Jess and Victorine sitting beneath the lonely tree, picnicking as they had just last month. Jess blinked. *Don't cry.* She forced a smile and the tree settled into benignity. It was time to go, before she found that she could not.

She held Victorine's hand as they walked back to the car, the tiny fingers clasping Jess's with such confidence and such trust. It was almost impossible to let go, to allow the child to climb into the jeep, to drive towards Paris, not knowing when or if she'd ever see Victorine again.

They hadn't gone far when the jeep began to rattle, the wheels to slip. A flat tyre. Far from being a nuisance, Jess was grateful for the extra pocket of time she could spend with Victorine while she fixed the car. Except the spare wasn't there. She cursed Warren under her breath. Perhaps they could keep driving to the next town. Jess checked the tyre but saw that it had a long nail in it, a slow leak that had done its work while they picnicked; they weren't going anywhere for now.

How long would it take for another vehicle to drive along this out-of-the-way road? Perhaps one of the workers from the nearby vineyards might come past. And it seemed her prayers were answered after not more than ten minutes by the noise of a car.

She almost cried with relief when she saw it was a US Army jeep like her own. She held out one hand to flag it down, the other shielding her eyes from the glare of headlights. The jeep pulled to a stop. A man climbed out.

Warren Stone.

'Got yourself in trouble?' he asked with a grin.

Jess's stomach twisted. No spare tyre. Warren taking her jeep and leaving her with his. The coincidence of him being the one to find her.

'Who's this?' he asked, looking into the back of the jeep where Victorine lay stretched out, sleeping.

'Dan's niece. Lieutenant Colonel Hallworth's niece,' she corrected herself.

'What a delightful child.' Warren stroked Victorine's cheek. It was the kind of gesture that might suit a doting elderly lady but coming from Warren, the gesture made Jess's skin crawl.

'*Maman*?' Victorine said sleepily, stirring and yawning.

'*Maman*?' Warren repeated. 'My, that is interesting.'

'She's Dan's brother's child. Born before I even knew Dan. She calls me that because she has no one else.'

'And nor do you. Have anyone else. Just me, and a dark road and a broken jeep. Sweet child, you'll have to excuse your *maman* and me for a while. We have some business to transact.'

And Jess knew that the thing she'd dreaded since his words, spoken to her in a bar in London — *One day, Captain May, you will regret this conversation very much* — had finally come to pass.

'No,' she said, but even she could hear the shock in her voice.

He shrugged. 'Do you want me to wake the child so she can watch?'

Jess felt her hands begin to shake. 'You wouldn't.'

'Wouldn't I?'

Her Colt was in her own jeep, the one Warren had taken that morning. She didn't have a knife. She had only herself.

But Warren was bigger and stronger and even though terror would make her fight and kick and punch and scream, she knew he'd win in the end. And although she couldn't believe that she would ever acquiesce to such a thing, she knew it was better to get it done quietly behind one of the trees at the side of the road while Victorine slept. She would never want Victorine to witness the violence of Jess resisting Warren, a violence that would scar Victorine for life in a way different to the scars Amelia bore, but perhaps the more powerful.

Her stomach roiled and she thought she might be sick. She tried to breathe, in and out. She tried to separate her mind from her body, to send her thoughts elsewhere and leave Warren with only her shell. But she felt one treacherous tear roll down her cheek.

Then she made herself nod, indicating a tree a little way down the road, hoping its carapace of leaves would screen from Victorine's sight, should she chance to wake, what was about to happen.

'Glad to find you're so amenable,' Warren said, excitement shining like flak in his eyes.

Jess leaned into the car to kiss Victorine, darling child, whose eyes were soft-shuttered with sleep.

Then she followed Warren to the tree. She tried to hold back the tears but she couldn't and Warren reached up to wipe them away, thumbs pressing into her cheekbones. It was the worst thing of all.

That he could take a gesture of kindness and turn it into something vicious made the first sob escape. He smiled.

And so she wept as she let him kiss her and unbutton her blouse and lift up her skirt and take what he wanted from her. He groaned loudly as he moved roughly into her, breathing hard as if it was a pleasurable moment, a wanted moment, a moment to cherish.

Jess closed her eyes. And still she wept.

When Warren was done he sagged against her, face pressed into her neck. Jess opened her eyes at last to see a five-year-old child standing sleepily before them, having parted the low-hanging branches that Jess had thought would conceal forever what had just happened. Instead, Victorine stared in confusion at the sight of a man's body pressed close to Jess, at Jess's skirt lifted far higher than it should be, at the tears on Jess's face.

'Victorine,' Jess gasped, pushing Warren off her.

He stumbled backwards, hands fumbling with his trouser buttons and Jess caught sight of his face. The expression he wore was not one of gloating, roistering victory as she'd expected. But something else.

He reached out a hand for her and Jess recoiled, thinking he was going to hit her now, not content with the physical violence he'd so far inflicted. But he touched her hair instead, almost tenderly, and said, puzzled, 'It wasn't what I thought it would be.'

Jess backed away, tucking Victorine behind her, outrage unleashed at last – that he would think the only abomination in what had just happened was his disappointment.

'Did you really believe I would fall in love with you just because you kissed me? Just because you did . . . *that*?' Her voice was as deadly quiet as a sniper tiptoeing through a defeated village, and colder than the bitter winter of the Ardennes. She could not yell or scream; her anger was so ferocious it was almost beyond her control. 'I loved Dan a long time before I ever kissed him,' she hissed. 'There is a very big difference between this . . .' She shifted her eyes contemptuously to his unbuttoned fly. 'And love.'

She turned from Warren, picked up Victorine and carried her back to the car, the child's sweet soapy smell pressed into her neck where Warren's mouth had been only moments before. She prayed to God it was too dark for Victorine to have seen very much. That she was too young to comprehend, least of all to commit to memory, what she had witnessed.

The most appalling part of the whole appalling evening was that, in an abhorrent way, Jess had won. Warren had got what he'd obviously long wanted but had found that the way he'd obtained it had made it not to his liking. A bathetic end to the game for him and a victory for Jess as hollow as any in Europe that had cost millions of lives.

For all of the long, silent ride back to Paris, Jess thought of three things. The US Army soldier saying *ain't nobody going to stop me having her.* Dan saying, *I love you.* And her terror at what those words would bring upon one of them.

The bomb, it seemed, had just gone off.

Twenty-nine

*J*ess was in London longer than she'd expected. The war in
Europe finished just as she arrived. Everybody cheered and
drank champagne and kissed. Jess didn't. Instead, she lost the
contents of her stomach at the thought that maybe if she and Dan
had stretched Amelia out just a few more days, then Amelia's threat
would have amounted to nothing. But then she heard that Dan's
division was likely being sent to the Pacific and while it didn't make
her stomach feel any better, it reassured her that she'd done the right
thing. Imagine if she'd been responsible for sending Dan's battalion
off to the unknowns of Asia with a new CO who was a stranger to
both the men and to decency?

She handed in her accreditation papers in London but it took a
month to organise passage for her back to New York. Troops being
repatriated had priority.

She received two surprises in London. The first was a letter,
forwarded from the Hotel Scribe and obviously opened by Warren
Stone. Warren had enclosed a note that read: *I couldn't let you leave
without seeing this.*

The letter was from Dan. It said:

Jess, I know it's a cliché that a writer like you will detest but you're the best thing that's ever happened to me. Better than the best; you were the miracle.

I keep asking myself — if I'd never gone to your party at the Scribe, would that be better? Then we'd still be the best of friends, and I'd still be able to see you. But I shake my head because half of you isn't enough. All of you isn't enough. None of you is unthinkable.

I was out on a raid last night and I thought perhaps I would die and that would be good because then I wouldn't feel like this but I know you left because of my men and to throw it in your face by dying would be too cowardly. Besides, I know how you'd feel if I died and I can't do that to you.

Be happy, Jess. I can bear this if I know you're happy. Otherwise my life has nothing in it at all.

Jess sank to the floor, brought to her knees by Dan's letter, as Warren Stone had intended her to be. It took her a long, long time to stand up, to splash her face with water, to pour herself a whiskey and light, then stub out a cigarette, unsmoked.

Because the other surprise, she knew now, was that she wasn't going to New York alone. She was taking a child with her, inside her womb. A child whose father was unknown. She and Dan had always been careful but she wasn't dumb enough not to know just how many rubbers had failed in wartime. And then there was Warren. He hadn't bothered with a rubber.

Only a couple of days separated the last time she was with Dan from that awful night with Warren. She would never know. And she would *never* want Dan to find out what had happened. He would kill Warren with his bare hands and then he really would be court-martialled.

All of which made it more important that Dan marry Amelia, if he hadn't already, and forget about Jess.

Love, she thought wearily as she stared out at the bombed husk of London. War makes us monsters or angels, but so too does love. And now she would leave behind in Europe the love that Dan had made for her out of the ashes of war, a love ruined finally by monsters.

⁓

'You're back!' Bel folded Jess into her arms when she appeared in her office two weeks later, skinnier than when she'd left, older – so much older – knowing too much and not as good at pretending as she used to be.

Bel held her at arm's-length after the initial hug and cast her eyes over Jess critically. 'Thank goodness,' she said, seemingly satisfied, sitting down to light a cigarette. 'You need to eat, Jessica May, get your curves back, but I don't see why we can't have you back on the cover in a couple of months. Nobody remembers Kotex now.'

Kotex. Even Jess struggled to think what on earth Bel was talking about. The dimmest memory of a field in upstate New York, a cow bellowing in the background, Bel stepping out of a car to speak to her, a conversation with Emile – God, she'd all but forgotten Emile too.

Jess fiddled with a cigarette and then put it away.

'We're doing a feature on Stella Designs and their patriotic dresses soon. You'd be perfect for it. I'll set it up.' Bel smiled as if it were just like old times; she hadn't even mentioned the war.

But how could anyone pick up the life they'd once lived, like a gown that had been tucked away in a forgotten cupboard, slip it back on and resume the smiling and the laughing?

'I thought I'd keep reporting for you,' Jess said.

'Reporting?' Bel tapped ash off her cigarette. 'I don't need any more war reports. Bar the Pacific, it's all but over. Paper supplies will be back to normal soon. You've done your job. You can have some fun.'

'I don't know if I can,' Jess said honestly.

'Of course you can.' Bel was adamant. 'No good comes from moping. Everybody wants to start afresh, to kick up their heels, and they need to know what to wear while doing it.'

Kick up their heels. Dance on the graves of the fallen. Whoop over the bodies of the living dead from the camps. Grind out their cigarettes on the memories of the missing. Jess shook her head. 'I might see what else I can pick up. Thank you though,' she added, resurrecting her manners from the place they'd been stowed, unneeded in war.

'Well,' Bel said, looking a little miffed. 'My offer will stand. I'm proud of what you did over there. But you don't have to do it any longer.'

Jess kissed Bel's cheeks and walked out onto the street, to an assault of buses and cabs and horns and neon signs and intact buildings and people wearing colours other than khaki and carrying purses instead of weapons, unhelmeted, not a gas mask in sight, or a jeep, or a drop of blood.

And so, for the next two months, Jess tried. Yes, everybody had heard of her, yes they all thought that her skill behind the camera and her ability to put words together was outstanding. They would be happy to have her. Except . . .

Except that the male correspondents were coming back. And the men in the US Armed Forces. Those men needed jobs more than she did, she was told, because they either did or would soon have a wife and children to support. She'd have someone to support her. She was a knockout! What man wouldn't want to support her? Wink, wink. In fact, why didn't they go out together and get a drink that very night?

'No, thank you,' Jess said. *No thank you, no thank you, no thank you,* over and over again.

In a city plastered with propaganda posters of red-lipsticked women in aprons cooking roast dinners, posters that exhorted women to lay down their tools and their pens and their minds and leave their jobs to the more deserving returned soldiers, Jess soon heard the news about Betty Wasson. Betty had been a CBS correspondent throughout the war and had returned, imagining she'd be employed by CBS in the States now that the war was over. They turned her down. And so Betty Wasson, who'd put together five broadcasts a day from Greece, who'd been wrongly detained as a spy and who'd kept her cool even under questioning from the Gestapo in Berlin, had returned to her pre-war job as an assistant to the food editor at women's magazine *McCall's*. Dorothy Thompson, former European bureau chief for the *New York Post*, was back writing fluff for *Ladies' Home Journal*. What hope did Jess, a mere reporter for *Vogue*, have in finding serious work when women like this couldn't get any?

Then she saw a piece in the *New York Courier* that said the brave and much-decorated Lieutenant Colonel Daniel Hallworth of the United States Army was returning to New York with his wife, Amelia. He would be taking up his position as Editor in Chief of the newspaper. And Jess, telling no one besides Martha what she planned to do, knew that she and the child she carried inside her had to get out of New York forever.

PART TEN

D'Arcy

Thirty

$\mathcal{A}$fter she stepped away from her embrace with Jess, D'Arcy went upstairs and did a lot of thinking in her Buly-perfumed tub. A lot of doubting. And quite a lot of hoping.

She knew Jess wouldn't answer a direct question. She'd made it clear that D'Arcy must ask Victorine. So, instead, the next morning, D'Arcy asked Célie to prepare another dinner in the folly and to deliver an invitation to Josh. She spent the entire day, her last at the chateau, tying up loose ends, terrified that he wouldn't come.

She dressed early, in a startlingly pink 1960s Miss Dior mini-dress with a high-buttoned neckline and elbow-length sleeves, and sat alone in the folly with her thoughts for half an hour before Josh arrived at the appointed time.

'Thank you for coming,' she said with a smile that wasn't teasing or flirtatious or anything other than just plain old D'Arcy. She poured him a wine, and refilled her own glass, already long since drunk.

'Will I need to catch up to you?' he asked, nodding at her glass.

Her stomach flipped and her heart squeezed at both the gentle humour and the note of worry she could hear in his words, at the way she could interpret him so much better than just last week when she'd have thought he was issuing a reprimand. 'I don't think so,' she said as Célie brought out plates of steaming, buttery dorade once more, along with crazily shaped, garden-fresh honeyed carrots and leaves of salad so green that even fine arts-trained D'Arcy couldn't name their precise shade.

D'Arcy waited until Célie had left before she began. 'I asked Jess this morning if she would come to the exhibition in Sydney.'

'What did she say?' he asked, thankfully not pointing out that, as Jess's agent, he really should have been involved in the conversation.

'I want her to see Victorine, my mother, again. Jess wants to as well. But she said she'd have to ask you to accompany her; that while she's done a lot of uncomfortable travelling in her life, age was rather limiting her adventuring now.'

'And you asked me to dinner to see if I would?' He sipped his wine.

As D'Arcy sat across the table from Josh, surrounded by beauty, the air between them thickset with something else entirely, she gathered her courage to her like a favourite dress. 'No,' she replied.

Josh frowned.

'Sorry!' she stuttered. 'I did mean what I just said but it came out wrong. God, I'm shit at this,' she added with a wry smile and he finally looked at her as if she'd piqued his interest and perhaps he didn't despise her.

'I know it's a lot to ask,' D'Arcy said, choosing her words carefully, very aware that he might say no and go back to the chateau, 'but could we go for a walk? I want to say something but it's hard enough with us both just sitting here . . .' It was hard enough just to say that, to admit she felt vulnerable and awkward and unwilling to resort to witty repartee.

Josh nodded and stood. They walked towards the canal, the last frantic rustlings of small animals and the buzzing of insects gathering their last supper agitating the air. In D'Arcy's muddled thoughts, one clamoured more loudly than the rest: that choosing what seemed to be the path of least hurt did not always have the intended consequences, if Jess and Dan and her mother were anything to go by.

She could just say that it was important for Jess to come to the exhibition, that it would only be possible for Jess to come if Josh came too; to put him in a position where he couldn't say no. But he needed to choose and she needed to ask. But first, she needed to explain.

'I found out that Victorine couldn't have children. And I've been so mad . . . no, that's a lie. I've been so . . . sad,' she made herself say it, '. . . because if Victorine's not really my mother, I thought that meant I had no one. Which is why I've been a bit of a bitch,' she finished. 'Finding out about her has made me feel a little lost.'

She stopped walking, realising they were beside the tree she'd sat beneath with Jess. The tree that had, like Jess, tried to tell her what she needed to know. The tree that unwound serenely to the floor of the little wood now and D'Arcy smiled. Because she knew the answer. She wasn't lost. In beginning to unravel the mysteries, she had found someone else inside her who was worthy of being freed.

Josh gave her the smallest and briefest smile in return. 'Thanks for telling me. You haven't been a bitch. But no matter what's happened, I'm not interested in a one-night stand.'

Are you still interested in anything else? D'Arcy wondered. But there was more she had to confess before she could address what he'd said. 'I sent an email to Dan Hallworth, inviting him to the exhibition too. I told him that Jessica May was still alive, and that she would be there.' Josh was back to frowning. It wasn't a good sign but D'Arcy kept going anyway. 'Just like I need to talk to my mother, Jess needs to talk to Dan. I think she thinks she did something he won't forgive her for but, like she said, forgiving someone is the bravest thing you can do. She needs to forgive *herself*. And she'll only do that if she speaks to Dan. You probably think I'm meddling but I feel as if

Jess and Dan aren't finished yet. I'd like them to finally have that promised kiss from the photograph. But if you want to tell her not to come because of it, I'll understand.' Her voice finally trailed off.

'That's very . . .' Wrong. Interfering. Presumptuous. She waited for him to condemn her. 'Romantic,' he finished.

A flicker of hope. It gave her the strength to keep going. 'Everything that's happened made me think that if the woman I'd believed to be my mother could hurt me so much, I couldn't imagine what kind of hurts might come from a person – a lover – who wasn't required by the bond of family to be always there and always kind.'

She dared to look at his face, which was surprised at best, unreadable at worst. 'I'd like you to come to Australia, not for Jess, but for . . . me.' The last word was a whisper that D'Arcy spoke to the ground, a far cry from her usual directness. 'I know that's probably not much of an incentive. And I need to say that it's a risk for you, coming. I don't know when I'll truly be un-lost. Which means I could easily be sad and grumpy and like I've been for the past week. You said you wanted a slower life, a more relaxed life. What's happening in my life right now isn't exactly relaxing.'

Josh hesitated, then asked, 'D'Arcy, how old are you?'

Which meant he wondered too. Would that make everything far too complicated for him? 'The right age to be Jess's granddaughter,' was all she said.

She felt his finger touch her under the chin and lift up her face so he could see her properly. 'Go back to Australia tomorrow like you'd planned to. Talk to your mother. And . . .'

And it was nice knowing you. She closed her eyes against the sound of his next words.

'And perhaps I'll see you next month,' he finished.

Perhaps. Which meant it might not all work out. But then again it might.

The things we do for might and for hope, Jess had said. D'Arcy had just been truly honest about the things that mattered for the very first time and, in return, she'd received a shard of hope. It was worth the discomfort and trepidation it had cost.

PART ELEVEN

Dan

Thirty-one

The hallways of a newspaper office were always busy and noisy but Dan didn't hear any of it. The clack-clack-clack of typewriters; the shrill peal of telephones; the shouts as somebody received a tip-off and jammed their hat on their head and their notebook and pencil in their pocket before charging out into the streets, a newshound on the trail of a story; it was all muted compared to the battlefield. Here, the sounds were steady, unpunctuated by mortar explosions or screams or white phosphorus. Nobody dropped down dead beside him or lost their legs or spilled their intestines onto the ground. Everyone was alive and unhurt at the end of each day.

Dan kept the radio in his office turned up so loudly that everyone who came in to see him complained about it. But he couldn't tell them why he was afraid of silence. Jess would know. He could tell her. Except he hadn't a damn clue where she was.

He'd been to see her editor at *Vogue*, who was equally mystified. 'I haven't seen her for months,' Belinda had said. 'Do you want to offer her a job? I'm afraid you'll have to duel it out with me. I'm still hoping she'll return to adorning my pages with her face and her smile.'

Dan flinched, knowing how Jess would feel about being asked to model again after everything she'd done over in Europe.

'She was looking for something more serious,' Belinda continued. 'The kind of job I imagine a newspaper like yours would be able to provide.'

He knew Bel was fishing, wanting to know why he'd come looking for Jess but he had no intention of telling her. 'Can I leave my card? Please ask her to call me if you speak to her.' His card. Like Jess was a business acquaintance. God, it almost destroyed him handing over that piece of paper to Bel. At least he knew she'd been in New York, which was something.

He'd also tried to speak to Martha, but she was doing a very good job of avoiding him. Too good. She knew something, and she obviously had no intention of telling him.

So he'd heard nothing more. It was, he supposed, unsurprising, but also as painful as having gas in your lungs, a kind of searing agony that left invisible scars, scars that burned in the middle of the night, that ached in the cold, that stung every time he had to leave the office and return to his home.

'Mr Hallworth?' His secretary, Constance, a sensible woman whose instincts he'd grown to trust over the past few months, opened the door after a quick tap.

He turned from his usual place by the window, staring out at skyscraper spires, bayonets of steel tearing into the sky. 'Yes,' he said, pulling his mind back into the present, to his role as Editor in Chief of one of New York's biggest daily newspapers, a role his father had gladly handed to him the moment Dan stepped back onto American soil.

'This came in over the wire,' Constance said. 'Addressed to you. I don't recognise the sender's name. Have we put on a new stringer to cover Nuremberg? Apparently there are pictures too.'

Dan held out his hand, frowning. 'As far as I know, Gareth Hogan's still our stringer. But he doesn't send pictures.' He glanced at the sheet of paper in front of him, expecting it was a mistake, that the cable operator had entered the wrong number and he was about to read a dispatch meant for the *New York Post* or the *New York Times*. But the page clearly stated both his name and the name of his newspaper. His frown deepened as he read the piece.

'This is good,' he said at last. 'Gareth is always too concerned with everyone's name, rank and serial number to get to what the story is all about. Who did you say it's from?'

Constance consulted her notepad. 'An I. Durant. Do you know him?'

'Never heard of him.'

Dan re-read the page in front of him. Monsieur I. Durant was well informed and had thought to speak to the spectators, the people who filed into the courts at Nuremberg to watch the trials, had thought to ask them why they were there, for whom they mourned, and whether any kind of retribution would be enough. There was even a direct quote from one of the Nazis on trial. He was a lesser personage than Goering or Hess for sure, but still. A quote from one of those to be tried was gold.

'Can you get Gareth on the line?' he said to Constance. 'I need to find out what's going on.'

'Sure.' Constance disappeared and, by some miracle, it only took her half an hour to locate their stringer.

She put him through and Dan didn't waste words. 'Why am I getting high quality stories from a Monsieur I. Durant, with quotes from former Nazi officials, when I haven't seen anything from you all day?'

Dan listened without sympathy to his stringer's tale of a broken leg from a drunken jeep accident which would put him out of action for at least a month. 'I survived an entire war without a drunken jeep accident,' he said curtly to Gareth. 'Someone who can't survive a couple of months in a hotel room covering a trial isn't someone I need on my service. You can make it up to me by finding out who Monsieur Durant is and I'll give you a reference that'll get you another job.'

After he'd hung up the phone, Constance knocked again. 'The pictures just came in on the wire,' she said. 'You'll want to take a look.'

She was right. The pictures hadn't been taken by a hack; they were the work of an artist. An artist who hadn't wanted to send film, but prints. The photographer had caught American Judge Francis Biddle with his head turned towards the man before him, one Otto Ohlendorf, who was admitting to having presided over the murder of ninety thousand Jewish people. But the judge's eyes were not fixed on the man. Instead they were turned unknowingly towards the camera and they shone with staunched tears as Ohlendorf spoke dispassionately about his concern for the welfare of those who'd had to administer the killings. *Where is your concern for all those who died?* the image seemed to say, through the suddenly unshielded face of the judge.

The next photograph was of Marie-Claude Vaillant-Couturier; a member of the French Resistance, she had somehow survived both Auschwitz and Ravensbrück and was the first survivor to tell her story to the court. This time, the photographer had caught the judge with the same damp eyes but they were fixed on the woman before him, honouring her by refusing to look away no matter how affecting her words were.

Dan let out a breath. 'Let's get everybody into the conference room to finalise the news budget. This is going front page tomorrow.'

⁓

'That's some Pulitzer-grade reporting you've got on your front cover this morning,' Walter Hallworth said to his son as they drank their coffee and ate their eggs with all of the city's morning newspapers spread out before them.

There had been no time for Dan to look for a home of his own; he'd returned from the war one day and started work at the newspaper the next so the old family home on the Upper East Side was where he now resided. The arrangement perfectly suited his father; Walter Hallworth might have retired but he still liked to know what was happening in the world of journalism and he still liked to have breakfast with his son, no matter that Dan was out the door by six, ready for the day ahead.

'Where'd you find your stringer?' his father asked now.

'He found me,' Dan said, and proceeded to tell his father as much as he was able to. Gareth had been next to useless, unable to find out anything, except that someone had told him that Monsieur Durant was American, but maybe had a French father, had reported sporadically throughout the war, and lived in France.

The bio note that had come with the images said much the same thing. Short of going to Nuremberg, Dan was at a loss, so he'd sent a message to the hotel Durant was staying in, arranging to pay him and to make him their official correspondent. No more drunken stringers stuffing things up.

'Gareth was a good man,' Walter protested mildly. 'Always up for a whiskey.'

'Exactly,' Dan said. 'He's a dinosaur. Does everything drunk and hopes we'll be too busy with national news to read his sloppy reports properly.' He stood up, putting his napkin down on the table, stopping at the running sound of tiny feet.

'Papa!' Victorine called.

Dan kissed her cheeks, soft and warm from her bed. No matter how early he left in the morning, Victorine had a sixth sense about it and would always wake up to kiss him and hug him before he was gone.

'Come here, princess,' Walter ordered.

Victorine walked dutifully over and placed a delicate kiss on each of her grandfather's cheeks, still reserved, Dan noted, even after all this time. Not that she saved her reserve for Walter; she regarded everyone with a graveness and reticence that was completely out of place on someone not quite six years old, never relaxing into friendliness the way she'd done with Jess.

Jess. Dan winced as he did every time he so much as caught himself about to think of her.

'Did you swallow an elephant, Papa?' Victorine asked mischievously, having noticed his grimace.

'Something like that.' He grinned at her.

'Can I come with you today?' Victorine wheedled.

'You'll be bored,' Dan said automatically, then relented as he always did. 'But you can come and have lunch with me.'

Victorine clapped her tiny hands and then sat herself at the table to start her breakfast with her grandfather, who would always try to clear the newspapers away, deeming them unfit for children. Nobody ever said that everything Victorine had seen up to that point in her life had been unfit for children.

That night, when Dan returned home, he stopped in at Victorine's bedroom. As always, she lay awake waiting for him and he tried to remind himself to be home by nine so she would get more sleep, except that he had strong reasons for staying out late. The light in the hallway wasn't on, as it should be, and he reached around for the switch, snapping it on, and crossing to Victorine's side when he saw her face. It bore the red and unmistakable mark of a hand slapped on it.

'What happened?' he said, lifting her out of the bed and tucking her into his lap, burying her head against his shoulder, stroking her hair.

'I was naughty,' Victorine sniffed.

He didn't ask her anything else. 'Never say that you're naughty,' he whispered, kissing her forehead and holding her tightly to him until her limbs relaxed and her breath evened out into sleep. He tucked her back into bed and then made himself walk to the room at the other end of the hallway. He opened the door.

From where he stood, it was impossible to tell that anything was awry. Lamps, carefully chosen for the quality of their shades and the low, soft light that pooled at the stand without casting more than a faint glow into the room, made it seem as if she were simply a wife, and a beautiful one at that, waiting for her husband. Her face was assiduously painted with powder and colour and all manner of creams and lotions, the dress selected to draw attention to her legs and her cleavage. It was only when she turned to his voice, asking, 'What did you do?' that she revealed a tumescent ridge of scar tissue, crawling like a worm over her face, and the sleeve from which nothing hung.

'What did I do?' Amelia replied. 'What do you mean?'

'To Victorine.'

Amelia's face changed, becoming suddenly as unlovely as the scar. 'She's a brat. She hates me. All she does is talk about Jess. Her *maman*.' She spat the word at Dan as if it were the filthiest thing she could say.

'She needs time.' Dan gave a compressed smile because what was at stake was Victorine and he would do whatever he had to do for her. 'It's strange for her, what's happened. It's strange for me too. As it must be for you.'

'What is strange about getting married?' Amelia enquired. 'I believe it's something that men and women all over the world do. It's actually rather ordinary.'

Dan sat in a chair opposite his wife, his body sinking into the plushness. Everything in the room was soft and sumptuous and so very English: brocades and swags and dark wood and velvets and shades of pink and red that Amelia insisted he must call rose. He pressed down the nausea that clogged his throat every time he stepped foot into her bedroom and reminded himself that rose was simply a colour and had nothing whatsoever to do with blood.

He shifted, trying to get comfortable, and eventually stood and sat on the edge of her bed, which was still cushiony and lush but at least it didn't envelop him, draw him down the way the chair did with its upholstered arms and back.

'You know that nothing about this is ordinary,' he said quietly, trying not to provoke a fight.

'It could be if you made a little more effort. Or are you so repulsed by me?'

'Don't,' he said sharply. 'I am not repulsed by your face or your arm.'

'But you are repulsed by what I did to get myself here.' Amelia filled in the subtext he wouldn't say. 'Don't you think it's time to forgive me for that and make the most of the situation we've landed ourselves in? Surely it's better for Victorine if we get along.'

Dan used all his strength to keep his face neutral. How could he ever forgive her for what she'd done? He studied her, her dark brown hair almost the same colour as his, shiny and clean and perfectly styled. Her blue eyes, large and soft and pleading, eyes that she was so good at having her maid enhance with her dressing table of tools. Eyes that she was so good at turning on people, who would be immediately charmed by her limpid and innocent gaze and her pitiful scars and her heartbreakingly missing arm. Her dress, he was sure, had cost him a fortune and it certainly flattered her figure. He wished he could see all the effort, all the polish, as a simple attempt to make the most of the features that were still undamaged, to assuage the pain of remembering what she'd once looked like. But all of it felt calculated, strategic moves to advance her position, or perhaps everything he saw about her was sabotaged by what she'd done to get here.

So yes, she was right. He hadn't forgiven her. And he realised now that his lack of forgiveness was there in everything he did and said, the tone of his voice, the rigid stance of his body whenever Amelia appeared in the room, the way he tried never to really look at her as if that might make her disappear. How must it feel to live like that? How must it make Victorine feel to witness his barely masked loathing? And what kind of man did it make him that he couldn't find even a grain of compassion in him for a woman he'd damaged?

He couldn't stop the sigh escaping and Amelia's face twisted. Even though he knew that, given her temper, he shouldn't ask this now, he did. 'What happened with Victorine?'

Amelia stared at him for a long moment and he waited, braced, for the lie. For the accusations that would be levelled at Victorine about her naughtiness, her wilfulness. For the demand that she be sent to boarding school in Europe. Instead, Amelia's face rearranged itself and, for the briefest instant, Dan thought he saw a trace of honest emotion, a sadness in her eyes.

'What happened is that Victorine would like me to be Jess,' Amelia said flatly. 'And I'm not. I can never be. So I became angry and I hit her. It was not, obviously, my finest moment.' She turned away to pick up her diamond-adorned, gold cigarette case.

Her candidness made his words come out honestly too. 'I'm sorry. Which is useless, but I am.'

'I know you are. And I know that if saying sorry a million times would fix my face and my arm, you would do it.' She paused and they sat, he perched on the edge of the bed, legs braced for escape, and she in the armchair by the fireplace, her cherry-coloured dress blending into the rose fabric of the chair as if she belonged there.

She lit her cigarette, breathed in the smoke, tapped the ash into the tray. He watched her, still waiting for the conversation to escalate into the inevitable argument.

'What will we do?' she asked instead.

'What will we do?' he repeated, surprised. It was the first time she'd asked for his opinion. Until now, she'd pushed and demanded and he'd resisted and ignored and he winced to think of all the quarrels, loud and hostile, all the accusations, all the shame, all the sorrow. 'What would you like to do?' he asked.

'I'd like for Victorine and I to get along. Every day that we don't, you hate me a little more.'

He began to protest, to say that he didn't hate her but she put up her hand. 'All right, you're not capable of hatred. You're too fine a man for that.' Her voice was wry. 'But you hate this situation a little more. Am I right?'

He nodded.

'So, I'm going to retreat,' she said. 'I won't expect you to take me to parties and hold my hand and wrap your arm around me. I won't take dinner with you. I'll stop insisting that we find somewhere to live that's far away from your father. I'll leave you alone. I will try not to hate myself because you can't bear to touch me . . .' Her voice faltered and she ground out her cigarette.

He imagined her sitting in this room every night while he worked late or went out without her and he realised she was wrong; he *was* capable of hatred and he hated himself right now. 'The most important thing is that Victorine be happy,' he reiterated. 'Her life, up till now, has been a shambles. She's had nothing that could be called stability or consistency and she's seen things that children shouldn't know anything about.'

'And you'll do anything for her, won't you?' Amelia spoke to her hands folded in her lap and he knew she understood perfectly well that yes, he would do anything for Victorine, but he would certainly not do anything for his wife.

'I will,' he said.

'Well then.' She looked up and met his gaze and he realised she'd flung the incendiary right back at him. It was up to him, what happened now. He'd been blaming everything on her and sure, some of it was her fault but he was an adult and he'd made a decision and he had to accept the consequences of that decision. Right now, the consequences were hurting Victorine.

And Jess had vanished. It seemed she had no intention, ever, of coming back. So should he blow up everything, continue arguing with and shrinking from Amelia, keep exposing Victorine to a household empty of love, keep loathing himself for what he'd done to Amelia and what he'd done to himself? Or should he do what he could to defuse the grenade before the precious remnants of Victorine's childhood shattered forever?

Thirty-two

*L*ater, as he left Amelia's room, head pounding, wanting to lie down in the dark and — yes, he could admit it — cry, he knew that in trying to fix it, something had shattered after all. His soul.

'Damn you, Jess,' he muttered for the millionth time since Germany. *One day, this will fade. You once told me that everything does. Why should this be any different?* But he'd been wrong. Like the coal seam fires burning beneath the earth's surface for thousands of years, flameless, persistent, the slow burn making them almost impossible to extinguish, what he felt for Jess would never fade.

He would have to pretend, for Victorine's sake, that he was happy. But he didn't know if he could ever do again what he'd just done with Amelia.

'Papa!' The cry made him swivel and turn into Victorine's room. Her face was wet with tears and he held her and shushed her until she stopped sobbing.

'Did you have a dream?' he asked.

And, not for the first time, she nodded and said, 'The man was there again.'

'What man? What did he do?'

But Victorine just shook her head as she always did, unable to articulate anything more about the man and why he had frightened her so. He slid her back down onto her pillow and straightened her sheets, frowning at a noise like rustled paper.

'What do you have in there?' He expected to see one of her many war souvenirs, the ribbons and peg dolls and scraps of khaki that she'd collected from nurses and soldiers alike but what he found were sheets of newspaper. He couldn't help smiling at her peculiar and endearing ways and he lay down on the bed beside her, wanting to keep her safe from dreams. He fell asleep himself, only to be plagued by dreams of his own, dreams about Jess.

Dan was at the breakfast table early as usual, having slunk out without waking Victorine, or so he'd thought until she appeared not ten minutes later, clutching the newspaper he'd found in her bed last night, the newspaper with the pictures from his new correspondent on the front cover.

Victorine's eyes were round and serious as she turned them on Dan. 'You saw *Maman*,' she said inexplicably.

Walter eyed Dan over his eggs.

Dan ignored his father and spoke to Victorine. 'I haven't seen Jess,' he said, picking up his hat even though he hadn't eaten anything.

'But she took these.' Victorine pointed to the photographs in the newspaper.

'A man called Monsieur Durant took them,' Dan said.

Victorine frowned at Dan as if she was disappointed in him. 'I'm not hungry,' she announced, slipping out of the room.

'She sure is a funny kid,' Walter said, studying Dan, who set his face into the most inscrutable expression he could muster. 'But do you know what I think?'

Dan didn't respond, which didn't prevent Walter from continuing. 'That whoever this Jess is, it'd be best if Victorine stopped mentioning her. A child can only have one mother.' Walter wiped his mouth on his napkin and threw it onto the table.

I'd have to cut out her heart to stop her from talking about Jess, Dan wanted to shout. Instead he turned on his heel and strode out the door.

That afternoon, another story came in. And more pictures.

As Dan studied them, he could see, now that Victorine had lifted the blindfold, that the pictures were taken either by Jess or a very skilled copycat. One was solarised perfectly, a technique that so few photojournalists would bother with, but which had always been one of Jess's trademarks. He read over the article and now he knew why yesterday's had punched him so hard in the gut: her phrasing was everywhere, the whisper of her voice in his ear as he read.

And so it went on, every day. Each time he went out for a quick drink at the bar down the road where newspapermen congregated, he was asked about his new correspondent. Everyone assumed the mysterious stringer was a man. Nobody suspected it was Jess.

Someone I met in the army, Dan would answer, and the person he was talking to would groan and slap him on the back and curse Dan's good fortune: to have survived the war unscathed, and to have unearthed a photojournalist from the rubble of that war who had lifted the bar so high, the rest of them could do nothing but walk underneath it.

He spent a week wound tight with fury, that she would reach out to him like this, professionally but not personally. Still, he read each dispatch from her as it came in, searching for a message, a clue, but he found nothing. And so he said nothing. Did nothing. Until he heard himself shouting at his editors in the morning meeting and realised that, even under intense fire from the Germans, he'd never shouted at his men before.

He closed the meeting, picked up his hat, locked his office door and left, driving upstate to nowhere, he'd thought, until he turned into a driveway at the house where Jennings' parents lived.

'Just the man I wanted to thank,' Mrs Jennings said as she embraced him and poured tea for him and cut him an enormous slice of cake. 'I think you had the hardest job in the war, keeping my son alive. I expected he'd be returned to me with at least a few scratches but he looks the same as always.'

Dan smiled. 'He didn't tell you about the broken bones?'

'I can't see those. They must have healed up just fine.' Mrs Jennings sipped her tea. 'I still can't believe the two of you used to hide frogs in the maids' beds but for three years gone you were fighting a war. And doing an excellent job of it too, I hear.'

'I did what everyone else did. No more. No less.' The reply rolled off Dan's tongue the way it always did, succinct and a little clipped, signifying that they should talk about something else. Because how could anyone do an excellent job of leading men to their deaths or, if not death, serious injury? How could anyone look at Amelia and say he'd done an excellent job?

'What's he doing now?' Dan asked. 'The end was such a rush that I didn't get a chance to find out whether he was coming up here to stay with you or going back to the city.'

Mrs Jennings pushed her plate away. 'I'd appreciate you speaking to him for me. He always listens to you. He's a little . . . lost.'

'That can't be right.' The vehemence in Dan's voice surprised them both. He paused and ate a mouthful of cake before he continued. 'I just meant that he was a stronger man at the end than he was at the beginning. I thought he'd land on his feet.'

'He *is* a stronger man.' It was Mrs Jennings turn to pause. 'But what does one do with the sort of strength one learns when fighting a war?'

Mrs Jennings' words played over in Dan's head as he drove back to the city, Jennings' address written on a piece of folded paper in his pocket. What had Dan done with everything he'd learned? Nothing. He'd become, in fact, a coward. Sitting behind a desk at the newspaper offices, restlessly shuffling his feet through meetings, avoiding his wife, pretending to Victorine that everything would work out fine.

At a nondescript block of apartments in Midtown, Dan rang the buzzer until a slurred voice answered.

'Jennings?' Dan asked uncertainly.

The door clicked open.

The man who greeted Dan held the shadows of Jennings in his face, overlaid by someone puffier, unshaven and slightly rank, still smelling of the night before. 'What are you doing to yourself?' Dan demanded as he snapped on the lights so he could see more clearly.

Jennings flinched and reached up to turn the lights off. 'Same thing as you,' he said to Dan. 'Forgetting. Except I'm not doing it with a wife and a child and a job as the editor of a newspaper. I'm doing it with this.' Jennings gestured to two empty bottles on the floor.

Dan couldn't help but stare at the cliché before him. The returned soldier who couldn't separate himself from everything he'd seen and who drank himself into oblivion because real life had become more terrifying than running into the maws of the Germans. 'You're wallowing,' Dan said sharply. 'I never thought you'd be the one to turn out like this.'

Jennings laughed bitterly 'And how many of your men have you seen since you've been back, *Sir*? None, I'll wager. I bet all you've done is avert your eyes from the ones like me weaving drunkenly down the street.'

Dan dropped into the nearest chair, rested his face in his hands and closed his eyes. It was true. He had averted his eyes each night from the ex-soldiers as they vomited in the street. Where had his compassion gone? In France, if one of his men had drunk as much as he could to steel his spine the night before battle, Dan would have talked to him. He'd have told him he had his back.

Behind his closed lids he could see Jennings' face as they'd driven back from the concentration camp. He could see Jess's picture of

Marie-Claude Vaillant-Couturier testifying about what had happened to her at Ravensbrück. And suddenly he knew the thing he'd been trying to ignore since he'd arrived back in America: it wasn't over. There was an aftermath. And that to turn away now was the most craven thing he'd ever done.

'Get in the shower,' Dan said, his CO voice coming back to him as easily as if it had never left. 'Shave. Get dressed. You have a new job and that is as editorial assistant on the *New York Courier*. Your first job is to come with me to see Sparrow's parents. I'm going to write about what's left behind after a war, and you're going to help me.'

And so he did. In some kind of frenzied response to Jess's articles, he wrote about the fallout in America. He didn't just speak to the men; he spoke to the women too, the ones who'd worked and earned money and looked after themselves during the war and who'd now had to give back their jobs to the returning men. Women whose contributions had been largely forgotten, who sat disconsolate in immaculate kitchens waiting for their husbands to come home from work. He spoke to Betty Wasson who confirmed what he'd begun to suspect: that the only job waiting for Jess in America would have been as a model once more.

In each edition of his paper he ran his stories and Jess's stories, lest anyone forget that just because the guns had been silenced and the bleeding had stopped, war lasted forever for those who'd been there. He had copies of the papers sent to Monsieur Durant at the hotel address he'd been given.

He never knew for certain if Jess read any of his words, but he felt the quality of her photographs and her reporting strengthen and, in turn, her brilliance made him dig deeper and recover the forgotten skills of reportage that he'd not used in all those long years of war.

He wasn't at all surprised when he received a telephone call from someone he knew he could trust that Durant was in the front-running for a Pulitzer Prize for Telegraphic Reporting. He was stunned though when he was also told that Dan Hallworth was leading the pack for a Pulitzer Prize for Reporting.

'You've taken us where we want to be, son.' Walter Hallworth clapped Dan on the back when he returned home that night to find his father waiting for him in his study. 'I'm proud of you.'

Dan was used to his father appearing in his study on an evening when some particularly toothsome story had broken and the news-papermen of the town had been vying for the disclosure nobody else had. Used to his father's need to chew over the news like a Sunday roast meant for savouring. But he wasn't used to his father compli-menting him. Even after he'd been made Lieutenant Colonel, Walter Hallworth hadn't seen the need to write to congratulate his son. Obviously Dan's source had seen fit to telephone Walter too and spread the report, even though nobody would know for sure until the Pulitzers were announced next month.

'Thanks,' Dan said awkwardly and was saved from having to accept any more unexpected compliments by the bizarre appear-ance of his wife.

He'd seen as little as possible of Amelia since that awful night when he'd tried to do the right thing and had almost destroyed himself. But he'd done enough – buying her jewellery and flowers and kissing her cheek – to keep her, he'd thought, reasonably happy. Victorine had certainly not sported any more red cheeks.

'Amelia,' he said, recovering from the surprise and chastely and automatically kissing the upturned cheek she offered him. 'I thought you'd be asleep.'

'How could I not wait up to congratulate my husband?' she said.

Dan shook his head at his father's loose tongue. Who else had Walter told of what was only a rumour at best or gossip at worst?

He saw his father grimace at Amelia's invasion of the study, a space Walter held as sacred and meant only for men. But still Amelia crossed to the sideboard and poured three whiskeys. 'Cheers,' she said, passing the glasses around.

'Cheers,' Dan said, sipping, although he felt like downing his in one go, a thought intensified by Amelia's next words.

'Your mysterious correspondent is a contender too?' she enquired.

Dan was thankful for his father's brusqueness. 'Mysterious?' Walter said. 'All correspondents are damn slippery creatures. Never where you want them to be but so long as they send in the goods, which this fellow delivers in spades, then they can be as mysterious as they like.'

'I wouldn't know,' Amelia said smoothly. 'I've only ever known one correspondent: Jess. Was she mysterious?' Amelia arranged her features to make it appear as if she was thinking. 'She never gave me that impression. She always had a face that was far too easy to read. Unlike mine now, of course. Nobody can read anything under this mess.' She gestured to her face and Dan felt a sudden need to sit down, which he resisted. Amelia couldn't know who Durant was. But if Victorine had worked it out . . .

'Who is this Jess that everyone keeps talking about?' Walter's irritation at having his tête-à-tête with his son ruined was palpable. 'A war is no place for a woman. And that's why.' He indicated Amelia's empty sleeve.

Dan heard Amelia's gasp and felt his own body stiffen. He knew his father hadn't meant to be cruel. And he also knew that Amelia would make Dan pay for that barb for months to come.

'You need to apologise to Amelia,' Dan said.

Walter shrugged. 'The war is no place for a woman,' he repeated. 'I'm sorry if you disagree.'

'That was hardly an apology,' Dan said sharply.

'My skin is thick, as you can see.' Amelia offered an ironic smile. 'The apology will do. And in answer to your question, Walter, Jess — otherwise known as Jessica May — was a photojournalist we knew in Europe. She reported for *Vogue*. I wonder what she's doing now? Not that it matters. She'd never be any competition for you or your Monsieur Durant. Women don't win Pulitzers, I believe.'

'You're damn right they don't,' Walter said.

With that Amelia floated out of the room, the waft of her silk nightgown sending a draught through the room, the thickness of her scent lingering behind her.

'Now, where were we,' Walter muttered. He raised his glass. 'Celebrating. May the best man win.' Walter tipped the whiskey down his throat and Dan at last allowed himself to sink into the nearest chair. *May the best* man *win.*

After his father had left, Dan went upstairs to his wife's room and prepared to do what he should have done months ago. He pushed the door open and walked across to Amelia's bed, where she lay feigning sleep.

Her eyes flickered and he saw, a millisecond before she was able to hide it, a look of resignation on her face. He almost laughed: that she seemed as uninterested in sleeping with him as he was in sleeping with her. Why then, continue with the charade?

'I haven't come to seduce you,' he said dryly. 'But rather to finish it. You can say I was the one who was adulterous in the divorce application. I'll pay you a generous allowance; you'll have the money you wanted, everyone will be happy.'

'You'll be happy.' She sat up, leaning against the upholstered bedhead, the low-cut neckline of her nightgown showing him more of her flesh than he wanted to see but it stirred nothing in him.

'I think you will be too,' he said.

'It's convenient for you to think so. But I'm happy with the way things are.'

'Really? You mean your first instinct when I sat down on your bed wasn't to think of a reason you were indisposed? You want me the way a woman ordinarily wants the man she's married to?'

'I think you're confusing sexual attraction with marriage. They aren't the same thing. One can be had without the other.' Amelia reached out to the bedside table, opened her cigarette case and lit up, blowing smoke into the room, reminding Dan of the smoke that had once danced through the Hotel Scribe when he'd lain in bed naked with Jess.

'Marriage is all about advancement and appearances,' Amelia continued. 'I'm just the kind of wife who enhances your reputation. Despite my deformities, Americans think I'm charming and just the sort of woman you ought to have by your side when you attend parties and dinners. It doesn't hurt that I'm deformed – in fact it makes you more of a saint to have taken me on. I'm not sure what they would think about –'

'Don't say her name.' He stood up. 'I'm done negotiating. I tried. I did what you wanted. It hasn't worked.'

Amelia was silent a moment, watching him. Then she surprised him by nodding. 'Wait until after the Pulitzers. You don't want to be dogged by an impending divorce, for which you will have to pretend to have committed adultery, when you're being judged on your professional abilities. Divorce is still the eighth deadly sin, you know. Then, if you still want to be free of me, I'll say yes.'

He was so stunned he didn't reply. He'd expected they would have this conversation back and forth for months until he eventually wore her down. 'Thank you,' he said, resisting the urge to leap into the air and cheer. For there was no possible reason why, after the Pulitzers, he would want to stay married to Amelia.

When he reached his room, he found Victorine in his bed, soundly sleeping, beside the newspaper, opened to the page with Jess's latest report. He lay on top of the blankets, hands clasped behind his head, smiling up at the ceiling. He would send a telegram to I. Durant – to Jess – urging her to come to New York for the awards; she had to. And then he would tell her that he was free at last to do what he'd asked in Germany: to marry her.

Thirty-three

$\mathcal{D}$an went to the gathering of journalists at The Onyx Club on the Upper West Side feeling much less certain. He hadn't heard a thing from Jess. Everybody at the club, awaiting the announcement of the award winners to come through while listening to Dizzy Gillespie sing a much-too-breezy song, asked him if his brilliant correspondent was there and he had to shake his head. Surely she would come? Surely she'd received his telegram? But why would she travel all that way for a rumour?

The only thing he knew for sure was that he'd barely eaten all day, had consumed nothing other than coffee and whiskey and he felt himself to be a little unsteady on his feet as he made his way over to the bar with his father and Jennings, and several of his top reporters.

They stood chatting for a while but Dan couldn't concentrate. His gaze raked the room, landing only on familiar faces, his wife thankfully absent due to an illness that had left her with little appetite for the past couple of weeks.

'So, you and Durant.' The *Times* editor slapped Dan on the back. 'The odds are so slim in each of your categories that I'm not even betting.'

'Excuse me,' Dan said, turning away too abruptly to be polite but needing to leave before he snapped. Who really knew which reporters the Pulitzer board was considering in any of the categories? Which is why it was ridiculous of him to imagine that Jess would come.

He stepped outside onto 52nd Street and breathed in deeply. He should eat something. He should definitely not have anything more to drink. The thought evaporated as a scent reached his nose. His head spun from side to side and then, there she was, more breathtaking than ever in a long, full-skirted gown that reminded him of the dress she'd worn the night they'd danced at the chateau. But it was blue, the colour of skies and oceans and impossible dreams, not the khaki colour of war and death and their love.

He couldn't speak. He didn't need to; everything he felt and thought was written plainly on his face.

Jess slipped in beside him. 'I don't need to ask how you are,' she said softly.

She'd obviously noticed that he was halfway to drunk and nervous as hell. He turned his body towards her so that he could see her face and discovered it was guarded in a way he'd never seen it before. What had happened over the past year?

'I've never seen you in anything other than a uniform,' she said, a small smile touching her mouth. 'The tuxedo suits you.'

The reference to their past gave him hope. 'I've been driving myself crazy with wondering if you'd come,' he said. 'I'm not staying married to Amelia. She's agreed to a divorce, after tonight. I don't know what kind of man that makes me – someone who'd put his life on the line for any man in his battalion but someone who can't stomach staying with a woman he's injured – so perhaps you don't want me anymore. But I love you, Jess. Those last days of the war messed with my head and made me think I had to save my men and that the only way to do that was to marry her. But I can only save myself. I want to be with you.'

As he spoke, her eyes filled with tears which then trailed over her cheeks in delicate streams that he wanted to kiss away, to let her know that, from now on, there'd be nothing to cry about. He saw her guard crack and then fall, exposing what he knew to be true: that she hadn't stopped loving him either. That the past year had been hell for her too.

He reached for her hand but she wouldn't let him have it. Instead she drew it up to her chest, her other hand clutching it, as if all she had to hold onto was herself.

'I went to see Victorine this afternoon,' she said, her voice low. 'I gather you haven't been home or you'd have heard. She's a wonderful child. I miss her so.' He heard her voice break on the last words and he again reached out for her, needing to draw her in to take away every hurt he'd inflicted on her but she refused to come any closer.

His heart began to pound, and his whiskey-addled stomach to churn.

'Amelia showed me out after I'd spent some time with Victorine. She said she'd been unwell. But it was an illness she was happy to celebrate. Morning sickness. You're going to be a father. Congratulations.'

The last word was desolate and this time she came into his arms gladly. He wrapped them around her and felt her cling to his back.

'Once.' His voice was a kind of animal moan. 'I slept with Amelia once. I didn't think I would ever see you again. Victorine was unhappy and I wanted her, more than anything, to know what it was like to have a loving family. So I thought I'd try . . .' He couldn't speak for a moment but made himself go on. He'd hurt Jess yet again so the least he could do was be man enough to confess. 'It was awful. How could anything have come of it?'

He felt her hold him more tightly, felt her forgiveness for him open up around him as she spoke into his chest. 'But it did.'

'It doesn't change anything,' he insisted. But he knew it did. How could he give another child the instability of beginning its life without a family, like Victorine had had to endure? Amelia would never let him have their child if they divorced.

'But this will.' He felt the effort it took for her to pull away, for her to speak while the tears were still wet on her cheeks.

'You haven't ever told Victorine about her parents, have you?' she asked.

Dan shook his head emphatically. 'I don't plan to tell her. Perhaps when she's grown up. But the last thing she needs right now is to know that she isn't even related to me. That she's the offspring of two French people whose names nobody knows.'

'I thought Amelia knew about Victorine. She's your wife so I just assumed . . .'

Dan reached out and stroked Jess's face. 'I have had possibly a dozen conversations with Amelia. I'm married to her yes, but she's not really my wife. She knows that. She knows we don't have anything.'

Jess drew in a sharp breath. 'I think she would disagree with you. You see, I was watching Victorine skip away to have her bath and she looked so clean and grown up and different to the girl in Italy and in France that it just came out. I said, *I wonder if her parents would recognise her if they were ever able to trace her?* Amelia said that was obviously impossible because they were dead. And I said, unthinkingly, that I meant her real parents, not your brother and his wife. Her birth parents.'

Dan's stomach twisted brutally. 'She said she'd tell Victorine, didn't she?'

Jess nodded. 'Only if you divorce her.'

He felt the locks snap shut. Amelia was carrying his child. Amelia would ruin Victorine if she told her that Dan wasn't even her uncle, let alone her father.

'Goddammit!' He swore loudly and pressed his fingers against his temples.

Rather than talking about it more, rather than trying to help him work out a way to stop Amelia – as if she'd already given up – Jess stepped back and fumbled in her purse. 'I have a favour to ask you.' She passed him a folded sheaf of typewritten papers.

He read over her words about all the things she'd wanted to write about in Europe but that Warren Stone would have obliterated with blue censors' ink. She'd even spoken to women in East Germany, some of the estimated three hundred thousand, she said, raped by packs of Russian soldiers, most women by more than one man.

It was the best thing she'd ever written. Despite the fact that she wasn't just singling out the US Army, she'd be hated for writing it. He didn't want anyone to hate her. He couldn't do it. He wouldn't publish it. He shook his head.

She gave a little shrug as if she'd expected him to refuse. Then she reached up and kissed him gently, far too gently, on the lips. It was the lightest of touches, brushing against him the same way his thumb had swept over her back the night they'd danced at the chateau, but its effect was such that it almost brought him to his knees.

When she drew away, she gave him the smile he remembered as being particularly and especially Jessica May's. 'One day, when your heart is mended, and you think of me, raise a glass for me, won't you?' she said. 'We're worth remembering.'

He stepped forward then, both hands on her tear-soaked cheeks, and his lips met hers far from gently. He felt her whole body sigh into him as she opened her mouth and kissed him the way she'd always done. As if she trusted him. As if she loved him. As if she *was* him. 'This is not the end,' he whispered against her lips.

She gave him a sad smile that seemed to say, *Yes it is*. Then she said, 'Congratulations. You deserved to win,' before she disappeared.

～

He had no idea for how long he stood outside after Jess had gone. His father eventually found him and dragged him inside. The awards had been announced. His secretary was on the telephone at the club right now taking down the names of the winners of each category.

And he vaguely heard, through the clamour in his head, his father say, 'The right *man* won,' as Dan's name was read out from the list. But not Monsieur Durant's.

Dan's eyes focused then, taking in his father before him, taking in that especial emphasis on the word *man*. And Jess's words. *Congratulations. You deserved to win.* Not you *deserve* to win as if it was something still in the future that hadn't yet been decided. But as if it had already happened, or as if she knew the outcome.

'You found out she was a woman,' he said to his father, his voice barely controlled, aware that all eyes were on him, wondering why he wasn't smiling.

'Your wife pointed out that Durant was not who he seemed. It's preposterous, posing as a man,' Walter sniffed. 'I informed some people of the deception.'

'She didn't pose. We all just assumed, because that's what we do. Assume that anyone who does anything that makes a difference is a man.'

'Pulitzers only go to men.'

Dan looked at the papers in his hand, Jess's story, the one he'd thought he wouldn't publish for her sake, but now he knew what he would do. He heard his name called again; he had to say something even though all he wanted to do was howl, loud enough that the windows might shatter, a loud and brutal noise that probably wouldn't make him feel any better.

Instead he pulled himself together, drew in a breath and, as the club quieted, began to speak. 'Thank you. But I'm not accepting the prize money in my own name.'

Dan felt his father's glare on him as he continued. 'I'm giving it to the people I've been writing about. I'm starting two endowment funds, one for the wounded and the damaged, for those who aren't the same anymore. It will be called the Sparrow fund, in honour of Mr and Mrs Sparrow and their son. The money will be used for the men you'll see on the streets tonight and who you might cross the road to avoid, and for the families of the men you won't see because they are no longer with us. The second fund is for the women who fought in their own way, as bravely as any man, and who now make chicken dinners. It will be called the Jessica May Foundation, in honour of a woman I met in Europe who was lion-hearted.' He paused for a long moment, almost undone by his own words. But he owed it to Jess to keep going.

'Jess wrote those stories, the ones you all admired,' he continued at last. 'She is Monsieur I. Durant. She should be writing for any of us, under her own name. So this fund is for women artists and writers and photographers and its purpose is to enable them to do the work that we all do unthinkingly, that we've never had to fight or struggle to be allowed to do.'

As he spoke, he heard the whispers. Of course most people suspected that he and Jess had done more than share a jeep in Europe. Journalists were the worst gossips and he was standing in a room full of them, naming a foundation after her.

But he didn't care. He had plenty of money and it was about time he did some good with it. About time he honoured Jess the way she should be honoured.

As he spoke, he caught a glimpse of blue silk swirling like a furious ocean right down the back of the club, almost hidden from view. Shoulders emerging from the blue, shoulders he'd kissed and caressed and held and loved. Jess's face. She smiled at him, raised her glass and mouthed the words, *I love you* – three words she'd never said to him before, three words he'd only said to her once – before disappearing.

He left the club as soon as he could and was unsurprised to find Amelia waiting for him in his study at home.

'I hear congratulations are in order,' he said stiffly.

Amelia stroked her stomach, expertly robed and decorated, the facade of the poor maimed wife still holding. 'I hoped you'd be glad.'

He laughed mirthlessly and his hand stretched out for the whiskey decanter but he caught himself just in time and lit a cigarette instead. 'Glad about your threat to tell Victorine about her parents or glad about the fact that I've realised my wife is such an expert in blackmail she should probably be a politician?'

'The world is different now, Dan. You shot men in order to survive. At least my bullets aren't deadly.'

Oh, but they are, he wanted to say. Except that would make him vulnerable, would show Amelia that his heart was so raw right now it was a wonder it was still keeping him alive.

'So there won't be a divorce?' she asked and in her voice he heard the slightest quiver, as if she wasn't sure, as if she was worried that, despite everything he'd done for Victorine, he would do no more.

'There won't be,' he said shortly, looking out the window, blowing smoke in a long, thin stream, knowing he couldn't blame Amelia for falling pregnant – he was certainly as much to blame for that as she was – but he could blame her for dragging Victorine into the whole damn mess and for making sure Jess didn't get anything she deserved.

He waited until he heard her leave. Then he sat down and poured himself a large whiskey. He remembered that last terrible question Jess had asked of him outside the club: *One day, when your heart is mended, and you think of me, raise a glass for me, won't you? We're worth remembering.*

And his reply: *This is not the end.*

'It's not,' he repeated now, stubbornly. How could it be? How could what they had *ever* be finished, ever be over. It was a denouement, that was all. And he would wait all the rest of his life for the resolution.

PART TWELVE

Victorine

Thirty-four

The minute the artworks were handed over to the gallery, D'Arcy went straight to Victorine's apartment. And as soon as she saw her mother, eyes the same sad, luminous blue they'd always been, face fearful, D'Arcy sank onto the sofa and swept Victorine into her arms. There was no question about whether Victorine was her mother; in every way that was important, she absolutely was, no matter if they shared no blood tie.

'Will you tell me?' D'Arcy asked when she thought she could speak.

'I think I'm overdue to tell you.' Victorine kissed D'Arcy's cheek, folded her hands in her lap, hesitated, and then began to speak.

In October 1973, Victorine stepped off the train at the station in Reims and ran like a three-year-old – even though she was more than thirty years old – to Dan, flinging herself into his arms. They embraced for a long, long moment. When at last they drew away, Victorine openly wiping her eyes, Dan surreptitiously doing the same, Victorine laughed.

'Needless to say, I missed you,' she said.

'And I missed you.' He kissed her forehead. 'I'm glad you could get away.'

They'd been planning this for a year so that everyone's busy schedules could align – Victorine was publishing director of a French magazine conglomerate and James, Dan's son, was working at World Media learning the business from Dan – and now at last they were to spend two weeks travelling around France. Dan had insisted on them all getting together; family should know one another, he said, and they didn't, not anymore. Victorine, knowing that Dan would declare all of Normandy off-limits because of wartime memories and wanting to begin the holiday not too far from Paris to min-imise travel after his plane journey, had suggested they begin in the Champagne region. After what she'd thought was a momentary hesitation in Dan, he'd agreed that it might be nice to look at cham-pagne caves and castles and forests and gardens.

'Here's James. You probably don't recognise him.' Dan gestured to the man beside him, blond and therefore unlike his father.

'James!' Victorine exclaimed. 'It can't possibly be.'

'I promise it is,' he said teasingly, just like the child he'd always been, able to find the funny side in any situation.

The two of them had always played together as young siblings, but had not known each other as adults. Victorine had insisted to Dan that she be sent to boarding school in France when she was ten years old – James had been four at the time – in order to maintain her French identity; she missed the country of her birth, she'd said. She'd really wanted to escape Amelia, although she hadn't put it like that and she knew Dan understood.

After she'd finished at school, Victorine began working in France, refusing Dan's offer of a place in the business in New York because she felt that it wasn't rightfully hers, although she hadn't said that to Dan; he'd told her about her true parentage when she was eighteen and while she still loved him as much as ever, she'd wanted to make her own way in the world and had done so. He visited her every year, including one trip to accompany her on an exhaustive and fruitless search to try to find out anything she could about her parents, but there had been so many lost children and lost families in the exodus from Paris, so many records destroyed in the war, that the mystery of Victorine's parentage would remain forever unsolved.

It suited her, a life consumed by work; she'd always been a grave and earnest person, never a true child, as her teachers used to say. Some people, she knew, mistook that seriousness for humourlessness, thought she was dour, but it was just that there was an impossible-to-shift weight pressing on her, one she'd borne ever since she could remember having feelings, one thàt seemed to push down all the more if she had moments of unoccupied time.

'How's your mother?' she asked James now, politely.

James looked across at Dan and quirked up an eyebrow.

Dan picked up Victorine's suitcase. 'Let's find our hotel and then we can sit down and talk about that over a drink,' he said.

Victorine couldn't help rolling her eyes at the thought of what Amelia might have done now and she thanked God for possibly the thousandth time that her father had finally divorced his wife when James turned sixteen and could look after himself. She followed them to the car and, once they'd driven to the hotel, checked in, unpacked and washed off the journey, they all sat on the terrace and watched the sun take a long and leisurely time to set, while drinking Kir Royales.

'You were right,' Victorine said to Dan as she sipped her drink. 'We should have done this years earlier.'

'Do you think we'll manage to drag ourselves away from here and do any sightseeing?' James asked, glancing up at the majestic autumn sky, tinged pink and gold, at the waiter approaching with fresh Kir Royales, at the ancient but lovely hotel in which they were staying.

'Yes,' Victorine said determinedly. Even on holiday, it was best to keep busy.

'It's not worth arguing with her,' Dan said lazily. 'I've lost every fight I've ever had with her from the time she could talk. As evidenced by her spending the first years of her life on a battlefield and now having lived in France for longer than she's lived in America.'

Victorine placed an affectionate hand on Dan's arm. He hardly ever mentioned the war, or her early years, of which she held memories like fog: opaque but leaden. 'You know why I did it though,' she said. 'And I don't love you any the less for mostly not having been in the same country as you.'

'I know. But I do miss you.' He sipped his drink. 'You asked about Amelia before. There's something I probably should have told you a while ago, but . . .' He sighed. 'I guess I've become tired of explaining Amelia. Do you want to tell her,' he asked James, 'or will I?'

'Let me do it,' James said.

Victorine steeled herself. If it involved Amelia, it wouldn't be good.

James began to speak. 'The day Dad told Amelia he was moving out, on my sixteenth birthday, Amelia shared something with me. She said Dad wasn't my father; she'd had an affair not long after they were married to make herself feel better about her injuries.'

Dan grimaced and Victorine knew it was because he didn't believe Amelia's motivation for one minute; if she'd had an affair, it was for selfish pleasure not to soothe her soul.

James continued. 'I was born early, which Dad had always jokingly said was because I've been in a hurry about everything all my life, but it was actually because the date she'd given him wasn't the right one. Then when Dad told her he was done with her, that I was old enough to be my own person and not be affected by her character, she thought I should be told the truth. I'm sure she told me because she thought I'd hate Dad if he wasn't my father. But it just made me dislike her all the more.'

Victorine stared at Dan. How a wonderful man like him had ever let himself get mixed up with Amelia . . . The fog of memory lifted a little and she remembered a woman, Jess, telling her that Dan had to marry somebody else. Some things hidden in the back of a cupboard in a box labelled 'War'. A span of time when there was only noise and bandaged men who kissed her cheek and called her Vicki. A woman sobbing beside a tree at night. The weight pressed down like a headache, making her feel both sad and afraid.

She shook her head and the memories retreated and her fists clenched with the effort of keeping them back where they belonged, in the past. 'That's terrible. How must you have felt?' she said to Dan.

Dan shrugged. 'James has been my son in every way that's ever mattered. And when James told me he wanted to live with me after the separation, rather than staying with Amelia, I knew that we were as much father and son as any two people connected by blood. It's too exhausting to loathe Amelia. She doesn't deserve for me to expend so much emotion on her, not when there are others . . .' He stopped.

'So you have two children who aren't really yours,' Victorine said softly, imagining she and James were the 'others' to whom he had referred, and on whom he would prefer to invest his emotions.

'But who I love as if you are,' Dan finished.

Both Victorine and James reached out at the same time to hold their father's hands.

They all went for a drive the next day. The hotel manager had marked on a map for Victorine the less touristy places, the ones with more character, he'd said, and told her to visit the region's several beautiful chateaux before they distracted themselves with the champagne caves. The first chateau was, indeed, lovely and then, opposite a sharp bend, just as the hotel manager had said, lay the entrance into the second.

The long driveway promised nothing, which was why Victorine was so surprised when she saw it. Untamed and unruly gardens that held the bones of something beautiful, tumbling down to a fairytale palace.

'Look!' Victorine cried, as if everyone's attention wasn't already drawn to the chateau. 'I hope it's open to the public. Let's go and see.'

She turned to the others. All the lines on Dan's face were discomposed and the colour had fled from his skin. 'Are you all right?' she asked at the same time as she felt the butterfly wings of memory flutter at the edge of her mind. The sensation quickly vanished in her concern for Dan.

'Did you come here during the war?' she asked, knowing that Dan loathed to visit war museums and the like. 'You were posted near Reims at one point, weren't you?' she said slowly, wondering if that was why he'd hesitated when she'd first suggested beginning their holiday in this part of France, cursing herself for not having thought more about it.

'No,' Dan said firmly, cheeks pinking up a little at last. 'I don't know this place at all.'

Victorine threw a puzzled look at James, who shrugged, pulled up near an actual drawbridge and said jokingly, obviously wanting to change the mood in the car, 'Do you think there are any princesses inside?'

As he spoke, the door opened. A woman stepped out, a beautiful woman, her hair long and dark, her limbs elegant and lithe beneath a white cotton summer dress, sprigged with embroidered flowers.

'Can I help you?' she called out in French.

'We were hoping to see inside the chateau. It's breathtaking,' Victorine said. 'Monsieur Clement from Chateau du Lac said we should visit.'

The woman smiled and even Victorine felt herself gape at how stunning she was.

'Most people miss the turn-off,' the woman said, 'but I think Monsieur Clement is sweet on my mother and he often sends people here so he has something to discuss with her whenever we visit his bar for a drink. I don't mind showing small groups through at all. We can start inside and then I'll show you the gardens, such as they are.' She gave a rueful smile. 'If you come back in a year or two, I promise they'll be spectacular. It's a work in progress.'

'The inside sounds like a good place to start,' James said.

'You're American. I'm so sorry.' The woman switched to perfect English, with the hint of an American accent herself. 'I'm Ellis. But everyone calls me Ellie.'

'That's an unusual name,' James said, stepping in beside Ellie.

'It's my godmother's middle name. Martha Ellis Gellhorn. You might have heard of her?'

Victorine took Dan's arm – she'd felt him stiffen by her side – as James smiled at the idea that they mightn't have heard of Martha Gellhorn.

'Oh yes, we've heard of her,' James said to Ellie. 'She's a wonderful journalist.'

'I used to know Gellhorn,' Dan said, surprising Victorine – but of course, being in the newspaper business, her father would have met someone like Martha Gellhorn. 'In fact I knew one of her friends very well. But you wouldn't have met her. She . . . she died a long time ago.'

Victorine heard Dan's voice catch and his face had paled once more. Ellie said something sympathetic as Victorine leaned in closer to Dan. 'Are you sure you're all right?' Victorine whispered. 'We can go back to the hotel if you're not feeling well.'

He shook his head but his face was grim. 'No. I suppose I just hadn't realised how it might feel to be out in the French countryside after all this time.'

James and Ellie moved on ahead, talking earnestly together, Ellie pointing out some of the features of the chateau. Victorine hurried forward to hear, bringing Dan with her.

They wandered through the interior until they reached a stunning room near the back, so grand it must once have been a ballroom.

The walls were a soft grey and it appeared that some images painted on the wood of an unearthly forest were being restored. The salon opened out onto a terrace and to gardens that had been tamed a little more than the front. The gardens led down to a canal, which seemed to beckon one to step out onto the lawn and revel in the sun and the scent of flowers and the dappled patches of shade.

'Who takes care of all this?' Victorine asked in wonderment.

'I'm a botanist,' Ellie answered. 'This is my, and my mother's, challenge. Like a naughty child, if you like. She bought the chateau for a song back in the fifties when nobody wanted a chateau ruined by the war. We'd come down here every summer from Paris and camp on the grounds and have a marvellous time. A few years ago, we decided to try to restore some of its splendour – it's called *Lieu de Rêves*, after all – while keeping the wildness that we both loved about it. She's upstairs, but she's working, so she asked me to look after you.'

'Can we walk down to the canal?' James asked.

'Of course.' Ellie and James set off across the garden but Dan didn't move.

'I think the jet lag might have got to me,' he said at last. 'Perhaps I'll wait in the car.'

'I'll come with you,' Victorine said.

They waited near the car for a long time, Victorine wandering off a short way every now and again to inspect a flower or to pick strawberries for Dan or to marvel over the peculiar stunted trees that were dotted about or to listen out for James and Ellie, who finally returned.

On the drive back to the hotel, Victorine watched Dan, who didn't speak. James was oddly reticent too.

'I hope you don't mind if I have dinner elsewhere tonight,' James said, once they reached the cool fans in the hotel lobby. 'There's a friend nearby who I'd like to see.'

'Sure,' Victorine said. 'It will give me a chance to catch up properly with Dan.'

The next few days were strange. They would all begin the morning together and then James would vanish for large parts of the day. Dan was as skittish as a kitten and Victorine honestly didn't feel as if he was enjoying himself. Then, one night when she couldn't sleep, she sat in the lounge of the hotel drinking espresso and she saw James come in through the doors with an expression of such misery on his face that her impulse to call out his name died on her lips. Instead, she watched him walk blindly across to the elevators, not noticing her at all.

The following day, they were to leave the area and drive to the Loire. On their way to the highway, James turned off at *Lieu de Rêves*, muttering something about having perhaps left his hat there. But the house was closed up, and it looked to have been vacated. He hardly spoke on the way to Amboise, where he dropped off Dan and Victorine and then departed early for Paris, and then New York.

It all became clear nine months later. As Victorine sat in her office in Paris, she received a phone call from Jessica May, a woman she'd never really forgotten, a woman who'd been hiding in her unconscious since the last time she'd seen her, when Victorine was almost six years old.

'Let me explain who I am,' the woman, Jess, said.

'I know who you are,' Victorine whispered, feeling it all now – the love and the joy and yes, the terror.

'I know it's a lot to ask but I need you to come and see me,' Jess had said.

And she gave Victorine an address: *Lieu de Rêves*.

Thirty-five

*V*ictorine left work and caught the train to Reims as soon as she hung up the phone from Jess. At the station, a woman she would have recognised anywhere waited for her. Nostalgia and the remnants of childhood love made her throw herself into Jess's arms. As she did so, the past – everything she'd entombed in her mind's most secret grotto since the morning Dan had appeared at breakfast with bloodshot eyes and whiskey-breath and told her that she would soon have a baby brother or sister and that they should remember Jess inside them but never speak of her again – was finally disinterred.

'It's so good to see you,' Victorine said at last, wiping her eyes and studying the older woman's face.

'I hope you still think that when we get to the house and I tell you why I've asked you to come,' Jess said in reply.

Which sounded ominous.

To Jess's credit, she didn't put it off. As soon as they reached the fairytale castle, Jess took Victorine straight upstairs to a bedroom and pressed a finger to her lips before opening a door. Both women tiptoed in. As her eyes adjusted to the dimness, Victorine made out a cot. Inside the cot was a baby, asleep. Victorine's hand flew to her mouth.

They stepped back outside the room and the pieces began to fit together in Victorine's mind. 'Ellie is your daughter,' she said. 'The baby is Ellie's.'

'Yes. But of course there's more, otherwise I wouldn't have dragged you all the way here,' Jess said.

They seated themselves downstairs on the terrace that overlooked the canal. Jess told Victorine that she'd been working upstairs and had seen them all from her balcony when they'd come to the chateau, had watched them step out of the car and had known she couldn't face them, except through her camera. Because there was the fact of Ellie to explain and that was still, even after almost thirty years, unexplainable.

'That night,' Jess said, 'James returned to the chateau and took Ellie out for dinner. The next day, Ellie and I had the worst fight of our lives when I told her she couldn't see James again. The excuses I used were pathetic. That he was from America and was just having a holiday romance. That he couldn't possibly be serious. Anything other than tell her the truth.'

'I don't understand,' Victorine said. 'Even if they did go out a few times, why was that such a big deal?'

Instead of answering her directly, Jess said, 'Luckily I'm a poor sleeper. I came downstairs one night to make some tea and I found her with her luggage, on her way to meet James. They'd been seeing one another in secret for days, not telling you or your father because Ellie didn't want it to get back to me. They were in love. They were going to run away and get married. Ellie cried and said she wanted a proper wedding with me by her side but I'd been so unreasonably opposed to James that she hadn't told me of her plans. Now that I knew, she wondered if I would relent. Would understand that marrying James didn't mean she was leaving me. She thought that was why I was so upset with her, so against the idea of James. She looked so very hopeful.' Jess's voice cracked and tears began to drip relentlessly from her eyes, staining her trousers. 'I had to tell her the truth. Part of it anyway.'

'Which was?' Victorine was aware that her heart had started to beat faster, as if she knew what the revelation would be somewhere in her subconscious, even though her thinking mind hadn't yet located the right pictures and arranged them in the proper order.

'That she and James were quite possibly half-brother and sister. That I couldn't be sure. That there were two possibilities as to whom Ellie's father was. Dan Hallworth or . . .' She stopped speaking.

The page in Victorine's head finally turned to the picture she'd forgotten: Jess with her back against a tree. A man holding Jess's neck so the red flush caused by the pressure of his fingers stained Jess's skin like blood. The noises the man had made. The look of anguish on Jess's face. 'You were raped,' she whispered.

Jess closed her eyes. Then she nodded.

'How can you ever tell your own daughter that she might be the outcome of rape?' Jess stood up and stared at the gardens. 'Instead I told Ellie that I'd been foolish and had slept with another man at the same time so I had no way of knowing if Dan was her father. Regardless, she couldn't marry James because of the possibility that they were related. She was furious with me. She left the house that night anyway. But not with James.'

A long silence filled the room, then Jess finally spoke again. 'I don't know where Ellie went; she never told me. Somewhere to try to mend her broken heart. She returned here the day before the baby was born, just last week. She was ill and sad and I don't think she'd been looking after herself. But that wasn't the problem. She haemorrhaged in labour. Her placenta wasn't in the right place, but because she hadn't had proper pre-natal care nobody knew.' Jess's tears were falling freely now, a ceaseless flood.

'Where is Ellie now?' Victorine asked fearfully.

'She died,' Jess said, looking upwards into nothing, a Mater Dolorosa asking the world to tell her why this had happened, searching for an explanation for that which was beyond understanding.

Victorine was unable to speak. Because the explanation she could offer wouldn't fix anything. Ellie, that beautiful woman, heartbroken by something that had happened back in 1945, would still be dead. How could she tell Jess that none of it needed to happen. Because James *wasn't* Dan's son. Which meant James and Ellie could not possibly be half-brother and sister, even if Ellie was Dan's daughter.

Victorine stood up and walked over to the doors. She leaned one hand against the frame, not seeing anything, mind racing with questions. Surely Jess would be relieved to know that Ellie and James weren't related? Or would that only make her blame herself for having kept the lovers apart needlessly?

Jess joined Victorine, both women staring down towards the canal, unspeaking. Then Jess reached out to take Victorine's hand, holding it tightly, painfully so, but Victorine didn't pull away. Instead she felt her own hand grip Jess's just as tightly, holding on to one another, to this secret, to loss and the past and the bitter legacy of a long-ago war.

'I had to separate them,' Jess whispered at last. 'But in doing so, I killed her.'

As Jess spoke, Victorine's eyes fell upon two trees, trees she remembered skipping gleefully around when she was a child, a child who had seen but didn't yet understand that all around her flourished the merciless. She'd named those trees, she recalled now; had named the one holding aloft its skirt of leaves 'the child', had named the one with its interwoven branches 'the mother'.

And so that last terrible sentence, and the anguish Victorine heard in Jess's voice, decided her. She made a choice in that moment, one she would keep to for all the years following, never knowing if it had been the right thing to do, hoping only to prevent more hurt. She could not possibly tell Jess that James and Ellie could have married and raised their child. Because she was sure that Jess, as

Ellie's mother, would not survive the knowledge that the whole awful tragedy – perhaps even Ellie's death, for if Ellie had been with James, she might have looked after herself properly – had been preventable, if only everyone had known the truth. Instead she would take the child and be its mother and she would remain silent, as Jess would, forever, the distant trees the only ones who knew what had really happened.

PART THIRTEEN

D'Arcy

Thirty-six

When Victorine finished speaking, D'Arcy was unable to do anything other than stare at her mother for several long minutes. Then she said, 'Jess asked you to take the baby, didn't she? I'm the baby.'

'You are.' Victorine kissed her forehead. 'I asked Jess if I could have you. I think that's perhaps what Jess was hoping for when she asked me to visit her in the first place, even if she didn't know it at the time. She was so grief-stricken over Ellie that she couldn't think straight, knew only that she suddenly had a baby to care for, and wasn't sure she had the strength right then to do it. She was so convinced that, because she'd ruined Ellie's life, she'd also ruin yours if she kept you. And she couldn't bear to tell Dan any of it, couldn't bear to burden him with a baby who might be the grandchild of Warren Stone, the man who'd raped her, the man he would rightly hate. So I told her about what had happened to me at school – that I couldn't have children – and said I'd take you somewhere far away, where tragedy and the past wouldn't find us.'

Victorine paused. Her lips quivered and her eyes misted with tears. It was the first time D'Arcy had ever seen her cry. She waited, knowing her mother would speak again once the pain had diminished to a less brutal degree.

'Jess would never tell Dan about the rape,' Victorine said at last. 'Nobody spoke about such things back then. Except in that one article she wrote and was condemned for. And I'd unknowingly blocked out, like a nightmare, the memory of her being raped and all I could think was that if I'd been able to tell Dan about it back when it happened, then the whole relentless future we'd been subjected to could have been changed.'

'No, no, no,' D'Arcy cried, holding her mother close to her as Victorine's words were eclipsed by her sobs. 'None of it is your fault. It's not anybody's fault. Except perhaps Warren Stone's,' she said grimly.

Victorine touched D'Arcy's cheek, which was wet also. 'I wonder if he even knows how much grief he's caused. So many men did so many terrible things to so many women during the war and all of those things had consequences nobody ever imagined or even knows of.' She sighed. 'Jess and I agreed it would be best if we had only minimal contact thereafter, as if that could assuage our own individual guilts. But every year I sent her photos of you, which she always wrote and thanked me for. And then she called me last week, said she'd been feeling her age and that she'd just wanted to see you. To know you a little. I understand why.' Victorine paused again, swallowing. 'Hence her agreeing to the exhibition here in Australia and requesting for you to be the art handler. She hadn't actually intended for all this to come out though. But I'm glad it has.'

'I am too.' Then D'Arcy confessed to her mother the same thing she'd confessed to Josh. 'I invited Dan Hallworth to come to the exhibition.'

'I know.' Victorine smiled at her daughter. 'He called me.'

'Oh.' D'Arcy couldn't meet her mother's eyes.

'Don't look so worried. One of the most difficult parts of all of this has been having to lie to him. After Jess gave you to me, I asked

Dan if I could set up the Australian arm of World Media, which he'd always talked about. He agreed. So I came here with you and I . . .' D'Arcy could see the struggle it took for Victorine to say the words. 'I told him not to visit me. That I didn't want him looking over my shoulder. That I would fly to New York once a year to see him. It was why you were always left with the nanny when I went. It broke my heart. And his. But I couldn't tell him what had happened. I simply refused to talk about my personal life in any interviews. I suspect Dan has been subtly keeping tabs on me in between my visits through colleagues who've moved from here to New York or vice versa. Just as I do with him.'

Victorine stood and walked to the dresser, picking up the newly reinstated framed photograph of Jess in her US Army uniform, arms piled high with bouquets of flowers, the happy faces of Parisiennes all around her. She talked to the photograph rather than D'Arcy. 'When I spoke to Dan yesterday, he told me he'd always believed that Jess was dead. That he'd tried for years to find her after the last time he saw her, in 1946, but the trail was completely cold. After I met with Jess in France, I honestly thought knowing everything might well destroy him, just as I'd thought the same about Jess. But perhaps I was wrong. Perhaps I made the wrong decision, keeping everything from them both.'

Victorine's voice cracked on the last sentence. And D'Arcy could feel her agony, that of having to make such a choice, of always doubting herself thereafter, but sticking to the course regardless because she'd believed that doing so would protect others. Victorine was the most selfless person D'Arcy knew. She was, in all of this, the true hero. 'Your life,' D'Arcy managed to say. 'Your life shrunk because of me.' Another act of selflessness.

'My life expanded because of you,' Victorine said, turning to her with a smile. 'I've *always* loved you as my own. The part of me that might have been capable of forming an attachment to a man died that night I saw Warren rape Jess. My relationship with you has always been the most important thing in my life and I wouldn't have it any other way.'

At that, D'Arcy ran to her mother and lay her head on her shoulder like a child and wept. After a long time, she asked two more questions. 'Do you think that if both Jess and Dan come to the exhibition, they might . . .'

'I hope so,' Victorine whispered into D'Arcy's hair. 'They deserve it.'

And then the final question. 'Did Jess never find out who Ellie's father really was?'

Victorine shook her head. 'There was no DNA technology back then. As far as I'm concerned, you've always been Jess and Dan's granddaughter. You have her elegance, his charm, and the courage of them both.'

The night of the exhibition, D'Arcy couldn't remember a time she'd been more nervous. Everyone would find out that the photographer was Jessica May. Jess and Dan would see one another again. She and Victorine would be reunited with their family. And Josh . . . might not come.

She'd deliberately asked not to be around when the exhibition was hung. She wanted to walk into it for the first time and be surprised. She wanted to see the looks on people's faces when the truth – that every photograph there from 1943 onwards had been taken by Jessica May – was revealed.

She and Victorine arrived right on time. D'Arcy gratefully accepted a glass of champagne and passed one to her mother, stopping when she saw the look on Victorine's face: one of adoration. And D'Arcy realised that a man had arrived who must be Dan Hallworth, that he'd seen her mother and D'Arcy together, and that the look on his face matched Victorine's.

Every last shred of the worry D'Arcy had been unable to dislodge from her mind vanished. The next part of the story was finally ready to be played out. Dan and Victorine shared the true bond of a father and a daughter even though they shared no bond of blood. It was the same with D'Arcy and Victorine. And Jess could finally tell Dan about the other things that might bind them all together: Ellie, and D'Arcy. D'Arcy and Victorine had agreed that Jess should be the one to tell him that they might have had a child together.

Dan joined them and D'Arcy could still see, in the cast of his face, the handsome soldier from last century who'd embraced her mother as if she were the most precious thing on the earth. Yes, his skin was worn with age, his hair white, his movements stiff but he still stood tall and his blue eyes held stories, and a sparkle for Victorine. He kissed her cheeks, after which she shyly introduced D'Arcy as her daughter.

'You have quite some explaining to do,' he said to Victorine teasingly, forgiveness wrapped up in every word.

'And we all have a lot of catching up to do,' D'Arcy added.

'Is Jess . . .' Dan hesitated and D'Arcy could see both uncertainty and hope in his eyes.

Victorine squeezed his hand. 'She's coming. You'll be able to see her again.'

Dan breathed out slowly. 'I can't quite believe it. After all this time.'

'I think you'll find she's exactly the same person as the one you used to know,' D'Arcy said with a smile, which Dan returned, and D'Arcy felt her heart expand – that love could make another person look the way Dan did right now. Shimmering, alive; the years suddenly stripped away.

Then she saw another familiar face across the room and her smile grew so big it almost hurt. She excused herself and went to greet Josh.

'Hi,' she said, wondering if she was imagining it or if he was smiling a little too. 'How are you? And where's Jess?'

'The flight knocked her around,' Josh said, eyes not leaving her face. 'She's resting. She said she'd prefer to come tomorrow when everyone won't be staring at her. I think she'd like the news of who she is to sink in a little with the media first. I'll bring her back in the morning.'

'Of course she'd feel like that,' D'Arcy said contritely. 'I really should have thought of it. I'll arrange for her to come through an hour before the gallery opens tomorrow morning. I'll organise for Dan and Victorine to come back then too. They both want to see her so much. And there's something Jess needs to tell Dan.'

'What?' he asked.

'I'll tell you everything later. The most important thing is for her to talk to Dan, and to see what she's done; that she's created a magnificent body of work.' D'Arcy flung her hand around as she spoke so the gesture took in not just the photographs, but also Dan and Victorine. 'Let me just tell them she's not coming tonight.'

D'Arcy slipped back over to Dan and her mother and told them they would all see Jess tomorrow.

Dan's face creased momentarily with disappointment, then he nodded his head. 'It would be good to rest up tonight. To see her tomorrow when we're both less disoriented from flying. Although,' he confessed, 'I'm not sure that rest is going to make me feel any less muddled when I see her again.'

D'Arcy kissed his cheek. 'I can't wait to see you both here, standing in front of the pictures that brought you together.'

'Me too,' Victorine said. 'I'll take you back to the hotel.' Victorine slipped her arm into her father's.

Which left D'Arcy able to return to Josh.

'Shall we look around?' Josh took her hand and D'Arcy's stomach flipped with the thought that maybe . . . Maybe Josh had come all the way to Australia for more than just Jess.

Together, they made their way to the beginning of the exhibition, to the photographs Jess had taken during the war of soldiers and survivors and nurses and the condemned at Nuremberg and the rape victims she'd never been able to ignore. Then on through the years when she was establishing herself in the fifties, sixties and seventies, to the last twenty years and the peak of her fame.

At the second-to-last room, a film played. D'Arcy's documentary. She'd had to work on it harder and faster than she'd ever thought possible. When the gallery had seen the rough footage, understood the context of the conversations D'Arcy had captured with Jess, the pieces of the larger story of a woman trying to be both artist and the conscience of the world, they'd insisted that it be shown.

And D'Arcy saw now that the room was almost full, that people were watching intently, some with tears in their eyes. She saw that her film had not been made by a dilettante, but by an artist too.

'You did it,' Josh said, smiling at her. 'I hope you're as proud of yourself as you should be.'

'I might actually be a little bit proud,' she admitted.

'And there's one last room we should see.' He indicated the exhibition signs.

'No, we've seen it all.'

'Jess insisted the gallery take a few extra images,' he said in a peculiar voice and D'Arcy stepped into the last room with trepidation.

Just six images lined the walls, large images, as if there'd been no possible way to contain the depth of feeling caught in the pictures. The images were of D'Arcy and Josh.

Josh tipping a handful of water down her back, D'Arcy's eyes shining, laughter pouring from her mouth like the canal water spilling over her. D'Arcy with a butterfly on her head and Josh looking at her in a way that made her heart sore. D'Arcy alone, standing in front of a table of crates and tools, staring outside as if something were missing. The two of them, sitting on a sofa, heads tipped back, faces exhausted, hands resting on the couch so achingly close that all the viewer wanted to do was to pick up those two hands and entwine them. Josh and D'Arcy lying on a picnic blanket, Josh's mouth open as if talking, D'Arcy listening intently with not just her heart, but her entire being in her eyes. The final picture was the photograph of Jess and Dan about to kiss, utterly in love, but separated for most of their lives.

The breath left D'Arcy's body. The D'Arcy in each picture was in love with the Josh in each picture. It was as plain to see as the love on Jess and Dan's faces. But how did Josh feel?

'Come with me,' she said.

She led him to the curator's office and shut the door behind them. Then, she made herself speak in a way she would never have spoken just two weeks ago. But what she'd learned so well over the past few days was that, in people not speaking, in the absence of words, everyone in her past had been hurt.

'I love you,' she said, surprising herself with the strength in her voice.

He smiled and she felt her heart turn over inside her chest.

'It's easier to pretend I don't feel the way those photos show that I do,' she continued. 'It will be much harder to be in love with you. Because I'm not very good at it. Because I live here and you live in Paris. Because of so many things. But I want to be with you anyway.' *Please say something*, she thought. *Your smile says a lot but I need to hear it.*

'D'Arcy Hallworth, I've been in love with you ever since you strode across the drawbridge at the chateau. Since even before you called me dashing,' he said, stepping closer to her.

She grinned and reached for him, arms winding around his neck, his hands sliding up her back. And then she kissed him.

Nothing prepared her for the way it felt to kiss a man she loved, and who loved her in return. The kiss went on and on, neither willing to stop, D'Arcy content for once to do nothing other than kiss until Josh reluctantly broke it off.

'After waiting all this time I'm not going to have sex with you in an office,' he said firmly.

'After all this time?' she repeated, laughing. 'You actually make it sound like you've been wanting to sleep with me.'

'Believe me, I have.'

The look in his eyes made her breath catch, her whole body flush. Without apologising to anyone for their sudden departure, they hurried outside and found a taxi.

It took too long to drive to her apartment where, the minute they were inside, he placed his hands on her cheeks, drew her in and kissed her again, not gently, not softly, not slowly, but exactly as she wanted to be kissed. *At last*, she thought as she searched out his tongue. *At last*, she thought as she felt his body pressed hard against hers.

Thirty-seven

The next day, after showering with Josh, which took much longer than it should have, they grabbed takeaway coffee, longing for Célie's coffee and baguettes, and hurried back to the gallery, only ten minutes later than the time they'd arranged to meet Victorine and Jess.

Nobody was there. Josh frowned. 'Maybe I should have collected Jess.'

They were interrupted by the clack of Victorine's heels on the floor.

'Mum, this is –' Before D'Arcy could introduce Josh to her mother, her words were stopped by the redness of Victorine's eyes. D'Arcy clutched Josh's arm. The crying was supposed to have stopped now that everyone was here at last. 'What is it?' D'Arcy asked with alarm.

Before her mother could reply, Dan Hallworth arrived, smiling broadly, obviously so incredibly happy to be on the cusp of seeing Jess again after all this time. But he also halted when he saw Victorine, concern replacing the joy that D'Arcy had wanted to believe would be fixed on his face forever.

'What a mess,' Victorine said, rubbing her forehead with her hand; the patina of tragedy had made the lines on her mother's face stark while everyone else in the room was soft-blurred with unawareness.

'What do you mean?' Dan asked.

'Jess had a baby,' Victorine said sadly. 'All those years ago. One of the reasons she stayed away after you'd married Amelia was because she found out she was pregnant.'

'Jess and I have a baby?' he whispered, and D'Arcy flinched as if his pain were hers too.

'That's just it,' Victorine said. 'She didn't know. Warren Stone . . .' D'Arcy could see the visible effort it took for her to keep speaking. 'Warren Stone raped her. I saw it. She could never be sure whose child it was. She knew what you'd do to Warren Stone if you found out. She didn't want to burden you with a child conceived out of hate. But she loved her daughter.'

'How do you know all of this?' Dan asked haltingly.

D'Arcy's breath held as Victorine told Dan about Ellie and James. That Jess had thought James was Dan's son. That she couldn't let James and Ellie elope because Ellie might be Dan's daughter. That instinct had told Ellie to go back to her mother's house when the baby she'd conceived with James was ready to come. That she'd haemorrhaged and died.

'Did the baby die too?' Dan's voice was barely audible.

Victorine smiled at last. 'No. This is the baby.' She gestured to D'Arcy. 'Jess gave her to me.'

'D'Arcy is Jess's granddaughter?' Dan asked, looking at D'Arcy with love spilling from his eyes.

'And quite possibly yours, too. In a real sense, not just through me,' Victorine said, her voice suddenly choking as if she couldn't bring herself to say any more.

What else was coming? D'Arcy remembered to breathe. And then she asked the question that had been sitting at the edges of her awareness since her mother arrived. 'Where's Jess?'

The silence said everything. It was a visceral thing, merciless, pressing itself down on D'Arcy's shoulders, almost making her legs buckle beneath her.

Victorine tried to speak. *Don't say it*, D'Arcy thought. She reached out a hand to Dan, who looked as if he might collapse too.

'I dreamed of Jess last night,' he said wretchedly. 'She was lying beside me, smiling her inimitable smile. Nothing has ever made me feel so good in all my life as receiving one of those smiles.' He stopped for a moment, eyes looking through them all and perhaps into the past, to a time when Jessica May smiled just for him. 'Then she kissed me. And she said . . . goodbye.' He breathed in sharply. 'In all the time I knew her, we never said goodbye to one another. You don't say goodbye to someone in wartime unless . . .'

'No, no, no,' D'Arcy cried furiously. 'That's not how it was supposed to be!'

'Nothing was,' Dan said dully.

D'Arcy almost had to walk out of the room to stop herself from crying. What right did she have to weep? She'd only known Jess for two weeks. Dan had mourned her and loved her all his life. She realised Josh was holding on to her as tightly as she was holding on to him. Because he had loved Jess too. Everyone did. It was impossible not to. And now she was gone.

Then she found herself held in an embrace, Dan on one side, Victorine on the other, her mother and her grandfather, two people she knew she loved unquestioningly, watched over by Josh, a man she knew she loved unquestioningly too. It was a love she never wanted to, in fifty years time, weep for because she'd had to surrender it.

'Champagne,' Dan said suddenly and gruffly. 'We need champagne.'

D'Arcy nodded a little uncertainly while Josh went to track down a bottle and some glasses left over from the opening party. Dan pulled the cork from the bottle and passed everyone a glass.

'Once upon a time,' Dan said, his words soft, 'Jess asked me to raise a glass for her. *One day, when your heart is mended, and you think of me, raise a glass for me, won't you? We're worth remembering*, she said. I never did raise that goddamn glass. Because I thought, I hoped . . . that it wasn't over. And far from being mended, my heart . . .'

He closed his eyes, unable to go on.

'Well,' he said after a long moment. 'I think you know how my heart feels right now. But she deserves all of our raised glasses. Because she is most certainly worth remembering. To Jess,' he said, his last words strong, as Jess deserved them to be.

'To Jess!' the others cried, proclaiming his toast to the gallery filled with her works, her artistic works and her works of flesh and blood, remembering her, celebrating her, vowing, as D'Arcy was doing, to live and to love the way Jess had never been able to.

Then Josh kissed her forehead and wrapped his arms around her. 'After the exhibition,' she said to him, the idea forming as she spoke, 'let's go back to the chateau and hang all her works there. Let's open it to the public so that they can see it. Let's make the world raise their glasses to her too. If that's okay with both of you.' She looked over at Dan and Victorine, who nodded.

'You should run the Jessica May Foundation from there too,' Dan added. 'Make it yours. Make the chateau a place where women can have time and space to make their art. Let Jess's legacy continue to grow, every day.'

'Really?' D'Arcy said, awestruck at the thought that a foundation to which she'd once looked to for support might now be something she could use to support other women artists like herself to achieve their dreams.

'Really,' Dan said.

'I think you'll find,' Victorine said with a teary smile, 'that you own Jess's chateau. When she gave you to me, she told me that she would bequeath it to you upon her death.'

'And you should also come to New York and meet James. Your father,' Dan added.

A father. Something D'Arcy never thought she'd have. She looked across at Victorine, who nodded, blinking hard.

There were almost too many things happening for D'Arcy to grasp them as individual hurts and losses, as well as wonders and astonishments. She suddenly felt as if she understood Balzac's belief that a person was made up of ghostly layers, layers that image-taking stripped away each time a photograph was taken. The photographs Jess had taken of D'Arcy had stripped away much of what D'Arcy thought she was, and everything she didn't need. She hoped that her documentary about Jess had done the same, that it had torn off the layers Jess had wrapped herself in after the war so she now appeared as she really was: bold and strong and beautiful and so well loved.

Then, as Victorine embraced Dan, Josh and D'Arcy turned to look at the images of Jessica May moving across the screen before them, smiling as if giving them her blessing. A blessing, D'Arcy realised now, Jess had bestowed on her when they'd embraced on the terrace of the chateau, an embrace D'Arcy could feel again now, reaching beyond death, bequeathing to Josh and D'Arcy the promise of a long and beautiful life. The long and beautiful life that Dan and Jess had never had, the long and beautiful life that D'Arcy had never imagined having, lay now, astonishingly, before her. She sealed the promise with a long and beautiful kiss on Josh's lips.

Author's Note

In some ways, this was the hardest book I've ever written. So many characters and storylines and time periods to bring together the way I imagined them in my head. In other ways, it was the easiest book I've ever written. Jess and Dan were two characters who came effortlessly to me; they were a true gift from the writing muse. But of course there were lots of reasons this happened, not the least because of all the amazing research material that couldn't help but inspire me to write.

I first became aware of Lee Miller when I was writing *The Paris Seamstress*. Her story was immediately captivating: a famous model and Man Ray's lover, she wrote and photographed some extraordinary stories for *Vogue* during World War II, but her work was largely forgotten thereafter. Her son, Antony Penrose, knew very little of his mother's remarkable past until after she'd died. It was his wife, when clearing out the attic at Farley Farm – Miller's home – who came across Miller's sixty thousand photographs and negatives, plus clippings, cameras and wartime souvenirs, stored haphazardly in cardboard boxes. Penrose resurrected her legacy and she is now widely regarded as one of the war's preeminent photojournalists.

How could anyone not be inspired by this woman?

But I also knew that I couldn't write her life story. Some terrible things happened to Lee Miller in her life, not the least of which was that a family friend raped her when she was just seven years old, infecting her with gonorrhoea. It was a tragedy that I wasn't sure I was equipped to write about; what could I possibly know about how that affected Lee throughout her life? Also, I wanted to write another dual narrative like my previous book, *The Paris Seamstress*, and I couldn't do that by sticking to the facts of a person's life. So I decided to use Lee as the inspiration for the character of Jess.

My story begins with Jess's modelling career hitting a major hurdle when an image of her is sold to Kotex to use in an advertisement. This actually happened to Lee Miller, although at a slightly earlier time than I have used in the book. It's hard for us to imagine how shocking appearing in a sanitary product advertisement was at the time and how it could possibly ruin someone's career, but it was and it did. Miller gave up modelling after that as nobody wanted to see the 'Kotex girl' in photographs designed to show off evening gowns. Condé Nast did discover Lee Miller, as he discovers Jess in this book, and Miller was one of his favourite models; his influence was instrumental in her successful modelling career. The pictures Toni Frissell is taking of Jess in the opening scene are based on pictures Frisell took for the cover of *Vogue* in 1942.

My descriptions of Italy when Jess arrives there in 1943 are based on Martha Gellhon's piece, 'Visit Italy', published by *Collier's* in February 1944, and Margaret Bourke-White's pieces, 'Salt of the Earth' and 'Fifth Army Field Hospital', taken from *They Called it Purple Heart Valley*, published in 1944, and from her piece, 'Evacuation Hospital', published in *Life* in February 1944. The scene set during the Easter service in Italy is based on 'Easter in Italy: Americans Pray Within Earshot of German Lines' by correspondent Sonia Tomara, published in the *New York Herald Tribune* in April 1944.

Martha Gellhorn tells Jess that a photograph of a naked woman painted in camouflage colours is used during lectures. This is true;

Roland Penrose, a photographer and Miller's lover – later husband – lectured in camouflage during the war and he used this image of Lee Miller as his 'startle slide' to make sure everyone was paying attention.

The letter that Warren Stone reads to Jess about the 'inherent difficulties' of having women in the war is taken from *The Woman War Correspondent, the US Military, and the Press* by Carolyn M. Edy. The other letter Warren Stone quotes to Jess, from a major in the Surgeon General's office, about the supposedly devastating effects on the 'female apparatus' from parachute training is taken from *Never a Shot in Anger*, the memoir of Public Relations Officer Colonel Barney Oldfield, as is the anecdote about Capa et al missing their parachute training school places because of a drunken party the night before.

Martha Gellhorn did stow away in a hospital ship to become the first woman correspondent to land at Normandy. I used her piece 'The Battle of the Bulge', published in *The Face of War*, as the basis of the scenes set in Bastogne and the Ardennes. I have tried as much as possible to only put Martha in places that accord with her actual movements during the war, but obviously her relationship with Jess is a fiction.

Many female correspondents wrote letters to SHAEF protesting the restrictions placed on them during the war, and thus the scene in which Jess writes a letter, supported by the other correspondents, is based on an amalgamation of those letters.

Iris Carpenter's visit to Omaha Beach and her subsequent court-martial is recorded in Carpenter's memoir, *No Woman's World: From D-Day to Berlin, a Female Correspondent Covers World War II*. I have also used Ernie Pyle's June 1944 wire copy (he was correspondent for the Scripps-Howard newspaper business) titled 'Omaha Beach after D-Day', published in *Reporting World War II: American Journalism 1938– 1946*, as the basis for Jess's descriptions of how Omaha Beach looked after D-Day.

Lee Carson's ability to avoid court-martial through the employment of her eyelashes is recorded in Oldfield's memoir. Catherine Coyne, Lee Carson and Iris Carpenter were all real people and I have tried to, once again, have their appearance in Jess's life accord with their actual movements during the war. Both Iris Carpenter and Lee Carson were given permission to access all areas at around the same time as Jess is granted this permission in my book.

The scene where a singer is brought into the Hotel Scribe to entertain the correspondents, as well as the sign propped on the piano, and the attempts at misogynist humour the following morning are all detailed in Oldfield's memoir, which is, quite accidentally, an awful chronicle of the widespread sexual harassment of women throughout the war. Also recorded in this book is the incident about the German girl bearing a note from a US soldier, which she thought was a special pass, but which is in fact anything but. Oldfield notes, seemingly without censure, that the writer of the note must have 'enjoyed himself and . . . had a sense of humour as well as generosity of spirit'. I have tried not to exaggerate the way women were treated during the war, but I know many of the incidents I've written about must seem unbelievable.

I wanted to write about Ravensbrück concentration camp, the only concentration camp exclusively used to imprison women during the war, but this camp, because of its location, was liberated by the Russians, not the Americans. So the concentration camp that I have used in this book is an amalgamation of Ravensbrück, plus other camps like Buchenwald and Dachau, and I have drawn on Lee Miller's and Iris Carpenter's reporting of those camps. After Lee Miller photographed Dachau, because the photographs were among the first taken of any of the camps and the sights were so shocking, she sent a cable to her editor at *Vogue* that read: 'I implore you to believe this is true.' I have borrowed this wording for Jess.

Many correspondents did not believe the concentration camps existed until after they came upon them, which Jess alludes to. General Collins did make the civilians in the town of Nordhausen bury the dead as punishment for turning a blind eye to the horror that existed right on their doorstep, and the practice of taking German civilians from nearby towns to the concentration camps to see what they had ignored is also noted in *The Women Who Wrote the War: The Compelling Story of the Path-breaking Women Correspondents of World War II* by Nancy Caldwell Sorel. Jess's experience of coming upon the camp and having machine guns trained on her is based on what happened to Marguerite Higgins, correspondent for the *New York Herald Tribune*, when she reached Dachau.

The view attributed to General Patton about 'fornication without fraternisation' is detailed in Oldfield's memoir.

The description of Hitler's apartment is based on Lee Miller's piece, 'Hitleriana', published in *Vogue* in 1945. I have appropriated the infamous photograph of Lee Miller in Hitler's bathtub and given this to Jess.

Iris Carpenter was the reporter who came upon a US Army soldier raping a German girl in 1945. She never reported on this incident for the *Boston Globe*, but wrote about it in her later memoir, published in 1946. She records the reaction of the officer to whom she reported the incident – that the main problem with war was that there were women near it. Jess's report, 'I've Got A Pistol and There Ain't Nobody Going to Stop Me Having Her' is based on Iris's recollections in her memoir.

The story about the 371st Fighter Group and Yvette, the injured girl who became their mascot and good-luck charm, is true. At a field hospital in Italy, an orphaned Italian boy stayed for several weeks and he also became a kind of mascot for both the nurses and the nearby battalion. Fiction is all about what is possible and both of these examples made me believe that it was possible for Victorine to have been accommodated in a field hospital for a few months.

Many other sources provided useful information to help me write this novel. For information about female correspondents during the war, as well as the sources listed above, I also used *Women War Correspondents of World War II* by Lilya Wagner; *Women of the World* by Julia Edwards; and *Where the Action Was: Women War Correspondents in World War II* by Penny Colman.

To understand Lee Miller's life, I read *Lee Miller's War*, edited by Antony Penrose; *Lee Miller: A Life* by Carolyn Burke; and *Lee Miller: A Woman's War* by Hilary Roberts. My description of the area around Carentan is based on 'Unarmed Warriors' by Lee Miller. Martha Gellhorn is another extraordinary woman and for details about her life, I referred to her collection of reportage published as *The Face of War* and Caroline Moorhead's biography, *Martha Gellhorn: A Life*. I also read Gellhorn's fiction to understand more about her turn of phrase.

Les Faux de Verzy do exist in a forest near Reims.

The division Dan belongs to is based on the US Army's 82nd Airborne Division, although I have occasionally had to take a little license with their precise movements; it is likely he would have been called out of Italy earlier than Easter to prepare for the invasion, the division fought at Anzio rather than Cassino, and it went across to Berlin, rather than Munich.

The intricacies of the battles of World War II and life in the US Army were drawn from Antony Beevor's *The Second World War*, David Drake's *Paris at War* and *The Historical Atlas of World War II* by Alexander Swanston and Malcolm Swanston. I also visited Utah and Omaha beaches as research for the novel as well as the Omaha Beach Memorial Museum, the American Cemetery at Colleville-sur-Mer, and the Airborne Museum at Sainte-Mère-Église. I confess to this being the most difficult area of research for me as I knew nothing about army ranks and the difference between a platoon and a company and a battalion when I began; any errors to do with this are mine and, while I have tried my best, I am not an expert and hope I have it mostly correct.

Susan Sontag's *On Photography* and *Regarding the Pain of Others* were useful in understanding the moral complexities of war photography.

The inspiration for two of the images I describe as part of the photographer's body of work comes from actual images: David Heath's *Vengeful Sister* and Mark Cohen's *Group of Children*.

The final word should, of course, be Lee Miller's. Something she wrote in a letter to Audrey Withers, her editor at *Vogue*, sat with me as I wrote this book and tried to imagine what it might have felt like to witness and then to record both the horror and the heroism of war: *'Every word I write is as difficult as tears wrung from stone.'*

$\mathscr{A}$cknowledgements

$\mathscr{A}$s well as all the sources listed on the previous pages, there are many people I wish to thank. The most important of these is Rebecca Saunders at Hachette Australia who makes me believe I can actually write books and that they are worth reading. Rebecca's faith in me, her support of me and her encouragement are unflagging and I know I wouldn't be publishing my fourth historical novel if it wasn't for her.

Everyone at Hachette Australia is wonderful and I'm pretty sure I say in the back of each book how lucky I am to be published by them. But it's true! Special thanks to Sophie Mayfield for her attention to detail and editorial assistance, and to Dan Pilkington for always galvanising the sales team behind my books.

Thank you also to Celine Kelly for her astute structural editing and for helping me turn the book into the thing I hoped and imagined it could be. Alex Craig is the world's best copyeditor and I am once again so fortunate to have had her working on this book.

Leah Hultenschmidt at Grand Central in the US and Viola Hayden at Sphere in the UK are both amazing editors to work with, and I am hugely grateful for their support, and their belief in me.

To all my writerly friends, too many to list, for laughs when things are good and tissues when things aren't so good, a big thank you. Special thanks to Sara Foster who always reads through my manuscripts and provides wonderful advice and suggestions just when I most need it.

David Scherman's words, in the epigraph on page 1, and the quote from Lee Miller on page 121 are both reproduced from the book *Lee Miller's War: Beyond D-Day* by kind permission of Palazzo Editions Limited and the Lee Miller Archive.

My three children are the loves of my life and their excitement about my books — especially about the research trips to Europe that they get to accompany me on — is inspiring and makes me want to keep writing to make them proud. To my husband also, for never once doubting, thank you.

As always, to my readers, the biggest thank you of all. Your emails and messages are the bright spots in my days, the sparks of encouragement whenever a book seems too tricky. I hope this book finds a place on your shelves too.

ALSO BY NATASHA LESTER

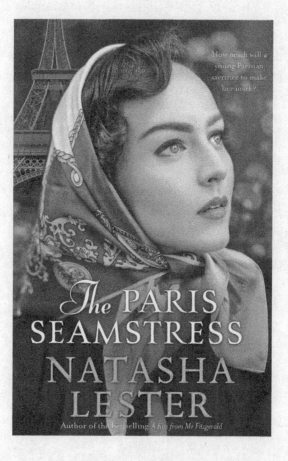

A transporting story of a grandmother
and her granddaughter as they attempt
to heal the heartache of the past

Author of
the bestselling
*A Kiss from
Mr Fitzgerald*

NATASHA
LESTER
Her
MOTHER'S
SECRET

A sweeping story of love and courage
from England to the Manhattan
of the 1920s and 1940s

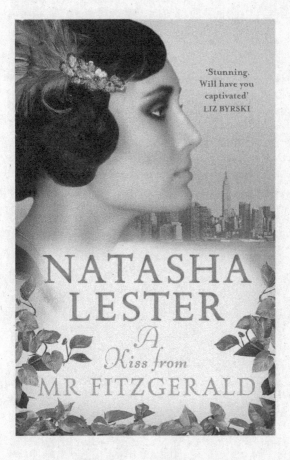

'Stunning.
Will have you
captivated'
LIZ BYRSKI

NATASHA
LESTER
*A
Kiss from*
MR FITZGERALD

A deliciously evocative love story
of a small-town girl with big
ambitions in 1920s New York